The
Mud Man

A novel

Donna Marie West

Print Edition ISBN: 978-1-7357289-8-8

E-book edition ISBN: 978-1-7357289-9-5

Manta Press, Ltd.
www.mantapress.com

Cover Design by Tim McWhorter
Edited by Lily Luchesi, Partners in Crime Book Services

First Edition

Acknowledgements

My deepest and most heartfelt gratitude to my partner, Serge, who has never once complained about the thousands of hours I've spent, month after month and year after year, with pen to paper or fingers to keyboard.

My most sincere thanks as well to my editor, Lily Luchesi, who found so many places where I could make my story better, and dear fellow writers and valued friends, Charles H.K. West (no relation as far as we know) and John Irvine, without whose input and encouragement this story might never have made it out of my computer.

And finally, but not least, a humble thanks to you, the people who take the time to read my stories. I hope you enjoy reading them as much as I enjoy writing them.

He has come at long last to the end of his life.

As he grows cold the pain fades until he feels nothing at all. He hears nothing. Sees nothing but the stars in his mind's eye.

Soon, his spirit will begin its journey to join the spirits of those who lived before him.

That is good.

He is ready.

1

DISCOVERY AT BENNETT LAKE

"I brought coffee!" Chloe McLean sang as she came into Veronica Booth's cluttered office at the University of British Columbia's Anthropology Museum. She carried two extra-large cups from Tim Horton's stacked in one hand, while a brown paper bag hung from the other. "And donuts. They had the maple glazed ones you like so much, and—"

"And chocolate glazed for you," Veronica finished with a smile.

"Well, yeah!" Chloe laughed as she put everything down on the one corner of the central table that wasn't covered by papers, boxes, and zipper lock plastic bags. "I figured if we're going to get that box of stuff from Campbell River sorted and catalogued today, we'll need some help from our good friends, caffeine and sugar."

"Thanks." Veronica reached for one of the cups. She popped the lid and took a satisfying sip. "You know you're the best assistant I've ever had, don't you?"

Chloe responded with a grin, her teeth flashing white against the tawny skin that came from her Coast Salish blood.

Coffee and donuts long gone, the two women were three hours into a disappointing day—all but one of the potential artefacts that had been donated to the museum were ordinary stone fragments or bits of bone, rather than anything fashioned by human hands—and Veronica was about to suggest a lunch break when her cell phone buzzed in the side pocket of her cargo shorts.

She glanced at the screen before taking the call. She didn't recognize the number.

"Professor Booth?" a woman blurted breathlessly.

"Yes? Who's this?"

"Anne Temple. You probably don't remember me, but I was in your Culture and Communication course two years ago. Anyway, I'm with Professor Sutherland's team up here at Bennett Lake. He gave me your number and asked me to call."

"I remember you," Veronica said as an image of the enthusiastic, red-haired young woman popped into her mind.

"You do? Well anyway, we found something interesting, and Professor Sutherland thought you might want to come up and take a look."

"Something… interesting?" Veronica shrugged at Chloe, who studied her with wide brown eyes. Gerald Sutherland had been her archaeology professor a dozen years ago. He remained her mentor now that Veronica was an assistant professor at the University of British Columbia, and they'd collaborated several times on research and the writing of peer-reviewed papers. "Like what?"

"Well, we're up here looking for artefacts from the nineteenth century Klondike gold rush, you know, but we've stumbled across something else: signs of habitation by Native Americans way earlier than that. I can't really say more over the phone, but I guarantee you'll want to see this *in situ*. And, um… it's time sensitive. So… do you wanna come?"

"Sure, I guess so," she said, as Chloe nodded and made wild shooing gestures with her hands, clearly having guessed the gist of the call. "I don't have anything pressing to do this week."

Anne gave Veronica instructions on how to get to the remote location: take a flight from the Vancouver International Airport to Skagway, Alaska, then the White Pass Railway to the station near the ghost town at Bennett Lake. She gave Veronica the number for the team's satellite phone and told her to call when she was on the train. Someone would meet her at the station. Veronica should dress warmly, pack to rough it, and bring a good, waterproof sleeping bag.

"Looks like I'm off to see what this big discovery is all about," Veronica said to Chloe after ending the call. "Can you handle things here for a few days? And take care of my kitties? Stay a couple nights at my place if you want to."

"Absolutely!" The twenty-two-year-old student still lived at home and frequently moaned about sharing her bedroom with her younger sister. Veronica knew she would love the privacy of the spacious two-bedroom apartment near Kitsilano Beach. "Go. Have fun," she said. "But keep in touch. I want to hear everything."

Thirty hours later, Veronica was on the vintage gold rush era train from Skagway, her nose nearly pressed to the window to take in the magnificent view as the route wound between mountain peaks. Even now, in the first week of July, they were topped with lingering caps of snow. As breath-taking as the scenery was, however, after an hour it grew somewhat monotonous, and her mind began to wander.

Two years ago, a novel coronavirus that came to be known as COVID-19 sparked the worst global health crisis since the Spanish influenza pandemic of 1918 to 1920. Millions died worldwide although, thank God, Canada hadn't been one of the countries hit the worst. Eventually, science prevailed, and vaccines effectively ended the pandemic. Still, after two years of periodic confinement, social distancing, classes cancelled or given online, field work postponed, and the wearing of face masks everywhere but in one's own home, Veronica was ready and eager to get out to a dig.

As the holder of hard-earned doctorates in cultural anthropology and anthropological archaeology, with a special interest in the First Nations of Western Canada, she was frequently called upon to participate in digs or study finds that might have a connection to First Nations people.

She expected to see the usual remnants of soapstone carvings, bone jewellery, and obsidian tools. Maybe a petroglyph or two, if she was lucky. But what if it was something more? Something that might help her advance her career and secure tenure at the university? Even though it was Professor Sutherland's dig and therefore, his find, they might collaborate on a paper as they had a few times in the past.

Anne and a young Native American man who introduced himself as Ed met Veronica at the station. Ed grabbed her bags while Veronica paused to zip her jacket closed against the crisp mountain breeze, and they walked to the team's campsite not far from the shore. The two students refused to answer any questions except to say she would see for herself soon enough, but Veronica could practically feel the excitement emanating from them.

She left her backpack and sleeping bag in a tent, and they headed out for the dig site.

After thirty minutes of hiking past sparse birch and spruce trees in the boreal forest east of the lake, they were joined by a young woman jogging towards them from the direction they were headed.

"He's completely uncovered now!" she began, her face flushed and the words tumbling one over the other. "Hurry up! I've never seen anything like—"

"He?" Veronica stopped in her tracks and glared at Anne. "You didn't tell me you found a body!"

"We discovered him yesterday morning," the student said with a grin. "We've been working ever since to dig him out."

They hurried another ten minutes along a deep, narrow chasm between two jagged outcroppings of rock. Several squares typical of archaeological exploration had been cut into the soil beneath the carpet of moss, but they seemed for the moment to be of no interest. Two students knelt almost reverently around a two-metre-long trench dug out of the thawing permafrost soil. Professor Sutherland, standing behind them, was taking photos with a compact digital camera.

Anne introduced Veronica to the other students. Veronica said a quick hello to them all as well as to Gerald Sutherland, before dropping to her knees on the soggy ground of the mini bog. She took one look and gasped at the sight.

A human body lay on its back in an almost metre-deep trench, its left leg bent beneath it, arms folded across its chest, head turned slightly to the right. Though it remained caked in mud, it appeared to be a man of average height with shoulder blade-length hair, wearing the tatters of a leather shirt and trousers, and what looked like a sealskin moccasin on the visible foot.

"He's amazing," Veronica murmured, her heart racing and eyes glued to the emaciated body. She looked up at Professor Sutherland, who nodded in agreement with everything she said, and around at each of the students. "He doesn't look as damaged as Ötzi, the famous iceman found in the Swiss Alps in 1991. Instead, he's been perfectly preserved, far better than any of the bodies found in bogs in Europe. I suppose this ground was frozen until recently, which might explain it." She paused. "How did you find him?"

"Anne and I were hiking up the mountain to get a view of the terrain," Ed replied at her elbow. "I tripped over something sticking out of the ground. Fell flat." He chuckled. "We began excavating and found part of a spear. Turns out that's what I tripped over. We kept digging and discovered a couple bone beads and a stone projectile point… and then we found him."

"Everything's in my tent," Professor Sutherland said. "The spear's in three pieces, but it's quite beautifully made. You can study all of it when we get back. As for him"—he stared down at the body—"we'll need to pack him in ice until he can be put into a freezer to prevent decomposition. We'll have him taken down to UBC for study. After that, I expect this site will become the object of a major archeological dig."

While Professor Sutherland was speaking, Veronica pulled

her cell phone from her pocket and began taking photographs of the site. Still snapping away, she leaned down to get a better look. All at once, she stumbled back, falling on her butt when she thought...

No way! That's impossible! You're hearing things, Vee.

She scrambled back to her knees to peer into the trench again. Another low, barely audible hiss came from the body.

"Did anyone hear that?" She looked around at the others, searching their faces.

Eyes narrowed. Heads wagged. No.

"Maybe ice melting inside him?" Anne suggested.

Veronica had almost convinced herself the younger woman was right, when she saw the man's blue-tinged lower lip twitch.

"Holy shit!" Ed exclaimed. By the stricken look on his face and the sound of his voice, he'd seen it too.

"I think this guy's alive!" Veronica yelled. "We've got to get him out of there. Now!"

As the students mobilized to carefully raise the body from its grave, Professor Sutherland gaped at Veronica as though she'd lost her mind.

"Professor Booth," he said with a shake of his head. "Veronica... That soil must be thousands of years old. It's not remotely poss—oh, Christ!" He fell back a step, his eyes nearly popping through his wire-framed glasses, as a gurgling moan came from below them.

A few minutes later, the thawing body was out of the trench and on the ground at their feet, still in the same position he'd lain in for however long it had been. Veronica had time to think they'd all been imagining things, that every sign pointed to this man having been dead and frozen solid for millennia, when he began to convulse weakly, limbs twitching and eyes rolling beneath their lids. Thin, pink-tinged saliva bubbled at the corners of his mouth.

Professor Sutherland marched away, shouting for Anne to get on her sat phone and call for a medevac helicopter.

Ed and Megan, the girl who'd come to meet them on the

trail, helped Veronica roll the mud-covered man onto his side, so he didn't choke on his saliva. As they turned him, she heard something crack inside. She prayed it was ice, but who knew? After a minute or so he grew still, his breathing shallow, raspy, and frighteningly irregular.

Anne got off the sat phone to tell them the helicopter was on its way, but there were too many rocks and trees for it to land here, or even lower a basket. They had to get the victim down to the shore.

"We can make a stretcher," said Ed, thinking on his feet, "with a couple tree branches and the tarpaulin. I know how to do it."

It took a few minutes to find adequate branches, and more valuable minutes to cut them using the hatchet in their toolbox.

Veronica grabbed the nearby tarpaulin, which she assumed the team had been using to protect the site from the elements. She gave it to Anne, who followed Ed's instructions to fold the tarp back and forth across the two branches. All the time they worked, she sat beside the mud man, unable to do anything to help him and fearing he would die for real before he got anywhere near a hospital.

He was hanging in there despite suffering another prolonged seizure, when Ed and Professor Sutherland got him onto the makeshift stretcher.

"Keep him on his side," Veronica said, as something from a long-forgotten first aid course came back to her. "He'll breathe easier than on his back."

"You call that breathing?" Megan said grimly. "Sounds like my grandmother did when she had pneumonia… just before she died."

Ed and the other male student—in all the excitement, Veronica hadn't caught his name—each lifted their end of the stretcher and headed towards the lake at the briskest pace they could manage without tripping over protruding rocks or roots and dumping their charge on the ground.

The rest of them followed, Veronica and Professor

Sutherland discussing how to proceed with this unimagined turn of events. By the time they exited the forest, they'd decided Veronica should accompany the victim to the hospital. Having found the man, the senior professor felt he should go, but he was reluctant to leave his students. Nor did he want to abandon the dig site, which might yet yield further surprises.

As they passed her tent, Megan ducked inside to grab a sleeping bag, which they used to cover the man once they reached the lakeshore.

While they waited for the helicopter, the poor man appeared to stop breathing. They frantically debated the pros and cons of trying CPR on him, but after half a minute he started again with a rattling gasp.

Finally, the medevac helicopter came into view, a big red bird heading straight for the group; it landed a few minutes later about thirty metres away. As the rotors slowed, the medevac team of two men and a woman jumped out and rushed over with equipment in hand. While the woman enquired as to how the patient had been found, the men got him off the makeshift stretcher and onto his back on theirs with a blanket wrapped snuggly around him. They slapped an oxygen mask on his face but gave up on putting in an IV when they couldn't find a vein in either of his emaciated arms. Then they hustled him, Veronica, and her baggage—minus her sleeping bag, which she left for when she came back—onto the helicopter.

Veronica strapped herself into the seat opposite the narrow bed and they took off for the hospital in the town of Whitehorse, just over the B.C. – Yukon border. All the time they were in the air, she watched the female paramedic monitoring the comatose man and tried to wrap her mind around the events of the past hours.

A human can live without eating for several weeks but can only survive for a few days without water. The mud man couldn't have been out there in the mountains for longer than that.

Unless he was. He was buried in a metre of thawing

permafrost soil . . .

She shook her head, refusing to let herself contemplate the ridiculous alternative. It occurred to her that she hadn't looked at the broken spear or other items the team had found, but of course they could wait. This man—whoever he was—couldn't.

The helicopter landed in the hospital parking lot and the patient was rushed into the emergency ward. Following the medevac team and the ER people, Veronica heard a few words pronounced with grim urgency:

"Multiple fractures… severe hypothermia… dehydration… "

Then curtains were drawn to keep her out, and she was steered towards the ER reception desk by a nurse who said she needed to get some information for the patient's file.

Veronica didn't have much information to give, but she feared the poor man wouldn't live long enough for it to matter.

2

GUARDIANSHIP

Veronica stayed over three hours in the waiting room lined with padded grey chairs—twenty in all, she'd counted them over and over again—sipping lukewarm coffee with powdered creamer from the machine in the hallway and trying her best not to imagine the worst. Finally, the senior of the two doctors—a Native American woman of around forty—who had disappeared behind the curtains with the patient came to see her.

"You're the woman who came in from the mountains with John Doe, right?" The doctor sounded as exhausted as she looked. As Veronica nodded and gave her name, she went on, "I'm Dr. Highwater. I'm sorry I didn't come sooner, but…" She hesitated.

"He didn't make it," Veronica guessed, her heart sinking. She'd stood up when Dr. Highwater came in, but now her knees gave out and she dropped back into the chair nearest the reception desk.

"On the contrary," Dr. Highwater said, sinking down into the chair beside her. "Against all expectations, we've been able to stabilize him. We've aspirated his lungs, put him on a ventilator, and managed to get an IV into him. He's being transferred to the ICU as we speak. If he survives the next twelve hours—and I have to be frank with you, I'm not at all confident he will—we'll get some x-rays and other tests done." She sighed heavily. "Since you're not a family member, I'm afraid I can't tell you more."

Veronica took a moment to let that sink in. "What if you don't find any? Family members, I mean. What happens if you can't identify him?"

"Then I'll have to sign a certificate confirming the patient is incapable of making decisions for himself. The court will appoint a Public Guardian and Trustee, who will be able to sign off on future medical decisions."

"Hmm, right." A thought popped into her mind. "What about his clothes? Can I take them, keep them for him?"

Dr. Highwater gave her a wry smile. "I suppose so, if you want to call them clothes. They fell off him in shreds when we tried to remove them. He had only one shoe, and it was more of a slipper, really. No wallet or cell phone. No watch or ring. My guess is he's an indigenous hunter, one of those guys living off the grid, subsisting on whatever he can hunt or gather, the way his ancestors lived. Probably took a fall."

"That makes sense," she agreed, although something about that scenario didn't feel right.

He was found buried a metre deep in an ancient, thawing bog.

Dr. Highwater pushed to her feet with a weary groan. "I've got to get back on duty. I'll send someone with the man's clothes, then I suggest you go home to wait. Call tomorrow morning to see if there's been any change."

"To see if he's still alive, you mean?"

"Well . . . yes."

"I don't live in town," Veronica said as the doctor turned to leave. "Is there a hotel nearby?"

"Closest one is the Coast High Country Inn. Ask the nurse for directions."

About twenty minutes later, the young nurse she'd spoken with earlier approached Veronica with a black plastic garbage bag in hand. "You asked for John Doe's things?"

"I did," she said, reaching for the bag. "Thanks. Oh! Can you tell me how to get to the Coast High Country Inn?"

The hotel was about twenty minutes away, across the bridge

over the Yukon River. If Veronica didn't want to walk, she could take the bus that stopped outside the hospital.

Veronica decided against the bus. Although the temperature had dropped considerably in the past few hours and gathering clouds threatened rain, the walk was relaxing and gave her a chance to replay the day's astounding events in her head. She found the hotel, booked a room on the second floor, and took a long shower. After dressing in clean jeans and a blouse, sneakers on her feet instead of hiking boots, she ventured down to the restaurant for supper.

She ordered a steak sandwich and a glass of red wine, followed by a slice of apple pie and a cup of coffee to which she happily added real cream. Back in her room, she stripped to her underwear and fell into bed, the long day of travelling and roller coaster emotions taking its toll. Within minutes, she was asleep.

Veronica woke up just after dawn to the sound of rain against the window. After dressing in last night's clothes, she opened the bag containing the scraps of the mud man's apparel and immediately regretted it—now thoroughly thawed, the dirty bits of leather and sealskin stank like wet dog and something rotten.

Breathing through her mouth to reduce the risk of gagging, she dumped the shreds of leather into the bathroom sink and brushed off enough soil to give them a cursory examination. From what she could see, the clothing was artisanal. There were no signs of buttons, zippers, or tags, though she supposed they could have been lost in the mud or during the trip to the hospital. She returned them to the bag, tied it shut, and pushed it to the back of the closet.

Leaving the "DO NOT DISTURB" card on the doorknob so housekeeping didn't inadvertently throw out her prize possession, she went downstairs for breakfast. After filling up on pancakes, orange juice, and coffee, she called the hospital for news about the mud man.

"Are you a family member?"

"Well, no," she said, rolling her eyes, as if this would have any effect on the receptionist. "If I were, he wouldn't be a John Doe, would he?"

The receptionist let out an exasperated sigh. "Hold on, please." Nearly five minutes passed before she came back. "He's still in the ICU. No change in his condition."

Veronica took this as good news. *He made it through the night.*

Back in her room, she took advantage of the hotel's free Wi-Fi and spent the morning doing research on her cell phone, looking up regional newspapers in search of articles about a man gone missing. She ended her fruitless search after going back two years and decided to go to the hospital. The rain had ended, and the clouds were parting to reveal a pale blue sky. On her way she stopped at a small grocery store, where she bought a box of zipper-lock plastic bags in which to properly store the bits of leather and sealskin, along with a prepackaged blueberry muffin and bottle of water for sustenance.

"I'd like to enquire about the condition of the John Doe who was brought in yesterday," she said to the grey-haired woman at the admissions desk.

"Are you a family member?"

"No. If I were, he—"

"Wouldn't be a John Doe," she finished, and Veronica realized this was the same woman she'd spoken to earlier. "Let me see what I can do. Have a seat in the waiting room. It might take a while."

Veronica munched her muffin and drank her water. Fifteen minutes passed before the receptionist came to say the doctor in charge of the patient in question would come to see her. Another half hour passed before Dr. Highwater showed up, wearing a fresh white lab coat but looking just as tired as she had the evening before.

She stood as the doctor reached her to meet her eye-to-eye. "Tell me what you can. Please."

Dr. Highwater hesitated, clearly choosing her words carefully. "Well . . . he hasn't regained consciousness, but he's hanging in there. He's suffering from severe frostbite, dehydration, and malnutrition. X-rays show fractures in the pelvis and left femur and four broken ribs. I'll be sending him for more extensive tests, which should give us some idea of the condition of his brain and other organs, and of course that hip needs to be repaired surgically as soon as he's stable. The RCMP are with him now, taking photos, making a dental chart, and collecting DNA samples in hopes they'll be able to identify him. I'm afraid that's really all I can say. Even if I knew more, I couldn't tell you because—"

"I'm not a family member. Right. Thank you, Dr. Highwater."

The doctor left and Veronica marched back to the admissions desk.

"How would I go about requesting guardianship of a comatose patient?" she asked.

"You mean the John Doe?" the receptionist asked in return. Her frown said she wished Veronica would go away and stop bothering her. "I'm not exactly sure, but I do know you'll need to go through the courts. I suggest you get yourself a good lawyer."

"Thanks, I will," Veronica said. She already had someone in mind.

In an ultimately unsuccessful attempt to put the mud man out of her thoughts, Veronica treated herself to a tour of the S.S. *Klondike*, a restored sternwheeler from the turn of the twentieth century docked on the river near her hotel. After an early supper at the hotel restaurant, she called Chloe to check in on her kitties and promised to tell the curious student all about the discovery at Bennett Lake when she got home. She called Anne to say she planned to return to the lakeshore camp tomorrow and spent the rest of the evening making arrangements for the trip.

First thing Thursday morning, Veronica called the hospital to be told only, "No change, critical but stable." She ate breakfast, paid her hotel bill, and took a taxi to the town of Carcross, an hour from Whitehorse at the northern tip of Bennett Lake. From there, she hired a boat to take her to the Bennett Lake station. She spent several hours at the archeology team's campsite looking over the artefacts they'd found so far. Even without referencing known artefacts, she recognized that the bone beads, stone projectiles, and broken spear were ancient and important. That afternoon, she caught the train back to Skagway, two bone beads, a stone projectile point, and a short piece of the spear nestled safely in her backpack, along with the remains of the mud man's clothing. After a quick supper in the Alaskan town, Veronica flew home to Vancouver with her mind full and a huge decision to make.

The following morning, she sent fragments of leather and sealskin, one of the bone beads, and a splinter of the wood from the spear to UBC-affiliated labs for DNA analysis and radio-carbon dating. While she hesitated to let her thoughts run rampant until the results of the tests came back, she couldn't help but entertain the possibility she'd inherited a discovery that would put her name up there along with the likes of Carter and Leakey, Mead and Boaz—and maybe make her rich in the process.

She spent the rest of the day on the phone with various people in the administration offices of UBC, the Whitehorse General Hospital, and her older brother Neil, the best lawyer she knew. By evening, she was on her way to making an official request for emergency guardianship of an incapacitated and unidentified adult. It was a complicated process, made ten times worse by the fact that while the man had been found in B.C., he was currently hospitalized in the Yukon, necessitating all kinds of inter-provincial communication and cooperation. At least Professor Sutherland, far more interested in the long dead than the barely alive, relinquished all claim to the man he believed to be an indigenous hunter who had met with a disastrous fall. He couldn't explain how the fellow had come to be buried so deeply and it seemed he didn't want to try, focusing, instead, on the disappointing prospect that the artefacts the team had found might be modern day reproductions rather than authentic Neolithic tools.

Saturday morning, Veronica received a phone call from the Whitehorse branch of the RCMP. The female officer had spoken to Professor Sutherland and his students, and she wanted to compare details in their statements with hers. Luckily, Veronica had discussed this with the team on Thursday, so she was able to give the exact same information—the truth, of course, omitting only the fact that the man had been found in millennia-old, thawing permafrost soil. When she finished her tale, the officer informed her that she was unlawfully in possession of items belonging to the man, and that she should send them back up to Whitehorse immediately.

"You mean the remains of his clothing? Dr. Highwater at the Whitehorse General gave them to me."

"Yes, I know, but she never should have done that. They may help us identify him."

I kind of doubt that, Veronica thought, but she agreed to send them by UPS later that day. She didn't mention holding back a few fragments for her own use.

The next five days sped by in a rush of legal paperwork and legwork, emotional ups and downs, including a shock Tuesday morning when Veronica called the Whitehorse General for an update on the Bennett Lake John Doe.

"He's no longer in the ICU," said the man who answered the phone.

"Wh-what? What does that mean?" Veronica could barely get the words out. "Did he… did he pass away?"

"No, uh… hang on." She waited with her phone clamped to

her ear until he came back. "He was transferred to Vancouver General Hospital yesterday by air ambulance. We're not equipped to keep a patient long-term in our ICU."

"Thank you," she said, and immediately called Vancouver General.

"I'm sorry, but we can't give you confidential patient information if you're not a family member or have legal authority," the man at the information desk said.

Veronica didn't think he sounded sorry. "That's fine," she replied, trying to sound like this didn't make her want to scream with frustration. "I'll have the legal authority before you know it."

Unfortunately, despite her best intentions and growing sense of urgency with the situation, the wheels of justice turned slowly. It was Wednesday afternoon the following week when she and Neil finally went to the Vancouver courthouse, having delivered the necessary paperwork the previous Friday.

"It's an unusual case, to be sure," admitted Judge Chamberlain after they explained everything verbally that he'd already received in written form. "If this man's identity is learned and relatives found, you will almost certainly have to relinquish your guardianship," he said after thinking for several long moments. "Do you understand this, Ms. Booth?"

"I do, of course," she said, "although to be honest, I don't think that'll happen. Either way, I want to make sure he gets the best medical care possible."

"Your commitment is commendable," the judge said as he began signing papers. "As I said, this is an interesting case. I've never seen anything like it, to be honest with you." This was something, given that the white-haired man looked to be in his sixties or more. "I'd like to know how it turns out."

"I'll keep you informed," Veronica assured him. "Thank you."

She collected her copy of the signed papers and left the courthouse with Neil. They celebrated this small victory with supper together at the Blue Water Café in downtown

Vancouver.

"I can't thank you enough for your help," Veronica said to Neil as they ate. Onlookers would have no trouble identifying them as brother and sister. They had the same ash blond hair, short, straight nose, and deep blue eyes, although he was slightly overweight from too many sumptuous business dinners while she was slim and athletic. He was actually six years older than her and had always been her protector and confidant.

There was one thing, however—at least for now—that she hadn't shared with him.

3

A FIRST SMALL STEP

Veronica was irrationally nervous Thursday morning as she headed to Vancouver General Hospital to see the mud man. She told herself she was ready to face anything, yet butterflies swarmed in her stomach as she parked her car and walked into the hospital's Jim Pattison Pavilion.

She rode the elevator to the ICU on the second floor and used the special phone in the cafeteria to let them know she wanted to visit the John Doe transferred from Whitehorse.

"I'm so sorry, dear," said a nurse in a lilting Irish accent, "but that particular patient is a special case. I'm afraid he can't have any visitors—"

"I've been awarded emergency guardianship by the courts," Veronica interrupted as politely as possible. "I'd like to get a report on his condition and I . . . I insist on seeing him."

"Oh!" The nurse took a few seconds to let this sink in. "In that case... have a seat in the cafeteria and I'll ask Dr. Webber to talk to you. Better have a cup of tea, it might be a while."

Veronica detested tea, but she took the nurse's advice and got some coffee and a banana-nut muffin, and settled down to wait. She should have brought a book. It was almost an hour later when a tall man with salt-and-pepper hair, wearing an open lab coat over street clothes, walked into the cafeteria. He took a moment to look around, somehow divined that she was the person he sought, and strolled towards her.

"Veronica Booth?" he asked.

"It's me," she replied.

He sat opposite her and placed a disturbingly thick file folder on the table. "I'm Dr. Webber. I've been taking care of the Bennett Lake John Doe since he arrived. I'm told you've been given legal guardianship of the man? May I see your papers?"

She'd expected this, of course. She pulled the folded documents from her satchel and held them out to him. She didn't think he would actually bother to read them, but he did. Carefully.

Finally, he handed them back to her. "What do you want to know?"

"Everything," she said frankly. "His condition, what kind of tests you've run on him, his prognosis."

The physician took a long breath in through his nose and blew it out through pursed lips. Opening the file folder, he began by telling Veronica what she already knew: the patient had been found half-frozen in the forest near Bennett Lake and medevacked to the Whitehorse General Hospital. He'd been put on life support and treated for frostbite, extreme dehydration, and pulmonary edema. Once he was stable enough, he was transferred to Vancouver General.

"Preliminary tests in Whitehorse showed a slow but steady heartbeat, and an EEG indicated minimal brain activity. He suffered two prolonged seizures in the week after he arrived and was each time given IV lorazepam, which was effective in stopping them."

"That all sounds really bad," Veronica said, unable to hide her dismay.

"Well yes, it is, but he's now on anti-seizure meds and hasn't had one since. He's undergone a multitude of tests..." He referred to the file again, skimming through several pages before continuing, "ECGs, EEGs, CAT scans, MRIs, blood tests, and bone marrow analyses. The femoral fracture was surgically repaired with a titanium rod and screws and the stable pelvic fracture should heal on its own. While he remains in a coma, the latest results seem to indicate his organ function and brain activity are crawling towards normal levels. To be honest with you, I've never seen a case like his."

Veronica caught her breath as hope sprang into her heart. "So... you think he might wake up?"

He shrugged. "There's something of a precedent, I suppose. In 2015, a young man in the US who froze in a snowbank for ten hours was revived and is now living a normal, happy life. But our man's not out of the woods yet, no pun intended. As his circulation came back, gangrene set in in his extremities and unfortunately last Friday, we had to amputate his toes, his fingers near the distal joints, and most of his left thumb. He has a serious middle ear infection with ruptured eardrums in both ears. There's damage to his eyes as well, but we won't know to what extent his vision might be affected until he wakes up. In addition to all of this, he has a generalized bacterial infection we haven't yet been able to identify. We've started him on broad-spectrum antibiotics, but it's too soon to know if they'll have any effect. Ms. Booth"—he leaned a bit closer to her over the table—"you need to understand. He may remain permanently in a vegetative state, or he may regain consciousness, only to be blind, deaf, and/or completely paralyzed, and we have no idea what his cognitive abilities might be."

"I understand. Have you any clue yet to his identity?" she asked, trying to sound calmer than she felt. To tell the truth, she felt vaguely sick to her stomach at hearing these details.

He shook his head. "He looks to be Native American, with those high cheekbones and dark hair. He's blood type O+, which is consistent with this hypothesis, as O is the most common blood type amongst North American indigenous people." He paused, frowning. "Judging from the imaging of his bones, he's in his mid- to late thirties, although osteoarthritis in many of his joints indicate an arduous lifestyle. His teeth look like he's never seen a dentist—they're straight enough, but quite worn, and he has no fillings although he's in need of some. He's missing two molars in the lower left jaw. Looks like they were knocked out quite some time before he died as the bone is healed, and he has several scars on his body indicating a number of injuries over the years."

"I want to see him."

"I don't advise you to—oh, very well," he said, interrupting himself. "It'll give you a better understanding of his condition. Follow me."

They walked down the hallway to the ICU, where the motherly Irish nurse instructed Veronica to wash her hands and put on a surgical mask and gown for her protection as well as the patient's.

After doing the same, Dr. Webber showed her to a private isolation room, opened the door, and gestured for her to go in ahead of him.

She walked briskly into the small room but stopped halfway to the bed, stunned by the collection of machines around it, and by the sight of the man himself.

He lay on his back with his head and chest slightly raised. IV lines and tubes ran in and out of various parts of his body, and he was patched into a heart monitor that showed a reassuringly steady if slow beat. A rhythmic hiss came from the ventilator plugged into the trach tube secured to the base of his throat. His hands were wrapped in thick, white bandages. His face was gaunt, his skin sickeningly pale and so dry it looked ready to crack, and his hair had been shaved close to the scalp.

"Oh God, the poor man. He... he looks more dead than alive," Veronica said under her breath, "like a survivor from a Nazi concentration camp." She turned to look at Dr. Webber. "Can I sit with him for a while?"

"Sure. Just don't touch any of the machines."

"Of course not. Thanks."

She sat with the mud man for nearly an hour, just watching the slight rise and fall of his chest as the ventilator breathed for him. She tried but ultimately failed to imagine what he might have gone through to end up where he had. In the end, although she wasn't particularly religious, she found herself praying that one day, sooner rather than later, he would open his eyes.

The first thing he is aware of is sound. A sort of buzz like a swarm of blood suckers inside his head.

The second thing is pain. So much pain he cannot feel where one ache ends and the next begins.

Is he dead, he wonders? No, he cannot be dead. Death would not hurt so much.

Veronica stopped by the hospital every afternoon for the next three days to sit for an hour or two with the mud man, even though there was no discernible change in his condition. On Monday morning, she went into her office to do some of the work she was paid to do.

She and Chloe had long since finished cataloguing the items in the box from Campbell River, but there was always something new to look at. Today's something new included two stone projectile points, a surprisingly sharp obsidian blade, four additional bone beads, and a bone needle Professor Sutherland had found around the mud man and sent down for her to examine. He thought these were probably in the man's pockets when he succumbed to whatever tragedy had befallen him. His take now was that the man had found and perhaps even used the ancient tools and weapons. He'd generously offered to share credit for the findings with Veronica if they came to the same conclusions as to the origin of the artefacts.

Veronica, however, wasn't sure they would.

"This doesn't look recent at all," Chloe remarked as she studied the rudimentary needle. "More like Mesolithic or early Neolithic. Are you sure it belonged to your mud man?"

Veronica reached for the artefact and held it for a moment before answering. As of yet, she'd only told Chloe the same thing the RCMP and Professor Sutherland's crew knew. Nothing of her suspicions. "Pretty sure," she said cautiously. "It was found right there with him, along with the other stuff."

"But where would he have gotten them? You don't just come across things like this while out on a hike."

"No, you don't. I think they're his."

"His? But that would mean..." The young woman's eyes grew round as saucers. "You don't really think... Seriously, Veronica?"

"I know it sounds crazy," Veronica admitted, "but I think it's possible, somehow. Imagine if he wakes up, what we could learn from him."

"What we could—? Right. Um... " She was silent for a moment, and Veronica thought her cheeks lost a bit of their usual colour. "I guess I'll start looking through online catalogues, see if I can find anything comparable to what we have here."

"Sounds like a good idea." Veronica put the needle down on the table as her cell phone buzzed in her pocket.

It was the hospital, asking her to come and see Dr. Webber. He wanted to talk to her about the results of some tests.

Heart in her throat and fearing bad news, she drove the usual twenty minutes to the Vancouver General in ten, weaving in and out of traffic, and practically ran from the parking lot to meet Dr. Webber in the hallway outside the ICU.

"We've been able to identify the bacteria in John Doe's system," he said carefully, as if he were having trouble getting the words out. "It . . . well . . . it appears to be a previously unknown, apparently mutated strain of *Bacillus F.* How he came into contact with *Bacillus F.* in northern B.C. and what caused it to mutate in the first place are huge questions, but I'm hoping to get some answers soon. I've contacted UBC and they'll be sending someone up to the place where the patient was found to collect soil and water samples."

"O—kay," Veronica said slowly, as this information simmered in her mind.

Dr. Webber went on, "The *bacillus* genus of bacteria includes some useful species, such a *B. subtilis*, which can be cultivated to produce bacitracin, a common antibiotic. Others are not so good. Some strains of *B. cereus* cause food poisoning. *B. anthracis* causes a serious illness called—"

"Anthrax."

"That's right. I'm worried about the load of bacteria still active in his body despite the antibiotics we're pumping into him. He's virtually filled with it—it's in his blood, spinal fluid, skin. And there's another thing." He paused. "The man's near-demise may not have been accidental. I've had a chance to go over the tests taken up in Whitehorse and I've found something . . . unsettling . . . in the report: remains of two extremely toxic plants were found in his stomach. *Veratrum viride*—common name Indian hellebore—and *Amanita muscaria*—a sort of poisonous mushroom. I believe he must have consumed a substantial quantity of both not long before he froze, but whether accidentally or deliberately, I couldn't hazard a guess.

"Contrary to that rather gloomy news," he added, while Veronica pondered the possible implications of this information, "he continues to make progress. His heart rate has increased, his blood pressure is approaching the low normal range, and his kidneys are beginning to function. His hands and feet and the surgical incision in his thigh are healing nicely, and his lungs are clearing up. He reacted to pain this morning by flinching when his wounds were dressed, and—"

"And that's a good thing?"

"Oh, it is. It indicates he's coming out of the deep coma towards what we call a minimally conscious state. If he continues gaining strength, we'll be able to give him a short spontaneous breathing test—see if he can breathe without the ventilator—in a day or two."

"That's the kind of news I want to hear!" Veronica exclaimed.

Sitting at the patient's bedside a few minutes later, dutifully washed, gowned, and masked, listening absently to the faint beeping of the heart monitor and the rhythmic hiss of the ventilator, she thought over everything Dr. Webber had said— the good, the bad, and the inexplicable. She recalled reading something about *Bacillus F.* Discovered a dozen or so years ago in Siberian permafrost soil, the mysterious bacteria, once thawed, had proved to be alive and perfectly healthy.

A bacterium that can survive long-term freezing? What if the bacteria in the mud man is what kept him alive while he lay frozen in the ground, sustaining its host until it thawed and became active again? There's no telling how long he might have been there. Weeks? Years? Millennia? Maybe I'm not so crazy after all.

She reached out and rested her hand on the mud man's left shoulder, wanting him to know—if he was aware of anything— that he wasn't alone. It was the first time she'd touched him since that day in the mountains, and while nothing more than skin and bones, his body was reassuringly warm beneath his thin, blue hospital gown.

"You're going to recover," she said in her most soothing voice, although she had no idea if he could understand or even hear her. "A man frozen and come back to life? You'll have so much to tell us, no matter who you are. But if you're what I think you might be… I can't even imagine… "

She rambled on for some time, telling him about herself, how ever since she'd found a stone projectile point in the garden of her home in Kamloops at the age of eleven, she'd been fascinated by other times and other cultures. How her obsession with her career had made relation-ships difficult. How it had cost her her marriage after only three years and how, although she had many acquaintances at UBC, only Gerald and Chloe were what she would consider friends.

Thinking what to say next, she realized the beep of the heart monitor had picked up a tick. She'd noticed it was at fifty-eight on the screen when she sat down. It was now at sixty-two.

"Hey, can you hear me?" She gave the patient's shoulder a gentle squeeze.

Seventy. His shoulder twitched beneath her hand, and his head turned ever so slightly towards her.

"You *can* hear me, can't you? Listen, um… you've had some sort of accident. You're in the hospital in Vancouver. They're taking great care of you, though. Don't worry about a thing."

His grey, cracked lips pressed together in a thin line.

Veronica could see his eyes rolling around beneath the lids. Suddenly, they popped open. His eyes were brown, but bloodshot and cloudy, and she wondered if he could see anything. She supposed he was lucky to still have eyes in his head, given what had happened to his fingers and toes.

After blinking rapidly a few times, his eyes narrowed, and he squinted to look at her. His mouth worked as if he wanted to speak, and he made a weak, gurgling sound deep in his throat.

"Shh, don't try to talk," Veronica said.

The gurgling continued. A single tear crept from the outer corner of his right eye and slowly slid down the side of his face. His right leg jerked and then his left arm, and suddenly his entire body began to spasm violently. The various machines he was plugged into all sounded alarms.

Before Veronica could run for help, Dr. Webber and the Irish nurse she now knew as Beatrice rushed into the room.

"He's having a seizure!" the doctor said, his voice steady but filled with urgency. While Beatrice turned off the alarms, he filled a syringe from a bottle on the stainless-steel table in one corner of the room and injected it into the patient's IV line.

Veronica backed up against the wall, her heart racing in her throat. The stench of fresh feces wafted up from the bed. She was as fascinated by the fact that someone in the mud man's condition could defecate as she was disgusted by the smell and distressed by the scene in front of her.

The seizure continued for another minute or so, then the patient gradually quieted.

Dr. Webber turned to Veronica. "I think we've got it under control," he said, as if she couldn't see this for herself.

"Okay, good." She took a long breath in an effort to steady herself. "He opened his eyes. I thought he was waking up, but"—she shook her head—"I guess that wasn't it at all, was it?"

"Maybe that's what provoked the seizure," the doctor suggested.

"You think?"

He raised one shoulder in a half-shrug. "I told you earlier: I've never seen a case like his. I have no idea what path his recovery might take, but I'm going to consider what just happened a first step forwards."

Veronica nodded. "Good. Then so will I."

"Please step out, Ms. Booth," Beatrice said. "I need to get the patient cleaned up."

"Of course. Actually, I'd better go back to work. I'll come tomorrow afternoon. Let me know if there's any change, if he has another seizure, or… anything."

"We will," Dr. Webber assured her, and they left the room together.

4

AWAKENING

He is not dead. He is not dreaming. He is sure of both now.
He tries to move, but the most he can do is open his eyes.
He sees pale light, like morning sun through fog. The light
makes his eyes burn and so he closes them again.

Everything hurts still, but now the pain has names. Hands
and feet. Eyes and ears and throat. His ears still buzz dully, but
he can hear other things too. Voices he does not understand
and sounds he has no words for.

Something is in his throat. He wants to cough it out, but he
cannot. He wants to scream, but he cannot do that either. And
so, he screams inside.

Bolstered by a pot of strong coffee and a box of Timbits she
picked up on the way home from the hospital, Veronica spent
Monday evening on her laptop, obsessively Googling about
specimens recovered from deep bogs, thawing permafrost soil,
or receding glacial ice. There were many: the famous Ötzi, of
course, who lived and died some 5,300 years ago. Hundreds of
human remains had been retrieved from peat bogs in Denmark,
Ireland, Germany, and elsewhere, the oldest of which had been
radiocarbon dated to 8,000 BCE. Animal remains found in
Siberia, including an incredibly well-preserved wolf's head, a

puppy, a baby horse, four baby cave lions, and a woolly mammoth were between 12,400 and 50,000 years old. The mammoth, it was reported, had *Bacillus F.* in its brain.

Reading on, she was amazed to learn that *Bacillus F.* found in the Yakutia region of Siberia was over three million years old. It was being touted by some of the scientists studying it as a possible "elixir of life" due to its perceived ability to prolong the life of its host. The Russian scientist who first discovered it in 2009 had even injected himself with it and subsequently declared he felt stronger than ever. As far as she could find, he was still alive and kicking.

Other types of microorganisms had also remained alive after being frozen for millennia. In 2005, NASA scientists thawed out something called *Carnobacterium pleistocenium.* After being frozen in a pond for 32,000 years, the bacteria began swimming around, apparently unaffected by their long siesta. Two years later, scientists revived an unspecified bacterium that had lain dormant beneath the surface of a glacier in Antarctica for eight million years. More recently, microscopic, multi-celled creatures called bdelloid rotifers that had lain dormant in Arctic ice for 24,000 years were thawed and subsequently began to reproduce in a Russian lab.

It boggled Veronica's mind to think the Bennett Lake mud man might go to the top of the list. And yet . . .

Although she'd told Dr. Webber she would go to the hospital, Veronica needed a break after three weeks of focusing on the mud man and tossing and turning during a mostly sleepless night. She got up to feed her cats—black and white Scout, who looked like a miniature cow, and Rusty, whose name came from his dark ginger colour—both rescues and probably the closest thing to children she would ever have. She called Chloe and told her to take the day off, then she went back to bed with a bagel and a glass of orange juice, and the historical novel she'd started weeks ago. When she got up for the second time, she called Neil to invite him and his wife, Becky, for a casual supper at her place. Becky was a documentary filmmaker with an independent company who always had entertaining tales to tell about her projects and the people she met during her work. She was the perfect person to distract Veronica for a few hours.

She'd managed to keep up with her jogging two or three mornings a week, but today she opted for an exhilarating swim in the nearby Kitsilano saltwater pool. She forced herself not to call the hospital, reasoning that if the patient's condition changed, someone would call her. She stayed busy with some long overdue housekeeping, laughing when the kitties dove under her bed at the sound of the vacuum coming out of the hall closet. Later, she showered and blow-dried her hair, noting that she was due for a trim, and put on a skirt and blouse for the first time that summer. Lastly, she ordered Chinese food from the local restaurant, knowing Becky and Neil would enjoy it as much as she did.

They arrived right on the dot of 6:00, about two minutes before the food. The three of them chatted about the usual things while they ate, draining a bottle of white Riesling in the process, and as much as she'd wanted to avoid it, the subject of John Doe from Bennett Lake came up. Neil had told Becky what he could and she enquired as to his condition.

Veronica told them he was still unconscious in the hospital and promised to keep them posted if and when the man's condition changed. She said nothing of her suspicions as to his identity.

Before leaving a couple hours later, Neil suggested Veronica call their parents—they hadn't heard from her in a month and were beginning to worry. He'd told their kid sister, Kim, that Veronica had become involved in a new project, and that she would tell them all about it herself.

She promised she would and she honestly meant to, but events the next day pushed all thought of such mundane obligations far from her mind.

By mid-day Wednesday, Veronica and Chloe were satisfied with their work. They'd identified the stone projectile points and the obsidian blade found with the mud man. Both were similar to artefacts previously found at archaeological sites on the coast of northern B.C. and Alaska—sites dated to between 8,000 and 22,000 BCE.

Veronica was typing up the report she would send on to Professor Sutherland when an email came in from the DNA sequencing lab where she'd sent her samples for analysis.

"It's about damn time!" she exclaimed before she thought to hold her tongue.

It was too late to take it back; Chloe was at her elbow, peering eagerly at Veronica's laptop.

With a sigh that was part resignation and part anticipation, Veronica scanned the document until she reached the summary.

Sample one, the leather, was *Cervidae*, a positive match to caribou. Sample two, the sealskin, was confirmed to be *Phocidae*, a positive match to harp seal. Sample three, the wood from the spear, was *Thuja plicata*, commonly called western red cedar. Nothing unusual about any of those. Sample four, however, which had come from what everyone assumed was bone, was in fact ivory from an extinct species of *Elephantidae*.

"Woolly mammoth?" Chloe read aloud. She straightened and added, "Haven't they been extinct since the last ice age?"

A quick Google search confirmed the massive mammals had died out on continental North America around 9,000 BCE, although they'd survived for several thousand more years on some isolated islands in the Arctic Circle.

"It doesn't mean the man was contemporary to mammoths," Veronica pointed out, although she felt as though she were trying to convince herself as much as Chloe. "He might've found a tusk somewhere, or even just a chunk of ivory, and fashioned the beads from it."

"Or, he might have found the beads," Chloe added. "Of course." She peered at Veronica through narrowed eyes. But you don't believe that, do you?"

"I . . ." Veronica shook her head. "I'm trying to hold back on drawing any conclusions until we get more pieces of the puzzle. Okay?"

"Um . . . okay," Chloe said, her voice filled with doubt.

Another puzzle piece came in an hour later when Veronica received a phone call from the Whitehorse office of the RCMP. After ending the call, she shared what she'd been told with Chloe. There was no reason not to, and talking about it helped her make sense of it.

"The mud man's dental records and DNA aren't in any of the RCMP's data bases," she began. "They asked the lab for a more detailed analysis in hopes of at least identifying what tribe he belongs to, but results were inconclusive."

"Inconclusive?" Chloe's dark brows knitted together.

"Well, basically, he doesn't belong to any known indigenous tribe, although he has a number of markers found in various West Coast Native Americans. The lab thinks the sample it was given was corrupted in some way."

"But you don't think it was corrupted, do you?"

"I don't. I asked them to send me what they have by email so I can look at it myself."

Veronica left for the hospital shortly after that, stopping for a sandwich in the cafeteria before heading up to the ICU.

The mud man looked much better than the last time she'd seen him, probably because the short trach tube sticking out of this throat was no longer attached to the ventilator machine, which sat silent against the wall to the right of his bed. He lay motionless on his back, but he apparently heard her pull the visitor's chair to the left of his bed, because he opened his eyes halfway and turned his head towards her.

She talked quietly to him, telling him about the artefacts that had been found with him and expressing her hope that he would eventually be able to tell her who he was and how he'd come to have them. He gave no indication he understood her, but after a while his mouth began to work as if he wanted to speak, and he made weak, whining sounds deep in his throat.

Veronica hesitated to touch him after what happened the last time, but she wanted to comfort him in some way. Finally, she rested her hand on his emaciated upper arm and gave it an encouraging squeeze. "Shh… don't try to talk just yet."

"He couldn't if he wanted to, what with the tracheostomy," said Beatrice as she came into the room. "His voice should return once the trach tube's removed and the incision heals." She let Veronica stay while she worked on the patient, taking his blood pressure, putting drops in his eyes, changing out his IV bag, and injecting medication into his IV line. "I'll change his catheter and get him cleaned up after you go," she said, and left Veronica alone with him again.

Veronica stayed for another half hour. The patient would drift off for a moment, then his eyes would pop open again and it would seem he was looking at her. Listening to her.

His throat worked as he repeatedly swallowed and he made another sound, this one more of a cough. His left arm rose a few centimetres beneath Veronica's hand, then dropped again. His shoulder gave a sort of shudder and then, either exhausted by these efforts or overcome by the medication flowing through his veins, he closed his eyes and fell asleep.

Veronica visited again the next day, and the day after that. While she waited in the cafeteria Thursday afternoon, the bandages were removed from the man's hands and feet and all of his stitches taken out. He was unplugged from the heart monitor, the tube had been removed from his throat, and the incision in his throat bandaged for the ten days or so it would take to close. A physical therapist began passive range of motion exercises as an initial step in what would certainly be a long and difficult rehabilitation. Dr. Webber told Veronica the antibiotics were slowly making a dent in the bacterial infection which, he added, remained unexplained as the soil and water samples from the Bennett Lake area showed no trace of *Bacillus F.* or anything else that might be considered unusual. Finally, as the patient's life no longer appeared to be in danger, he would be transferred out of the ICU to what was called the step-down unit next Monday.

The mud man was fully awake when Veronica entered his room on Friday. His eyes were open, and he turned his head in her direction as she pulled up her chair. He seemed somehow stronger today, and there was a little bit of colour in his hollow cheeks.

"Hey there," she greeted him. "I've got great news for you."

He looked up at her face, squinting and blinking repeatedly in an effort to focus. Tears welled and rolled slowly from the corners of his eyes.

Veronica grabbed a tissue from the box on the bedside table and gently dabbed his cheeks dry. As she repeated the good news the doctor had given her, the mud man painstakingly raised his right hand onto his chest. He stopped to rest, then slowly slid it up to his throat to touch the bandage there with his intact thumb. He didn't need to speak for her to understand his question.

"Yeah, um… that'll heal soon, and then you'll be able to talk. You were on a ventilator, you know, but now you're off it…" She stopped. There was no expression of comprehension on his face. Of course, if he was who she suspected he was, he didn't speak English.

His right leg kicked weakly beneath the sheets. He coughed as if clearing his throat. His mouth opened and he ran his tongue along the edge of his lips, which Veronica noticed were still dry and cracked.

"Oh God, are you thirsty? I'll go see if you can drink some water." He was being administered liquids through the nasogastric tube inserted in one nostril and taped in place to his cheek. She had no idea if he could drink the normal way.

She went out to ask Beatrice, who paged Dr. Webber. He came and said yes, if the patient was able to swallow properly, he could try to take a couple sips.

They made Veronica wait outside the room, but when they emerged a few minutes later, they were smiling.

"He choked on the first sip and spluttered all over me," said Beatrice, gesturing down at the wet spots on her uniform. "But then he swallowed three little sips like a champion."

It was wonderful news and Veronica went home hoping his progress would be smooth from now on.

This, however, proved to be what her dad called magical thinking.

5

FOR THE GOOD OF ALL CONCERNED

"He's agitated today," Leslie, the young weekend nurse, told Veronica Saturday afternoon.

"Agitated? What do you mean?" she asked.

She raised a pencil-thin black eyebrow. "Well, you know. Agitated. Moving so much we had to give him a sedative to take care of him this morning."

"A sedative? He's just awakened after being comatose for"—Veronica caught herself before she said something she would have to explain—"weeks!"

"I know. It sounds terrible, but we had no choice. He was flopping around so much he pulled the IV needle out of his arm. He could've hurt himself... or me." Tears stood in her eyes. "I'm sorry."

"Call me next time something like that happens, will you?" Veronica admonished her, although really, what difference would it have made?

She washed her hands and donned a mask and gown, and went in to see the patient.

He was sleeping soundly, still under the effects of the sedative. She didn't stay long before heading home, frustrated and disappointed by this turn of events.

She was in for more disappointment when she received the DNA analysis results from the RCMP. Considered corrupted, as the officer had said, they were, in fact, incomplete and inconclusive. Useless.

She wanted to scream.

Damn it! Fine then, I'll have to take things into my own hands.

When she returned to the hospital on Monday, she found the mud man had been transferred as scheduled to a semi-private room in the step-down unit. Masks and gowns were no longer necessary as he was no longer considered a risk or at risk for contagion. She took this as good news—until she saw him.

The steel guard rails were up on the sides of his bed. He'd been restrained with padded cuffs around his wrists that were attached to the bed frame. A peek under the sheets at the foot of his bed confirmed his legs were equally restrained with cuffs around his bony ankles.

"What the hell?" Veronica exclaimed, staring at him.

Roused by her voice, he opened his eyes and immediately began to struggle against the restraints. His movements were small and weak, but definitely intentional.

"Shh… don't do that, you'll hurt yourself," she said, dropping her voice to the soothing tone she used when talking to her kitties. She pulled up the visitor's chair to sit beside him and tried to comfort him by gently rubbing his upper arm. God, he was nothing but bones and sinew and dry, paper-thin skin.

He ceased moving and attempted to speak. His voice was barely a whisper, his words uttered in whatever language he spoke scattered amidst frantic, huffing sounds.

"Shh," she said again. She shook her head, hoping he could see well enough to make out the gesture, hoping it meant the same thing in his culture as it did in hers. She pressed the buzzer that would bring a nurse to the room.

"What's with the restraints?" she demanded as Beatrice hurried in.

"Oh, Veronica, I know. But when we moved him here this morning, he became so distraught! He hit me"—she pointed to a bruise rising on her cheek—"with his elbow. I don't think he meant to, but still…"

"He's disoriented. Confused. Probably scared to death,"

Veronica said, "and I'm pretty sure he doesn't understand a word of English."

"I agree. But we have a protocol to follow, and we have to keep everyone safe, the staff as well as the patients. I'm sorry," she said again.

Veronica took a deep, calming breath. "How is it you're even here? Aren't you an ICU nurse?"

"Dr. Webber arranged it. He thought it best the patient kept the same nurses, given his . . . unusual situation. And to tell you the truth, I wanted to."

She nodded. "Okay. Good. I'm sorry I got mad." She looked at the mud man, who had settled down as she and Beatrice talked. "He's calm now. Can't we remove the restraints?"

"No, I'm afraid we can't. We can help him sit up though, and drink some juice." She cranked the bed up a bit and poured a small amount of apple juice into a Styrofoam cup from a pitcher on the table at the side of the room.

"Here you go, love, drink this," she said. She put a straw in the cup and raised it to his mouth.

"Can I do that?" Veronica asked when she saw him close his lips around the end of the plastic straw and obediently take a drink.

"All right. Be careful, though. He's . . . unpredictable."

"I'm sure I'll be fine." Any fear she might have of the mud man was overcome by her fascination. She waited for Beatrice to leave before putting the guard rail down and sitting on the edge of the bed. She held the cup for the patient, and he obediently drained the juice one careful swallow at a time. Once he was done, he whispered a few halting words to Veronica in his pained, rasping voice, and she had the definite impression he was thanking her.

She thanked him, too, as she slipped the straw and the tissue she used to wipe saliva from the corners of his mouth into a plastic zipper bag she'd brought in hopes of such an opportunity, and stashed it in her oversized handbag.

Later that day, she dropped the specimens off at the DNA

lab where she'd sent her other samples, requesting a rush job on a complete analysis of the man's genome.

As the week went by, the mud man's physical condition continued to improve. It became clear he had some hearing and vision and was not paralyzed, although how fully he might regain function remained to be seen. The feeding tube remained in place, but he was started additionally on a nutritious liquid diet fed to him by hand. Unfortunately, as he grew stronger, he also became increasingly distressed and hard to handle.

Having asked for them, Veronica began receiving reports of difficulty changing out the patient's feeding tube and catheter, bathing him, or basically giving him any of the care he required daily. The physical therapist abandoned all hope of working with him, citing fear of bodily injury to herself or him.

Attempts to communicate with him by bringing in speakers of Heiltsuk, Tlingit, and Inuit languages failed miserably. The suggestion was made that the problem might stem from neurological damage in the language centre of his brain, rather than the man's having come from some isolated indigenous tribe who spoke an obscure dialect that had nothing in common with any other language. This made sense to the hospital staff but not to Veronica, although she wasn't willing to risk her reputation or her job by sharing her personal theory.

At least not yet.

Thursday morning while Beatrice was bathing him, the mud man managed to dislodge his feeding tube so that he nearly choked on it. That afternoon, after informing Veronica of this latest complication and receiving her reluctant agreement, Dr. Webber decided to keep the patient mildly sedated. He wouldn't be so groggy he couldn't sit up to drink, but he should remain calm enough to ensure his own safety and that of everyone concerned.

Twenty-four hours later, however, this plan was no longer feasible.

"I'm sorry, Veronica, but he can't stay here any longer," Beatrice told her at the end of a disappointing visit in which she'd found the mud man once again restrained and so heavily sedated he could barely acknowledge her presence or keep his eyes open for more than a few seconds at a time. "Dr. Webber has had word from the board of directors. I hate to say it, but I have to agree with them. Despite the miraculous recovery he's made so far, your John Doe should be in a long-term facility where he can receive the medical care he needs, along with physical and occupational therapy, and whatever other rehabilitation…" She paused, shaking her head. "Unfortunately, I can't think of any place that would take him the way he is that can offer that sort of care."

"I can," Veronica said. "Just give me a few days to set things up."

His arms and legs begin to obey him, although they are shaky like those of an old man. He has none of the strength he once knew. This frightens him.

He sees something through the fog now. Vague shapes. Dull colours. Tiny black spots float in front of him that no amount of blinking can make go away. These frighten him more.

People talk to him in that language he does not understand. They do things to him. Most times they are gentle, but sometimes they hurt him. He thinks they do not mean to. They are caring for him.

Something bad has happened to him. He tries to remember what, but he cannot. He cannot even remember his name. This frightens him most of all.

6

BREAKTHROUGH

Veronica spent the weekend and most of Monday on the phone or in meetings with Neil, Professor Sutherland, hospital administrators, and the Vancouver branch of the RCMP, who evidently all needed to be involved in her plans.

She might have begun asking herself if it was worth the effort if she hadn't received an email that afternoon that steeled her resolve. By the time she sat down to supper at the Blue Water Café with her ex-husband, Walter Cooper, she was sure she was doing the right thing.

She and Walter had been neighbours growing up in Kamloops. Despite his being six years her senior and Neil's best buddy all through school, they'd been close friends, first dates, and later, lovers. When they were both in university—she in her freshman year and he headed towards a PhD in medicine— they'd been driving home late from a Vancouver Canucks hockey game, of all things. They'd both had a beer, but they weren't drunk. Walter, who was behind the wheel had, however, missed a bend in the road and crashed his BMW coupe into a telephone pole. Neither of them were injured, but concerned that a DUI would jeopardize his future, they'd told the police Veronica had been driving and momentarily dozed off. No charges were filed. Strangely enough, the shared lie had brought them closer together, and they married the year after she graduated.

It wasn't love in the traditional, romantic sense although

they were, of course, fond of each other. Rather, it was a marriage of convenience, both of them too preoccupied with their respective careers to care much for date nights, cocooning, or starting a family. Unfortunately, their work got in the way of even this commitment, and their three-year marriage ended in an amicable divorce four years ago next month.

Walter was now a doctor running a private medical facility that treated patients with traumatic brain injuries. Veronica suspected he had some unauthorized and questionably ethical gene and stem cell procedures going on, although he'd steadfastly declined to share details with her. She also knew that, with the high level of security at the facility, it would be the perfect place for the mud man to continue his recovery. Although they remained what Walter called "friends with benefits," their work continued to get in the way, and they hadn't seen each other since his birthday early in May.

Veronica called him and asked to meet.

"So... you think this guy is... what? 10,000 years old?" Walter asked after poring over the file Veronica had given him to read while they ate. He looked across the table at her, hazel eyes narrowed behind his wire-rimmed glasses.

"The carbon-14 dating I got back today suggests he could be." She was amazed at how calm she sounded—she'd screamed and done the happy dance all around her office when she received the email from the lab. In fact, the samples of leather, wood, and ivory had all given the same results: 7,000 to 9,000 BCE, give or take a few hundred years either way. "The DNA test the RCMP had done on him is inconclusive. They think the sample was corrupted, but I think they just weren't expecting what they found. I'm having another one done. I should get the results back in the next few days."

Walt scrutinized one of the pages of the report she'd typed up on her laptop and printed out.

"And you think the mutated *Bacillus F.* bacteria has something to do with him surviving having been frozen in some ancient mud hole for millennia?"

She drained her second glass of red wine in one long swallow. "I do. I don't have any proof—yet—but I'm hoping eventually we'll find a way to communicate. My God, Walt, can you imagine it? A Neolithic man right here with us? Alive in the 21st century?"

He guffawed and retorted, "When he gets a look at how things are now he might want to go back to the Stone Age." He didn't say anything more until they were halfway through dessert and coffee.

"Okay, Vee, I'll take him . . . on one condition."

Veronica didn't much like the way that sounded. "And what would that be?"

He ran his fingers over his neat, dark blond mustache and took his sweet time answering her. "I want unlimited access for tests and research purposes. No questions asked. I want to know what, where, and how he was infected by that bacterium, and if it really... If there's any way to reproduce, replicate, or simulate whatever allowed him to remain alive while frozen, I want to find it. Do you understand? I want it!"

He gave her a pointed look. "In exchange, he'll get the best care my facility can offer, and all the privacy you want for him. We'll re-evaluate the arrangement in... let's see... six months?"

With a sudden sinking feeling she might eventually regret it, that perhaps this wasn't the best solution after all, but unable to see another, she agreed.

The next two days were crammed with meetings between lawyers—Neil and a no-nonsense, red-haired woman called Fiona Harrison, who represented Cooper Medical—Walter, and Veronica herself. By the end of Wednesday's business supper at a five-star restaurant near the facility, arrangements had been made and comprehensive non-disclosure agreements and contracts drawn up and signed. NDAs would be sent to everyone so far involved in the mud man's case, including Professor Sutherland and his students, doctors and nurses who had treated him both in Whitehorse and at Vancouver General, and of course Chloe, who was already privy to more than anyone else besides Walter himself. As Walter had suggested previously, the situation would be re-evaluated in February of the following year.

Veronica visited the mud man for the first time that week on Thursday. While he wasn't in restraints and he'd been turned onto his right side—Beatrice had explained how bedridden patients needed to be moved periodically to prevent bedsores and other complications—she was dismayed to find him once again too doped up to pay any attention to her.

She'd arranged to see Dr. Webber, who gave her a detailed protocol for the patient's ongoing care and a list of the medications he was receiving, including but not limited to antibiotics, pain meds, anti-seizure lorazepam, a laxative to ensure that he didn't become constipated—apparently a problem with bedridden patients—and anti-inflammatory eye drops. He'd already forwarded the patient's file electronically to Cooper Medical, and asked to be kept up to date on the patient's progress. Veronica assured him she would do so, and she signed the necessary papers to have him released.

Twenty-four hours later, the mud man was transported by ambulance to Walter's facility in North Vancouver. He was placed in a spacious basement room equipped with all the necessary medical paraphernalia as he was still hooked up to his feeding tube, IV line, and catheter. A heart monitor and oxygen tank stood in one corner of the room, ready should they be required. A video camera had been installed so he could be observed 24/7 from the nurses' station at the end of the corridor. Veronica sat in a comfortably padded folding chair to the right side of his bed, waiting for him to wake up. Although she hated to admit it, he'd needed to be heavily sedated to avoid any problems during the transfer.

In her hand she held her cell phone, open to her email inbox and the PDF attached to the message she'd received only moments ago from the DNA lab. It confirmed her wildest suspicions and then some. The mud man's DNA contained markers found in ancient East Asian and North Eurasian ancestry and the recently discovered but now extinct Ancient Beringian genome. These various peoples were believed to have migrated to North America over the Bering Strait land bridge in separate waves between 40,000 and 13,000 years ago and were credited with being the ancestors of modern Native Americans. He also had nine percent Neanderthal DNA—more than twice that of any modern human—and while he had a number of markers found in Heiltsuk, Tlingit, and Tagish people, his DNA matched none of the genomes for the known tribes. It was what she'd been hoping for, what she'd been preparing herself for, but it still seemed too good to be true.

No wonder the RCMP lab techs thought the sample was corrupted. They weren't expecting to find the DNA of a 9,000 or 10,000-year-old man.

She wanted to shout it to the world, but she'd settled for discreetly showing Walter the PDF. The information was confidential, history-rewriting-explosive, but a public announcement would have to wait until she published her first paper.

Walter stood by Veronica's side now, as anxious as she was for the mud man to awaken.

Thinking the sight and smell of the forest might comfort him, Veronica had sent Chloe out yesterday to buy two potted ferns and two dwarf cedars, which were tidily placed along one side of the room. The young woman had also procured a black bear rug which was freshly cleaned and now lay spread on the floor near the trees, and two tanned deerskins, which Veronica had draped over the foot of the bed. The sound of the ocean wafted from her old CD player on the table in one corner of the room.

It seemed to help.

The patient remained calm as the sedative wore off. His

eyes still closed, he began to chant, his voice hoarse and frequently cracking, but stronger than it had been a few days earlier.

After a good ten minutes, his monotone chant dropped off and he opened his eyes. He turned his head left and right in an effort to take in whatever he could make out of his surroundings. His eyes had cleared somewhat over the past weeks, giving Veronica hope that his vision was improving.

"Hey there," she said in the gentle voice she always used with him. "You've been moved to a new hospital, but don't worry, you're going to be okay here. We'll take good care of you." She knew for certain now that he didn't understand a word, but she hoped he understood her tone.

He looked up at her, blinking and squinting in an effort to focus. He took a number of long, deep breaths, perhaps noticing the odour of the animal skins mingled with the hospital smell, and almost smiled.

He tapped weakly at his chest with the palm of his right hand. His mouth worked silently for a moment, then he whispered something that sounded like, "*Xat Dom-ma.*"

It meant nothing to Veronica, but apparently it was important to him, as he repeated it over and over. After a couple minutes, however, his energy waned or he simply gave up trying to communicate with her. His arm dropped to his side, and he turned his head the other way, towards the pristine white wall.

When they were certain he'd fallen asleep again, she and Walter left the room. Veronica headed to the university's administrative office, where she officially deposited her request for a year's sabbatical from teaching to work on a special and, for the moment, confidential project.

He lets them believe he is asleep, but he is not sleeping. He is thinking. He remembers things now, remembers who he is

and where he comes from. He remembers being cold—so very cold—and he knows he has lost his toes and fingertips to the ice.

He does not know where he is now, only that it is a different place from before. Here, there are some familiar smells amidst the strange, bitter ones, giving him hope that he is not so far from home.

Walter had on his staff a burly Native American man named Ty Forestall, who had been with him since the opening of the facility six years ago. He was the perfect nurse-slash-therapist for the mud man's daily care and physical therapy. Although he'd been required to sign the NDA, he, like the rest of the staff, had been told only that the patient was a member of a remote northern indigenous tribe recovering from frostbite and multiple traumatic injuries, the best lie being one close to the truth.

Ty joined Walter and Veronica the next morning on their tour of the hospital.

In spite of herself, Veronica was impressed. Everyone they encountered was pleasant, polite, and professional. The handful of nurses and orderlies wore crisp, white uniforms while the security crew of three wore navy blue. Everything about the facility boasted "state of the art," beginning with the fourth and top floor, where labs and an operating room were located. The third floor held a dozen private rooms, about half of them occupied by patients in various states of consciousness, as well as a two-bed ICU. On the second floor, one wing of the L-shaped building held examination rooms and the security hub, while the opposite wing was home to a comfortably furnished sunroom, a cafeteria, and a handful of offices. On the first floor were the reception area, which was really a glorified security desk where all arrivals were required to sign in and out, a cozy lounge, and the radiology department. In the basement, in the opposite wing from the mud man's room, was the physical and occupational therapy department, complete with a variety of equipment for patients to use in their rehabilitation. A second room in the mud man's wing was reserved for special cases but, Walter admitted, had never been used. The remaining space was taken up with storage rooms and closets.

Ty accompanied Veronica when she went into the mud man's room after the tour, part of Walter's protocol being that she should not be alone with the patient until they were certain he posed no threat to her. Once again, they wore no masks, Dr. Webber having told Walter in his email that he saw no continuing need for them as long as no one had symptoms of a cold or the flu, or—God forbid—COVID-19, which still caused occasional outbreaks in the general population.

Ty had given the patient his liquid breakfast before the tour. He was still sitting up halfway, one of the deerskins draped over his bony shoulders, covering most of his blue and white striped hospital gown. His colour was good, and he looked more fully awake than he had in the past week.

"Good morning, you!" Veronica said cheerfully.

The mud man began to babble in his native tongue, clearly recognizing her and determined to communicate.

Ty followed her to the bed and stood beside her chair, as if to protect her should the patient become agitated. He'd been made aware of the troubles at Vancouver General.

The mud man struggled to push himself further upright against his pillows, managing with help from Ty. Cupping the fingers and thumb of his less damaged right hand, he brought it to his mouth and made the universal sign for drinking. "*Ti-en*," he said, his voice almost pleading. "*Ti-en*."

"Can he have something?" Veronica asked over her shoulder.

"Sure." Ty brought a Styrofoam cup of water, which he held for the man to drink.

When he'd drained the cup, the mud man nodded. "*Taa*," he said with a faint smile. "*Ti-en*."

"*Ti-en*?" Veronica pronounced it "tie-en," the way he did. "I think that means 'water' or 'drink.' "

"Either way," Ty agreed behind her, "it looks like he knows what he's saying, even if we don't."

"Get him some more, please." This time, Veronica held the cup to the mud man's lips herself.

He raised both hands towards the cup, but in his awkward effort to clasp it between them he knocked it out of her grasp, spilling water onto his chest and lap.

"Holy crap!" Ty muttered, reaching for the cup that had fallen to the floor.

But far from being upset, the mud man was chuckling softly. "*Ti-en*," he gasped when he stopped laughing. "*Taa. Taa!*"

"*Ti-ęn*," Veronica repeated as she patted the front of the patient's gown dry with a towel handed to her by Ty. "Water."

The mud man looked at her, blinking, his face creased with puzzlement. Then his dark eyebrows shot up. "Wat-er?"

"Water," she said again, nodding. "*Ti-en*. Water."

"Wat-er. *Taa!*" His face brightened and he poked his wet chest with his thumb. "*Dom-ma.*" Another poke. "*Dom!*"

"Dom? Are you telling me that's your name? My name's Veronica." She tapped her sternum with her hand. Then, uncertain whether he could clearly see the gesture, she reached for his hand, careful to avoid the sensitive ends of his amputated fingers, and placed it on her shoulder. "Veronica."

His forehead creased. "Vee-orn-a?"

"Vee," she said, thinking that perhaps "Veronica" was too much for him. "Vee."

He grunted. "Vee." With great effort that showed in the grim set of his mouth, he raised his hand to touch her cheek with his calloused palm. Then he lowered it to tap his chest. "Dom."

"And I'm Ty," said the nurse, leaning in close to the bed. He gently took Dom's hand and touched it to his chest. "Ty."

"Ty," Dom said, nodding. He pointed to himself. "*Xat* Dom." Then, gesturing towards Veronica and Ty respectively, he added, "*Xat* Vee. *Xat* Ty. *Taa*!" He gave a satisfied smile and continued with a string of words in his language, his tone questioning, until he seemed to realize no answer was forthcoming, and he fell silent, his hand dropping heavily onto his lap.

"Poor guy," Ty said with a sympathetic shake of his head. "Can you imagine what it's like to be in his condition, no idea where he is, surrounded by people who don't speak his language? And no one's come to claim him?"

"They haven't," Veronica said. She wished she could tell him why, but she held her tongue.

"That's crap," he commiserated. "Well... I've gotta give him his meds, get him washed and changed and all that. Do some physical therapy with him. You can watch on the monitor in the station down the hall, if you want to."

"I will." She gave Dom's skinny arm a squeeze and left the room, hopeful that today's breakthrough would lead to even better things tomorrow.

7

LEARNING CURVE

Forcing herself to trust Dom's care to Walter and his staff, Veronica took a personal day Sunday. She went swimming and spent some quality time with her kitties. She called her parents and Kim to give them as much news as she could, and she promised to visit them in Kamloops as soon as possible. Ultimately unable to take her mind off him, she spent the evening on her laptop, putting order into everything she'd written up so far about the mud man and planning how to proceed.

She arrived at Cooper Medical at 10:00 Monday morning to find Beatrice at the nurses' station, dressed in the requisite white uniform with the Cooper Medical insignia on it.

"What are you doing here?" she asked, her voice rising in pleasant surprise, but she'd already guessed at the answer before Beatrice replied.

"Your Dr. Cooper came to see me last week," the older woman said. "Thought it a good idea to have someone familiar caring for Jo—oh, it's Dom now, isn't it?—and well, he made me an offer I couldn't refuse. I took my vacation days and told the hospital I wouldn't be going back. I'll be working days Sunday and Monday, and nights Wednesday through Friday. Started this morning." She glanced at the monitor and Veronica followed suit. "He's had breakfast and I'll be back in for his morning care as soon as the orderly comes down to help—ah, here he is now!"

Veronica watched on the monitor as Beatrice and Alex, a young African American orderly built like a football player, gave Dom his medications through his IV line and took care of his morning medical and hygiene needs, with Alex doing the turning and lifting of the patient.

After a few minutes, it occurred to her that Dom was unnaturally calm, barely moving as he was washed and clothed in a man-sized diaper and a clean, striped gown. Seconds later, she was in his room.

"Don't tell me you sedated him?" she demanded, hands on her hips. "He doesn't need—"

"Dr. Cooper's orders," Beatrice said. "Dom's scheduled for examinations today—blood and tissue samples, x-rays and MRI imaging—and he thought it would be easier if the patient slept through it all. I'm afraid I had to agree. He said you'll get the results as soon as he does."

"You better believe it," Veronica grumbled, but she did see the sense of this. "Okay then." She looked down at Dom, sleeping peacefully now under the effects of the sedative. "I'll come back this afternoon."

With nothing to gain by staying at the facility, Veronica spent the day shopping for items she hoped would contribute to Dom's comfort and progress. She returned late in the afternoon with a box of wooden plates and bowls, cups and spoons. She dropped these off in the cafeteria with a request that they be kept exclusively for use by the patient in room B1. Then she went to Dom's room and deposited a bag of clothes—half a dozen tee-shirts and three pajama bottoms for him to wear instead of those embarrassing hospital gowns, a grey terry cloth bathrobe, and a pair of moccasin-style slippers—in his closet. Finally, she placed a toothbrush, toothpaste, and a comb for when his hair grew long enough to need it beside the sink in the small bathroom adjoining his room.

Ignoring Walter's order that she not be alone with Dom, she quietly pulled up the folding chair and sat beside the bed. The first thing she noticed was that the feeding tube had been removed from his nose, an encouraging sign that he was now able to take in sufficient nutrition the normal way. The second thing was the way he lay, on his back with his arms crossed over his chest, reminding her of the position he'd been in when he was found. His eyes were closed, but he wasn't asleep. Rather, he was chanting under his breath. She listened for a few minutes, trying to make out individual words but ultimately unable to catch more than the most frequently repeated syllables which, of course, meant absolutely nothing to her.

The enormity of teaching the mud man about the modern world suddenly struck her. Never mind he didn't speak English; he would have no word in his own language for most of the things around him. No concept whatsoever what they were. As much as she wanted to learn about his world, she realized that teaching him about hers might prove the more difficult of the two.

She feared she wouldn't be up to the challenge, but she would do her best. Like someone at NASA famously said, failure was not an option.

Beatrice came in just then, followed by Alex pushing a cart with a tray holding two of the newly purchased wooden bowls and a wooden spoon.

The activity roused Dom, who ceased his chanting and opened his eyes to peer expectantly from Veronica to the others.

"Supper's here, love," said Beatrice as she began to raise the bed. "Let's get you sitting up."

Alex rolled the narrow table that fit over Dom's legs into place and put the tray on it.

Dom immediately reached for the tray, groping around the nearest bowl before grasping it precariously between his palms.

"Easy there!" Alex exclaimed, reaching for the bowl before Dom sloshed what looked and smelled like chicken broth everywhere. He helped Dom raise the bowl to his lips, held it steady while he took a few sips, then lowered it again to the table.

"*Taa*," said Dom, nodding. A smile spread slowly across his face. "*Dom doo. Sen. Sen!*" With help from Alex, he raised the bowl and drank on his own, spilling only a few drops as he returned it to the tray.

Dom finished all the chicken broth a few minutes later and reached for the second bowl, which contained applesauce.

"No, Dom, not like that!" Veronica gently took the bowl from him. Balancing it in one hand, she placed the spoon in Dom's right hand. His shortened fingers were weak and stiff, but she managed to fold them around the stem of the spoon. Holding his fist closed, she guided it to scoop up some applesauce and raise it to his mouth.

"Oh my," Beatrice said under her breath. "Who is this poor lad that he doesn't know how to use a spoon?"

"He must have some sort of brain injury," Alex suggested. "Some of the patients here can't talk or pick up a spoon, or even remember their own name."

After a couple misses that resulted in applesauce on his cheek and chin, Dom got the idea of pushing the spoonful of applesauce into his mouth. "*Sen,*" he said, scraping the bottom of the bowl with the spoon. He looked at Veronica. "*Sen?*"

"I think that means 'more,' " Veronica said, turning to Beatrice. "Can he have more? Look at him, he's skin and bones."

She shook her head. "He's on a strict diet, with a slight increase in quantity and calories every few days. Too much all at once would do him more harm than good." As she spoke, she gently wiped Dom's face clean with a paper napkin from the tray.

"Right. Of course." Veronica turned to Dom as Alex cleared the table and pushed it away. "I'm sorry, Dom. You can't have—"

"*Sen!*" he insisted, adding a string of words in his language. His voice cracked and he stopped to clear his throat. "*Sen. Taa!* Yes!"

There was no way to explain to him the need to gradually increase his food intake. Instead, she asked, "You want some water?" She gestured for Beatrice to fill a cup. "*Ti-en*? Yes?"

"*Ti-en. Taa*," he replied grumpily. "Wat-er."

With help from Veronica, he held the cup between his hands and drained it in a few long swallows. "*Ti-en. Lah-taa*," he said with a nod of satisfaction.

Assuming "*lah-taa*" meant "good" or maybe "thank you," Veronica took the cup back and said, "You're welcome."

She left shortly after that, but was back Tuesday morning to watch Ty begin Dom's therapy session. After a few minutes, however, she realized observation on a computer monitor in the nurses' station wasn't enough for her. She wanted to be involved.

She ventured into the room and told Ty of her intentions. He reluctantly agreed it was a good idea, and so she began learning the exercises that would eventually get Dom out of bed—in a wheelchair at first but, hopefully, one day on what was left of his feet—and using his hands well enough to take care of himself.

Contrary to his behaviour at Vancouver General, Dom was now cooperating during PT without being sedated. He had reasonable control of his arms and legs, but no strength to speak of. Any sustained effort brought tremors to the involved limbs and tears to his eyes. He grimaced in pain when Ty manipulated his left leg, which bore a thick, red surgical scar along half the length of his thigh, but he didn't cry out, as if this was a weakness he wouldn't allow himself.

After Ty gave Dom his lunch of chicken broth—this time with minute bits of chicken and vegetables in it—more applesauce, and milk in a wooden cup, he and Veronica went to the facility cafeteria for their lunch. They then spent an hour doing occupational therapy to improve Dom's fine motor skills—at this stage, moving his fingers individually and holding a cup or spoon was an achievement. Finally, Veronica left the room to allow Ty to get Dom changed from his hospital gown into a tee-shirt and pajama bottoms.

By Thursday, Dom was strong enough to turn onto his side

on his own, and sit properly upright in bed to consume his meals of fruit-vegetable smoothies, beef or chicken soup, and applesauce or vanilla pudding from a cup or bowl. They hit a speed bump, however, when it came to taking pills meant to gradually replace his IV medications. He chewed the first one Ty gave him and immediately spit it out on the floor, following this action with a stream of words in his language that were almost certainly curses. He batted away Ty's hand and refused to open his mouth when Ty tried to force the issue. As a last resort, Ty and Veronica swallowed a couple Tylenol each to show Dom how it was done and prove that it was perfectly safe to do so, and finally Dom conceded to taking his first pill by mouth, swallowing it with a long drink of water.

Dom must have been confused and terrified by the strange people and things all around him—and understandably so—but he also proved curious and eager to learn. He was better at retaining words in English than either Veronica, Ty, or Beatrice were in his language. After only a few days, he knew several dozen useful words—mostly parts of the body, food items, and simple words like, "yes," "no," "more," "good," "eat," and "drink." Veronica was taking notes with the lofty goal of compiling a dictionary of English words and their phonetic equivalent in what she had come to think of as Post-Beringian although, as she'd suspected, Dom had no word for modern items such as pajamas, therapy, pill, or toothbrush.

His physical condition continued to improve as well. By the following Tuesday, he was eating limited portions of soft food with his fingers or a spoon, although he could only handle a few bites at a time, throwing up within minutes if he ate too much. With help from Ty and Veronica, he could sit up on the edge of the bed to do some of his PT, but his balance was poor, and he needed support so he didn't fall over. Ty made a priority of working on his core muscles so that he could sit up on his own. The x-rays and MRIs taken the previous week showed that the fractured ribs, femur, and pelvis were sufficiently healed to envision getting him out of bed in the next few weeks. They also revealed a previously torn but healed ligament in his right ankle. Mild osteoporosis and osteoarthritis in his right shoulder and wrist, and in both knees and ankles indicated long-term poor nutrition and an arduous lifestyle.

On the other hand, Dom's blood cell count and other values were within normal range, and blood, urine, and tissue tests indicated that the *Bacillus F.* had either been vanquished, or had fallen to such low levels as to be undetectable. After discussing it with Dr. Webber, Walter halted the antibiotics that Dom had been on for weeks, noting that this would probably help with his nausea issues as well.

Ty removed Dom's IV line and exchanged the disgusting and degrading diapers Dom had by necessity worn for a slightly less disgusting and degrading bedpan, and spent the morning teaching the patient how to use it. The catheter would remain in place until Dom was able to get to the bathroom when he needed to. He'd suffered two brief seizures since arriving at Cooper Medical, both at the end of the day, possibly brought on by fatigue, and he remained on a daily dose of lorazepam in hopes of preventing any further episodes.

Things were unfortunately slowing down on the communication front. Everything about living in the modern world had to be painstakingly explained to Dom: pills, bedpans, toothpaste, toothbrush, sheets, and pillows were only the beginning. Veronica couldn't even fathom how she might explain electricity and running water, let alone currency and the internet.

Every two days or so, Walter came to see how the patient was doing. Although he appeared to be genuinely interested in Dom, Veronica suspected he only wanted to keep an eye on his investment. Every evening, she wrote up a report on her laptop of Dom's progress that day, in addition to the phonetic form of any new words she learned in his language.

Thursday afternoon, reflecting on how early indigenous people had left records of their lives in the form of rock art and petroglyphs, Veronica bought a whiteboard and a box of erasable markers, hoping that Dom's impaired vision wouldn't preclude his using them. If she wanted to teach him about her life and culture and learn anything about his, they needed to get past the language barrier, and while she took for granted that he would have no writing system, she figured he could draw stick figures at least as well as she could.

"This is a board," she told him, setting it flat across his outstretched legs and sitting down on the edge of the bed.

He looked down at it, blinking and tilting his head this way and that as he tended to do, his forehead creasing in puzzlement. He touched it with his fingers, then he rapped on it with the knuckles of his right hand. "Board," he said. "*Tah.*" Yes. He shrugged as if to say, "What's it for?"

Veronica pulled the cap off the black marker and carefully wrapped his right hand around it so that he held it like a dagger. "Marker."

Frowning, Dom said, "Mark-er." He sniffed it and made to put it in his mouth, but she stopped him with a hand on his wrist.

"*T-lay doo,*" she said firmly, although she wanted to laugh. "No eat." She guided his hand to the board and helped him draw a large circle, then a spiral, two figures common in prehistoric art.

He peered down at the figures and a smile slowly appeared on his face.

She picked up the eraser brush and wiped the board, never expecting the reaction this would engender.

Dom let out a distressed yelp, dropping the marker, and would have flung the board away if Veronica hadn't stopped him. He pushed himself as far away as he could against the headboard of his bed, clearly horrified by the disappearing drawings.

Veronica and Ty, who had been hovering behind her, did

their best to explain to Dom what the board was and how they could use it to talk to each other. After some prolonged, distressed babbling in his language, he calmed down and allowed Veronica to put the marker back in his hand. She drew another circle with him, then she replaced the marker with the eraser.

"Eraser," she said, repeating it until Dom nodded and said the word back to her. She guided him to erase the circle.

Marker. Eraser. Draw. Erase. Catching on, Dom placed his left hand on the board, his fingers spread apart, and traced around it. Then he changed hands, fumbling to hold the marker in his more severely crippled left hand, and did the same thing.

Leaning down to peer closely at the board, he carefully drew two circles, one inside the other, in the space between his index fingers and thumbs—or at least between his right thumb and where his left thumb should have been. The image looked vaguely familiar to Veronica, but she couldn't place it.

"Dom-ma," he said, tapping his right hand against the prints on the board and then touching his chest. "Dom." He held the marker out. "Ve-roni-ca," he said, using her whole name for the first time. "Hand. *Denzi*. Draw."

"Just like we see in caves and rock art all over the world," she said to Ty. She took the marker and traced her hands on the board to the right of Dom's prints.

He looked at Veronica's handprints for a moment. Then, with his right index finger, he traced the concentric circles between his own prints, half erasing them, but seeming not to notice.

"*Xat* Dom," he repeated, tapping his chest. He pointed to the faded black tattoo about five centimetres in diameter of two concentric circles on the inside of his right forearm. "Dom." He touched Veronica's prints with his finger. Pointed at her.

"Okay, I get it!" she exclaimed as it came to her. "I have to make a mark between my prints, like a signature." After thinking about it for a few seconds, she went with the obvious choice and drew a large "V" in the diamond between her handprints.

Dom nodded with satisfaction and turned towards Ty. "Ty?" he said. "Ty. Hand. *Denzi.*"

Ty took the marker and traced his prints below Veronica's, adding a thick "T" between them.

"Good," Dom said, suddenly beaming a smile at them. "*Lah-taa.*" He tapped the board with his knuckles again. "Board good." Then he lay back against his pillows and closed his eyes, clearly exhausted.

Veronica put the board and markers on the table and left Dom to rest.

The people in this place are kind to him, especially Vee and Ty and Bee-a. Vee brought something called a board and marker. This is a good thing. It will help him learn their words. Help him teach them his words.

His pain is less, except for his left leg. His ribs when he takes a deep breath. And his toes. How can toes hurt when they are no longer there?

His eyes are not good, but they are better than before. The fog is thinner, with a few clear patches, even though the black spots remain. His right ear is good, but his left ear hears only a faint buzz. He hopes his sight and hearing will return to normal, but if they do not, he will adapt.

If there is one thing he knows how to do, it is to adapt.

8

THE FINE ART OF COMMUNICATION

The whiteboard turned out to be a stroke of genius. Friday, in between meals, therapy, and Dom's afternoon nap, Veronica used it to teach him basic English words like the colours of the markers and simple directions—up, down, left, right—and how to count to ten. In turn, Dom proved to be quite an artist despite his questionable vision and damaged hands, painstakingly drawing large, simple figures of items from his life—in the appropriate colours—and exchanging words for them with Veronica and Ty.

Fish. Tree. Mountain. River. Bird. Man. Woman. Baby.

It was late afternoon and Ty suggested stopping for supper when Dom drew the image that would change everything.

"*Choo-ka-too*," Dom informed them, tapping the image of what looked like an elephant with huge, yellow tusks and shaggy, brown fur.

"An elephant?" Ty guessed, his tone doubtful.

"No." Veronica worked her tongue around inside her mouth to produce some saliva, which seemed suddenly to have dried up. "It's a woolly mammoth." She pointed to the image and said to Dom, "Mammoth."

"Mam-moth," said Dom, nodding. "*Choo-ka-too*." He looked from Veronica to Ty and back to Veronica, obviously pleased with the response this drawing was getting. "Good." He rubbed his stomach and grinned. "Mam-moth. *Lah-ta doo.* Good. Uh, much eat."

"That's impossible," Ty objected. "Mammoths died out thousands of years a—oh, God." His jaw dropped and his normally dark tan face paled to a chalky beige. "He . . . no." He shook his head. "No way."

"We're still trying to figure out how it can be true, but it looks like it is." Veronica turned away from Dom and lowered her voice to avoid him catching any of her words. "He comes from a time when the last mammoths still roamed northern Canada." She steered him away from the bed and explained where and how Dom had been found and what she knew so far, finishing with, "You can't tell anyone, Ty. Aside from them thinking you're crazy, you've signed the NDA. You—"

"Don't worry," he interrupted, nodding slowly as he recovered his senses. "I get it now. I get why he doesn't know a word of English, or how to use a spoon or brush his teeth. Why you and Doc Cooper have been giving him such extra special treatment."

"Walt wants to know what kept Dom alive while he was frozen for something like 9,500 years," Veronica said, "and I want to know everything about his life before whatever happened to him happened. That's why it's so important we learn to communicate with him."

"No friggin' kidding." Ty looked past her to Dom, who sat motionless, staring blankly at his mammoth, clearly plunged into memories from his past. "I'll do everything I can to help all three of you."

Although Dom asked for the whiteboard and markers as soon as Veronica and Ty entered his room Saturday afternoon, Ty confiscated them for his own use. Sitting beside Dom on the bed, he made a series of line drawings to help explain how today they were going to get Dom out of bed and sitting in a wheelchair.

Dom indicated that he understood and seemed eager, but Veronica worried that he wasn't ready for such a major move without getting upset or having a seizure.

Thankfully, her fears proved to be unfounded, as Ty more or less lifted Dom into the wheelchair he'd brought into the room earlier that morning.

Once Dom was settled in the chair with his catheter clamped off and his feet safely on the footrests, Ty took his pulse and blood pressure. Both were elevated, but not alarmingly so. He gave the patient a few minutes to get used to sitting in the chair, then he slowly wheeled him around the room with Veronica walking beside him.

"Ah, good," Dom said, although he clutched the armrests for dear life for the first few minutes. When he finally relaxed enough to let his hands drop onto his lap, Ty showed him how to make the wheelchair move.

With Ty providing a little extra power from behind and Veronica still at his side, Dom wheeled himself clumsily once around the room. When he stopped, he was breathing hard and beads of sweat stood out on his forehead, but he was smiling.

"Good job, buddy," Ty said. Taking a critical look at his patient, he added, "I think that's enough excitement for today."

They got Dom to bed without a fuss and left him to rest before suppertime came around, but they were confident he'd taken a big step forward.

They were right.

Only five days later, Dom was able to get into his wheelchair with minimal help, the biggest obstacle being the catheter and urine bag he still wore.

This afternoon, he was determined to wheel himself all around the room, touching everything he encountered and asking, "*Oh-cho?*" What?

While Ty pushed the cabinet containing medical supplies out of the room to avoid any possibility of an accident now that Dom was mobile, Veronica gave Dom words for everything— walls, table, chair, bed, potted ferns, waste basket. When he ran into the bear skin rug, she picked it up and laid it across his legs.

He clutched the fur for a moment, then nodded in recognition. "*Shashay*," he said. He raised his arms, short fingers curved into claws, and growled ferociously. "*Shashay*."

"Bear," Veronica said as Ty returned.

"Bear." Dom dropped the rug on the floor and wheeled himself back to the table, where he'd found the board earlier. Veronica helped him place the board across the arms of his chair and handed him the box of markers.

He chose the black marker and, stopping only once to rest, he drew the form of a man with a spear held high, poised to fly, facing the figure of a bear standing up on its hind legs. He dropped the marker in his lap and tapped the human figure with his palm. "Dom," he said. He tapped the bear figure and made a swiping motion with his left hand. "Bear." Then he pulled up his tee-shirt to reveal four long, white scars across the left side of his chest. "Bear," he said again, running his remaining thumb along each of the scars in turn. "*Oon.*" Hurt.

Veronica moaned. "Oh God. You mean a bear did that?"

He nodded. "*Taa.* Bear bad . . . Eraser?" Ty handed him the eraser and he wiped the board clean. Then he drew a group of five men close together and the bear, this time on its back with its feet in the air. "*Den-no-ny.*" He tapped the group of people. "*Den-no-ny.* Bear good eat."

"So, he got hurt hunting the bear, but in the end they killed and ate it," Ty surmised.

"Looks like," Veronica agreed, her heart picking up a tick at this peek into Dom's life; it was exactly the kind of thing she wanted to hear. She chastised herself for not taking photos of the images he'd drawn so far and vowed to bring her cell phone with her from now on.

Without warning, Dom pushed the board away. As it fell to the floor with a clatter, he wheeled himself towards the side of the room.

Too surprised and curious to make a move to stop him, Veronica and Ty watched as he placed his left hand on the pristine white wall and began tracing around it with the marker. When his two handprints were on the wall, he drew the now familiar double circles between them, effectively signing the wall.

"Vee. Ty," he said, gesturing towards them and then the wall. He held the marker out for one of them to take it.

Veronica grasped the marker and put her prints on the wall, just beside Dom's. Ty did likewise, tracing his hands above Dom's.

"Doc Cooper's gonna shit bricks when he sees this wall," Ty said with a chuckle. He took a step back and gave Dom a heartfelt thump on the shoulder. "Good job, Dom!"

"Yes," Dom said, nodding. "Good Vee. Good Ty. Good draw hand wall."

Dom's progress continued slowly but steadily over the next week, with one complication. Even after the laxatives were withdrawn from his daily medication, he suffered from loose stools, frequent stomach cramps, and occasional nausea, and everyone had assumed these were side effects of the antibiotics that were being pumped into him. He was off them now, though, and through trial and error they finally realized he was somewhat lactose intolerant, suffering the consequences if he consumed too much milk, cream soup, or cheese. That made sense to Veronica and confirmed the hypothesis that early indigenous people were hunter-gatherers rather than farmers. Dairy products would not have been part of their diet once a baby stopped nursing from its mother.

By Wednesday, Dom was eating slightly more substantial portions of food and chugging non-dairy protein drinks boosted with vitamins and minerals. He was able to slide from his bed to his wheelchair, although he still needed help getting back into bed. He could get himself to the bathroom to wash his hands and face and use the toilet with a minimum of help from Ty or Alex, although it took him two days to get over the shock of running water and the sound of the flushing toilet. This allowed Ty to finally remove the catheter, and it was about time too. Now that he had better use of his hands, Dom had begun pulling it out at night, making a mess and risking harming himself in the process.

He understood close to a hundred words and used them, along with his drawings, to communicate. When he wasn't in therapy, doing the range of motion exercises Ty had given him to do whenever he could, or resting, he kept himself busy watering his trees and ferns with the plastic watering can Veronica had brought in or covering the walls within reach with his unique brand of art. He drew credible images of people, trees, birds, fish, and animals including caribou, bears, rabbits, wolves, and another mammoth. He even drew a couple pot-bellied horses that looked remarkably like the ones painted on the walls of the famous Altamira and Lascaux caves in Europe. There was an orange sun, a silver full moon, and wavy blue lines representing water. Most striking—besides maybe the mammoth—was the tipi tent he called an *isaah*, similar to the summer houses made by modern indigenous people from poles and skins of seals or caribou.

It was Dom's world as he remembered it—a rich, colourful world in harmony with nature. Veronica watched him create it from the monitor in the nurses' station and took photos when she went into his room.

Surprisingly enough, far from being angry at the desecration of his walls, Walter was thrilled to see that efforts to communicate with Dom were bearing fruit.

"Keep it up," he said to Veronica after his visit with Dom the following Tuesday. "He has to learn enough English to tell me what I want to know."

Over the weekend, Dom had got Beatrice and Alex to trace their handprints close to the others. After his therapy Wednesday morning, he took a blue marker from the box on the table and wheeled himself over to the wall with the prints. Groaning as he stretched to reach high enough to do so, he drew a shaky square around the five sets of handprints.

"Dom," he said, tapping his prints. "Vee. Ty. Alex. Bee-a." At each name, he tapped the corresponding prints. Then he traced the box around them. "Wall." He dropped the marker in his lap and wheeled himself to where he'd drawn the people and tents. "*Den-no-ny*," he said, the word Veronica guessed meant his people. "Sun. Mountains. Birds. Good."

He wheeled himself to the next wall and slapped it with his hand. "Wall." Then on to the next. "Wall." He pushed on to the wall with the door. "Wall. Bad!"

"He's fed up with being cooped up here," Veronica said. "Of course, he is. All he's ever known is the great outdoors and the endless sky. He's probably worried his world doesn't exist anymore."

"It doesn't," Ty said grimly.

"Well, it sort of does. I mean, the mountains and trees and sun are still there, even if his people aren't. I think some fresh air and sunshine would do him good. Is there any reason why he can't go outside?"

Ty frowned, thinking this over. "Medically, no, I guess not. But just for a few minutes. The last thing he needs is to catch a cold." He got Dom wrapped in his bathrobe over his pajamas, the deer skin over his legs, and put his slippers on his feet while Veronica explained as best she could that they were going out to see the sun and trees.

Dom's eyebrows shot up and he nearly nodded his head off. "*Tah.* Sun good. Trees good. Yes. Go."

Veronica grabbed her jacket and Ty's from the closet in the nurses' station and they shrugged them on, but Dom moaned as he looked around him from left to right and up to the ceiling.

He reached out to touch the nearest wall and exclaimed, "More wall? No! Go sun. Yes. Trees. Yes. Go—"

"Wait just a minute, Dom," Veronica said. "We'll be outside soon." Of course, he had no concept of the size of the building as he'd never been outside his room while awake.

Ty pushed Dom down the hallway and used his pass key to open the back door. They emerged on the back patio. Probably due to the unseasonably cool weather, no one else was there.

Dom took a long, deep breath and turned his face blissfully toward the sky. "Blue sky.

Yellow sun. *Laa-tah*!" After about ten seconds, however, he sniffed the air and shook his head, his expression one of disgust. "Smell," he said, "no good." He shrugged and rattled off a few words in his language.

Of course, the city air smelled nothing like his long ago home in the northern wilderness. Veronica sucked in a deep breath. The first thing that hit her was the aroma of roasting chicken coming from the cafeteria. Then what? Car exhaust? Cigarette smoke?

Dom gave up trying to figure out what he smelled. He peered hopefully around, blinking owlishly, and pointed ahead of them. "Green. *Choo*?" Trees?

Veronica was happy to know that he could see enough to distinguish the cedar hedges hiding the chain-link fence around the perimeter of the property. "Yes," she said, "we have trees," as Ty began pushing him across the lawn.

"Yes! Trees," Dom exclaimed as they drew closer. He reached out to touch the lower branches, grasping fistfuls of needles, practically inhaling them. Then he surprised them by trying to pull himself upright.

"Woah, hang on, buddy!" Ty yelled, grabbing him by the shoulders as the deer skin fell to the ground. "No standing just yet! Sit. Sit!" It sounded like he was talking to a dog.

Dom fell back into the chair with a grunt. "Dom stand. Stand!" he insisted, trying again.

For the first time, Veronica saw in Dom something of the powerful man he'd once been, rather than the invalid she'd known these past weeks.

He must be frustrated to no end at the way he is now. I sure as hell would be.

"Wait, Ty. Let him try," she suggested.

"He's not strong enough yet. He'll fall on his face."

"And what if he does? Ty, this guy hunted mammoths and fought bears. I don't think falling down on the grass will end him." She rested a hand on Dom's shoulder. "Hang on, Dom, we'll help you."

He nodded. "Yes. Help Dom." He bounced impatiently in the chair until Ty put the brakes on it and pushed aside the footrests.

Veronica picked up the bear skin and hung it over the back of the chair. She and Ty positioned themselves to support Dom on either side. Despite what she'd said, she was aware he'd just recovered from multiple fractures and couldn't risk any kind of fall.

"Stand. *Lah-taa*. Good," Dom said once he was on his feet, but after a few seconds, he began to sway. His arms trembled and sweat broke out on his forehead to run down his cheeks. His left leg faltered and folded, and he sat down heavily again.

"That was a good first try," Veronica said in her most encouraging voice while Ty got Dom's feet back on the footrests. "We'll do it again tomorrow, okay?"

"*Taa*. Dom stand tomorrow," he said between pained breaths. "*De-ne-land*. Thank you."

Veronica and Ty sat on the grass at Dom's feet. She said in a hushed voice, "I didn't teach him 'thank you,' Ty. He just picked it up. He's learning English so fast . . ."

"Dom learn En-glish," he said above them, a satisfied grin on his face when they turned to look at him. "Dom stand. Walk. Go *den-no-ny*." He went on for a bit in his own language, seeming to talk to himself rather than to them.

Veronica didn't understand a word, but his tone was crystal clear.

When he was well enough and strong enough, he intended to go back to his people.

9

A DRAWING ON THE WALL

Veronica resigned herself to heading to her childhood home Saturday morning for her parents' fortieth wedding anniversary. Neil and Kim had planned a big celebration, and not going would certainly mean alienating her family further than she already had. Pitching in her share to pay for her parents to take a Princess cruise up the Inside Passage to Alaska next May wasn't enough. She had to show up in person, no matter how badly she wanted to spend every day with Dom.

She'd called Chloe Friday afternoon to come and kitty-sit. The young woman arrived bright and early in jeans and a hoodie, a bulging backpack over one shoulder and a book bag over the other.

"You know," Chloe said as she put her things in the guest room, "you might've taken a year off teaching, but the museum still thinks you keep office hours."

"I do. I've just been really busy with . . . you know . . ."

"The mud man. I know. I've been putting in a couple afternoons a week on stuff I can do, but I'm back to class now and the work's piling up. You really need to come in soon."

"Dom," Veronica blurted. "The mud man? His name's Dom." She paused while Chloe gaped.

"How do you . . . He . . . he's conscious? He told you that?"

the young woman finally stammered.

"He is. He did. In fact, he's completely lucid and getting stronger by the day. I'm sorry I haven't kept you in the loop. Time got away from me, I guess. He actually tried to stand for the first time on Wednesday. He's picking up English really fast too. I can't wait for him to be able to tell me all about his life and his people. He could fill the huge gap in knowledge we have about Neolithic man—sociopolitical structure, hunting methods, medicine, toolmaking, religious beliefs. Everything! I want you to meet him, Chloe, when he's ready for visitors."

"Seriously? Oh my gosh, I want to meet him, too!" Chloe grinned, recovering from her shock of a moment ago. "Who knows? He might be my many thousand-times great-grandfather."

"I never thought of that," Veronica admitted. "It's kind of a nice idea though, isn't it?" She thanked Chloe for coming, kissed her cats goodbye and promised to see them soon, and left for the four-hour drive to Kamloops.

It turned out to be a pleasant weekend. Her parents were thrilled about the cruise. Neither Kim nor the handful of aunts, uncles, and cousins she hadn't seen in years gave her the grief she expected for being virtually absent from their lives. The dinner party Saturday was a great success and the following morning she had a chance to catch her parents, Neil, and Kim up on her work with Dom.

She described him as an indigenous hunter from an isolated northern tribe who'd been found almost dead from hypothermia and was now recovering at Walter Cooper's medical facility. Neil and Becky already knew some of this, but they seemed as eager for details as the others. Veronica saw Neil's face cloud with doubt once or twice—he knew she was keeping something from them but was discreet enough not to say anything. Kim wanted to know why no one had come forth to claim the man. All Veronica could say, quite truthfully, was that no relatives or tribe members had been located. She promised to keep in touch more often and drove home Sunday evening, anxious to see

Dom the next day.

"Dr. Cooper asked to see you as soon as you came in,"
Beatrice said upon Veronica's arrival Monday morning.

"What? Why? Is Dom okay?" A glance at the monitor
showed the patient sitting quietly in his wheelchair while Alex
changed the bed linens.

"He's fine," Beatrice assured her. "It has something to do
with his test results, I think."

Not feeling particularly comforted by this, Veronica headed
to Walter's office.

"What's up?" she asked after the obligatory greetings.

"I just want to keep you up to speed," Walter said, gesturing
for her to pull up the chair opposite his desk. "First of all, the
latest round of urine, blood, and tissue tests still show no sign
of the mutated *Bacillus F.* bacteria. Second, DNA tests confirm
markers for—"

"You had DNA tests run?" Veronica demanded. "I already
showed you the results in my file on him."

Walter nodded. "You did, and now I have them in my file
as well. They correlate with yours," he added. "Markers for
Haplogroup D, for North Eurasian, East Asian, Ancient
Beringian genomes, as well as several modern tribes. And the
kicker, of course, is the percentage of Neanderthal DNA, far
more than anyone else on earth today." He let the last words
hang in the air.

"So, you believe me now . . . about who he is?"

"I believed you before, but you know me, Vee. I have to
find my own proof of things. Now, the third thing I wanted to
tell you . . ."

Veronica clenched her fists and resisted the urge to lean
towards him.

"We'll be doing further tests on Dom today. A spinal tap,

bone marrow aspiration, and a couple tissue biopsies to confirm whether or not the *Bacillus F.* has been completely eliminated, or if a trace remains—"

"Those are invasive tests," she said, "and painful too, aren't they?"

"They are. But don't worry, he won't feel a thing. He'll be under general anesthesia for all of it."

"Again? Come on, Walt, that's—"

"Veronica," Walter cut her off, "I'm telling you this as a courtesy. As per our agreement, I'm not obliged to ask your permission for any test or procedure I choose to have performed on the patient."

"I want to see the results of all the tests."

"Of course," Walt said smoothly. "Now, my fourth point. While you seem to be making progress on the communication front, I want to remind you how important it is that he be able to tell us where and how he was infected with the *Bacillus F*, especially if it really has been eradicated from his system."

"You're assuming he even knows. Prehistoric people had no concept of germs, bacteria, or any of that. He may have no clue whatsoever."

Walter tented his fingers on his desk and sighed. "That would be unfortunate, wouldn't it?"

Veronica stared at the Rolex on his left wrist in an effort to avoid looking at his face. "You gave me six months."

"And I'll respect our agreement, as I expect you to do as well. Draw on every damn centimetre of his walls if you must, but get it out of him."

Veronica pushed to her feet. "Is that all for today?" she asked, doing an admirable job of sounding calm when really she felt like screaming with frustration. "I want to spend some time with Dom before you dope him up again."

"One last thing," Walter said as she reached for the door handle.

She gritted her teeth and turned to look sideways at him. "What is it?"

"Now that Dom's mobile, and I assume he'll gradually become increasingly so, we'll need to control him. I don't want him having any contact with the other patients or their families. We can't have him talking about mammoths and tipis, or asking them how to work a zipper or peel a goddamn banana."

Veronica left the office, slamming the door behind her.

"I'm so sorry," Beatrice said as Veronica burst into Dom's room to find him flat on his back in bed with an IV line in his right arm. "Dr. Cooper told me to get Dom on a sedative drip at 10:30 sharp. He made me promise not to tell you before you spoke to him."

"He was asking for you," Alex said.

Veronica sat down on the edge of the bed and took Dom's hand in hers. "Hey, I'm here," she said. "Everything's okay. You're just going to sleep for a while."

Groggy but still conscious, Dom opened his eyes to peer blurrily at her. "Vee," he said, his voice so low she could barely make out the words. "Vee come. Dom no want sleep medicine."

"I know," she said. "I'm sorry. I'll be here when you wake up." She gave his hand a squeeze.

After fighting to stay awake for as long as he could, he closed his eyes and drifted into a drug-induced slumber.

With no choice but to accept she had a few hours to kill, Veronica drove to her office where, as Chloe had said, she found a box of stones in from a private collection to identify and catalogue. There were recent issues of *Archeology* and *Canadian Anthropology* magazines, as well as a printed copy of the paper Professor Sutherland had written up on the Bennett Lake finds for her review and comments.

After skimming through the magazines, she sat down to read the paper which, as usual, was succinct and precise. There was no mention of the mud man. The artefacts, the professor asserted, had been found in thawing permafrost soil—well, that was true enough—and pointed to human habitation in the area roughly 7,000 to 8,000 years BCE. She made a couple minor notations in the margin and put the paper in an envelope she would deliver personally to Gerald's office.

Next, she looked at some of the stones, half of which may or may not have been flakes created by human hand, but she stopped herself from investigating further as a brilliant idea came to her.

She took the envelope to Professor Sutherland's office, leaving it on his desk as he wasn't there, came back for the box of stones, and left the university. She stopped at Tim Horton's for a quick, late lunch before returning to Cooper Medical.

Dom was in his room, lying on his left side in bed while Alex held an ice pack to his lower back. Upon approaching, Veronica saw that Dom was also holding an ice pack, this one to his throat.

"What the hell?" she exclaimed. "What's wrong with his throat?"

"Thyroid biopsy," Alex replied. "Didn't anyone tell you?"

A couple tissue biopsies, Walter said.

"Yeah, Walter did, sort of," she grumbled. "Here, can I do that?" She practically wrenched the ice pack from Alex's hand and plopped down on the edge of the bed. "Shh, don't move," she said to Dom, who tried to turn towards her at the sound of her voice.

"Vee here. Good," he said. "Dom *oon*." He wasn't whining about it, just letting them know. "Throat. Back. Hurt."

"I know," she said, hoping he understood. "You'll feel better tomorrow." She glared at Alex, who threw up his hands in a gesture of innocence.

"I'll go get his supper," he said and fled the room.

Fifteen minutes of ice seemed to help, and by the time Alex came back with Dom's supper of poached salmon and steamed vegetables, he was able to sit up in bed.

Veronica stayed with him while he ate—sometime over the past week the protocol of not leaving her alone with the patient seemed to have fallen by the wayside—and afterwards, when he lay down again.

After a few minutes, he closed his eyes, crossed his arms

over his chest, and began to chant under his breath.

Veronica pulled her cell phone from her jeans pocket and videotaped ten minutes of it before leaving, frustrated and feeling helpless, and hoping for Dom's sake that tomorrow would be a better day.

Dom proved to be too sore Tuesday morning for any meaningful physical therapy. Ty helped him into his wheelchair as he could barely move his legs, and accompanied him to the bathroom in case he required assistance there.

When he came out, Dom said he wanted to go outside, but it was a windy, rainy day and Ty said no, it wouldn't be good for him.

Veronica, recalling something Walter had said to her the day before, went to the cafeteria.

Walt was right about one thing: Dom doesn't know how to peel a banana.

She knew he'd eaten bananas, but they'd come blended into a smoothie or sliced in a bowl. She procured a bag filled with two bananas, an orange, an apple, a lemon, and a little basket of strawberries, and returned to Dom's room.

She and Ty spent the morning teaching Dom the names of the fruit and words like "sweet," "sour," and "juicy," while they shared the fruit with him. Dom learned how to peel his banana, although with his hands the way they were, even this simple task was something of a chore.

"*Roo-shaw*," he said of the strawberries, as if he were familiar with them.

Roo was his word for "red," so Veronica assumed *roo-shaw* meant something like "red fruit" or "red berry." His language was nothing if not logical.

"This last one," she said to Dom, holding up the lemon, "is a lemon. It's really sour." She cut it into quarters with the knife she'd borrowed from the cafeteria kitchen and nibbled at one of them. The sour face came automatically and she had to force herself to swallow. "Ew, lemon! Sour!" she repeated as Ty chuckled at her elbow.

"No way I'm eating that!" he said, although he'd happily tasted all the others to show Dom how good they were.

"Dom eat lem-on," Dom said, reaching out with his right hand.

Veronica put a lemon quarter in his palm.

He sniffed it, then tentatively bit into it. His eyes shut tight and his mouth puckered, and uninhibited by the restrictions of modern social norms, he spit it out on the floor. Then he burst into a hearty laugh. "Lem-on sour! Eww, no good!" Still chuckling, he tossed the lemon back to Veronica. "Lem-on no good."

"Looks like tastes haven't changed so much over the years," Ty remarked drily.

"*Denzi!*" Dom said suddenly. "*Denzi.* Draw. Draw wall. Fruit."

"That's a wonderful idea," Veronica said, and she went to fetch the box of markers.

Dom faithfully reproduced images of the fruits on a fresh section of wall—red apple, yellow lemon, and so on. He even added some *maa-shaw.* Blueberries. He took a break when Ty brought in his lunch, but he went back to work when Veronica and Ty left him to grab their own meals in the cafeteria.

When they got back, Dom was working on a new image.

"That's no fruit," Ty said. "What the hell is it?"

Veronica gazed at the red and orange figure that looked eerily like a bomb exploding into a dozen pieces. "I have no idea."

They stood back until Dom rolled his wheelchair away from the wall, nodding with satisfaction at his art.

"Dom? What is that?" Veronica asked him, pointing at the new image. "Is it the sun? Fire?"

"*T-lay,*" Dom replied. "No sun. No fire." He raised a hand

and made it travel through the air above his head, accompanied by a faint humming sound. Suddenly he made an explosive sound, "*Pfffttt!*" and threw both hands in the air. Then he lowered his hands, his fingers wiggling as if to indicate rain—or something else—falling from the sky.

He said something in his language, stopped to think for a minute, then said in English, "Fire. Yes. Fire fall. *Taats* . . . Uh . . . Sky. Ground."

"I think he means a meteorite," Veronica suggested. "He must've seen it at one time and it made an impression."

"Must have," Ty agreed. "Must've been terrifying back in the day when they didn't know what it was."

Dom spent the rest of the afternoon putting finishing touches on his drawings. He made no effort to talk, preoccupied by something in his mind.

Veronica filmed him for a while on her cell phone and left before supper for home and an evening writing up the events of the past two days. Reading back over her notes from the beginning, she was certain she had the makings of a best seller, maybe even a Pulitzer Prize winner.

He laughed today with Vee and Ty. The sour lemon tasted bad, but laughing was good.

He remembers the last time he laughed. It seems a lifetime ago. He remembers other things too.

Painful things.

Things better left forgotten.

10

MOVING SMARTLY ALONG

By Wednesday, Dom had recovered sufficiently from Monday's tests to resume his physical therapy, which Walter had arranged for him to do in the PT department for two hours every morning from Tuesday to Saturday.

As much as she wanted to be there, Veronica had to admit it might be best to leave the guys alone in the mornings. Ty was just as apt as she was to communicate with Dom, and he agreed to tell her of any new words he learned or other observations he might make.

She did, however, insist on spending her afternoons with Dom. Thursday morning, having conferred with Ty the previous day about sizes and other details, she went shopping for things Dom would need in the upcoming weeks. She came back loaded with bags bulging with two pairs of sweatpants and a pair of jeans, a black hoodie, dark blue, button-up sweater, underwear, socks, a pair of slip-on sneakers, and personal items like shampoo and deodorant. She would let Ty show him how to use the latter. One thing she didn't buy was a razor—not because he wasn't allowed anything sharp or pointy, but because she'd noticed that, like some indigenous men, Dom didn't grow a beard. He had sparse, dark hairs on his arms, legs, and chest, but none on his face.

While Dom ate his lunch, Veronica and Ty went to the cafeteria for theirs.

One of the facility's other patients was there with his family.

Ty took a moment to go and talk to them. After sitting down with Veronica at their own table, he motioned with a tip of his head towards the family.

"That's Everett," he said of the young man with a buzz cut and several jagged pink scars on his face and head. "I took care of him before Dom arrived. He suffered devastating head injuries in a car accident a couple years ago. Doctors said he'd never come out of the vegetative state he was in, but after three or four of Doc Cooper's treatments, he woke up. Got a long way to go still, but he's gradually recovering his memories and functions."

Veronica glanced over at the guy. He sat in a wheelchair, but he was smiling crookedly and eating on his own. She reminded herself that while Walter's treatment of Dom might well border on insensitive and unethical, his experimental procedures were evidently doing some people a lot of good.

"Dom go out. See sun. See trees," Dom suggested when they returned to his room.

"It's pouring rain, buddy," Ty said. He grabbed the whiteboard and drew a fluffy cloud with fat, blue raindrops falling from it to the green ground. He tapped the board. "Rain. *Ti-en.*"

Dom shook his head. "*T-lay!* No *ti-en. Taats ti-en.*" Sky water.

"We'll go outside tomorrow," Veronica offered, hoping the weather would cooperate.

"To-mor-row. *Tah,*" Dom grumbled.

They spent the afternoon showing Dom his new clothes, teaching him how to put on the socks, how to work the zipper on the hoodie and the buttons on the sweater, simple tasks made difficult by the condition of his hands. The way he peered owlishly down at what he was doing, blinking repeatedly, tilting his head this way and that, it was clear his vision hindered him as well.

"No good!" Dom exclaimed in frustration over his fumbled attempts to do up the buttons after Ty's third demonstration.

"Here, let me help you." Veronica reached out to gently clasp his hands in hers before Ty could step in and do it himself. With her fingers guiding his, Dom eventually managed to fasten the five buttons. "There, you see? You can do it, you just need practice."

He stared blankly at her, then shook his head. "Dom no . . . uh . . ." He said a word in his language that sounded like "*aa-wax-ay*," and repeated, "Dom no *aa-wax-ay*." Suddenly he slapped his forehead viciously with the palm of his hand.

"You don't—no understand," Veronica guessed.

"No und-er-stand," he said through gritted teeth.

"But you will," she said, taking his hands again. "Now let's undo the buttons."

After a minute or two he settled down to the task and, an hour later, he was able to fasten and unfasten the buttons on his own.

"You did good," Ty said, giving Dom a manly thump on the shoulder. "Real good."

"*De-ne-land*," Dom grumbled. Thank you.

As they worked, Veronica and Ty had given Dom the corresponding vocabulary. Naturally, he had no words in his language for zipper or buttons, nor for socks, underwear, or sneakers, although he did have one for shoes, which he called *teeli*.

"You'll never guess what we did in therapy this morning," Ty said to Veronica on Friday.

She'd spent the morning working in her office and arrived in time to find Ty and Dom eating lunch together at the table in Dom's room.

"I'm sure I won't." She pulled out the second chair and dropped into it. "Tell me."

"Well, as you know, we've been working on assisted

standing all week. He's still having trouble with his balance, but today, Dom took his first steps."

Catching the gist of Ty's words, Dom announced, "Dom stand. Walk. Walk one. Two. Three steps." He grinned proudly.

"Three steps?" Veronica repeated. "That's wonderful! *Lah-taa*. Great progress!"

"He was so good I promised him we'd go outside after lunch," Ty said.

"That's a great idea," she agreed. "It's sunny today, and warm, too."

Dom was already wearing sweats and a tee-shirt. He put on his hoodie, socks, and sneakers with minimal help, and even wheeled himself down the hallway to the door, stopping only once on the way to rest. Ty took over the job of pushing his wheelchair outside and across the lawn to the trees.

While Dom sat calmly, his face turned up to the early autumn sunshine, Veronica and Ty chatted about what the next step with their extraordinary patient should be.

"I've been thinking about it," Veronica said, "and I'm realizing that if we want Dom to tell us about his life, we need to tell him about ours. Our past and . . . well, what modern life is like, I guess. Electricity and cars and books, and . . . everything. Slowly, of course," she added hastily. "I don't want to blow his mind."

Ty nodded in agreement. "It's probably a good thing he can't see so well. Otherwise, I think his mind would already be— Hey Dom, what're you doin' there, buddy?"

Dom had put his feet on the ground and was preparing to rise.

"Dom stand. Walk," he said. It wasn't a question.

"Um . . . Okay, then. Hang on."

Ty helped him stand. With Veronica and Ty steadying him on either side, Dom walked half a dozen steps before stumbling and stopping. As he began to tremble with the effort of remaining upright, he let out a sudden, strangely maniacal laugh. Then the laughter subsided, and he let himself collapse to the grass.

Ty and Veronica had no choice but to follow him to the damp ground.

"Dom? What is it? Are you okay?" asked Veronica, afraid he might be suffering a seizure while Ty grabbed his wrist to check his pulse.

"Pulse is fine," Ty said.

Dom shook his head in reply to Veronica's question. "*T-lay*. No. Dom no okay," he blurted between heavy breaths. "Feet no good. Hands no good. Eyes no good. Dom no good!" His words were raw, filled with frustration, and he pounded the ground with his fist to accentuate the last few words.

With her clinical objectivity in serious jeopardy, Veronica, on her knees, shimmied closer to the distraught patient. Wrapping an arm around his shoulders, she said, "Oh, you're so wrong, Dom. You've lived through something no one else has. You're strong and brave. You're going to teach us things we've never imagined and, one day, everyone's going to know your name."

There was little chance he understood more than a few words of this, but she hoped at least her tone of voice would soothe him.

"Dom's a good man," Ty said, doing a better job of using simple words than Veronica, the supposed communication expert. "*Denzi lah-taa*. Draw good. Talk English good. Talk Vee and Ty about . . . uh, about *den-no-ny*. Dom people."

After a moment of silence which Dom used to collect himself, he said, "Dom understand." He nodded and looked from Ty on his one side to Veronica, who had withdrawn her arm from around his shoulders, but remained close. "Hands no good. Feet no good. Eyes no good." He said something to himself in his language, then took a long breath. "Dom good. Good man. Yes. Stand now!"

They helped him to his feet and he walked slowly back to his wheelchair, leaning heavily on them and gasping for breath by the time they reached it. Veronica could feel his pulse, rapid but strong and steady, in his arm. After giving him a few minutes to recover, they were heading back to the building when Walter opened the back door and called,

"Veronica! Come up to my office! We need to talk."

"Ooh, Walter talk Vee," Dom said, shaking his head wearily. "No good."

She doubted he'd seen Walter poke his head out the door, but he'd obviously recognized the voice. She couldn't blame him for not thinking highly of Walt, who only spent a few minutes with him every couple days.

It turned out Walter simply wanted to give her the results of Monday's tests.

"You demanded to know, so I'm telling you," he said. "Everything came back normal, except for two things."

Veronica caught her breath. "Two things? What are they?" She wasn't actually sure she wanted to know.

"Well, . . . First, we found a minute amount of *Bacillus F.* in Dom's bone marrow. I'm not sure whether that's good news or bad or whether it has any bearing on anything moving forward, but I'm going to hold off on ordering a new course of antibiotics and see what happens."

"Not very ethical," Veronica observed. "What's the second thing?"

"We did a testicular sperm extraction and—"

"A what?"

"Veronica, really. Do I have to explain to you what that is?"

"No!" she snapped. She knew it meant extracting a small amount of tissue from a testicle for analysis. "I just can't believe . . . why would you do that?"

"Isn't it obvious? I want to know if and how the *Bacillus F.* might have affected the production of sperm or their properties."

"And . . .?"

"Unfortunately, his sperm count is minimal and the ones that are present are atrophied and inert. Whether the cause is the bacteria or the freezing, the result is the same. He—"

"He's sterile." She sighed. "Do you think the condition's

permanent?"

"I haven't the foggiest idea," he admitted. "It's not like there's been any studies about the effects of long-term freezing on the human reproductive system."

"But I assume you're going to do one?"

Walter thought for a moment. "It's not quite up my alley, but yes, I'll have Robin, my head lab tech, initiate it."

"You're disgusting," Veronica said.

"Am I? Is what I'm doing any worse than the study you're making of him, preparing a book that'll certainly make you rich and famous, planning how to present your prehistoric man to the world like you own him? You're as self-centred and egotistical as me, Veronica." His voice rose as she headed for the door. "You can pretend otherwise, but we both know better!"

Veronica slammed the door closed behind her and stomped down the hallway towards the stairs, her heart pounding and her face on fire. She found herself fighting back hot tears, not because what Walter said was mean or hurtful, but because, deep down, she feared he was right.

Not wanting the guys to see her in this state, she didn't go down to Dom's room. She didn't go home right away, either. Instead, she signed out, drove to Kitsilano Beach, parked her car, and walked in the sand along the edge of the calming waves, until she'd burned off most of her rage at Walter and stopped mentally kicking herself in the butt for making that damn arrangement with him in the first place. She went home to take a shower, eat leftovers, and sit up in bed half the night with the cats curled up beside her as she tried to figure out what to do about Dom.

As dawn broke, she decided the only thing she could do for the mud man was stay her course: learn everything she could about him and prepare him as thoroughly as possible for modern life. She didn't see any alternative. She couldn't turn back time or take him back to his people, could she?

To that end, she stopped on the way to Cooper Medical for three cups of Tim Horton's original, along with a supply of cream and sugar, and a box of muffins. Dom was still on a specific diet to help him gain weight, build muscle, and solidify his bones, but she didn't think a cup of coffee and a couple bites of field berry muffin would do him any harm. He hadn't thrown up in weeks, not even after biting into that lemon.

"Hey guys," she said as she entered the room just after 8:00.

"You're early today," remarked Ty, "and you brought coffee?" His face lit up at the sight and smell of it.

"I did." She closed the door with her elbow and set everything down on the table. "I figured it was time we introduced Dom to this staple of the modern Canadian diet."

"Vee!" said Dom, squinting at her from where he sat on the edge of his bed, wearing only his pajama bottoms.

"Hi, Dom," she said back.

"I guess getting dressed can wait," Ty said, "until we've had a cup—Hey Dom! Come over here."

Dom got himself into his wheelchair and rolled to the bathroom. When he came out, his face and chest still damp from washing, he joined them at the table.

"This is coffee," Veronica told him. "Good drink," she added in his language. She put the paper cup in his hands after removing the lid to add a little packet of sugar. Who knew how he would like it? "Be careful. It's hot."

"Yes. Hot," he repeated dutifully. "Cof . . .?"

"Coffee."

"Cof-fee." He took a careful sip, then another. "Cof-fee good. Good drink. Thank you."

"You're welcome," she said, feeling slightly happier with herself than she had last night. Judging by appearances, Dom seemed to be back to his usual curious and determined self. He was nothing if not resilient.

He drank half of his coffee and ate half of his muffin, which was all Ty would allow him. Then he dressed himself in a tee-shirt and sweatpants—no underwear, Veronica noticed—and the guys went to the physical therapy room.

Veronica returned to her car for her laptop and sat at the

table in Dom's room to work and ponder how she would approach things this afternoon.

Ty brought lunch for the three of them—vegetable soup and egg salad sandwiches, oranges, bottles of water, and a protein drink for Dom. After they ate, he showed Dom how to open the water bottle by holding it against his chest with his left hand and twisting the cap off with his right hand.

Dom practiced until he could do it on his own, grumbling all the while that bottles were no good; water should run in a river.

It was an overcast but warm day, and they decided to spend the afternoon outside. Dom put on his sweater—he'd obviously been practicing with the buttons—and Veronica brought the whiteboard and markers, the bottles of water, and the remainder of Dom's muffin. Ty pushed Dom's wheelchair through the grass to where a picnic table had been placed near their usual spot beside the cedar hedge.

Using the board and about a dozen new words, Veronica told Dom about her family. She had a big brother called Neil and a little sister called Kim. A mother and father. She lived in a house—she thought explaining what an apartment was might be too much for him to grasp just yet—with two cats called Scout and Rusty.

They all chuckled at her pathetic drawings of the cats. Ty took his turn, drawing his large family of grandparents, parents, two sisters and two brothers. He drew himself smaller than the others, the baby of the family, and they laughed some more. Then he erased this and drew himself as a man, a woman and two little girls beside him, a dog between them, and told Veronica and Dom about his family.

Dom soaked it all in and when it came his turn, he readily began to draw.

Veronica placed her cell phone out of sight beside her to record whatever Dom had to say as she'd done frequently over the past weeks. She would figure out how to write whatever he said in his language phonetically later.

Dom drew a board full of people of all shapes and sizes. His *den-no-ny*. Then he erased these and drew a smaller group, taking pains to name each figure to Veronica and Ty. One grandmother. Two grandfathers. Mother. Father. Sisters. Brothers. Dom. He was the oldest of seven children, big brother to four little sisters and two brothers. He drew the adults standing side by side, the children sitting cross-legged at their feet. Finally, he added two grey, pointy-eared dogs, which he called *oohshay*, confirming the notion that indigenous people domesticated a wolfy sort of dog early on.

By the time they went inside to get ready for supper, Veronica had enough information to keep her busy all weekend.

11

STORIES SHARED

Dom did, in fact, keep Veronica busy for the next two weeks. She spent her mornings working at home or, when necessary, in her office. She drove to Cooper Medical for lunch, sometimes bringing coffee and a muffin, to spend the afternoon with him.

When weather permitted, they sat outside with the whiteboard, teaching each other new words and phrases. On rainy days they stayed in Dom's room, talking and playing games like tic-tac-toe on the board, or checkers on a large black and white cloth grid Ty bought online, these activities being incorporated into Dom's ongoing occupational therapy.

Ty had stuffed Dom's slippers and sneakers with balls of cotton wool so they would fit better, making standing and walking more comfortable for him. Dom had subsequently begun walking with the assistance of a two-wheel walker, pushing it ahead of him at every step, until his strength and balance would allow him to go without it. Ty hoped this was a question of only a few weeks.

Once he could stand for more than a minute or so with only his left hand on his walker, Dom began filling up more of his walls with his art. Making good use of the whiteboard as his command of English improved and she mastered a few words in his language, he told Veronica something about his people.

It was more than she could have hoped for.

Dom's *den-no-ny* had had a semi-permanent settlement near

the coast where they built huts with stone bases and grass or skin roofs, and a summer village further inland, where they erected *isaahs*. They had a structured social system with a council of elders who made decisions affecting the tribe, and who doled out justice when necessary. They made tools of stone, bone, or antler, and clothes of skins and furs. The men hunted and fished and occasionally fought amongst themselves for position or a woman. The women took care of the children and most of the cooking. Everyone gathered wild berries, plants, and roots, and adults possessed quite sophisticated knowledge of their medicinal properties. Dom himself was a teacher and a healer, what Veronica took to be a sort of shaman, and eventually an elder of his tribe.

He drew forests and beaches, mountains and rivers, and asked Vee and Ty if they knew these places. They assured him all these could be found nearby and they would take Dom there when he was able to go.

Veronica and Ty gradually began introducing Dom to everyday items in the modern world. They drew pictures of square houses, tall apartment buildings, a structure with four rows of windows they told him was the hospital where they were now, other square buildings full of fruits and vegetables, shoes and clothes, or coffee and muffins. Stores. They explained where his new clothes came from and how they were made. They tried to explain running water and how they could turn on lights in the dark. Veronica was pretty sure he didn't understand the workings of these technological wonders—hell, she barely understood them, herself—but he seemed to accept them as they were.

When Dom was safely away in the therapy room or the bathroom, Veronica took photos of each new wall drawing. She recorded his tales on her cell, which she placed out of sight on the high shelf above the table. It wasn't that she didn't want him to know what she was doing; she simply didn't know how to explain a cell phone to him. Not yet anyway.

"Do you think he's ready to confront the cafeteria?"

Veronica asked Ty Tuesday upon her arrival.

"Um, yeah, I guess so," he said, "although we'll have to explain the elevator to him."

This took a while, Dom looking vaguely confused but mostly excited—understandably, he was becoming increasingly impatient with spending so much time in his room.

"Yes. Dom go up. Eat lunch in big room with Vee and Ty. *Lah-taa!*"

"Okay then," Veronica said, hoping this venture wouldn't turn out to be a mistake. "Let's go."

Dom was already dressed in a tee-shirt and sweats. He declined his wheelchair, so they ambled at his speed to the elevator, out on the second floor, and down the hall to the cafeteria.

Everett and his family sat at one table, and a few staff members were scattered at others, drinking coffee or cola or eating lunch. The place went eerily silent for a moment when Veronica, Ty, and Dom entered, then everyone went back to their meals, although Veronica was fairly certain their conversations now revolved around the newcomers.

Once seated at a table, Dom began looking left and right, alternately widening his eyes, squinting, and blinking as he tried to focus on everything around him. He stared at the large windows for a moment, then shook his head and looked away.

We've got to get his eyes examined, thought Veronica, observing him. *Maybe something can be done about his vision.*

"Much people. Much talk," he said, his voice growing tighter with each word.

"About twelve people," she confirmed. "It's okay. Be calm. Ty will bring your lunch."

Ty nodded and headed for the counter.

Veronica reached over and put her hand on Dom's arm. "It's okay. I'm right here. You're okay."

He swallowed and nodded. "Dom okay. *Taa.*"

He was clearly terrified. *Of course, he is. Who wouldn't be, in his situation?*

Ty came back with two trays holding plates of beef stew and dinner rolls—Dom was managing closer to normal portions now—and Dom's protein drink. He put these down on the table and went back to the counter, returning with three cups of coffee, slices of apple pie, and their utensils.

Dom ate and drank in silence. His hand trembled slightly holding his spoon—he still wasn't allowed a fork or knife—but it steadied after his first few bites.

"Good. Good lunch," he finally said as they finished up. He turned to the windows again, frowning. "Blue sky. Go outside?"

Ty sighed.

Veronica said, "Those are windows, not doors. We can only look out. We can't go out."

They accompanied Dom to the nearest window. He touched it and rapped on it and groped around the edges of it in hopes of finding a way to open it. Finally, he nodded and said in a disappointed voice, "Go Dom room. Rest."

"That's a good idea," Ty agreed. "You've had enough excitement for one day."

Veronica took advantage of Dom's naptime to see Walter. He wasn't in his office, but she tracked him down on the fourth floor. He came out through a door labelled "No Unauthorized Admittance Beyond This Point," wearing a white lab coat over his usual slacks and button-down shirt, a surgical mask hanging loose around his neck.

"Veronica? What can I do for you? As you can see, I'm busy here."

"I want to get someone in to examine Dom's eyes. See if we can do something to improve his vision . . . Glasses or something?" she prompted when he didn't answer.

But then again, Dom's easier to control if he can't see properly.

"Oh, come on, Walt! You said you'd give him the best care possible, and our six months are far from over. You can't deprive him—"

"All right!" he exclaimed. He lowered his voice, as if

realizing someone might overhear them. "I'll get in touch with a specialist I know. She'll have to come here, though."

"Of course."

Two days later, ophthalmologist Dr. Ruth Russell came to examine Dom. The task was complicated by the language barrier and the fact that he didn't know his letters, but after doing the best she could using cards with numerals and coloured symbols she confirmed what Veronica already suspected: Dom had suffered serious damage to the interior as well as the lenses of his eyes, resulting in a general clouding of his vision and numerous tiny blind spots she called "floaters." She wasn't optimistic that his vision could be improved with corrective lenses, but she suggested surgery might be a possibility.

She impressed upon them the importance of bringing him to her clinic for a thorough examination as soon as it was feasible. Observing the artwork on the walls, however, she remarked that he was making good use of what sight he had. Fortunately, she didn't seem to notice the mammoth.

"You'll explain all this to him, I assume," she said to Walter, who had been present for the examination.

"We will," he said. "Thank you."

But they didn't need to tell Dom anything. Judging by the grim look on his face, he knew.

He is learning to ignore the ache in his leg and the frequent burning pains in his fingers and feet. Learning to listen with only his good right ear.

His hands work better now. His legs are growing stronger. His eyes . . . It seems he will have to live with his new, poor vision, like an old man.

The thought makes him want to both laugh and cry, but he does neither.

He will put all his energy into learning about Veronica's world and teaching her about his. He suspects she wants

*something from him. Dr. Walter wants it too, but he does not
know what it is.*

Dom was uncharacteristically shut down the next day,
unmotivated in his physical therapy, disinterested in talking or
drawing. And who could blame him?

Veronica felt sick at heart at seeing him this way, but with
nothing helpful to offer, she left the hospital to get ready for
supper with Becky and Neil at their place. Becky had called last
night to invite her, saying she had news she wanted to share.

She already had a suspicion what it might be, so she wasn't
as surprised as she was happy when Becky announced she and
Neil were going to have a baby. She would be an aunt for the
third time, as Kim and her husband, Rick, had two young sons.

Saturday afternoon, with much drawing and erasing on the
whiteboard, Veronica shared her good news with Ty and Dom.
When a big smile appeared on Dom's face, indicating he
understood, she realized this was a great opportunity to ask him
if he was a father. She shook off the solemn thought that he
certainly never would be again. This wasn't the time to tell him
that.

"*Taa.* Dom *ecka.* Uh, father," he said readily enough in
response to her question. He drew on the board the figures of a
naked, well-endowed man with shoulder-length black hair, and
an equally well-endowed woman with longer hair and a large,
round belly. "Dom," he said, adding the concentric circles that
identified him over the man. There was no mistaking the pride
in his voice. "Woman name Lil-lia." He pointed to the woman.

He drew three other figures of varying height—two slender
boys and a small, plump girl. His sons and daughter.

"Boy Seen-ee. Eight summers," he said.

Veronica understood he meant the boy was eight years old.

"Boy Saawli. Six summers. Girl Woo-shaax. Three

summers." Then he pointed to Lil-lia's belly. "Baby."

Of course. She was pregnant, hence the round belly.

"They're beautiful. Beautiful family," Ty said. "Good family."

"Yes. Good family. Good Dom family." His face clouded and he frowned.

Veronica could have sworn there were tears in his eyes.

He sniffed and cleared his throat, and turned away for a moment.

"You think he knows?" Ty asked under his breath.

Knows what? That he probably won't have any more kids, or that the ones he had have been dead for 9,500 years?

"No. I don't," she said. The answer was the same either way. "I think maybe something happened to them, though. We'll find out eventually."

Ty replied with a nod and a little noise in his throat.

They ate in the cafeteria. Afterwards, Dom insisted on going outside. It was pouring rain—typical for a fall day in Vancouver—but they sat out on the covered end of the patio for a while anyway. Ty told stories from his childhood, silly things like getting lost on a walk in the woods and collecting little fish in tidal pools at the beach. With help from the whiteboard, Dom understood the gist of what he was saying, and he smiled, nodded, or frowned in all the right places.

Dom spent the rest of the afternoon drawing on his wall, a colourful and elaborate scene of himself, Lil-lia, and the children sitting around a campfire, a baby in Lil-lia's arms. A grey dog lay curled at the bigger boy's feet. When he left to go to the bathroom, Veronica took photos. Upon his return, she asked him to tell her about this time around the fire.

"Good time," he said. "Summer. Good eat. Good talk. Lil-lia baby."

"I see that. The baby was—I mean, is—a boy or a girl?"

"Girl baby. Li-anni."

"Beautiful." Now it was Veronica who had tears in her eyes, and she fled to the bathroom before they began to flow. Dom might not notice, given his poor eyesight, but Ty definitely would, and she didn't know how to explain this lack of scientific objectivity. It was completely unlike her to let a subject affect her emotionally and the truth was, she didn't know how much longer she could hide the fact that she cared about Dom more than anyone could guess.

12

GOOD DAYS

Early the following week, Ty got Dom pedalling a stationary bike in the PT room to improve his strength and stamina. That Friday afternoon, he brought a gift—a beautifully carved wooden cane for Dom to use when he was ready to abandon the walker.

"This cane belonged to my grandfather. He made the carvings on it himself," Ty told him. "I want you to have it. Go ahead, take it."

Dom grasped the cane in his right hand and proceeded to shuffle around the room with Ty at his other side to steady him.

"*Lah-taa*," he said, smiling widely. "Good. Cane more good walker. Dom like!"

"I figured you would," Ty said, smiling just as broadly. "We'll work on your walking with it tomorrow in PT, okay?"

"Yes, good. Dom walk with cane tomorrow."

Taking advantage of Dom's present good mood, Veronica went to the place on the wall where he'd drawn the red starburst image. "Dom? Can you tell me what this is? *Oh-cho denzi?*" What draw?

Using his walker again as Ty had prudently taken away the cane, Dom came to her side to contemplate the image for a moment. Finally, taking a step back and looking at Veronica, he said,

"People see in sky. Dom—" he stopped to search for his words "—fourteen summers. Yes." He nodded, more to himself than to them. He went to the table and sorted through the markers. He shoved the ones he wanted into the pocket of his sweatpants and went to an empty spot on the wall.

Veronica and Ty watched as he drew a craggy mountain with the green marker, adding a snow-capped peak in light blue. With the red marker, he added several chunks of something— presumably from the explosion in the sky—falling into the side of the mountain not far below the tree line.

He made a rumbling sound in his throat. "Big noise. Sky fire. Mountain fire. Elders say no go. Sky fire much bad. Sky stone place bad."

"Right," Veronica said, certain now what his people had seen. "We call it a meteorite. A stone from the sky."

"Dom bad!" he exclaimed. "Go see met-or . . . uh, sky stone." He tapped the image of the mountain and spoke for a moment in his own language. "Dom fifteen summers. Go alone boy. Stay sky stone place one moon. Come home man."

"Oh! A rite of passage," Veronica said as she grasped what he was saying. "You went to this place when you were fifteen?" She tapped the mountain on the spot where the red chunks landed.

"Yes."

"And you stayed a month? Um, one moon?"

"*Taa*. One moon."

"While you were there, did you . . . were you sick?" She moaned and feigned throwing up for emphasis.

With a frown of puzzlement, he shook his head. "Dom no sick." He thought for a moment. "Dom fall. Hurt arms. Hurt knees." He held out his arms so they could see his elbows, which bore numerous faded, white scars. He shrugged and went on, "Dom wash in good cold water. Drink water. Eat berries. Hunt. Feel good. Dom strong. Go home."

"Why do you think the elders told you not to go there, if it was such a nice place?"

He frowned. "Dom no understand."

Veronica tried again. "Why did elders say the sky stone

place was bad? A bad place?"

"Uh, elders say . . ." He continued with a few words in his language, then gave up with an emphatic shake of his head. "Dom no words. No En-glish for say. Sorry."

"It's okay," she said with a sigh of exasperation. "I'll ask you again when your English is better."

"What do you think?" Ty asked Veronica later, as they left the building together. "Could he have been infected by that weird bacteria up on the mountain where the meteorite landed? Either by ingesting it or maybe through his blood when he fell and hurt himself?"

Veronica stopped to look him squarely in the eyes. "You know, I thought it was a crazy notion, but maybe it's not so crazy if you're thinking it too. Maybe the meteorite had some property—chemical, organic, radioactive, or whatever—that mutated the *Bacillus F.* in the ground or the water. Or maybe it brought the bacteria here itself."

"Space bacteria? Like . . . alien?" Ty chuckled over the words. "Seriously?"

She shrugged. "I honestly have no idea. But Ty . . . don't tell Walt about this. Dom's not ready to be interrogated about it. Not yet."

"Hey, I'm just the nurse and therapist, taking care of the patient's medical needs. Anything else . . ." He shrugged. "You comin' in tomorrow?" he asked as they continued walking.

"I am," Veronica replied. "I'll see you then."

Ty came in Saturday morning for Dom's PT, but he excused himself after lunch to be with his twin daughters for their fifth birthday, leaving Veronica alone with Dom for the afternoon.

It was a sunny fall day, so Veronica suggested going outside. Dom immediately agreed. Before they went out, however, she hurried to her car for the box of stone artefacts she'd put in the trunk weeks earlier and picked up the board and markers from his room.

"Dom? Will you look at these?" she asked once they were settled at the picnic table and Dom had recovered his breath after the effort of pushing his walker across the lawn. "Can you tell me what they are? *Oh-cho*?"

"*Taa*, Dom look," he said agreeably. He peered into the box, then reached in and brought out one of the stones. Reached in for another.

Veronica took the opportunity to study him while his attention was on the stones in his hands. Although he was still severely underweight, he'd gained tremendously over the past three months. His face had filled out and his colour was good, a pale tan tone. He was barely average height and he wasn't handsome in the modern, movie-star sense of the word, but he was striking, with his high cheekbones and forehead, and long, wide nose. His eyes were slightly almond-shaped, hinting at his Asian ancestry, and brimming with intelligence despite the nebulous spots marring them. His hair was growing out thick and straight, deep brown rather than black, with the odd grey strand mixed in. The tracheostomy incision had healed beautifully, leaving only a circle of puckered red skin at the base of his throat.

He was adapting as well to his condition as anyone could, she supposed. Aside from that one episode a month ago now, he never complained about his disabilities, nor the periodic tests, nor even the fact that he'd discovered he was fenced in, although sometimes she caught him staring blankly at the hedge or up at the sky, a far-away expression on his face.

Sitting there across the table from him, Veronica finally admitted to herself that Dom had evolved from being her research subject to something more. She'd never become emotionally attached to anyone involved in her professional life, but she was becoming dangerously fond of him, and there was nothing she could do about it, except hide it from all concerned.

She wondered what he thought of them: herself, Ty,

Beatrice, Alex. Even Walter. He'd drawn them all on the wall near their handprints—Veronica with yellow hair and blue eyes, Beatrice with her brown eyes and hair, Walter with his wire-framed glasses, Alex with his dark brown skin and dreads, and Ty with his round face and short, black hair.

"Dom teach Vee!" he said suddenly, looking across the table at her. He'd lined up the eight stones along the side of the table. Reaching for the board and a marker, he drew a simple figure of a woman on her knees, scraping a hide with a stone in one hand. He collected three of the stones and placed them on top of the board.

"*Adish*," he said, pointing to the object in the figure's hand.

"So those are scrapers. Just what I thought." Veronica reached for another of the stones and put it on the board too. "What about this one?"

Dom took the stone in his hands, turning it over several times and holding it so close to his face to get a better look that he nearly went cross-eyed. "*T-lay*." He dropped the stone on the ground. "Stone no good," he said in disgust.

"Okay then," she said, stifling a giggle. She didn't want him to think she was laughing at him.

He erased the image and drew one of a man poised to throw his spear. He stopped to think, then added a bear opposite the point of the spear. He put two of the stones, which Veronica had already identified as damaged projectile points, on the board. He picked up a third stone, handled it for a moment, then reached across the table to give it to Veronica.

"*Adika-shay*," he said, tapping the board. "Stone—" He gestured with his chin towards the stone in her hand. "Start. No finish."

"That's exactly what I suspected," she agreed. "You're good, Dom. Really good."

He nodded, a satisfied smile on his face. "Dom good. Yes." He grabbed one of the scrapers and put it in the pocket of his hoodie.

"Dom, no! You can't keep that." Veronica held out her

hand. "Give it to me, please."

"No keep. Go Dom room. Dom teach Vee."

"Oh. Okay then," she agreed, as she realized how much more important Dom might become to her future research than she'd previously imagined.

Back in his room, Dom picked up one of the deer skins that lay over the foot of his bed, and lowered himself to his knees on the bear skin rug.

Veronica sat beside him, and he showed her how to use the sharp edge of the stone to scrape the underside of the deer skin.

"Woman work," he said, looking sideways at her and giving her a sly smile.

"Right," she said, taking the scraper from him. As she simulated scraping the deerskin, she began to contemplate the writing of two books—one for her scientific peers about Dom's people, language, and culture, and a second one for mass consumption, all about Dom himself and the story of his adapting to the modern world. While the first would earn her academic recognition, the second would hopefully make her wealthy enough to provide for all Dom's future needs, whatever they should prove to be.

She liked the sound of that.

After lunch Tuesday, Ty went out to his car and came back with a large cardboard box.

"My folks came over for my daughters' birthday," he said, more to Veronica than Dom. "I told them about Dom. Just the stuff fit for general consumption, of course," he added hastily.

As she nodded, he went on, "My grandfather was about Dom's height—that's why the cane fits—and the last two years before he passed away, he lost a lot of weight. Had to buy a bunch of new clothes. I remembered Pop kept them to give away, but he hasn't got around to it, so I went over to his place and picked up some stuff I thought Dom could use."

"Dom clothes?" Dom asked, having understood that much.

"You bet, buddy," Ty said. "Let's take a look."

It seemed Ty's grandfather, a full-blooded Haida elder, had had a penchant for jeans and flannel shirts, but there were also a couple turtleneck sweaters, wool socks, a pair of winter boots, and a yellow windbreaker. They all smelled vaguely of cedar and moth balls, but after wrinkling his nose at the odour, Dom began to inspect the clothing.

"Clothes good," he said a couple hours later. Uninhibited by modern social norms, he'd tried on every item with Veronica and Ty right there, watching and in some cases, helping him, and explaining what each piece was called and what it was used for. Unfortunately, he still refused to wear the jockey shorts Veronica had bought for him, so she discreetly averted her eyes at the appropriate moments.

That week, Veronica accelerated her teaching of Dom about the modern world. Her first step was bringing back the old CD player she'd removed from his room once he was lucid, afraid at the time that the unexplained sounds might confuse and upset him rather than comfort him.

It took her a while to explain to Dom that the black box could play music and voices of people who weren't in the room. Although the technology behind it must have passed light years over his head and he was clearly wary of it at first, he eventually seemed to accept it as just another strange thing in this new world in which he found himself.

Over the next few days, Veronica brought in a variety of CDs. Classical music. Pop. Country. Rock. Rap. Piano. Dom appeared to prefer the relaxation stuff with the sounds of birds and ocean and, surprisingly, the rap, maybe because it sounded a bit like a boisterous version of his tribal chants.

For his part, Dom recited a couple of his chants for her. Veronica recorded them on her laptop, hoping to write them down when she had the vocabulary for it. She planned to have him help her translate them when his English was good enough.

Ty left when Veronica arrived on Saturday, promising to come back with a surprise in a couple hours. Dom should dress warmly after lunch and go outside with Veronica when Ty called her. They'd spent the previous afternoon explaining what a telephone was. Dom had looked close to passing out when he heard Ty's voice on Veronica's cell, but after the first few seconds he grew quite enthusiastic about talking over the phone to someone in another room.

Veronica's cell chimed in her pocket. When she answered it, Ty asked to speak to Dom.

Dom listened to whatever Ty had to say, phone pressed to his right ear, and handed her back the cell. "Ty say go outside." He grinned, clearly pleased with himself for relaying the message.

They went out to their picnic table, Dom walking across the lawn with his cane, which he'd insisted on using rather than the walker, Veronica at his side should he need her. Ty joined them a few minutes later, a rambunctious husky straining at its leash beside him.

"Dog!" Dom exclaimed when he spotted the animal.

"You're right," Ty said, reaching them. "She's my dog. Her name's Daisy."

"Dog. Daisy," Dom repeated, reaching out to pat her.

"She's a bit excited," Ty admitted. "Only a year old. Uh, one summer, you know? But she's a good dog."

"Dog good. Dom like. Yes! Dom like much!" He leaned down so that Daisy practically jumped into his arms and laughed when she licked his face.

"Yeah, we're trying to discourage her from doing that," Ty muttered with a shake of his head. He pulled a green tennis ball from his jacket pocket. He gave it to Dom and explained what it was. Then he took it back, unclipped Daisy's leash, and tossed the ball.

Daisy raced after it, leaping into the air in her exuberance to catch her toy, and trotted back, tail wagging, to drop it at Ty's feet.

"Ah! Dog good," Dom said as Ty handed him the ball.

"Go ahead. Throw the ball," Ty said, making a throwing gesture with his arm. "We'll put it down to your OT."

"Dom throw ball. *Taa*!" He threw the ball and Daisy ran after it.

They spent nearly an hour throwing the tennis ball until the enthusiastic dog finally wore herself out and, for the first time, Veronica saw Dom truly relax and enjoy himself. Dressed in jeans, a heavy sweater, and sneakers, he looked like an ordinary guy enjoying an ordinary fall day, and her heart leapt at the thought that he might eventually live a normal, contented life.

Well, maybe not completely normal. Once her books were published, he would become a worldwide sensation.

She suspected she would have her hands full preparing him for that.

13

OUTSIDE THE BOX

He awakens in the dark, heart racing, breath catching in his throat.

A dream. A bad dream. He was running. Stumbling and running again. Falling. Falling far.

When his heart has slowed to normal, he swings his legs over the side of the bed and sits up.

Too fast. He sways for a moment and grips the bed sheets until he feels steady enough to stand.

He gropes for his cane on the floor at his feet. With his bad eyes he sees almost nothing in the dim light from the lamp on the wall, but he knows where he is. He walks to the bathroom and moves the little stick on the wall inside the door that turns night to day.

The light blinds him for a few seconds, but gradually what passes for his sight returns and he answers his body's call. When he has finished, he does not turn out the light and return to bed as usual. Instead, he pushes his feet into the shoes called slippers and shuffles to the other door, the one that leads out of his room. He opens the door and steps into the hallway.

One of the cats leapt onto her legs as Veronica's cell phone chimed on her bedside table, the combined disturbance only waking her halfway.

She reached for her cell, blinking to focus sleepy eyes on the number.

Unknown.

Noting the time—4:08—she hit "Ignore," dropped the cell on the table, and closed her eyes.

The kitty, Scout, who often slept on the bed, decided to stay and curled up beside her.

Thirty seconds later, her cell chimed again. She groaned and answered it.

"Veronica? Sorry to bother you so early," said a woman. "It's Gayle Adams, the night nurse at Cooper Med—"

"Gayle? Wait—what? Is Dom okay?" Veronica sat straight up in bed, instantly alert.

"He is. Or he will be. There was some trouble a little bit ago." She went on to explain that Dom had gotten out of bed—not unusual, he often rose to use the bathroom—and ventured from his room down the hallway to the facility's back door. It was securely locked as always, and when he tried to force it open, an alarm had gone off.

"He panicked at the sound of the alarm," Gayle told her, "and before we could get him calmed down, he had a seizure. A shot of lorazepam got that under control quickly enough, but—"

"Oh, God," Veronica moaned. "And now he's—"

"Sleeping. I'm afraid we had to sedate him."

"Thanks. I'll come—"

"Take your time. He'll be out for a few hours."

"Right. Okay."

Veronica tried to go back to sleep, but it was hopeless. She rose with the sun, showered and dressed, fed the cats and cleaned their litter box, and gave them a brushing they needed but didn't appreciate. When she could find nothing more to do, she headed for Cooper Medical.

Gayle, a blond woman around Veronica's age, was at the nurses' station, dressed in street clothes and obviously waiting for her before leaving after her night shift. Beatrice, in uniform and ready to start her day, was with her. Veronica walked past them to peer at the monitor offering a view of Dom's room.

The mud man looked to be sleeping peacefully, although she noticed the railings were up on his bed.

"What happened? How could he just walk out of his room without anyone seeing him?" she demanded of Gayle.

"There was an emergency on the third floor," the nurse explained, "and I was called to help. A good emergency," she added, offering an apologetic smile. "A comatose patient woke up!"

"Oh! Well, that's great, but still . . . I thought Dom was being watched—"

"He doesn't need to be monitored 24/7," Beatrice said in Gayle's defense. "If you ask me, he doesn't even need to be here. Aside from his weight and his eyesight, he's quite healthy. He—"

"He just had a seizure!" Veronica exclaimed. "You call that healthy?"

"Lots of people live with epilepsy," Beatrice replied patiently, "and this was his first episode in over a month. He should go home to his people, Veronica."

"Well, he can't!" Veronica snapped. "Gayle?" She turned to the woman, who was pulling on her coat. "Thanks for taking care of Dom and for calling me."

"Of course. Hope he feels okay today."

Leaving Dom to sleep off the sedative, Veronica walked four blocks to the local Tim Horton's to eat and cool off. When she got back to Cooper Medical, Dom was stirring in his bed.

They gave him another ten minutes before going into his room. Beatrice lowered the guard rails and Veronica sat down on the edge of the bed, close to Dom but not touching him.

"Dom? Hey, are you okay?" she asked gently.

He opened his eyes and looked at her, squinting and blinking to focus. He rubbed his hands over his face, then clasped them to his head. "Oh, Vee! Dom head hurt. Water. Dom want drink water."

"Of course." She fetched him a cup from the bathroom as Beatrice raised the bed so he could drink comfortably.

"Thank you." Dom chugged the water down and dropped the empty wooden cup on the bed.

Veronica picked up the cup and turned to Beatrice. "Why's he wearing that?" she asked, motioning sideways to the striped hospital gown on Dom.

"It was the easiest thing for Gayle and the orderly to get him into. I'm afraid the poor lad soiled his pajamas when he had the seizure. It's a common occurrence."

"Oh, God," Veronica moaned. "How embarrassing. I can't imagine what that felt like."

"From what Gayle said, I don't think he was aware, Veronica."

Still holding the cup, Veronica asked gently, "Dom? Can you tell me what happened last night? You went out?"

It was a few minutes before he replied. "Dom go bathroom. Go out room. Go . . ." He squeezed his eyes shut and shook his head, as if trying to clear the remnants of drugged sleep from his mind. "Big noise!" He clapped his hands to his ears. "Big noise! Dom no like!" He removed his hands from his ears and spoke in his language, his words coming in a long rush until finally he ran out of breath and fell silent.

Veronica didn't understand more than a couple words, and yet she did. He'd been terrified. Disoriented.

Of course, he was.

"The noise is called an alarm. It tells us if the door is opened without using the pass card."

"Al-arm." He grimaced. "Bad noise. Hurt Dom head."

"Dom? Why did you go out? *Aatay?*"

A shrug, followed by a few words in his language. Whatever the reason, he hadn't the vocabulary to say it in English. He ended with, "Dom bad?" It was definitely a question.

"No! Not bad. It's just . . . you can't go out at night."

"No go out night." He frowned. "*Aatay?*"

Why? Oh, God, what to say? It's dangerous out there? The guy hiked mountains, fought bears, hunted mammoths, and had wolves for pets, for God's sake. But what else could she say?

"You don't know enough about my world," she said, careful not to make Beatrice suspicious about his identity. "If you go out alone, you might get hurt."

He pondered this for such a long time, she began to doubt he'd understood her.

"Dom go out alone. Dom hurt," he said finally, his words slow and thoughtful. "Why hurt?" Before she could produce an answer, he went on, "Vee teach Dom more Vee world. Dom go out?"

He finished on such a hopeful note that Veronica feared she might burst into laughter. Or tears.

"Yes. Vee teach Dom, then Dom can go out." She already had the beginnings of a plan in her mind.

"We need to talk," Veronica said to Walter as he arrived at his office door the next morning. She'd been waiting there for almost an hour in order to catch him first thing.

"Better make it quick," he said as he bustled past her, his coat over his arm and briefcase in hand. "I have a procedure to do in an hour."

"It better not be on Dom," she said through her teeth.

"As a matter of fact, it's not. So, what do you want?" he asked as she followed him into his office.

"I want to take him out."

That stopped him in his tracks. He turned to face her. "I'm afraid that's not—"

"I don't mean out of the facility. I mean like, take him for a walk." God, that made him sound like a puppy. "Go to the playground down the street. Tim Horton's. Stanley Park. Whatever. He's used to the wide-open spaces and now he's getting stronger, he needs to get out of his room. Out of the hospital. He tried to go out Saturday night. On his own. In his pajamas."

"I heard," Walter grumbled, "and that particular event won't be repeated."

"How do you know?" Veronica's voice rose a notch. "Don't tell me you're going to sedate him every—"

"We'll be locking his door," he said, cutting her off, "from 9:00 pm to 6:00 in the morning, when the day shift comes—"

"You're not!" she exclaimed. "You can't. What if something happens? A fire or something? He wouldn't be able to get out. Look, I'll explain to him that he mustn't go out at night."

"And you'd trust him to not go out because you tell him not to?"

"I do," she said. *I'd trust him more than I trust you not to go back on your word.* "And if he stays in his room at night, you've got to let him go out during the day. To the sunroom, the lobby, outside when the weather's nice."

"And off the property? I'm sorry, Veronica, but I can't allow it—"

"You will allow it!" Her voice rose another notch. "He's not a damn guinea pig you can keep in a cage, and he's not a prisoner, either. We've got to stop treating him like one."

By now Walter had hung up his coat, sat down behind his desk, and removed some papers from his briefcase. He looked these over for several minutes, long enough for Veronica to think he planned to ignore her until she gave up and left.

"Be very careful, Veronica," he said eventually. He put the papers in order and pushed to his feet. "If anything should happen to him—"

"Yeah, I know. You'd lose your precious supply of Neolithic genetic material."

He gave her a long look. "I was going to say, we would have some difficult questions to answer."

He's right. Dom has no family name, no birth certificate, no social insurance number. How would we explain him to police or EMTs if anything should happen?

"Don't worry, I'll be careful. I'll get Ty to help me."

When she told Dom he would soon be able to go outside further than the medical facility's back yard, he was thrilled and wanted to go right away.

No, she insisted, there were things she had to teach him first.

She spent the afternoon explaining in the simplest words possible and lots of drawings on the whiteboard what a city was: buildings, streets, sidewalks, and cars. She told him the name of the city. Finally, she told him he mustn't leave his room at night, explaining once again that this could be dangerous.

"Dom understand," he said at last. Drawing several tall buildings on the board, he said, "Big city Van-couv-er. Cars roll fast street. People walk sidewalk. Dom walk street, car hit Dom. Dom hurt." He erased the previous drawing and made one of a car—a sort of oval with wheels on the side—with a man lying flat in front of it. The man held a cane in his right hand. "Dom," he said, tapping the image of the man, as if she hadn't figured that out. "Dom no like hit car. Walk on sidewalk."

"Good. And what about the night? You'll stay here at night? You won't go out?"

He actually rolled his eyes. Sighed. "Yes. Dom stay room night. Stay good. Go bad."

"Yes!" Veronica agreed. She wanted to hug him out of sheer joy that she'd got this important point across to him, but she managed to restrain herself. Who knew what a hug meant in his time and culture? Instead, she nodded. "You do understand."

"*Taa*. Dom understand. Go outside now?"

"No, not today. Tomorrow," she promised, "when Ty is with us."

"Tomorrow," Dom said grudgingly. "Dom, Vee, Ty go outside. *Lah-taa*."

Between Dom's physical therapy and lunch on Tuesday, Veronica told Ty of her plan. He thought it was a wonderful idea, as long as they took it one small step at a time.

As a precautionary measure against the anxiety they feared Dom might suffer when he began to venture outside the protective box of the medical facility, Walter and Ty had decided to put him on a low dose of anti-anxiety medication. Trusting Ty now, Dom agreed to take the new pill every morning. All his other medications had been stopped, except for a preventative dose of an anti-seizure drug and the occasional pain killer when he deigned to ask for one.

That afternoon, they had Dom dress warmly in jeans, jacket, and boots, and the three of them went out through the yard to the staff parking lot at the side of the building. Dom spent nearly two hours prowling around the cars, touching the hoods, roofs, and doors, caressing bumpers and actually smelling the tires and exhaust pipes, marvelling at the windows and the colours of the vehicles.

On Wednesday, they walked to the playground a block away. Cooper Medical was located in a residential area, bordered by quiet, tree-lined streets with little traffic. Cars did go by, however, giving Dom a start each time until after half a dozen or so, he got used to them. The walk took ten times what it should have, as Dom stopped not only to rest, but to examine parked cars, lamp posts, stop signs, fences, and little stone walls, frequently asking what they were and what they were for.

They walked around the block Thursday, this time stopping only occasionally when Dom needed to rest. He'd permanently exchanged his walker for the cane, but he still wasn't one hundred percent steady on his feet.

Friday dawned cool and overcast, but the rain held off as Veronica, Ty, and Dom strolled to Tim Horton's after lunch. Veronica had told Dom as much as she could about the place. She'd also told him they would meet a friend there, a prospect that clearly excited him.

She'd called Chloe yesterday to invite her here. The young

woman had no classes Friday afternoon, but even if she had, she said she would ditch them in a heartbeat for a chance to meet Dom.

Anti-anxiety meds notwithstanding, Dom tensed noticeably and edged closer to Veronica as they entered the restaurant.

"Much people. Much noise," he said, hesitating at the usual hustle and bustle of a place like this, and for a second Veronica worried that coming here might prove to be a mistake.

She hooked her right arm through Dom's left and replied, "You're okay. Vee and Ty are here. Oh, and there's our friend, Chloe," she added when she spotted the girl waving them over to a window-side table. She led him to the table, helped him shrug off his jacket, which she hung over the back of the chair opposite Chloe, and got him seated.

She sat to his right with Ty to his left. She introduced Chloe to Ty and Dom.

Chloe's cheeks flushed and she gushed, "Oh, Dom! I'm so happy to meet you! Veronica's told me so much about you. I can't believe—" She clapped her hand over her mouth and giggled like a schoolgirl, while Veronica glared at her.

Veronica had warned her to be calm and keep things simple, and it seemed she suddenly remembered this. She took a deep, centering breath. "Um, sorry," she said more carefully. "Chloe's happy to meet Dom."

Dom smiled across the table at her. He hadn't taken his eyes off her since sitting down. She was a pretty girl by anyone's standards, and she looked lovely today in a white turtleneck sweater that brought out her colour, her ebony hair loose on her shoulders. She was also the first woman he'd met who looked anything like any woman he'd ever known. Evidently, he could see well enough to notice this.

"Dom meet Chloe. Yes. Good."

Ty cleared his throat and stood up. "I'll go get our stuff. What do you guys want?"

Chloe and Veronica gave him their orders. Dom wanted coffee—after numerous taste tests, he'd told them he preferred it black—and a honey-glazed donut, for which he'd recently acquired a taste.

They spent a pleasant ninety minutes enjoying their food and chatting about simple things. Dom was mostly quiet and visibly nervous, reacting several times with a start to a sudden sound or movement, but managing to keep himself together enough and behave normally enough so as not to attract attention from the other patrons.

Chloe's gaze frequently fell to Dom's hands as he picked up his cup or donut, an expression of sympathy in her dark eyes. Most of the time, however, it was firmly on his face as she told him about her family and how she knew Veronica.

He seemed to relate when Chloe said Veronica was her teacher. "Dom teach Vee Dom world," he said. "Family. Animals. Stone tools. Vee teach Dom Vee world. Cars. Streets. Coffees." He looked all around. "Good place," he said suddenly, nodding with approval. "Dom like. *Taa.* Dom like much."

After draining second cups of coffee and promising to meet up again soon, Veronica, Ty, and Dom took their leave of Chloe and headed back to Cooper Medical, arriving as a light rain began to fall.

Dom had slowed down considerably over the last block, favouring his left leg and leaning heavily on his cane. He didn't complain, though, and in fact looked as happy as he had while playing with Daisy the dog.

Clearly, today's trip hadn't been a mistake after all.

14

DOM'S STORY, PART ONE

True to his word, Dom remained in his room at night, occasionally rising early to listen to music—Veronica had shown him how the player worked and left a stack of CDs, two of which were Native American tribal chants—or elaborate on his wall drawings.

He was autonomous for all his personal daily needs, although the state of his hands made mundane tasks difficult and he tended to fumble or drop things, causing occasional outbursts of frustration. He was growing steadier on his feet, and he'd suffered no further seizures. On the downside, however, Ty discovered Dom had little hearing in his left ear beyond persistent tinnitus.

Veronica and Ty took him to the sunroom, where he enjoyed watching television, pulling up a chair directly in front of the flat screen on the wall so he could make out something of the small, moving images in front of him. Walt had relented somewhat on his Dom-must-have-no-contact-with-anyone policy, so they introduced him to Everett and his family, and an older female patient called Molly, with strict instructions not to talk about himself or his people. While the frown on his face indicated he didn't understand why this was important, he agreed. Veronica suspected he would agree to just about anything to get out of his room.

He was fascinated by the magazines in the lobby and the sunroom, although he seemed to enjoy the feel of the glossy pages more than anything he could glean from their contents.

This gave Veronica an idea. She brought Dom an oversized pad of drawing paper and a mega box of wax crayons, so he didn't have to erase everything after he'd drawn it, as he did with the board.

Things were going well, but that was not to say perfectly smoothly. Dom's first car ride—an attempt to drive to Tim Horton's for a second visit with Chloe—resulted in a full-blown panic attack, complete with hyperventilation and frantic clawing at the door in his effort to escape the moving car. The trip was aborted, and Ty had to give him a shot of mild sedative to calm him down, but at least he didn't have a seizure.

Veronica called Chloe to explain the situation and arranged for the young woman to visit Dom at Cooper Medical the next day.

Ty's Saturday afternoons were now dedicated to the patient who had recently awakened from her coma, so Veronica was alone to greet Chloe in the lobby after she got past the security desk—Veronica had given the guard her name—cups of Tim Horton's finest and a box of Timbits in hand. They walked together to Dom's room, where they sat at the table to drink their coffee and munch their snack.

Dom apologized in his broken English for the missed visit yesterday, essentially admitting he'd been claustrophobic and scared to death.

"Car go fast. Much fast." He hesitated, searching for his words. "Car big box. Dom no like." He shuddered dramatically.

"That's okay," Chloe said, reaching over to take his hand in hers. "Chloe understands. I'm happy to see you today."

Dom nodded and grinned widely. "Yes. Dom happy see Chloe." He popped a cherry Timbit into his mouth. "Mmm. Good."

Veronica told Chloe about Dom's progress during the week, but the student seemed hardly to be listening. Her gaze swivelled between Dom and the drawings on the walls, until finally she got up to admire the images close up. Suddenly, she turned to Veronica and asked,

"Can he read and write?"

"Well, no," Veronica replied. "I'm sure his people had no written language, just as later Native Americans didn't."

"Oh, I know that. What I mean is, with his eyes the way they are. Do you think he can see well enough to learn?"

Veronica nodded slowly. "I suppose so, if we write in big, bold letters. He can write his numerals to twenty and, as you see, he draws all the time. Why?"

"I want to teach him!" She stared at the mammoth for a moment, then went on, "I've been thinking about it all week. I want to write my bachelor's thesis about teaching someone with no concept of written language how to read and write. I want to use . . . I mean, not use . . . teach. I want to teach Dom and document everything for my thesis."

"You won't be able to identify him," Veronica reminded her after considering this for a moment. "At least not until after the NDA is lifted and I've published my first paper."

"Oh, I wouldn't. He'd just be The Subject. A completely illiterate indigenous man—"

"Chloe teach Dom?" the subject in question piped up. "Teach Dom what?"

We've got to stop talking in front of him like he isn't there, Veronica thought. *He understands far more than we give him credit for.*

Chloe spent the rest of the afternoon explaining to Dom what letters were, how each one represented a sound and how, by stringing them together, they could make up a word. When she was done, he nodded enthusiastically.

"Dom draw words. Draw tree, say word 'tree.' Chloe, Vee, draw letters. Letters say word. *Taa.* Dom like. Yes. Dom learn letters." He grinned. "Start today!"

Veronica sat on the bed and watched the two of them, sitting side by side on the bear rug, the whiteboard between them. She couldn't help noticing they made a cute couple and she wasn't sure how she felt about that. Better not to think of it—at least for now.

"So, the first letter is A," Chloe told her student. She wrote a huge capital letter "A" on the board and drew an apple beside it. "A for 'apple.' Understand?"

"Yes, Dom understand." An hour later, he knew A, B, and C, and they'd thought up as many simple words as they could that began with those letters.

Dom was clearly elated with this discovery, and when Chloe and Veronica left him at suppertime, he was busy printing A, B, and C in every combination possible, along with drawings of apples, cats, and bears, on his drawing pad.

"You had an amazing idea," Veronica said to Chloe. "I wish I'd thought of it myself, but I guess I'll have to be content with buying more paper and crayons."

They laughed together, both of them thrilled with this turn of events and the possibilities unfolding before them.

It wasn't long before Walter heard about Dom's visits with Chloe and Veronica had to explain. He wasn't happy, but Veronica insisted the young woman could be trusted. She'd known who Dom was for months, she'd signed the NDA and, on top of that, she and Dom had an obvious connection.

Reluctantly admitting defeat, Walter condoned Dom's socialization, but he picked up the pace as far as tests and the collecting of samples were concerned. Declaring Dom strong enough to serve as a veritable donor bank, he extracted blood, stem cells, bone marrow, spinal fluid, and whatever else a person could donate while still drawing breath.

Veronica and Ty retaliated by taking Dom out as often as possible. They walked to Tim Horton's and explored the convenience store across the street from the restaurant. A second short car ride proved successful. Dom became anxious but was able to control himself. A third went so smoothly they were able to reach their planned destination of Cates Park, a half hour from Cooper Medical.

Chloe met them there to take a walk on the beach, something Dom had been expressing through words and drawings that he wanted to do.

He touched everything—the trees above the beach and driftwood along the shore, even dropping to his knees to run his hands through the coarse sand—but most of all, he wanted to go in the water. Argue as they might that it was too cold for that, there was no stopping him, so finally they all pulled off their shoes and socks, rolled up their jeans, and waded into the frigid waters of the Vancouver Harbour. Dom tottered a bit as his toeless feet sank into the wet sand, but he steadied himself with his cane and ploughed ahead until the water reached his knees.

When Veronica could no longer feel her feet and she actually heard Chloe's teeth chattering, she herded them all out as if they were her children.

"Holy crap, I'm cold!" exclaimed Ty, stomping his feet to get the blood flowing again. "Don't know how in hell those Polar Bear Swim people do it in January."

"Yes, much cold," Dom said, beaming even though his lips were tinted blue. "Good cold. Good water. Dom like. Make fire. Warm. Dry," he suggested.

"Sorry, buddy, we can't do that," Ty said as Chloe giggled behind her hand. "No fire here."

They sat to rub their feet dry and put on their socks and shoes. There were a few other people on the beach. An older couple were walking with a Yorkshire terrier that trotted up to them to investigate.

"Uh . . . cat?" Dom asked, squinting to focus on the shaggy creature.

It sniffed from one of them to the other, then let out a little yip.

"Dog?" he exclaimed. "*Taa*. Small dog. Pfft! No good."

They headed back to their cars, Dom still chuckling and muttering that the little dog was too small to do any good. His dogs, Veronica reminded herself, had barely been one evolutionary step removed from wolves.

By the beginning of December, Dom was halfway through the alphabet with Chloe, who came every Friday and Sunday afternoon, and Veronica had taught him the Arabic numerals to fifty. He continued to do two hours of PT with Ty Tuesdays to Fridays, and he was walking more easily, using his cane but relying less on it as his balance and strength improved. He'd gotten into the habit of spending an hour or so after lunch in the sunroom, where he watched TV and sometimes had a simple conversation with Everett and his mom, or Julia and Manuel, the parents of the little girl who recently came out of her coma. Molly had gone home with her family, although Walter would still see her on an outpatient basis for a few months to come.

One afternoon when she found herself alone with Dom in his room, Veronica asked him to tell her more about his life.

"Start at the start," she suggested. "When you were a little boy."

He thought this over for a moment, then shook his head. "*T-lay*. Dom no talk Vee today. Draw today. Talk tomorrow. Good?"

She nodded. "Good." She told herself the wait would certainly be worth it.

And it was.

Dom must have spent the evening and a good part of the night drawing. When Veronica arrived the next morning with coffee and one of his favourite field berry muffins, he had nearly a dozen full-page pictures spread out on the corner table. He always printed or drew everything as large as possible, the better to see them, she supposed.

"Ooh, berry muffin," he said, taking a bite. "Thank you, Vee."

She waited, sipping her coffee while he drank his and finished his muffin. He collected the drawings, looking closely at each one and taking care to put them in a particular order, and went to sit on the bearskin rug. He seemed to prefer this to sitting on a chair.

Old habits die hard, that's for sure.

Veronica followed him, turning on her cell phone recorder and placing it between them when she sat down to his right.

"Dom old fa—no," he corrected himself. "Grandfather. *Taa*. Grandfather. Grandmother." He placed the drawing of three people with wrinkled faces and grey hair twisted into long braids on the rug in front of her. One of the men stood stooped over and held a long walking stick. "Elders Dom people. Much good. Teach people much." He looked sideways at Veronica. "Vee understand?"

She nodded. She didn't ask why he had only one grandmother, assuming she'd passed away when he was young or even before he was born. "Your grandparents were elders to your people. I understand. Tell me more."

"*Taa*." Another drawing, this one of two adults and a boy who stood to their waist. "Dom." He pointed to the boy, who was naked. The adults wore minimal light brown clothing—presumably made of animal skins—that hung loosely to their mid-thighs. "Mother. Father. Father good. Teach Dom much. Teach hunt. Teach—"

"What did you hunt?" She hated to interrupt him when he was on such a roll, but she wanted to know. He knew enough animal names in English to tell her.

"Hunt bear. Car-ibou. Horse." He ticked them off on her fingers. "Rabbit. Squirrel. Seal. Beaver. Frog. Fish . . . uh, sa-mon. Clam. Bird."

"Don't forget the mammoth," Veronica prompted.

"*T-lay*. No mammoth. Mammoth, uh . . . more after."

"More after? You mean later?"

"Yes. Mammoth much more later." He took a long breath and went on, "Father teach Dom make stone scraper. Knife.

Points. Make *issah*. Uh, tent."

A third drawing, this one of a man and a boy holding stones. Two finished projectile points lay at their feet.

"Mother good. Teach Dom much. Make baskets. String. Clothes. Medicine. Good drink." He placed a drawing of a woman with a large woven basket in her arms, piles of leaves, flowers, berries, and branches or roots all around her.

The next drawing was of several older people and three children sitting around a campfire. "Elders teach Dom people stories. Songs. Dom remember." Eyes closed, he hummed for a minute or so, tapping his hand against his thigh to keep the rhythm.

His sixth drawing showed a tall boy with shoulder-length hair surrounded by smaller children, four girls and two boys. His younger brothers and sisters. He gave Veronica all their names, and she was grateful everything was being recorded because it would take her hours to figure out how to write them phonetically. "Dom help mother care small brothers. Sisters." He went on for a moment in his language, before abruptly cutting himself off. "Sorry, Dom no much good English."

"It's okay. You're doing great. Please go on."

"Yes. Dom fifteen summers. Go sky stone place. See old fire. Trees old fire." He placed the next drawing in front of Veronica.

It showed the side of a slope with a shallow hollow cut into it. Brown trees with bare branches stood around it. Green trees remained behind them, along with low bushes full of plump blueberries. Obviously, the meteorite had made an impact crater in the side of the mountain and caused a limited fire but outside the perimeter, the forest was making a comeback.

"Dom stay one moon. Go home man."

"Right." She nodded. He'd told her this before, of course.

"Man alone no good. Want woman."

"Right."

Another drawing, this one of a naked woman with long, dark brown hair decorated with yellow flowers, and the bulging belly of late term pregnancy.

"Dom woman."

"Lil-lia. Right?"

Dom's eyes narrowed slightly, and he shook his head. "*T-lay*! No Lil-lia. Roo," he said. "Dom woman name Roo."

"Oh! So . . . Roo was your first woman? Before Lil-lia?"

A curt nod. "*Taa*. Dom first woman Roo." He placed the final drawing in front of her, on top of the others. It showed the young couple with a male toddler at their feet and a second baby wrapped in some sort of fur in the woman's arms.

"Dom good father. Roo good mother." He pushed suddenly to his feet, stumbling in his haste, but quickly catching himself with his cane. "No more talk today."

"But I have questions. Can I—"

"No!" he snapped in a tone Veronica had never heard him use before. "No more talk today. Eat lunch. Walk outside."

Veronica sighed and turned off the recording. "Thank you, Dom," she said. "Can I keep your drawings?"

He shrugged with his back to her. "Yes. Keep."

She collected the drawings and her cell phone and stood. Dom was clearly holding something back. Perhaps it was the painful loss of Roo early on? He was, however, as stubborn as he was persistent, and she knew there was no point pressuring him. She'd heard enough today to keep her busy for hours, if not days. She would get the next part of his story when he was ready to tell it.

15

HAPPY HOLIDAYS

"It'll be Christmas Eve in ten days," Veronica said to Walter. She'd actually booked an appointment to make sure she got an uninterrupted half hour alone with him in his office.

"I'm aware," he said flatly, as though he'd been expecting her to say something else. "We'll be having our Christmas dinner here on Friday the 23rd, for staff, patients, and their families. I assume you'll be coming?"

"I wouldn't miss it for the world. After that, I'll be going up to my parents' house from the 24th to the 27th, like I do every year." She paused, recalling with an unexpected twinge of nostalgia that they'd spent many a nice Christmas vacation together at his or her family home.

"Tell everyone hello from me," Walter said, "and tell Neil I'll call him sometime soon for drinks and a chat."

"I will."

"You didn't come up here just to tell me you're going home for Christmas, did you?"

"I didn't. I came to tell you that when I get back, I want to bring Dom to my place for a few days. My apartment, I mean."

Walter blinked. He drew in a long breath and tented his hands below his chin. "I'm afraid that's out of the question."

Veronica was prepared for this. "Actually, it's not," she said. "That agreement we signed stated you'd provide Dom with medical care, which you have, and that I'd grant you permission to use him for tests and research, which I have. It didn't say anything about my not keeping guardianship and the right to make decisions for him. There's no reason he can't be allowed out for a holiday.

"His tests have all come back normal—again—and there's even an improvement in his bone density. He hasn't had a seizure since the night he set off the alarm. He's as intelligent and reasonable as anyone you've ever met and more so than many. His English is getting better every day, something you'd notice if you bothered to actually talk to him instead of just sticking him with needles or ripping bits and pieces out of him."

"I'll have you know I've talked to him plenty," he said, his tone defensive. "I've asked him repeatedly where he comes from—"

"You what?" Her voice rose an octave.

"He hasn't told me a damn thing that's of any use. He lived near the ocean, he lived in the mountains, he lived in the valley. He could've come from goddamn Timbuktu for all the good—" He threw his arms in the air and emitted an exaggerated sigh. "Take him out, Veronica, show him a good time, but don't forget I'm counting on you to drag the information I need out of him. That was the most important part of our agreement."

"Believe me, Walt, I haven't forgotten. And just in case you're worried about it, I'll take every precaution. I won't be alone with him." Veronica elaborated on her plan, having thought it through over the past few days. "I've already talked to Ty. He'll come for the first day and night or two. I'll ask Neil, too, and damn it, you can stay with us yourself if you feel the urge. But he deserves—no, he needs—to get out from between these four walls before he loses his mind."

"Fine," Walter said after about thirty seconds. "Maybe I'll take you up on that offer." He sat down behind his desk and slumped in his chair, as if this conversation had exhausted him. When he spoke again, his voice had lost its sharp edge. "What are you going to tell him about Christmas?"

"I don't know," she admitted. "I'll think of something before then."

In hopes of avoiding awkward questions, Veronica, Ty, and Chloe agreed not to tell Dom about Christmas dinner until the day before. They also agreed not to mention God or the traditional Christmas story of the birth of Jesus Christ. None of them could fathom how they might explain those concepts to him in a way he would understand.

However, despite his poor vision Dom had, in fact, noticed something was going on as the holiday approached. Veronica guessed the decorated fir trees in the lobby and sunroom and the holly wreaths on the doors he passed on his way to them gave it away. When he asked about them, she told him they were decorations to make houses beautiful in winter and that seemed to satisfy him, at least for the time being.

"Big supper tomorrow? Why?" Dom asked after they finally told him about Christmas dinner.

Ty groaned and ran his fingers through his short, spiky hair.

Veronica rolled her eyes, the imperceptible action wasted on Dom. "To celebrate the middle of winter." Then, concerned he might hear something about the true meaning of Christmas from someone else, she added, "We also celebrate the birth of a great man. Sort of an elder, who taught us how to be good people. Better people."

Chloe pulled a face at her.

She shrugged as if to say, *That's all I've got.*

"Ah, elder," said Dom, nodding. "Elder come supper tomorrow?"

Another groan from Ty.

"No, Dom," Chloe said gently. "He's dead. He's been dead for a long time."

"He what?" A frown. "Dom no understand word. What mean word 'dead'?"

"Holy crap," muttered Ty, who'd been against them saying anything about Christmas for this very reason.

They were sitting in a circle on the fur rug and deer skins on the floor in Dom's room. Chloe jumped up to get the box of markers and the whiteboard, which was by now turning grey from use, and knelt down beside Dom.

After thinking for a moment, she drew a barely recognizable animal standing on four thick legs. Art, as she frequently pointed out, wasn't her specialty.

"This bear," she said, tapping it with the marker, "is alive."

She drew a second bear, this one on its side. For good measure she added a spear sticking out of its chest and a pool of red blood around it. "This bear is dead."

"Way to be graphic, Chloe," said Ty.

Ignoring him, she erased the bears and drew a tree full of green leaves. "This tree is alive." Beside it she added a second tree, leaning slightly, its branches black and broken. "This tree? Dead."

Dom picked up the eraser and wiped the board clean. Taking the black marker from Chloe, he drew a man standing. "Man alive." He erased this and drew a man lying flat. He went through the box of markers until he found the red one. He added a jagged red line in the man's side. Then, using a brown marker, he drew a horizontal line above the prone man and finished by scribbling all over him, essentially covering him up.

His people buried their dead, thought Veronica, the clinical part of her mind clicking into gear. *So, there's the long-sought answer to that question.*

"Man dead," said Dom, pointing solemnly to the covered man. "Elder . . ." He paused and looked at Chloe. "Elder name?"

"Oh. His name is Jesus." She wrote it along the top of the board in big, block letters, spelling it as she went. "J-E-S-U-S."

"Je-sus." He nodded. "Je-sus dead. People remember Jesus. Big supper."

"That's right," Veronica said. She tried to sound upbeat, when really, she was thinking bitterly, *Wonderful. Now he'll know the word "dead" when it comes time to explain why he can't go back to his people.*

Dom smiled as he put the thought of death behind him. "Dom understand. Dom people celeb-rate much. Baby. Man fifteen summers. Woman fifteen summers. Spring. Summer. No celeb-rate winter. Cold. No much food. Winter bad."

"I'm with you there, buddy," said Ty, but Dom wasn't finished.

"Big supper. Much people. Much noise. Talk. Music. Vee, Ty, Chloe go big supper. Celeb-rate Je-sus. Dom go big supper. *Taa?*"

"*Taa*," agreed Veronica agreed, relieved that explanations were over. "We'll all go together."

The supper in question turned out to be a festive affair. The cafeteria was tastefully decorated with red garlands and fresh holly wreaths. The four patients who were mobile enough to come and Molly, who'd returned for the occasion, along with their families and the staff with their significant others, filled the place with cheerful chatter over a background of traditional Christmas music.

Veronica, Dom, Chloe, and Ty, along with Ty's wife, Amanda, sat at one table to eat a traditional turkey dinner. Beatrice and her husband, Alex and his companion, and Gayle, Dom's night nurse, ate at the table beside them. Everyone was dressed in something colourful, and Dom looked particularly Christmassy in Ty's grandfather's red turtleneck that Veronica had suggested he wear above his jeans.

"Mmm, good," Dom said, nodding with satisfaction as he tasted stuffing and cranberry sauce for the first time. He was able to use a fork now, although Veronica cut his turkey up for him. "Much good food! Dom like."

Halfway through their meal, Walter brought his plate and utensils and sat down in the empty chair between Veronica and Chloe.

"Everett will be going home next month," he told them after they all exchanged polite greetings. He practically glowed with pride. "And do you see the girl?" He pointed with his chin across the cafeteria to a dark-haired, pre-teen girl Veronica had seen in the sunroom the previous week.

She sat between Julia and her husband, Manuel, inclined in a deluxe wheelchair and plugged into an IV line and other paraphernalia. She was conscious, however, nodding and smiling and carefully chewing spoonfuls of mashed potatoes her mom raised to her mouth.

"Gracie went swimming last May in a lake down in Florida," Walter said, "and was infected by microscopic *Naegleria fowler.* The brain-eating amoeba," he added at the expressions of confusion on his companions' faces. Everyone at Beatrice's table seemed to be listening as well. "By the time doctors figured out what was wrong, she was in a vegetative state, half of her brain reduced to grey mush. After three months, her parents were advised to turn off life support and let her go. Instead they did some research, found a paper on the internet I wrote a couple years ago, and contacted me. She'd been here for three months, completely unresponsive, until one night—well, the night our friend here had his encounter with the alarm system—she woke up."

Veronica already knew this, having spoken to the girl's parents several times.

"At the moment she's almost completely blind and paralyzed, but she can hear and respond when spoken to, and she's beginning to eat soft food. I have great hopes for her progress over the next few months. A year from now, I plan to present my findings and the details of my patients' recoveries to the powers that be. I'll apply for patents, all of that, and get my combination gene and stem cell therapy for victims of traumatic brain injury into a recognized, large-scale clinical trial."

He gave Veronica a long look. "I know you don't agree with all my methods, but I really do want to help as many people as I can."

"I know, Walt," and she felt her heart softening somewhat towards her ex-husband.

Walter pushed to his feet as soon as he finished his meal. "I've got to visit the patients who aren't well enough to be here," he said and left, taking his empty plate with him.

Alex and Beatrice kept their chairs turned to chat with Veronica and her companions about their plans for the holidays, until people began drifting out to return to their home, room, or work shift. Dom contributed a word or two, but mostly he listened quietly, a frown of concentration on his face as he endeavoured to understand something of the conversation.

Eventually, Veronica told Dom that she would be away for four days, but Chloe would come to see him once or twice. When she got back, he could come and stay at her place for a few days, if she wanted to.

"Dom go Vee house?" he repeated, his eyebrows rising, the frown instantly gone. "Yes, Dom want. Please. Dom want much."

"Okay then," she said. "I'll get that all set up." She gave his arm a squeeze and rose to leave.

Christmas at the Booth house was, as always, hectic but happy, filled with family, Mrs. Booth's home cooked meals, the exchange of presents, and the retelling of childhood stories everyone knew by heart but loved hearing all over again.

Veronica managed to forget about Dom for brief periods of time, although she called Chloe every afternoon to ask how he was doing. She found herself telling her family about him, as much as she could without violating the NDA. It was all fine until she asked Neil if he would stay over for a day and night or two when she brought Dom to her apartment for a few days so she wasn't alone with him.

"Are you out of your friggin' mind?" he exclaimed. He grabbed her by the elbow and steered her into his boyhood bedroom. He shut the door. "I repeat, are you—"

"I'm absolutely not!" she snapped. "And I'm not afraid he's going to assault me or anything, either. It's just in case he has a panic attack or seizure or some other kind of medical emergency."

"Jesus, Vee, who is this guy that everyone falls over

backwards for him? And why can't he go home to his people? Surely someone's found someone with a connection to him by now?"

"Well, they haven't. And they won't."

His eyes narrowed to blue slits. He dragged her to the bed, sat her down, and plopped down beside her. "You've never been good at hiding stuff from me and I've known from the beginning that you're hiding something about this Dom character. Come on, Veronica, spit it out, will you? You know you can trust me and on top of that, I signed that damn NDA Walt's lawyer cooked up. What was that all about any—"

"Okay! I'll tell you!" she exclaimed. And out it came, everything, until she stopped because she had nothing left to tell.

"Sweet Jesus," Neil said when she was done, the sound more a breath than actual words. He rubbed a hand across his eyes, cleared his throat, and tried again. "So, that's it then. No wonder you kept it quiet."

The lack of doubt in his voice and the expression of utter shock on his pale, freckled face told her he believed her.

He shifted sideways on the bed to look straight at her. "I'll stay with you however many days you want. Do whatever you need."

"Thanks, big brother." She threw her arms around his neck and hugged him tight. "I know I can count on you. I always have." She withdrew a bit and looked him in the eyes. "You can't tell anyone what I've told you, though. Not Becky. Not even Dom. He doesn't know yet, I mean, about the time that's passed since whatever happened that ended up with him being buried in the bog."

"The poor guy. It's going to be a hell of a shock for him when he learns the truth," Neil said with a shake of his head. "Don't worry, little sister, your secret's safe with me."

Much has happened over the past moon. Walk on beach. Play with dog. The best thing, though, is making friends. Everett. Chloe. Especially Chloe. She is kind and patient and teaches him many new things. He likes writing letters to make words in English. In his head, he puts letters together to make words in his language. When he goes home, he will bring this new and useful skill to his people.

This time, they will welcome him back. He will take his rightful place amidst them, his woman and his children at his side.

16

HOUSE GUESTS

Veronica got an early start and arrived home just before noon on Tuesday. She took some time to cuddle her kitties, who wrapped themselves around her ankles and purred like little outboard motors. She knew Chloe had taken good care of them, but it seemed they'd missed her as much as she'd missed them. She unpacked, put on a load of laundry, and sat on the sofa with Rusty curled up beside her while she wrote a list of the groceries she would need for the next few days: red meat, lots of vegetables, eggs, multi-grain bread, brown rice, lactose-free cheese, soy milk, and so on. Once the laundry was in the dryer, she told her cats she would only be gone for a few hours this time and headed to Cooper Medical.

She signed in at the reception-slash-security desk and headed to Dom's room with the items she'd bought at yesterday's Boxing Day sales at the Aberdeen Mall in Kamloops: a warm jacket, knitted tuque and scarf, and large gym bag, all in his favourite colours of forest green and ocean blue. She also had a pink ski vest for Chloe, as she knew the young woman preferred these to actual jackets, and a box of handcrafted chocolates—dark, not milk—for them to share.

Dom wasn't in his room. Given the hour, she thought—hoped—she knew where he was. She deposited her purchases on the bed and went up to the cafeteria. He was there, thank God, dressed in a tee-shirt and jeans, eating lunch with Everett at a table near the windows. She was glad he'd made friends with the courageous young man. She took a moment to settle herself, then she picked up her own lunch of the inevitable turkey pot pie and a cola and walked to their table.

"Hey guys, mind if I join you?" she asked as she pulled up the chair to Dom's right.

"Vee!" said Dom. "Come. Sit. Dom happy see Vee!"

"Oh! I'm happy to see you too."

"Hello, Veronica," Everett said, "and belated Merry Christmas." He was already speaking more clearly than he had mere weeks ago. Walter's experimental therapy truly was miraculous.

"Vee happy see family?" Dom asked.

"Yes, very happy," she replied.

"Good." He nodded. He seemed genuinely happy for her.

"So, what did you do while I was away?" she asked him after she'd eaten enough to take the edge off her appetite.

"Oh, he's been busy," Everett said with a crooked smile.

"Dom do much. Chloe come two days. Dom and Chloe write words. Go sunroom. Watch TV. Ty come yesterday. Bring dog Daisy. Dom, Chloe, Ty throw ball Daisy. Good day." He was positively beaming now.

"Wonderful," Veronica said. "I'm happy you had a good time."

Back in his room after taking their leave of Everett, she gave Dom the things she'd bought and showed him all the compartments in the bag.

"Thank you, Vee. Beautiful bag. Beautiful clothes," he said enthusiastically. "Dom fill bag, go Vee house now?"

"Tomorrow," she promised him. "Today, I have a lot to do to get ready for you. Tomorrow morning Ty will come, and you and he will come to my place."

She waited for Chloe to arrive and presented her with the vest while they munched chocolates.

"It's perfect, I love it!" the girl exclaimed, shrugging off her old black vest and modelling the new one for them. "My favourite colour. Thank you so much!" She gave Veronica a warm hug.

"It's nothing," Veronica said, "compared to what I owe you for taking care of my kitties"—she lowered her voice—"and Dom."

"My pleasure on both counts," she whispered back. Raising her voice to a normal level, she added, "Now go on and run your errands. Dom and I have some reading and writing to do. I'll come by your place tomorrow afternoon, promise."

Veronica thanked her again, told them goodbye, and headed outside under a rare light snow.

Ty joined Veronica in Dom's room after breakfast the next morning. He would accompany Dom to her place, staying until Friday morning. Neil would take over from him, staying until the afternoon of the 31st. Finally, Walter would come for supper and New Year's Eve, then they would bring Dom back to the facility on New Year's Day. Chloe would spend as much time with them as she could, although she had to be home for New Year's Eve or she might be forced to explain to her family more than she was able.

Dom was already dressed to go outside in a grey turtleneck sweater and jeans, thick wool socks on his feet, the toes flat where they were empty. His jacket and boots rested on his bed. All he needed to do was pack his other clothes in his bag.

Veronica helped him do so, insisting he fold everything rather than just throwing it in. Ty had collected Dom's medical necessities: anti-anxiety and anti-seizure meds; Tylenol and Celebrex for the pain he continued to experience in his hands, feet, and left leg; calcium-vitamin D and glucosamine supplements for his bones and joints. He'd also packed IV and oral lorazepam should Dom suffer a seizure, and half a dozen cans of the protein drinks he still guzzled once a day.

"I think that's everything." Veronica looked around the

room as Dom watered his plants, talking to them under his breath in his language. She had the whiteboard under one arm, the pad of drawing paper and boxes of markers and crayons in a shopping bag to take with them. "Dom? Are you ready to go?"

"Yes, Dom ready. Go Vee house. Yes."

Ty heaved Dom's gym bag over his shoulder. "Don't worry about your plants, they'll be here when you get back. And bring your cane, you'll need it if we walk outside."

"Dom no more need cane," he protested. "Walk alone. No—"

"Dom?" Veronica interrupted in her sternest professorial voice. "We talked about this. If you come to my house, you must do everything we tell you."

"*Taa*," he grumbled. "Dom no do Vee say, come back here." He grabbed his cane from where it leaned against the wall. The truth was he still needed it for balance, and he knew it. "Dom ready. Go!"

Yesterday's light snow had turned to sleet, and they hurried across the parking lot as quickly as Dom could walk. Veronica bustled him into her car while Ty got in his SUV.

Dom was quiet on the drive, peering intently out his window at whatever he could see of the passing scenery, until they drove up the slope to the Lion's Gate Bridge.

"Ooh!" he exclaimed. He stretched to peer over the low wall running along the edge of the bridge. "Oh no! Go . . . high . . . Fly high!"

Veronica glanced over to see that all colour had drained from his cheeks and his hands were clenched tight against his thighs.

"We're not flying," she told him as she turned her gaze back to the road. "We're on a bridge. Relax, Dom, please. We'll go down again in a few minutes. Maybe close your eyes?"

He promptly squeezed his eyes shut, but continued to mutter in his language in a voice that shook with terror until they crossed the shorter and lower Burrard Street Bridge, and she told him they'd returned to street level. He opened his eyes, but his face remained a distressing shade of chalky green until they pulled into the parking lot behind Veronica's apartment building twenty minutes later.

"Here we are—" she began, but Dom had already opened his door. By the time she jumped out and ran around to his side of the car, he'd staggered a step or two and dropped to his hands and knees in the slush to throw up his breakfast in a steaming, lumpy puddle.

"Oh, God, Dom, I'm so sorry!" she said as Ty pulled up and hurried to join them.

"What the hell?" he asked, peering down at Dom.

"It's my fault. I didn't think to tell him about the bridges. He completely freaked out about the height, and I think . . . I think he's just motion sick, Ty."

Dom wiped his mouth with the back of one hand and pushed to his feet. He looked from Veronica to Ty and shook his head. "Dom no understand," he said weakly. He was still pale and tiny beads of sweat stood on his forehead just below his tuque. "Car fly? No fly?"

"No fly," Veronica said, putting a steadying hand on his shoulder. "I'll explain when we get inside. We can't stay out here in this weather, we'll all get pneumonia."

Dom's brows furrowed. "New . . . what?"

"Never mind. Are you okay? Can you walk?"

"Yes. Dom okay. Go inside."

Ty parked his car in the spot Veronica pointed out and grabbed the bags. They went in through the back door, Veronica gently propelling Dom forwards with a hand on his back. Although she usually took the stairs to her second-floor apartment, for Dom's sake she led them down the hallway to the elevator.

A minute later, she ushered the two men into her apartment. Once Dom finished fingering the cedar wreath on the door, they hung their wet jackets in the hall closet and left their boots on the mat beside the door.

Rusty came to greet them while Scout, more apprehensive

of strangers, scurried for cover beneath the coffee table.

"Cat?" Dom asked as he reached down to stroke the creature rubbing its head against his ankle. He seemed to be recovering quickly enough from the drive. "Soft fur."

"Yes, that's a cat and yes, they're soft," Veronica agreed. "That one, the orange one you're petting, his name is Rusty. The black and white one you'll see when he comes out from hiding is named Scout."

"Cat Rusty. *Taa.*" He straightened and turned to her with an expression of puzzlement on his face. At least his colour was back to normal. "Why cat? Dog good . . ." He paused to rethink this. "Big dog good. Hunt. Guard. What good cat?"

"Oh, cats are wonderful! They hunt mice and they tell us if something is wrong, if a fire is starting or something. These two are my babies. Fur babies."

Dom chuckled. "Vee no children. Two cats. Fur babies. Dom like, yes."

Veronica showed Dom and Ty around, explaining to Dom what each room was. Ty put the bags in the spare bedroom where Dom would sleep. He would be camping out on the sofa, but he'd assured Veronica he didn't mind a bit.

Dom already knew the name and purpose for everything in the bedroom: bed, dresser, mirror, bedside table, lamp, closet. Veronica instructed him to change his wet jeans for dry ones, put on his slippers, and place the clothes from his gym bag in the dresser drawers. This done, she took him back to the bathroom to put his personal items in a drawer beneath the counter.

As they paused there, he took two deep breaths through his nose and grimaced. "Smell, uh . . . bad smell."

"Oh!" Veronica said with a laugh. "That's the cats' litter box. For their, um, pee and poop." She pointed out the green plastic tray between the toilet and the corner of the room. "I clean it out every day but yeah, sometimes it smells a bit. You'll get so used to it you won't even notice it anymore."

When he had no reply to that, she showed him how the

faucets worked in the sink and shower, since they weren't the same model he knew from the hospital. She explained what the bathtub was and how he could soak in it for as long as he liked. She told him which set of towels hanging on the rack were his— the navy-blue ones, of course—and explained what the washing machine and dryer were. She didn't mention the medicine cabinet, which she'd locked to be on the safe side.

"Do you understand?" she asked when she was done. He gave her a look she was seeing more and more frequently these days, one that said, *I understand. Maybe my English isn't so good yet, but I'm not an idiot.*

"Okay then. I want to tell you about the bridge."

"Great idea," Ty said from the doorway.

They sat on the sofa with Dom between them. On the whiteboard, Veronica drew a bridge over some squiggly blue waves and explained to him how they hadn't taken to the air, but simply driven over the span.

"Dom understand. No see ground. Car go bridge. No fly." He let out a long sigh of relief and managed a smile. He took the marker from Veronica and wrote "BRIJ" above her drawing. "Bridge," he said.

"Close enough," Ty said. He gave Dom a clap on the back. "Good job, buddy."

"I'm sorry I didn't tell you about the bridge before," Veronica said for about the fourth time. "Are you feeling okay now?" She glanced at Ty. "We can give you a pill to help you feel better. Calmer."

Ty nodded in agreement but Dom said,

"Dom okay. No pill."

"Okay then. Do you want some lunch?"

"Lunch? Yes. Cafet-eria?"

"No. At home we usually make it ourselves." She looked from Dom to Ty. "Come to the kitchen and help me."

She made minestrone soup from a mix, adding some frozen vegetables and cans of tomatoes and kidney beans for extra nutrition. After warning him that the front of the stove and the saucepan would become very hot, she put Dom to work stirring the soup with a wooden spoon.

She and Ty slapped together ham and lactose-free cheese sandwiches, and when the soup was ready, they all sat down at the kitchen table with glasses of iced tea for Ty and her, and water and his protein drink for Dom. She watched Dom carefully for any signs of recurring nausea, but he seemed to have recovered completely from his earlier episode, which she was certain now had been brought on by his sensation of flying over the bridge.

Chloe arrived as they finished eating with a bag of Christmas presents for the three of them. They sat in the kitchen to open their presents: ceramic coffee cups with their names handwritten on them, a box each of varied coffees and cocoa mixes, and a new drawing pad for Dom.

"Well, I feel like a crumb," Ty admitted. "Protocol at Cooper Medical forbids staff giving presents to patients and vice versa, but I didn't even think about . . . here." Then he brightened. "Next stop at Timmy's or wherever is on me."

"Sounds good," Veronica said. Dom had thanked Chloe for the gift but didn't seem to equate it with needing to give one in return, which she was relieved to see.

Veronica and Chloe showed Dom the kitchen appliances—toaster, microwave, refrigerator-slash-freezer, dishwasher, and the all-important coffee maker—and the cupboards filled with food or pots and pans and Tupperware. They spent most of the afternoon telling him how everything worked before returning to the kitchen. Not relying on his sight alone, he touched everything, turning knobs and pressing buttons, until he told them he understood.

For supper, Veronica ordered sushi, which they'd previously discovered Dom liked, and made a tossed green salad to go with it.

Chloe left not long after their meal. Veronica, Ty, and Dom went to bed early, every one of them exhausted by the emotions of the day.

Thursday dawned sunny and warmer than the previous days had been. With some guidance from Ty, Dom took his first bath and dressed, toasted a bagel, and spread it with peanut butter and strawberry jam. Following Veronica's instructions, he even made the coffee.

After breakfast, Dom announced he wanted to go outside. After discussing it with the guys, Veronica called Chloe and, once she arrived, they walked to Kitsilano Beach Park a few blocks away. While they didn't go in the water this time, they strolled along the shore until Dom began to slow down—even with his cane, the going was strenuous through the damp sand—and they sat on a large, round log to rest and chat.

They took a different route on the way home, stopping at Starbucks for coffee and a light lunch paid for by Ty as promised. Chloe and Veronica decided it was time Dom learn about currency, so when they got back to the apartment, they introduced him to coins and paper money, which he quickly learned to differentiate by the size of the coin and colour of the bills. Once he caught on, he wanted to know the cost of everything he could name. They stopped for supper—a pork roast and potatoes Veronica had put in the oven upon their return and the rest of the salad—and continued until they ran out of items to price. Almost giddy over this exercise, Chloe took lengthy notes about everything for her bachelor's thesis.

While he and Chloe had their heads together, Veronica took the opportunity to study the marvellous puzzle that was Dom. On the one hand, he was an innocent child, with no knowledge of the world around him. On the other hand, he had an intellect at least equal to their own and life experience they would never match. He was still a long way from being able to function alone in the modern world, but one day he would. Of that she was certain.

"Dom people no money," Dom offered suddenly. "*Den-no-ny . . .*" He said a few words in his language then, realizing they didn't understand, he pushed to his feet and fetched the whiteboard and a marker.

Sitting down cross-legged and balancing the board across his knees, he drew a man holding a large bundle. Facing him, he drew another man with nothing.

"Man much deer skins," he began, using his marker to tap the image of the man with the bundle. He tapped the second man. "Man cold." He drew an arrow from the first man to the second, then he erased it and the bundle, and redrew half of the bundle in the second man's arms. "Man no more cold."

"They shared based on need," Veronica said, nodding, but Dom wasn't finished.

He erased everything and drew two new figures: a man with a bundle of furs—differentiated from the hides by the hairs sticking out of them—and a woman with a basket of fish.

"Man hungry," he said. "Woman cold." He erased the furs and basket and redrew them, the bundle in the woman's arms and the basket in the man's. "Woman now warm. Man now eat. Woman happy. Man happy." He looked around at them, a smile on his face, obviously happy as well to give them this information.

"We call that trade," Chloe said. "One person gives something to another person and gets something back." She leaned over to point to the figures on the board. "Trade furs for fish." She picked up Scout, who had decided the strangers weren't so bad and was curled up between her and Ty, and handed him to Dom. She took the board and marker and wrote the word TRADE above the figures. "Trade cat for board. You understand?"

He nodded. He gave Scout a cuddle and put him down. "Trade. Yes. Dom understand. Dom people trade much."

Veronica wanted to kick herself for not having recorded such an informative conversation, but she would write it all down on her laptop this evening after everyone else went to bed.

17

DOM'S STORY PART TWO

Ty left when Veronica's brother arrived mid-morning. After pausing, literally rooted to the spot without drawing breath for a good thirty seconds at seeing Dom in the flesh, Neil moved himself and his overnight bag into the apartment.

A few minutes after he arrived, Neil asked Veronica what she had planned for the day. The weather had turned again—heavy rain and sleet would keep them indoors today. Dom suggested going to the beach, only desisting after Veronica dragged him, still in his pajamas, out onto the balcony to experience for himself the sleet and freezing rain he couldn't distinguish through the closed window.

"Has he been to the mall yet?" Neil asked after Dom dressed in a t-shirt and sweats. "I'm not thinking downtown, but maybe—"

"You hate malls!" Veronica exclaimed, bursting into a laugh.

"Becky's had some influence on me," he replied with a grin and a shrug.

Veronica considered the suggestion. She looked at Dom, who now sat on the sofa, chanting to himself as he drew on his pad. He'd spent most of the previous evening drawing on his new pad, refusing to show anyone what he'd done, even taking it and the box of crayons with him to his bedroom for the night.

"I don't think he's ready for the mall," she said under her breath. "How about we stay in? Make some cookies and . . . I don't know, play checkers or something?" Checkers was Neil's all-time favourite pastime.

Neil's sandy eyebrows shot up in surprise. "He plays checkers?"

She grinned back. "He does."

In the end, they spent a pleasant day indoors. They had a veritable checkers tournament, with Neil the eventual but not surprising grand champion. For lunch, they made toasted bacon and egg sandwiches. Then they made peanut butter cookies, and Chloe, who arrived after lunch, taught Dom basic fractions by drawing pies cut in half, thirds, and quarters on the whiteboard.

"You know, I never quite understood your passion for the people of the past," Neil admitted to Veronica as they watched Chloe and Dom from a discreet distance. "But I think I do now. He's friggin' amazing. I never would've believed it, though, if you weren't involved. If you didn't have proof. If I wasn't seeing him with my own eyes and actually talking to him myself."

"I know," Veronica said, her voice reverent even to her own ears, "but one day—hopefully pretty soon— the whole world will have to believe in him."

Saturday dawned overcast but warm enough that the thin layer of slush on the sidewalks was melting, so Veronica, Neil, and Dom bundled up to walk to Starbuck's for breakfast. Veronica helped Dom make his choice and gave him a twenty-dollar bill to purchase two scones and a cup of coffee for himself. While they ate, he practiced counting with the change he'd received. To go home, they reversed Sunday's route, strolling along the beach on the way.

Walter came after lunch, earlier than expected, dressed more casually than usual in a sweatshirt, jeans, and a brown leather jacket. His overnight bag hung from one hand, a sack holding a token loaf of bread and bottle of champagne from the other. He and Neil hung out together for a while, chatting over a game of checkers, which Walter won, and promising to get together soon for supper or drinks, before Neil left for his New Year's Eve dinner with Becky and her parents.

"What do you think about doing something for New Year's Eve?" Walter asked after their own supper of leftover pork roast, lots of steamed vegetables, Walter's bread, and too many cookies.

"Um . . . like what?" Veronica asked warily. "Dom's not ready for dancing and drinks."

"No dancing and drinks," he assured her with a chuckle. "I was thinking maybe watch the fireworks at Canada Place? We wouldn't have to go downtown. We could watch from the—"

"Stanley Park sea wall," Veronica chimed in, "just like we used to do." She glanced at Dom, sitting on the floor with the cats rolling themselves into pretzels in front of him. They seemed to like him and he obviously liked them too, which was funny since the only cats he'd ever known had probably wanted to eat him.

"Okay. I'll have to explain it to him so he doesn't freak out."

"We've got a few hours," Walter said. "Explain away."

Dom caught on quickly to the notion of coloured fire in the sky—the best Veronica could do, along with a drawing on the whiteboard—and was eager to see it. When the time came, they bundled up again and drove in Walt's luxurious Mercedes sedan to a parking lot in Stanley Park. From there, they strolled over to the famous concrete path known as the sea wall, which circled the park's nine-kilometre perimeter.

A few people were already there and a few more showed up, but it wasn't a stifling crowd, the falling temperature and slight breeze keeping less intrepid citizens indoors to watch the ball drop in Times Square on television.

The fireworks show was short but impressive. It had Dom edging closer to Veronica with the first explosions and subsequently "oohing" and "aahing" and calling out every colour as flares arced into the sky.

Standing between these two men who were so very different yet intrinsically connected, Veronica felt strangely complete, as if she were in just the right place at just the right time.

Upon returning to Veronica's apartment, Walter brought out three stemmed glasses from the kitchen cupboard and popped the cork on the champagne, which had been chilling in the refrigerator since he arrived. He poured generous portions for himself and Veronica, but wisely only a few sips' worth into the third glass, which he handed to Dom.

"This is champagne," he said, "and this is called a toast." He clinked his glass to Dom's.

Dom frowned. "Toast? No." He shook his head. "Toast dry bread. Put peanut butter."

"It's a different kind of toast," Walter explained with unusual patience. "Same word, different meaning. So… to health, happiness, and"—he looked from Dom to Veronica and back to Dom—"a new life." He and Veronica touched their glasses together. To Dom, he said, "Now be careful, you want to drink that stuff one little sip at a time."

Dom sniffed the glass and took a cautious sip. He grimaced, swallowed, and took a second sip. He shook his head and declared, "No good drink. Dom no like."

"Your loss, Dom," Walter said as Dom handed the glass back to him. He set it down on the table, then looked at Dom and chuckled. "This is the expensive stuff."

"Dom people make more good drink," Dom replied.

"Really?" asked Veronica, seizing the opportunity to learn something new about his culture. "Can you tell us about it?"

"*Taa. Maa-shaw, roo-shaw, nan-shaw.* Uh . . . blue berries, red berries, black berries. Honey. Water. Wait. Wait more long time, drink more good." He licked his lips at the fond memory.

"Sounds delicious," Walter retorted, "but I'll stick with the Moët & Chandon, thank you very much."

After Dom took a bath and retired to his room, Walter poured himself and Veronica another glass of champagne.

"You don't honestly expect me to sleep on the couch, do you?" he asked Veronica in a smooth, seductive tone.

She didn't. They drained their glasses in her bedroom and went to bed where they made love as quietly as they could so as not to disturb Dom in the next room, before falling asleep comfortably wrapped in each other's arms. Tonight, their union felt like a celebration rather than the usual simple fulfillment of sexual need.

Dom gave them a narrow look when Veronica and Walter came out to the kitchen together late the next morning. He didn't say anything about suspicious sounds the night before, and they didn't ask if he'd heard anything, but Veronica was pretty sure he knew what they'd been up to. She wondered what he thought of it, but again, she didn't ask.

Having risen earlier than them, Dom had dressed and come out to make coffee for the three of them, which they sipped while Veronica and Walter cooked French toast and sausages. Walter concocted mimosa with orange juice and the remainder of the champagne but when asked, Dom declined. He would take his orange juice straight.

They returned to Cooper Medical after watching some of the New Year's Eve celebrations from around the world on TV. This time, Dom braved the drive over the Lion's Gate Bridge with his eyes open, understanding now that the car had not, in fact, taken to the air.

Veronica ate lunch in the cafeteria with Dom, Ty, Everett, and Everett's mom, then she went home to write up all the past few days' events on her laptop. It took well into the night.

Dom must have been equally busy Sunday evening because when Veronica came to see him the next day, he had a pile of drawings to show her and another part of his life story to tell.

"Dom good father," he began. "Roo good mother." They sat

side by side at the table in his room and as he spoke, he pushed two drawings over to her.

The first one showed a powerfully built man with shoulder-length hair tied back in a ponytail and a woman with long, black hair, a baby in her arms. In case it wasn't obvious, he'd written ROO above the woman's head and DOM above the man's. The second drawing was of six youngsters of varying size and sex, the youngest a female toddler and the oldest a tall, wide-shouldered boy, probably mid or late teens. All were scantily clothed, only the important parts covered.

"Good family. Good life," Dom said, tapping the second image with the crayon in his hand.

"I see that," Veronica said. "You had a beautiful family."

"Beautiful family. Yes." He paused. When he went on, there was a note of sadness in his voice that made Veronica apprehensive about hearing what was coming next.

"Big sick come *den-no-ny*. Elders say people bad, make sick come. Much people sick—"

"Oh, God," she murmured, her stomach sinking. "That's not why—"

"Much people dead," he continued, ignoring her. "Elders dead. Dom father dead. Roo mother dead. Dom four children"— he pointed out four of the youngsters in the drawing, sparing only the second oldest and the second youngest, both girls— "dead. Roo dead."

He retrieved the second drawing and used the dark red crayon to put spots all over the faces and bodies of Roo and the kids he'd pointed out, then pushed them back to her.

Smallpox, thought Veronica, *or measles or maybe even Bubonic plague, all of them diseases that have caused deadly epidemics throughout history.* She recalled how measles and smallpox had devastated large swaths of the Native American population when Europeans brought the viruses to the New World in the sixteenth, seventeenth, and eighteenth centuries.

"Oh, Dom, I'm so sorry," she said, but she had to ask. "What about you? Did you get sick?" She wondered if the

Bacillus F. had rendered him immune to other infections.

He shook his head. "*T-lay.* Dom good man. Strong. No sick. Dom make medicine. Try help people. No good. No help. Much people dead. Dom help, uh, care dead . . ."

"You helped bury the dead?" She grabbed the whiteboard and a marker, and quickly sketched a body beneath the ground.

He shook his head. "No. Much people dead. Much bad smell." He pushed the next image over to her.

It showed a red and orange bonfire with bits of brown wood sticking out of it.

Oh, God no, not wood, she realized, taking a closer look and covering her mouth to hide her horror. *Body parts. They burned the dead. Of course, they did. It was the only way to stop the contagion, whatever it was. They almost certainly knew nothing about germs, but they knew enough to do that.*

"Dom now elder," he went on after a moment. "Good father, two daughters. Fifteen summers, girls go with man. Much summers . . . uh, years go. Dom daughters good mothers, make much children. Elders say Dom take more woman. Dom no take woman. Dom hunt with men. Tell much. Teach much. Dom try hard. No happy. Much hurt." He touched his heart, indicating he meant emotional pain. "No more stay people. Go alone."

Two more drawings, one of him sitting with a group of children around him, apparently teaching them how to make a spear. The last drawing showed a man from behind, walking with bags hanging from his shoulders and waist, a hairy, grey dog at his side.

"Dom people talk, trade with people far"—he waved an arm to indicate distance—"far cold mountains. Dom see far people three time. Come trade with *den-no-ny.* Good people." He paused, steeling himself to spit out what was coming next.

"Dom go with dog look good people. Dog name Po. Good dog. Dom and Po alone five . . . no, six . . . years. Walk. Go beach winter. Go mountains summer. Hunt. Fish. No find good people. One day hunt bear. Po want help Dom kill bear. Dom want help Po. Bear kill Po. Want kill Dom." He pulled up his tee-shirt to expose the scars across his chest. "Dom bad hurt. Think soon dead. See Roo. See children. See parents. *Laa-tah*." A fleeting expression of peace crossed his face at the memory.

"You were ready to die," Veronica said, more to herself than to him. Something was niggling at the back of her mind but for the moment, she couldn't identify it.

"Far cold mountains people hunters find Dom. Kill bear. Take Dom village." He took a deep breath and let it out in a long sigh. "No more tell today."

"That's okay," Veronica said. She didn't think she could take any more, anyway. She reached over to lay a hand on his arm. "Thank you so much. I'm happy to know about your life."

He nodded. "Dom want Vee know. Vee tell Chloe. Yes?"

"Only if you want me to."

"Yes. Dom want tell Chloe. Tell Ty." He reached for two more drawings that remained face down on the table. "Vee, Chloe give Chris-mas present Dom. Dom no give. Now give Chris-mas present Vee." He handed her the two sheets of thick paper.

She turned them over and let out a gasp. He'd drawn her kitties—Scout sleeping curled up in a black and white ball, Rusty on his feet, batting at the fluffy purple mouse he liked to play with.

While far from masterpieces in any sense, they were fair representations of the cats, drawn with care. He'd written their names, SCOWT and RUSTEE across the bottom of each image.

"Oh Dom, thank you!" Whatever professional reserve Veronica had left went straight out the window and she threw her arms around his neck, immensely touched by his heartfelt gesture. "Thank you, they're beautiful!" She gave him a quick kiss on the cheek before recovering herself and releasing him. "I'll keep them always."

"Yes. Vee keep Dom drawings paper. Dom draw wall for Dom." He smiled, but the smile didn't reach his eyes, which shone with unshed tears. "Dom keep here"—he tapped his head and then his heart—"keep here."

18

FLU SEASON STRIKES

The holidays ended and Chloe went back to university, although she faithfully continued to visit Dom every Friday afternoon and Sunday. Along with Chloe and Ty when he was available, Veronica endeavoured to teach Dom everything he needed to know to survive in the modern world, while steadfastly continuing to protect him from the knowledge that millennia had passed between the life he remembered and the day he woke in the hospital.

During the month of January they visited a variety of places, including Stanley Park, the Shipyards Friday Night Market, and the Park and Tilford Shopping Mall, slowly familiarizing Dom with the city. They returned twice to the mall, not for the shops, but for the indoor botanical garden that Dom so fell in love with, he practically had to be dragged away when the doors closed.

In between these activities, Walter put Dom through another round of spinal fluid and bone marrow aspirations. This time, however, by way of repayment or perhaps because Veronica harped on it, he had an orthopedic specialist come in to give Dom injections of cortisone in his knees and left hip. After a few days, this reduced the chronic inflammation in the joints, making it less painful for him to stand or walk for extended periods of time.

Dom spent some time most days watching television in the sunroom, sitting close to the screen and sometimes asking Everett or Gracie's mom what something was. He spent most evenings drawing in his room, either on paper or on the walls, filling the latter with birds and animals, and scenes from happy times in his life, fishing, hunting, or teaching children how to make tools and weapons of stone or bone. There were no sick or dead people in sight. There were also no scenes giving any further clues as to how or where Dom had become infected with the *Bacillus F.*, or how he'd come to find himself buried alive in a soon-to-be-frozen-solid bog.

Veronica told Chloe and Ty everything Dom related to her because Dom wanted her to. She'd told Walter because Walter wanted her to.

Walter reminded her that the six-month limit was fast approaching, but he admitted he didn't yet have a plan about what to do with Dom beyond that point. Veronica had an idea or two, but she didn't share them. Not yet.

She let herself into Dom's room that Thursday afternoon with every intention of discussing her thoughts about his future with him.

He wasn't there.

The twenty-four-hour monitoring of Dom had ended at Christmas. Beatrice and Gayle had been assigned to a recently admitted ICU patient and the nurses' station, as it often was now, was unoccupied.

Veronica returned to the lobby. The security guard at the desk hadn't seen Dom since yesterday. She went to the sunroom, and then the cafeteria. Becoming increasingly worried by the second, she walked the floors, peeking into the patients' rooms, asking staff she passed if they'd seen Dom. By now everyone knew him, but no one had seen him since breakfast in the cafeteria. Finally, as a last resort before alerting Walter, she went out to the back patio.

She spotted him sitting at their picnic table near the trees. Despite today's close-to-freezing temperature, he wore only a tee-shirt and sweatpants.

Breathing a sigh of relief at the sight of him, she marched across the lawn, hands on hips, relief giving way to anger for giving her such a scare.

"Dom, hey, what are you doing out here? Without even your jacket?" A quick glance at his feet confirmed that he'd put on his sneakers, but no socks.

"Dom hot," he said simply. "Want more cold."

She noticed then that his cheeks were flushed. She reached out to clap her hand to his forehead, finding it hot and damp with sweat. "Oh, God! You're burning up!" She'd heard him sniffle and clear his throat a couple times yesterday, but she hadn't thought anything of it.

"Come inside," she said, taking his hand and pulling him to his feet.

He rose slowly, propping himself up with his cane and swaying slightly before following her toward the building.

"You're sick," she said when they reached his room.

"Yes, Dom sick," he said, and the fact that he didn't deny it concerned her. "Throw up breakfast. No eat lunch."

"You threw up? Here, sit down." She sat him on the edge of the bed and pulled off his sneakers almost without thinking about it, the way she'd done many times when Kim was a little girl. "Get undressed. Take a nice cool shower. Put your pajamas on and get into bed. I'm going to tell Walter you're sick and he'll give you something to help you feel better. Do you understand?"

"Yes. Cool shower. Go bed. Walter make Dom better." He sounded exhausted.

"I'll be back soon," she told him and left in search of Walter.

Within the hour, Walter and Ty, who'd been summoned from his post with Gracie, were examining Dom. Veronica hovered by the bed, the three of them taking the precaution of wearing gloves, gowns, and surgical masks for their own protection as well as his.

Walter took the usual vital signs—temperature, pulse, and blood pressure, all of which were elevated, although not dangerously so—as well as listening to Dom's heart and lungs. He finished by drawing blood and performing several swabs of

Dom's throat and nasal passages.

"You don't think it's COVID, do you?" Veronica asked the question that had been swirling in her mind since she found Dom outside. "You told me you vaccinated him last fall."

"I did," Walter confirmed as he collected the handful of test vials from Dom's bedside table. "He's fully vaccinated against COVID-19, tetanus, and the usual childhood diseases. I suspect he may simply have the flu."

"I hope that's all it is." She gave a long look to Dom, prone in his bed, his face red and slick with sweat. "I'll stay with him until you get the test results back."

Half an hour later, Ty returned with mixed news: Dom had tested negative for COVID-19 but positive for this winter's dominant strain of influenza.

"We get sick like this sometimes," Veronica told Dom in a reassuring voice while Ty took his vital signs again. "Walter, me, and Chloe, we've all been sick and got better."

Ty gave Dom two Tylenol and a Tamiflu and told him to try to sleep. "Don't be worried," he said. "A few days' rest and you'll be good to go."

Over the next three days, Dom experienced the worst manifestations of the flu. His head and body ached. His throat hurt. He was nauseous and couldn't keep anything down beyond a few sips of water or fruit smoothie, or the echinacea tea Chloe plied him with. His fever spiked dangerously several times despite the maximum dosages possible of Tylenol and Tamiflu, the ice packs applied hourly to his forehead and neck, and the IV drip administered to keep him hydrated. Ty, Beatrice, and Gayle were all assigned shifts with him so that he was once again monitored around the clock.

He rose only to use the bathroom, and only with someone at his side as he was too weak and lightheaded to walk on his own. He slept much of the time although when he was awake, he summoned the strength to talk to Veronica and Chloe or at least listen to the upbeat tales they told to keep up his spirits. Walter's worries that the high fever might cause Dom to have a seizure were realized Saturday afternoon, although this time, it was a mild and brief episode that ended without the need for medication.

"Why Dom sick?" he asked Sunday afternoon during one of his better moments. "Chloe no sick. Ty, Beatrice, Walter no sick. Vee no sick. Dom alone sick. Dom bad?"

"No!" Veronica said, as she gently placed a fresh ice pack under his neck. "No, Dom, being sick has nothing to do with whether we're good or bad. You have a sickness we call the flu. I told you before, it's common. We've all had it before. Everyone has. It's caused by . . . um . . . tiny animals so small we can't see them," she offered, trying to keep things simple, while wondering, *Are viruses animals?* "We call them germs. Sometimes germs are in the air, or water, or food, and they can make us sick."

His brow furrowed as he thought this through. "Small germs make Dom sick?"

"Yes."

A full minute passed before he asked, "Germs make *den-no-ny* sick? Make people dead?"

"Yes, I suppose so, but it's not the same—"

"Dom soon dead?"

"No!" she and Chloe exclaimed in unison.

"No," Veronica went on, "people don't die from the flu." Sometimes they did, of course, but she wasn't about to tell Dom that. "Look." She grabbed his hand, pushed up his pajama sleeve, and held his arm up in front of his face. "Can you see you have no red spots?"

He blinked a few times and squinted to focus. "Yes. No see red spots."

"You don't have the same sickness that killed your people, Dom," Chloe put in. "You might feel like crap right now, but in two or three days, maybe, you'll start to feel better."

"Three days Dom better?" he asked, his voice hopeful.

"Um, yeah, more or less."

This seemed to comfort him. With a low sigh, he settled back against his pillows and closed his eyes. A few minutes later, he drifted off to sleep.

When his people were sick with the red spots, he wanted to make them better. When he was attacked by the bear, he wanted death to end his pain. This time, as he sweats and shivers day and night, he wonders if he is not already dead.

If he is, death is not the joining with his ancestors in a beautiful place of peace, as his people believe. It is this place, full of strange people with white skin. Full of strange things that can give pain or take it away.

But that makes no sense. If he is already dead, no one would try to save him. No one would tell him he will not die. But Vee tells him this. Chloe and Ty and Walter say he will feel better soon.

Vee says something else too. Sickness is not caused by bad actions or bad thoughts, or a curse put by one person on another. Sickness is caused by tiny animals people cannot see, that we breathe or eat or drink without knowing it.

He is not sure he believes this, but it might explain why he is sick. He wonders if it might explain something else too.

Dom's fever broke midday Monday, but that Friday, just as he was recovering his strength, he suffered a relapse. His temperature rose suddenly to a dangerous level, and he began coughing up copious amounts of thick, green phlegm. He said his chest hurt when he breathed. He wanted to make tea from his cedar trees, but Veronica and Walter insisted that wasn't going to happen.

Walter suspected bacterial bronchitis, a common but serious complication after the flu. X-rays confirmed his diagnosis, and Dom was put on bed rest, oxygen, and antibiotics.

For the first time in months, Veronica found herself actively worrying about Dom's health. She was convinced the *Bacillus F.* had helped him fight off disease in the past, but now it was no longer in his system, he was as vulnerable to illness as anyone.

She spent most of Saturday with him, sitting by his bed when he was awake, and working on her laptop at the table while he slept.

That night, however, she woke up with a tickle at the back of her throat that signalled the start of a cold. By the next morning, she had the sniffles and a dry cough. She had no aches and pains or fever, so she suspected a run-of-the-mill cold rather than the flu. Still, there was no way she would risk bringing any more germs anywhere near Dom, regardless of any mask or other protections offered.

She called Walter to tell him she wouldn't be in for a few days, and asked him to explain her absence to Dom. He promised he would, and he assured her that Dom would continue to receive the best of care.

With nothing much to do but take care of her kitties, catch up on housework, and organize her notes, Veronica found her mind wandering to places it hadn't yet gone. She wondered if Dom's incredible survival might have as much to do with where and how he died as it did with where and how he'd been infected with the *Bacillus F.* After hearing his story of leaving his people and travelling for six years before finding new people, she realized now that he'd lived in two different places, possibly dozens or hundreds of kilometres apart.

She had to get him to tell her about the rest of his life, and more particularly, the end of it. Then maybe they could sew the pieces together and figure out not only what had kept him alive, but if the process could be repeated or synthesized or whatever exactly Walter was hoping for.

She forced herself to stay away from the medical centre until Friday, when she'd been symptom-free for over twenty-four hours. By then, Dom was mostly recovered from his bronchitis, although he would be on oral antibiotics for a few more days.

As he'd begun feeling better, he'd kept himself busy drawing a lovely scene of mountains and forest on the previously bare wall by the door. He'd also practiced his writing, as evidenced by the stack of pages with letters and words all over them that lay scattered on the table.

Ty and Walter had kept her up to date with phone calls every evening, but it was good to see all of this for herself. It was even better to see Dom up and dressed in jeans and a hoodie, his hair freshly washed and his cheeks back to a healthy tone.

After conferring with Walter and receiving confirmation that Dom was recovered enough to gradually resume his activities, she promised him that, if he was patient until then, they would go out somewhere with Chloe on Sunday.

19

DOM'S STORY PART THREE

Sunday at noon, Veronica and Dom dressed warmly and walked to Tim Horton's to meet Chloe for lunch. It was Dom's first time away from Cooper Medical in over two weeks, but aside from stopping once when he suffered a brief fit of coughing, he seemed well on his way to recovery.

Chloe was already there, wearing her pink Christmas vest, a broad smile on her face. She waved them over to her table in the far corner of the café.

They ate a leisurely lunch of soup and sandwiches, donuts and coffee, enjoying the meal and the conversation. Finally, as they prepared to leave, Veronica took a chance and asked Dom if he would tell them about his life with the people who had cared for him after he was attacked by the bear.

He took a minute to think this over. "Yes," he said finally. "Dom tell all."

"Wonderful! I'll come see you tomorrow and—"

"No. No tomorrow," he protested. "Tomorrow Dom draw. Next . . . uh . . . next tomorrow."

"The day after tomorrow," she said helpfully.

"*Taa*. Day after tomorrow. Dom tell all. *Lah-taa*." He nodded, more to himself than to them. "Tell all."

"I'm going to come," Chloe said, "if you guys don't mind. I'm sure it'll be worth missing my afternoon class."

"Yes. Dom want Chloe come. Want Ty."

He apparently didn't want to share his story with Walter,

but Veronica knew she would have to tell him afterwards, especially if Dom revealed something important. Dom didn't have to know that, though, at least not right away.

Veronica spent Monday in her office, working on some things the anthropology department had sent her weeks ago. She called Chloe and Ty Tuesday morning and they agreed to meet in Dom's room at 1:00.

When she let herself into the room, she immediately noticed a new drawing on the far wall, one of five men with rocks and long spears bringing down a mammoth with shaggy brown hair and huge, curved, yellow tusks.

The mammoth.

Dom had clearly been working on his pad as well and, when Chloe and Ty joined them, the four of them sitting in a circle on the bear rug and the deer skins, he brought a collection of drawings on paper with him.

Veronica turned on her cell phone recorder and put it down beside Dom so it wouldn't miss a word.

"Dom tell life Vee and Chloe and Ty," he said, with a sort of resigned tone to his voice. He presented them with the first drawing, one of a man lying on a bed of furs, four red gashes across his chest.

"Bear Dom bad hurt," he said, indicating the gashes with his thumb. "Much sick. Fever."

Of course, he was, thought Veronica when he paused. *He must've had one hell of an infection that even the Bacillus F. couldn't keep at bay. He's lucky he didn't get rabies or the flesh-eating disease.*

"People take care Dom. Girl—Lil-lia—take good care. Two months . . . Dom better." He looked at them as if to make sure they understood.

Ty said, "Go on. Tell us more."

"New people . . . *den-no-ny*. Good people. . . People want Dom stay. Dom happy stay. Hunt. Make medicine. Two years more. Lil-lia fifteen years. Woman now. Dom ask elders take woman Lil-lia. Dom want take woman Lil-lia. Man Shay-shoo-wa want take woman Lil-la."

Chloe's hand flew to her mouth to cover her gasp.

Ty chuckled.

"You had competition?" Veronica asked.

Dom frowned, not knowing this word, but perhaps understanding the rise in her voice. He nodded.

"Elders say most good, strong man take Lil-lia. Dom and Shay-shoo-wa fight." He presented a drawing of two men locked in hand-to-hand combat.

"Please tell us you didn't kill him," Chloe said.

"*T-lay*. No kill. Shay-shoo-wa break teeth Dom." He pulled his lip back to expose the space where he was missing two lower molars. "Dom break arm Shay-shoo-wa. Elders say Dom take woman. Dom happy. Lil-lia happy. Lil-la want Dom take. No want Shay-shoo-wa." He grinned proudly in spite of the serious topic of conversation.

"Dom strong man. Go with hunters, kill mammoth. Good kill. Much meat. Much bone. Much, uh . . ." He gestured to form tusks in front of his face.

"Ivory," Veronica said, thinking of the beads that had been found with him.

"Beautiful iv-ory. *Lah-taa*." Still grinning, he pulled up another drawing, this one of a young couple, the woman holding a baby. "Lil-lia good woman. Make family." He'd written their names—LIL-LIA and SEEN-EE—above them. The man— Dom, of course—had a second tattoo of concentric circles identical to the one on his arm, this one on his right thigh. She'd seen this on his leg when he changed clothes in front of her and guessed it was a tradition amongst members of his new tribe.

The next drawing extended the family to five children, from a baby to a teenage boy. He'd written their names above their heads: The oldest boy was Seen-ee; the second, Saawli; then two girls, Lana and Ma-ri; and finally, the youngest boy, Do-ni. In the drawing after that, the two oldest boys were muscular young men, each bearing a distinctive tattoo on his right thigh. Each had a well-endowed woman with long, dark hair at his side.

Veronica noticed in the final drawing that Lil-lia now wore a necklace bearing seven white beads similar to the ones found with Dom. She suspected they were the same ones and she meant to ask him, but Chloe spoke, and the opportunity passed.

"They're growing up," the young woman observed.

"Yes. Children grow more old." He put down a drawing of a much older woman, her face wrinkled and hair grey, wearing that same necklace above a brown, presumably leather, tunic. "Lil-lia much more old."

He paused, but whether he was thinking about what to say or simply dealing with a memory, Veronica couldn't say. Either way, his expression was pained.

He put down the image of a man, clearly in his prime, bearing the familiar black tattoos, and said, "Dom elder. No much more old."

And there it was, the thing that had been niggling at the back of Veronica's mind for weeks.

That's it! Of course! He had a family and his children grew up. He became an elder in his first tribe. Then six . . . no, eight years passed and he had a second family and those children grew up. He became an elder in his second tribe, yet he looks no older than forty, at the most.

She was so lost in thought she barely heard him when he added, "Lil-lia grey hair. Face lines. Dom no grey hair."

She looked at him then, as he grabbed a fistful of the thick, dark hair that now hung to his ears. "Dom no grey hair. No face lines."

The Bacillus F. not only allowed him to remain alive while he was frozen all that time. It slowed down his aging process. Oh, God.

"Shay-shoo-wa no like Dom. Elders no like Dom. Afraid

Dom. Tell Dom go. Dom say *t-lay*. No go. Hunters make Dom go. No come home. Tell Dom come back, kill Dom."

Chloe let out a soft sound that might have been a gasp or a sob. Ty cleared his throat and stared at the wall.

Veronica didn't dare look at either of them. She sat in silence, waiting for Dom to go on.

After a minute of heavy silence, he did.

"Lil-lia say Dom go. Live. Lil-lia give Dom, uh… " He pointed at the necklace around Lil-lia's neck. "Much years before, Dom give Lil-lia seven ivory… small balls. *Aa-wax-ay*?" As they all murmured yes, they understood, he continued. "Five children. Five balls. Lil-lia, Dom two balls. Give back Dom seven balls string. Ask Dom no forget Lil-la. No forget children. Say Lil-lia no forget Dom. Dom say no forget Lil-lia.

"Dom go alone. Four years alone. Dom no more want stay alone. Want see Lil-lia. See sons. See daughters. Return people. Elders say no stay. Hunters… Shay-shoo-wa and son Me-shoo hunt Dom."

He turned over the next to last drawing and placed it in front of Veronica. It showed a man running, three others behind him, spears and knives in hand.

"Dom run many days. Dom much tired. Fall. Fall far. Bad hurt. Leg. Ribs. Dom no can stand. Hurt for breathe. Hunters see. Laugh. Leave Dom."

"Holy crap," Ty exclaimed. "They left you there to die?"

"*Taa*. Three days. Three nights. Dom much cold. No eat. Drink rainwater. Seen-ee come. Saawli come."

"Your sons?" Veronica asked. "They found you?"

"Yes. Dom sons good sons. Good men. Come after hunters go." He shook his head. "Dom bad hurt. Sons no can help Dom live. Help Dom dead."

Chloe made another sound, this one definitely a sob, and pressed her hands to her face.

Dom turned over the last drawing, one of a man on his knees holding out a shallow cup to a second man lying on the ground.

"Seen-ee say, go kill Shay-shoo-wa. Kill Me-shoo. Take

care Lil-lia. Good son," he repeated. His eyes glistened with tears now, but he stoically finished his tale. "Saawli make good drink for people. Make medicine for people. Saawli make strong sleep drink for help Dom dead. Give Dom drink. Saawli good son." He stopped and shrugged. "Dom no dead. Dom sleep in cold. Wake up here in Vee world."

His sons gave him a drink with those toxic plants in it, expecting it would kill him. They probably buried him too. Oh, dear God, they buried him alive!

Veronica had no words. She dared to glance at Chloe, who sat motionless as a statue, a horrified expression on her face. Tears ran freely down her cheeks.

Ty got up and walked a few steps away, his back turned to them.

Dom sniffed and swallowed and then asked, as if he already knew the answer but just wanted to make sure, "Dom no dead?"

Veronica summoned her voice and croaked, "No, Dom is alive. We're all alive."

He nodded, satisfied. "*Lah-taa.* Dom alive. Summer come, Dom go... Go Lil-lia. Go sons, daughters. People no want Dom? Afraid Dom? Dom take family go home Dom first people. Good people. Happy see Dom. Dom teach letters for write words." He smiled then, a real smile that went all the way to his cloudy brown eyes. A dreamy look came over his face. "*Taa.* Dom go home."

20

A LONG, LONG LIFE

"He's much older than he looks," Veronica said, her voice barely above a whisper.

Ty grunted. "No friggin' kidding."

Along with Chloe, they sat in the cafeteria, where they'd been staring at their untouched cups of coffee for the past ten minutes, each dealing in their own way with the tale they'd just been told.

"I don't mean the 9,500 years," she said, and four solemn brown eyes fixed on her. "I mean . . . Dom was a teenager when he took his first woman, Roo, wasn't he? They had six children, and his two daughters who survived the measles or whatever it was, grew up and had kids of their own."

Two dark heads slowly nodded.

"After he left his people, he spent what—six years?—alone with his dog before being injured by that bear and integrating his new tribe. Two years after that, he took Lil-lia as his woman. They had five kids. The older ones were at least in their late teens before Dom was driven out. Four more years passed before he . . . well, you know. Do the math, you guys. He appears to be in his mid-thirties, forty at the outside, but he's got to be twice that age."

Chloe blinked. She'd stopped crying on the way upstairs, but her eyes were still red, her cheeks flushed beneath their usual tan tone.

"You're right," she croaked. She took a sip of coffee and

went on, "But he knows that, doesn't he? What he doesn't know about is—"

"The thousands of years since," Ty finished for her.

"He's smart. He probably suspects something. Too much has changed for him not to," Veronica said, "but we have to tell him straight up. He thinks he's going to go back to his people this summer and tell them about all the cool stuff he's seen and learned here."

Chloe nodded. "He wants to teach them to read and write."

"Crap." Ty glanced down at his watch, took a gulp of coffee, and pushed to his feet. "I've gotta get back to Gracie, but . . ." He looked from Chloe to Veronica. "You're gonna tell him now?"

Veronica sighed. "I don't think I have any choice."

"I'll come with you," Chloe said in the resigned voice of someone heading to her doom.

"Well, good luck with that, girls. I mean it. Let me know how it goes." Ty left them to head back to work.

Chloe and Veronica drank their lukewarm coffees and planned how to go about their next step. When they returned to the basement bedroom, they found Dom sitting cross-legged on the bear rug, chanting under his breath and rocking slowly back and forth.

"Hey, Dom, can we come in?" They'd agreed to let Veronica do the talking, at least to begin with.

"Yes, Veron-ica," he said, using her full name for only the third or fourth time. He waved absently for them to come in. "Come. Sit."

As they lowered themselves to the floor, Veronica to his right and Chloe opposite him, he said, "Dom no more tell. Finished. "

"That's okay," Veronica said. "This time we have something to tell you."

He stopped rocking and looked sideways at her, his brows knitted.

"I . . . um . . . I think I know why you didn't grow old as fast as everyone else. Why Lil-lia got grey hair and Dom didn't."

"Vee know? Tell Dom."

"Well, remember when we told you about germs? Even though we can't see them, sometimes they make us sick or even kill us?"

"Yes, Dom remember." His tone said, *Dom's not an idiot.*

"Well, we think . . . " She glanced at Chloe, who nodded encouragement. "We think the summer you went to the sky stone place, you got a different kind of germ. One that made you feel strong and made you grow old slower than other people."

His eyes narrowed and she could practically see the gears turning as he worked through this. Finally, he said, "Sky stone germs no make Dom sick. Make Dom strong? Live old?"

"Yes. I think so."

"Dom no more strong. Hands no good. Feet no good. Eyes no good. One ear no good." He slapped his left ear with his hand for emphasis.

"The germs couldn't prevent some damage from freezing even though they kept you alive. But you don't have them inside you anymore. When you were in the other hospital, they gave you medicine that killed them."

"Dom no more have sky stone germs?"

"No. No more. But you had them in you when your sons gave you the Indian hell—the sleep drink. I think they buried you in the mud and then you froze, and I don't understand exactly how or why it happened, but you didn't die. You just sort of slept there in the ice, until the ground thawed and we found you."

Dom was quiet for a long moment. Then he looked straight into Veronica's face and said, "Vee tell Dom. Much years go Dom sleep in ice?"

"Oh, God." Her heart plummeted, even though she'd been expecting this. "Yes, Dom. Many years went by. Too many to count."

He nodded. "Lil-lia no old woman. Lil-lia dead. Children dead. Dom people dead." He blinked hard twice. "All *den-no-*

ny dead?"

"Yes," she croaked over the lump in her throat.

"We didn't know how to tell you," Chloe offered, her voice husky with emotion. "I'm so, so sorry."

"No sorry." He reached out with his right hand and touched the young woman's wet cheek gently with his palm. "No good cry." He got to his feet, his own face a mask of shock and grief. "Go now. Chloe go. Vee go. Dom want stay alone."

Knowing there was nothing they could say to help him, the women left. Chloe continued to weep quietly all the way to her car. Veronica managed to hold herself together until she got home.

She called Ty and told him briefly what had transpired. Then she fell onto her bed fully clothed and cried herself to sleep.

Veronica got up in the middle of the night to shower and put on her pajamas. She made a cup of decaf and took it to bed, sipping it while she tried to start reading a new novel to take her mind off Dom.

It was useless. After reading the same page three times over, she put the book aside. All she could think about, all she could see, was that look of devastation on Dom's face when he realized everyone and everything he'd ever known were gone.

She finally fell asleep, only to be awakened by her cell phone. Walter's ringtone. Eyes still closed, she groped for the phone on her bedside table.

"Veronica?" Walter's voice.

"Who else?" She opened her eyes, only to squint against the light of the rising sun streaming through her window. Her stomach rumbled, and she registered absently that she hadn't eaten supper last night.

"What did you bunch do with Dom yesterday?"

"What? Why?" Her eyes popped open now and she sat up straight in bed. "What's happened?"

"What's happened is he didn't come upstairs for supper. Beatrice checked on him around nine. He was in bed and refused to talk to her. I've had her up in the ICU with that new patient these past couple weeks, so she didn't stay with Dom. Sometime later, he tossed his room and then early this morning he tried to leave the hospital. Apparently, he was in a terrible state, babbling about going home to see for himself and completely out of control. It took the security guard and an orderly to hold him until the nurse could get a sedative into him."

"Oh. God."

"What the hell did you tell him?"

"The truth." Veronica swung out of bed. "Are you at the hospital?"

"I'm on my way now."

"I'll meet you there." She threw on jeans and a sweater, coat and boots. She dumped some dry food into the kitties' bowl and headed to the hospital, her mind spinning so fast she arrived there without remembering the drive.

"Veronica," said Bill, the aged but still imposing security guard, as she approached. "Your boy there gave us quite a turn this morning. He's stronger than he looks. Nearly broke my arm." He rubbed his left elbow for emphasis.

Veronica recalled how Dom had bested Shay-shoo-wa to win Lil-lia as his woman. Evidently the breaking of an arm was his go-to move. "Oh. I'm so sorry about that, Bill. He got some bad news yesterday and . . . I guess he hasn't dealt with it yet." She scribbled her initials on the sign-in sheet and hurried to Walter's office.

He was already there, dressed in sweats rather than his usual neat shirt and slacks and looking as flustered as she felt. He motioned for Veronica to take a seat. When she declined, he remained standing as well.

"Why do I feel as though I've been left out of the loop?" he asked.

Veronica sighed. "Dom told us about the last part of his life yesterday afternoon. I was going to tell you as soon as I had the chance." She dug her cell from her handbag, pulled up the recording she'd made the previous day, and played it for him.

"Jesus Christ," Walter cursed as the recording clicked off.

They'd both sat down at some point while the recording played, and they took each other's measure from across Walter's desk.

"That doesn't explain his meltdown last night," Walter said after a crackling silence.

"It doesn't. But this might." Veronica went on to tell him about her discussion with Chloe and Ty, and her subsequent conversation with Dom.

"So, you think the mutated *Bacillus F.* not only allowed him to remain alive while frozen but prolonged his natural life as well?" Of course, the scientific part of his mind would kick in before the compassionate part Veronica knew was in there somewhere.

"I do. And I think maybe it's the combination of the bacteria in his cells and the way he died, with the Indian hellebore and toxic mushrooms in his system, that caused him to . . . well, not die. The bog he fell into must've frozen soon after he was buried, and he stayed there until the ground started to thaw and Gerald Sutherland's team found him. I know it sounds crazy, but he's here, isn't he?"

"And now he knows he's some 9,500 years old? Knows his world is long gone?"

"He doesn't exactly know how many years it's been, but yeah. He knows the world and the people he knew are gone."

"Hence the meltdown."

"Yeah."

Walter groaned and pushed to his feet. He walked around the office a couple times, stopping to stare at the books on his bookshelf and out the window at the back yard, as if they were of supreme interest to him, before facing Veronica, who had also risen.

"Your six months are over, you know," he said. "What do you propose we do with Dom now?"

"Why? You don't want him anymore?" Veronica lashed out, angry that he should be more concerned with logistics than Dom's anguish at losing everything he'd ever known.

"On the contrary," Walter replied, going smoothly into doctor mode. "I've been using his stem cells and genetic material in my treatment of Gracie. Her progress is astounding. She clearly knows who and where she is now and she's beginning to speak. Moving her left arm and leg. I'd keep him here indefinitely as a living donor, but of course you won't—"

"You bet I won't! He's not a prisoner, and he's not a goddamn petri dish, either. If he continues to give you bits of whatever you want from him, it has to be with his consent. And mine. And he should get something back for it."

Walter's eyes narrowed. "You mean in addition to the many thousands of dollars' worth of room, board, and medical care he's received since last summer?"

Veronica stood her ground. "I do. Starting with letting him come to my place on weekends. He's going to go insane if he stays cooped up here any longer. He needs to get out in nature, get out . . . just out."

"Is that all?"

"I don't know. Let me think about it. In the meantime, I'm going to see him."

"I'm coming with you," Walter said in a tone that let her know it wasn't a suggestion.

Ty was at the nurses' station near Dom's room, keeping one eye on the monitor from the camera in the room while he punched notes into a laptop.

"Beatrice told me what happened before she left," he said to Veronica and Walter without even looking up. "He should be awake soon."

Veronica glanced at the monitor to see that Dom was, in fact, moving restlessly on his bed, still dressed in a black sweatshirt and jeans. The room looked like a hurricane had hit it. She headed for the door, only to discover it was locked.

"You locked him in?" she demanded, turning on her heels to confront Ty.

"Beatrice did," he replied as he came to her side to punch in the key code. "I think she was really scared."

"Scared?" She glowered at Ty. "Of Dom? Or for him?"

He shrugged. "Maybe both."

Things looked worse up close. Dom had overturned the table, the chairs, and the dresser. The whiteboard was broken in two. Markers, crayons, torn up pages of drawing paper, and lengths of toilet paper littered the floor. There were a few items of clothing as well, but it looked like most of his clothes were stuffed into his gym bag, which lay with his jacket and boots near the door.

"I'll sit with him until he's properly awake," Veronica said. She righted the nearest chair and dragged it to the side of the bed. "You two go do whatever you're supposed to be doing. I'll call you if I need you."

"I'll stay," Walter said. "I want to talk to him."

Veronica turned on him, venom in her voice. "Seriously, Walt? How about you wait until he's processed what he learned yesterday before you start questioning him about where he found the meteorite or how much sleep drink he drank before he didn't die, or whatever the hell it is you want to know?"

Walter drew in a long breath and actually took a step back. "Right. You're right, of course. The poor man. I'll wait a while."

Ty went out with Walter, leaving Veronica alone with Dom. It was a good half hour before he was conscious enough to notice her there.

"Vee?" he said, his voice raspy from the sedative. He moved cautiously to sit up on the edge of the bed, where he swayed and gripped the sheets to remain upright. He coughed and gagged, but managed not to vomit, then clamped a hand to his forehead. "Dom sick?"

"No, not sick. You were upset. You could've hurt yourself or someone else. They had to give you a sedative." She fetched his wooden cup from the floor, rinsed it—seeing in the process that he'd cracked the bathroom mirror—filled it with cold water, and pressed it into his right hand.

He drank the water in silence, then dropped the cup on the bed beside him.

"Do you remember what happened?" she asked him, noticing at the same time that his sweatshirt was torn at one shoulder. Bill hadn't exaggerated when he'd described his earlier encounter with Dom as violent.

"*Taa*. Dom remember. Chloe and Vee tell Dom no more Dom world. Dom want go . . . want see . . ." He continued in his own language.

Veronica caught a few words, enough to understand he'd wanted to go home to see for himself that it wasn't there anymore. He'd assumed, rightly, that they wouldn't let him go, so he'd set out on his own.

"Your world is still there, Dom," she said as gently as she could. "The mountains and trees, the ocean and beach, the birds and fish and animals. Well, most of them, anyway," she added, glancing in spite of herself at the mammoth on the wall. "But your home is gone. Your people are gone. They've been gone for many, many years."

He gave her a doubtful frown. "Chloe and Ty look *den-no-ny*. Hair, skin, eyes."

"I know. They're maybe many, many times removed from your people. Like, your children's, children's, children's, many children's children. Do you understand?" This was certainly not genetically accurate, but it was the best she could do under the circumstances.

He nodded slowly. "Yes. Dom understand." His eyes welled with tears, which he promptly wiped away with the heel of one hand.

"Hey, it's okay to cry," Veronica said, while thinking, *Oh, God, what have I done?* She moved from her chair to the edge of the bed, her hip touching his. She put a hand on his shoulder. "You've just learned your family is dead and your home is gone.

You're sad."

He sniffed. "Yes. Dom sad." He shut his eyes, but this didn't stop the flood of tears coming. As they slid silently down his cheeks, he abandoned all effort at being stoic and leaned against her.

She wrapped her arms around him and held him tight, giving him the only comfort she could while his body shook with the sobs of a man whose heart was broken.

21

A TENTATIVE SOLUTION

He thought he knew loss and sadness when Roo and his children and half of his first people died from the red spot sickness. Thought he knew anger and despair when he was driven from his new people, from Lil-lia and his second family, by Shay-shoo-wa and the others he convinced to side with him.

All of it rolled up together does not compare to the way he feels now. Vee and Chloe told him what happened to him. Told him his people and everything he knows is gone. He does not understand why they waited so long to tell him this, but he does not doubt it is true.

The weight in his chest, like a stone in place of his heart, makes it hard to breathe. Tears come at night no matter how much he tries to hold them in. He wants to believe he still has something to live for, but he cannot think what.

Dom refused to see Veronica all the rest of the week, but reports came to her daily from Walter, Ty, and Beatrice of him spending his waking hours chanting in his language, elaborating on his wall drawings, or simply staring blankly in front of him. He resisted attempts by his nurses and even Walter to involve him in conversation, declined efforts to get him out of his room for physical therapy, a meal in the cafeteria, or a walk in the back yard. He barely touched the food brought to him, until Ty threatened him with a feeding tube and IV line in order to get adequate nourishment into him, and that got him ingesting enough to stave off these drastic measures.

Veronica drove out to Cooper Medical on Saturday and Sunday but found she couldn't bear to watch Dom on the computer monitor at the nurses' station, knowing it was as close as she could get to him. She was, if not equally as miserable as he was, more heartsick than she'd ever been for anyone. Almost as bad as knowing Dom suffered was her own self-doubt, which hung like a heavy, wet blanket over her every thought. She repeatedly examined everything she had or hadn't done, every decision she'd made since the day Professor Sutherland's crew uncovered Dom at Bennett Lake, and questioned whether she'd made a mistake in filing for guardianship of the comatose man in the first place.

Having limited choices as to whom she could turn with her woes, and Walter being as self-centred as she was, she confided in her brother.

"Ask yourself, Vee," Neil said as they sipped drinks in her kitchen Sunday evening. "Where would Dom be now if you hadn't got custody of him? Would someone else have seen to his best interests as well as you have? Would he be in a warm, safe room, with free food and access to all the medical care he needs? Or out on the street? Or worse?"

"But I did it for my own benefit as much as his," Veronica moaned. "Maybe more, at first. I wanted tenure, fame, fortune. All of that. You know me, Neil, I've always tended to put my needs and wishes before thinking of others."

He nodded in reluctant agreement and took another swallow of his gin, smacking his lips as it went down. "But you care about him now, don't you?"

"Oh, God. I do. More than I've ever cared about anyone, except you and Kim and Mom and Dad. More than I ever cared for Walter, if I'm being honest."

"And you've protected him?"

"I've tried to. I'm not sure I'll be able to once my first paper is published," she admitted. "It's almost ready, written and revised and waiting to go to Professor Sutherland for a proofread. I'll be asking for the NDA to be lifted soon and then . . ." She shrugged.

"Then you should start preparing Dom for the consequences." Neil finished his drink and got up to pour himself another two fingers from the bottle on the counter.

Veronica raised her glass for a refill as well. "I hate knowing he's in so much pain. I mean, I keep telling myself he'll get over it. He's been through so much already—before waking up in our time, I mean." She shook her head, words failing her. She downed half of her gin and tonic in one gulp.

"If he's half as resilient as you think he is—and I think he must be, to have lived as long as he did at a time when survival was certainly a daily struggle—he probably just needs time to process and accept everything. Then he'll start to bounce back."

"Right." She drained her glass. "You're right. I just hope for his sake—and mine, if I'm being honest, and the sake of everyone concerned—that it doesn't take him too long."

Veronica gave herself a personal day on Monday, not because she felt she deserved it, but because it helped take her mind off Dom. Instead of jogging, she went swimming at UBC's indoor pool. Then she treated herself to a Starbucks café mocha and spent the rest of the day watching DVDs of her favourite movies, one or the other of her kitties curled up on her lap. She ordered Chinese take-out for supper, but after a dozen bites the food seemed to stick in her throat. She was stricken by an acute pang of guilt. Here she was in her cozy apartment, her favourite meal in front of her, while Dom languished alone in his hospital room, probably feeling like he had nothing and no one to live for.

She gave a few bits of chicken soo guy to her kitties, stored the rest of the food in the refrigerator, took a long, hot shower, and went to bed. Tomorrow, she was determined, she would find a way to make things right with Dom.

Veronica began her mission Tuesday by calling Walter and arranging to see him before noon. She did some housework , biding her time until she could pack up last night's leftovers and head to the medical center.

She arrived before Walter and let herself into his office to wait.

"Sorry I'm late," he said when he came in ten minutes later. "I had a procedure on Gracie this morning."

"You did? How'd it go?"

"Great. I'm expecting her to regain some sight in the next few weeks." He grinned.

"That's wonderful, but . . . um . . . Oh, God, Walt, we have to talk about Dom."

The grin faded. "I know."

"We have to do something to bring him out of the despair he's fallen into. He can't go on the way he is."

"I agree," said Walter, sinking into his chair. "Any ideas how?"

"Actually, yeah. As much as I hate it, I think we need to tell him what you do with the genetic material you take from him. That you use it to help people like Everett and Gracie. We need to tell him we want him to show us where his sky stone landed so we can search for the bacteria that gave him such a long life. I think the prospect of taking us up north, into the forest and the mountains, will cheer him up."

"And you think he can do that? Find the right spot? He can barely see to cross the street on his own."

"I think he can probably draw his homeland well enough from memory that we might figure out where it is on a map. And I think his English is good enough now to understand all of this when we tell him."

"We won't be able to go up north until this summer."

"Perfect. That'll give us time to get him strong enough for

the trip."

Walter gave her a long look. "This will make for a few interesting chapters in your book."

"I suppose it will," she acknowledged, "but that's not nearly as important as giving Dom a purpose."

"Or perfecting my procedure to heal traumatic brain injuries and maybe extend the human lifespan to boot."

Veronica caught her breath as a thought suddenly popped into her head. "Speaking of lifespan… Now that the mutated *Bacillus F.* is out of his system, do you think he'll age normally?"

Walter frowned and gave a shrug. "That's something we'll have to keep an eye on, isn't it? But my opinion is, yes, I suspect he will." He glanced at his watch. "Do you want to talk to him before lunch?"

"I do." She'd left the Chinese take-out in the cafeteria refrigerator before coming to the office. If things went well with Dom, she would mention it. If they didn't, she probably wouldn't have any appetite anyway.

She and Walter took the stairs down to Dom's room.

Steeling herself for a negative response, Veronica pushed the door to Dom's room open. "Hey, Dom," she said as cheerfully as she could. "Can Walter and I come in?"

Dom looked up from where he was sitting on the bear rug, surrounded by his ferns and cedar trees, his own private forest. He was half-dressed in sweatpants, his chest and feet bare. From his position, cross-legged, hand on his knees, Veronica guessed he'd been meditating or praying to whatever he conceived God to be.

That's another thing I want to ask him about, when the time's right.

"No," he said, his voice as cold as the ice he'd lain in for millennia. "Dom no want talk Vee. No want talk Walter. *Esk. Esk!*" Go! He waved his arm towards the door.

"We won't go," Veronica said, stepping closer. "I know what we told you hurt you. I know you're sad—"

"Yes, Dom sad. People gone. Family gone long time before. Dom alone. Stay alone now."

"But you're not alone." Reaching him, she knelt down beside him but refrained from taking his hand the way she wanted to. "You have us. Me and Chloe and Ty and Walter. Even Neil. We're not family, but we all care about you. We're your friends. Do you understand that word? Friends?"

He didn't look at Veronica, instead fixing his gaze on Walter as the doctor moved a dwarf cedar out of the way and lowered himself to the floor opposite Dom. When he didn't reply, Walter said,

"If you don't want to talk to us, that's okay. Just listen. We have something to tell you."

Dom's eyes narrowed as he looked from Walter to Veronica and back to Walter. "*Den Dom oh-cho?*" Tell Dom what?

Walter began, using the simplest words possible to explain to Dom why he was so important to Walter's work in the hospital.

"So, for whatever reason, however it happened, we think the bacteria—uh, the germs—you had inside you from the sky stone place allowed you to live much longer than a normal life. You're special, Dom, the only person in the whole world like you. The tissues I've taken from you—blood, spinal fluid, bone marrow, all of that—are special too. I'm using them to make medicine to heal people like Everett and Gracie, and a couple others you haven't met yet. People who have been hurt bad in their head. But what I really, really need is for you to tell me or show me where the sky stone place is, so maybe I can collect some of those germs—if they're still there—and use them to help heal more people. Do you understand?"

Dom wore such a frown on his face and was silent for so long, Veronica feared he hadn't understood the half of it. She was about to re-explain things when he said,

"Dom blood and . . . uh, other"—he tapped his hip where the bone marrow aspirations had been done—"Dr. Walter take from Dom. Make medicine for people hurt bad in head?"

"That's right," Walter said with a sigh of relief and a cautious smile. "Veronica tells me you were something of a healer, that you knew how to make medicines and such for your people? You still want to heal people, don't you?"

Slowly, he said, "Dom want heal people. *Taa.*"

"Good. You're a good man, Dom," Walter said, nodding encouragement.

"So, Dom, what we were thinking," Veronica picked up, "is that maybe you can draw the place where you lived when you were a boy? Draw your homeland? And draw the sky stone place, show us what it looked like, so maybe we can find it on a map. You know what a map is?"

"Yes. Dom see map. Big place Can-ada map. Chloe show Dom where, uh . . . where Van-cou-ver ocean one side. Mountains one side." For the first time, he began to sound interested.

"Exactly. And then," Veronica went on, "this summer, maybe we can all go to your homeland, Dom and Vee and Walter and maybe Chloe and Ty, and find the place of the sky stone together."

It was a moment before Dom replied, his words coming slowly as he thought them through. "Yes. Dom want go homeland. Dom know sky stone place. Show Walter and Vee. After . . . Dom stay homeland?"

"Well, no," Veronica blurted, "you can't stay—"

"We'll see about it," Walter cut her off, shooting her a scowl as she raised her hands to say, *What the hell are you talking about?*

But Dom was nodding and smiling at the thought, and Veronica couldn't break his heart again by insisting it was impossible for him to stay in the mountains.

And who knows? Maybe there's a town or village or First Nations reserve nearby where he could spend some time. Maybe that's something I could arrange.

"There's something you have to do before we go anywhere," Veronica said. "Dom, you have to eat and exercise and get strong. Will you do that?"

"*Taa*. Dom eat, make Dom strong, go walk mountains. Walk far."

"How far is the sky stone place from your people's village?" Walter asked. "Do you remember?"

"Yes, Dom remember. Walk six days. Sleep five nights. Six day noon, reach sky stone place."

"Very good, Dom. Thank you."

"It's lunchtime now," Veronica said. "I brought something to the cafeteria for the three of us. Chinese food like we ate that time in the shopping mall, remember? You liked it? So will you come and eat lunch with Walter and me?"

"Yes," he said solemnly. "Dom eat good Chin-ese food." He pushed to his feet.

"Wonderful. Just one more thing, though," Veronica said as she and Walter rose.

"*Oh-cho*?" What?

"Put on a tee-shirt and shoes. You can't go to the cafeteria half-naked."

He gave her the faintest of smiles. "Yes, Vee. Dom put on tee-shirt and shoes."

He knows now what Walter and Vee want from him, what they probably wanted from the beginning. He will do his best to give it to them. In return, they will take him back to his homeland. It is a good trade.

22

STONES AND CHERRY BLOSSOMS

It took some time but by mid-March, Dom seemed to have put the worst of his grief behind him. He doubled down on his reading and writing with Chloe and applied himself to improving his strength and stamina by working out with weights and the stationary bike in the PT room. He began walking short distances without his cane, but he continued to use it on longer outings.

No longer needing to hide anything from him, Veronica gave Dom lessons in basic geography, so he understood where he was in the world, and history, so he learned of the major events that had taken place since his day. He was hindered—frustratingly so, at times—by his poor vision, but by greatly enlarging the image on the laptop screen, he was able to read and make out photographs of places and things. Veronica bought him a pair of black-framed magnifying eyeglasses, which helped him to read text on paper, although wearing them for more than an hour or so tended to give him a headache. Working in the evenings, he filled a new drawing pad with pictures of his childhood village and its surroundings, images that were fascinating to Veronica and Chloe, but had yet to reveal any actionable information. Hopefully they would do so in the near future, before Walter lost all patience with the situation.

Accompanied by Chloe and Ty, Veronica took Dom twice to Stanley Park. They explored the trails and strolled the various beaches. They ate lunch at the Pavilion and admired the First Nations' totem poles at Brockton Point. Dom was fascinated by the totem poles and wanted to know what they represented. His people had carved small forms in wood and bone, he said, but nothing like the monuments in the park.

They spent one Sunday afternoon shopping for clothes, since most of Dom's things were becoming too tight as he gained weight and muscle mass. Thinking ahead, Veronica bought him a pair of sturdy hiking shoes and a waterproof jacket for when they would venture out into the wilderness.

Ty invited Veronica and Dom out to his house to meet his adorable twin daughters and to play with Daisy. They were treated to a traditional Haida meal of smoked salmon, fried whole grain bread, and raw vegetables prepared by Amanda, who was discreet enough not to ask any intrusive questions of or about Dom. The girls were too young to suspect Dom was anything other than an indigenous man who didn't speak English very well.

As planned, Dom slept over weekends at Veronica's apartment, each time learning more about ordinary things like laundry and dishes, taking out the garbage, and preparing simple meals in a modern kitchen. He fed Rusty and Scout and cleaned out their litter box, and he told her he enjoyed caring for the cats even if he still preferred dogs.

Having determined that he should be at least peripherally involved in the life he and his students had saved, Professor Sutherland had called Veronica for updates a number of times following his return from Bennett Lake. He admitted to having had great difficulty believing it when Veronica told him after Christmas who Dom really was. Trusting him with the information, she'd sent him copies of the radiocarbon and DNA analyses, and he hadn't contacted her again in over two months. Now, however, he was eager to meet Dom.

She didn't see any reason to make him wait any longer, so after explaining to Dom who Gerald Sutherland was, she invited the professor to her apartment the first Saturday of spring for them to meet.

Professor Sutherland arrived wearing his teaching clothes of grey trousers and a turtleneck sweater, and carrying the hefty plastic crate Veronica had asked him to bring. He stuttered a step and his jaw dropped at the sight of Dom standing by her elbow, but by the time Veronica closed the door behind him, he'd recovered his composure.

He placed the box on the floor with a groan, said hello to Veronica, and offered his hand to Dom. "Gerald Sutherland," he said. "Please call me Gerald."

Dom's brow furrowed and he squinted down at the professor's hand.

"You take it," Veronica instructed him as she realized they'd never shown him how to shake hands. "Like this." She shook Professor Sutherland's hand. "It's a greeting, a sort of 'hello' between people."

Dom nodded and shook the man's hand.

"I can hardly believe it," Professor Sutherland began. He pushed his glasses further up the bridge of his nose, staring at Dom although he addressed Veronica. "The last time I saw him . . . I mean to say, you told me how he was doing, but I never imagined . . . Are you sure?"

"Sure about what?" Veronica was probably enjoying this momentary one-up on her mentor more than she should.

He blinked and dragged his eyes over to her. "Everything."

"I am. Radiocarbon dating of his clothes and the other artefacts found with him confirm it—you know they do—and his DNA is unique. Dom confirms it, too, in what he tells us about his life. You know those ivory beads you found with him? He and his people hunted the mammoth themselves. He made the beads and gave them to his wife, seven in all, one for himself and her, and each of his children."

"Flabbergasting," Professor Sutherland said, the word barely audible.

"It is," Veronica agreed, "and you haven't heard anything yet. Come and sit down." She hung his coat in the closet. He shucked off his shoes, and the three of them sat in the living room, Veronica and Dom on the sofa and Gerald opposite them in the armchair.

Not generally known as someone who couldn't find his words, the esteemed professor simply gaped at Dom.

While Veronica had to refrain from bursting into laughter, Dom broke the awkward silence.

"Thank you, Gerald. Vee tell Dom. Gerald people find Dom in ground. Take out. Help make Dom alive again."

"Oh. Of course, yes. Well, you're welcome," the professor managed. Then he shook off the last of his shock and told Dom how pleased he was to see him looking so well.

Veronica had made tea, knowing the professor preferred it to coffee. As they sipped their hot drinks and nibbled on grocery store cookies, Gerald asked Dom to tell him something about his life and his people.

Dom obliged but kept things general—hunting and fishing, the building of homes, the making of fire pits and stone or bone tools—with no mention of Roo or Lil-lia or how he'd watched two batches of kids grow up. Veronica hadn't told him not to talk about his families, but she suspected this was still too personal and painful for Dom to bring up voluntarily.

Despite the lack of personal details, Professor Sutherland was clearly enthralled, and Veronica imagined him trying to memorize every word Dom said until he could rush home to write it all down. He had, however, signed the NDA, so he couldn't do anything with what he learned until it was lifted.

When Dom ran out of things to say or words with which to say them, he pointed to the box Professor Sutherland had brought.

"What in box?" he asked.

"Oh! I'll show you," Veronica said. She fetched the box and put it down on the coffee table, opening it to reveal about two dozen fist-sized chunks of chert and obsidian. She handed a piece of the glass-like obsidian to Dom and took one for herself.

"Do you know what this is?" she asked him.

Dom weighed the stone in his hand. He ran his only thumb around the edges, his confused frown slowly turning into a smile.

"*Taa*. Dom know. Good stone for make tools. Knife. Axe. Scraper. Point." He delved into the box like a little boy at Christmas, removing each stone and turning it over several times in his hands before placing it to his left. Once the box was empty, he turned to Veronica.

"Dom need… uh… work stone. Hard stone for make tools."

"I know," she said. "We can go to the beach and pick up some stones there."

"*Taa*. Go beach now." He shot up from the sofa.

"Okay, wait a minute!" Veronica exclaimed, laughing. "Gerald? How do you feel about a walk on the beach?"

"Yes, absolutely," the professor said, pushing to his feet. "After you."

They drove in Veronica's car to Kitsilano Beach, where they strolled in the sand until they found a spot liberally scattered with granite stones worn smooth by eons of ocean tide that would be perfect as hammer-stones. Dom plopped himself down to examine the specimens around him.

Veronica and Gerald did the same, chatting as they chose prime cobblestones of their own.

"I've finished writing my first paper," Veronica told him, "about Dom's recovery after you found him, and how we came to identify who and what he is. I've been holding off on sending it to you because . . . Well, I don't know why, exactly, but I'm ready to have you give it a read. Then I guess I'll start the process of having the NDA lifted. We both want to publish, and my assistant, Chloe McLean—you know her, don't you?" As he nodded, she went on, "She's writing her major thesis about Dom . . . Well, not about him, per se," she explained when the professor's grey eyebrows shot up, "but about teaching someone who's had no prior contact with writing in any language how to read and write."

The eyebrows remained up. "And he can? Read and write?"

"He can. He's at second grade level now, but he has such a good mind and memory, Chloe thinks he'll be at third grade this summer."

"Third grade is considered literate."

"I know. Unbelievable, isn't it?"

"It's going to be a circus when word gets out," the professor said suddenly. He jerked his head towards Dom and gave Veronica a long look. "You realize that, don't you? The two of you will be in demand for speaking engagements, interviews, the talk show circuit, the whole nine yards."

"Oh yeah, I'm counting on it." She couldn't keep the grin off her face.

They left after an hour on the beach, coat pockets bulging with cobblestones. Veronica gave Professor Sutherland a printed copy of her paper, which he promised to read and return to her with his comments as soon as possible.

Dom spent much of the next few days sitting on the floor of his room or outside on the back lawn of Cooper Medical, a deer hide spread across his thighs to protect them, while he happily knapped his stones. Dozens of the small, useless flakes recognized by archeologists as an indication of human habitation in prehistoric times lay scattered around him. These, along with numerous cuts and scrapes on his hands attested to a struggle on his first attempts. Gradually, however, he adapted his techniques according to his capacity to hold and manoeuvre the stones with his damaged hands, and the flakes started to fall large enough for him to make something of them.

Veronica asked him to show her and Chloe how he made tools—she knew the basics well enough to demonstrate them to students, but she couldn't pass up the chance to learn from a master—so a week after he'd been given the box of stones, they sat out in her back yard and he showed them the tricks of the ages-old trade.

While his students laboured like the beginners they were on chert, Dom fashioned a beautiful and deadly sharp point from the less forgiving obsidian. Watching him from the corner of her eye, Veronica wondered if she might someday get him to give a workshop at the university—after the brouhaha about his very existence died down, of course.

On Monday, Veronica took Dom to the supermarket. He'd been asking where food came from as no one seemed to hunt or fish or gather it, but she hadn't conceived of the difficulty in preventing him helping himself to the fruits and vegetables in the produce section until they paid for everything at the checkout counter.

"Hey! You can't do that!" she cried as he picked up a McIntosh apple and bit into it. "I thought you understood. You—"

"Dom understand," he said around his mouthful of apple. "Eat now. Pay after." He grinned.

"It doesn't work that way," she muttered, but looking at him, she realized with a jolt that he didn't care.

The incident with the apple brought to mind a subject Veronica hadn't yet broached with Dom which clearly needed to be addressed: the laws and regulations of modern society. She couldn't risk having him arrested for shoplifting or trespassing or some other minor offense.

To this end, she asked Neil for help. Wednesday afternoon, after spending an hour with him as well as Walter and Walter's lawyer, Fiona Harrison, to work out details for getting the NDA lifted in one month's time, Veronica told Neil about the supermarket incident and her subsequent worries. He agreed to explain to Dom the importance of the rule of law, and they headed to Dom's room.

He wasn't there, but they found him soon enough on this rainy day, watching television in the sunroom. After chatting there for a few minutes, the three of them returned to Dom's room. Neil admired the drawings on the walls that he'd previously only glimpsed on Veronica's cell phone, then they sat at the table and he gave Dom the basic dos and don'ts of living in modern day Canada.

"Much laws," Dom said, shaking his head in dismay as Neil finished up. "Do. Do. Do. No do. No do. No do."

"I totally agree," Neil said, standing to leave. "But if it wasn't like that, I'd be out of a job."

Dom frowned. "Neil job make laws?"

"No. But I help people abide by them. Follow them," he added at the look of confusion deepening on Dom's face. "If you break the law, you get in big trouble."

"What trouble?"

Veronica wasn't sure if he really wanted to know, or if he was simply being obstinate as she knew he could be. Either way, Neil gave a sigh and sat down again to answer.

"Well, it depends what you did. You might get a ticket, you know? Have to pay some money to the city. Or you might have to go to court and if you're found guilty, you—"

"What mean word 'guilty'?" Dom interrupted.

"Oh. It means, um, if you really did the bad thing, you have to go to prison for some amount of time."

"What mean word 'prison'?"

Neil turned to Veronica. "A little help here, please?"

"Yeah. Hang on." She hadn't brought her laptop this afternoon, so she pulled up the new whiteboard from where it rested behind the table and grabbed a marker from the box.

She drew a stick figure standing behind bars and wrote the word "prison" above it.

"You're locked in all the time in a small room called a cell, smaller than this room," she told Dom. "You can't go outside except in the prison yard. There are no flowers, no trees, no mountains." She gestured around them. "No drawing on the walls. And there are bad people there, Dom. Very bad people. No friends."

"Dom understand," he said slowly. "Prison bad place. Dom no want go prison. Dom good man. Follow laws."

"How did it work with your people, if I might ask?" Neil enquired. "You must've had some sort of laws. What did you do when someone did a bad thing?"

"*Taa.* Yes. Dom people elders talk. Choose, uh . . . choose price bad person pay. Give furs. Give food. Give help. Much bad person . . . Elders say go, bad person leave *den-no-ny.* No come back. Come back . . ." He hesitated, and Veronica realized he must be recalling his own experience with his adopted tribe. "Come back, elders tell hunters kill bad person."

"Oh, jeez," Neil responded. "That's harsh."

"But necessary to their way of life," Veronica offered. "They had to trust each other implicitly to survive."

"I guess." He cleared his throat and looked at Dom. "So, Dom, be good, don't break any laws, and you won't have anything to worry about. Do you understand?"

Dom nodded. "Dom understand. No break laws. No go prison. Go mountains summer." He sat back, looking pleased with himself.

"And my job here is done," Neil said, standing. "I've gotta go. Becky's waiting supper for me. I'll see you guys again soon."

April was cherry blossom month in Vancouver, but the cherry trees weren't the only things blooming.

Veronica's recent conversations with Gerald Sutherland had inspired both of them and they met again—this time in her office and without Dom—to hatch the outline for a joint academic paper about the mud man's people and culture.

Chloe spent several evenings a week with Dom in a final push to improve his reading and get ahead on her thesis. Dom, on the other hand, wanted to be outdoors as much as possible, so every day became something of a balancing act between exercise, lessons, and excursions to nearby parks and beaches.

When Becky called to invite Veronica and Dom to join Neil and her at the Big Picnic in Queen Elizabeth Park on Easter Sunday, she immediately accepted.

Veronica arrived early with Dom, giving them time to visit the dancing waters fountain and the arboretum before meeting Becky and Neil on the lawn near the duck pond.

"Hi, Dom, I'm so glad to meet you," Becky said with a big smile. "Neil's told me a little bit about you." Emphasis on "little bit."

Dom glanced several times at Becky as they sat—she in a folding chair and the others on a blanket brought by Veronica—the expression on his face impossible to decipher.

They got the food out of the coolers. Becky and Neil had brought sushi along with disposable plates and utensils, while Veronica had packed vegetables, soft drinks, juice, and water, and a box of donuts proudly bought by Dom at Tim Horton's on the way to the park.

After a few minutes of casual chatting during which he sat silent, Dom pointed at Becky's belly and blurted, "Becky baby come soon?"

"Yes!" She rested a hand on her bulging stomach. "Three weeks. I can't wait to see my feet again."

They all chuckled along with her.

After a moment, Becky asked, "What about you, Dom? Do you have a fam—?"

She was cut off by Neil's sudden bout of coughing. She gave him a look that said, *Well, I had to try*, shrugged, and went for something less intrusive.

"Do you like Vancouver, Dom?"

He frowned and gave his head a quick shake. "Vancouver city much noise. Bad smell. Many cars. Many people. Dom more like mountains. Forest. Ocean. Sound of birds and river."

"So I guess that'd be a 'no,' " she said with a sigh as Neil gave her the stink eye.

"Dom go mountains soon," he offered, his face lighting up at the thought. "Show Dr. Walter and Vee Dom homeland.

Show sky stone place. Find germs for make people hurt in head better."

"Wow! Well, that sounds like a wonderful mission. What do you mean by 'sky stone'?"

"Oh look!" Veronica exclaimed in an effort to change the subject before Dom innocently gave away more than he should. "We have a little visitor." A plump, black squirrel had ventured down from a nearby cherry tree to creep cautiously towards them.

She tossed a carrot stick to it.

After sniffing it delicately, the creature grabbed the carrot, stuffed it in its mouth, and scampered a safe distance away. It munched the carrot and came back for more.

"Why give food to squirrel?" Dom asked as Becky tossed another carrot stick its way.

"Why? Because it's cute. And because it came to us. It trusts us," Becky replied with a soft laugh. "Some people even have one as a pet, like a cat or dog. What? Don't tell me you don't like squirrels?"

"Yes, Dom like squirrels," he said matter-of-factly. "Good eat. Soft fur."

Becky's jaw dropped and her hazel eyes rounded in horror as Neil covered a chuckle with another cough.

Frightened by the sound, the squirrel darted back up the tree to safety.

They ate their fill of sushi and veggies and downed their drinks, and Veronica managed to limit the conversation to safe subjects like what Dom did with his days and what the rest of them did with theirs, and Becky and Neil's hopes and dreams for the baby.

At length, Becky rose with a groan and a hand pressed to her lower back. "Excuse me, but I have to make a trip to the ladies' room," she said with a rueful grin. "Pregnancy is hell on the bladder, let me tell you."

"I'll go with you," Veronica offered. "You boys behave yourselves," she added over her shoulder as she and Becky headed for the public restrooms.

Once they were out of the guys' earshot, Becky said, "Sorry about the questions. Neil's told me just enough to make me curious and, well, you know me."

"No harm, no foul," Veronica replied. "I know you suspect there's more to Dom than just some guy from a northern tribe. I'll tell you everything as soon as the NDA's lifted, I promise. Believe me, it'll be worth the wait."

"That's fine. I'm too exhausted these days to go into filmmaker mode anyway."

They were on their way back from the restroom and still some distance from their spot when Veronica noticed something awry. Neil sat on their blanket, but Dom was nowhere in sight.

"What the . . . oh, shit!" she exclaimed, heart pounding against her ribs. She jogged towards Neil, leaving Becky waddling in her wake. "What the hell, Neil? Where's Dom?" She could barely keep the panic out of her voice.

"Relax, Vee, don't give yourself a stroke. He's right over there." Neil jerked his head towards the stand of cherry trees a couple dozen paces away.

Peering at the trees, she spotted Dom's sneakered feet. He was sitting behind a tree, his back against the trunk and his legs stretched out in front of him.

"What's he doing there?" she asked, her heartbeat stabilizing as Becky joined them.

"Beats me," Neil said. "He cut a bunch of thin branches off the cherry trees and said he had something to do. A surprise, he said."

"He cut branches? With what?" They'd brought Styrofoam plates and plastic utensils.

"Oh. He had sort of a . . . I guess a sharp stone in his pocket."

Of course, Veronica thought with an inward sigh. *One of his little obsidian blades. They're as sharp as scalpels.*

They sat and waited, Becky and Neil elaborating on planned renovations to their house until Dom returned about ninety minutes later with what appeared to be wreaths made from branches full of cherry blossoms he'd twisted together.

"Beautiful cherry flowers," he said with a pleased-as-punch look on his face. "For beautiful woman. Put on head. Make more beautiful. Smell good."

He handed one of the wreaths, which Veronica now realized were a sort of crown—chaplets, they were called—to her and the other to Becky.

While not particularly intricate or even perfectly round, given the condition of his eyes and hands, they were veritable masterpieces.

"Thank you, Dom, it's lovely," said Becky, placing the crown delicately on her auburn curls.

Veronica followed suit, but she couldn't immediately speak. Knowing what Dom was, knowing what he'd lost and could never get back, this unexpected and generous gesture brought unbidden tears to her eyes and a lump to her throat.

"Vee no like?" Dom asked, squinting and blinking to focus on her face.

"Oh, no—I mean yes, I do," she blurted. She cleared her throat. "It's beautiful. Thank you, Dom." She hoped he didn't hear the emotion in her voice but suspected he did, although he chose to ignore it.

"Now," he said, "no more eat sushi. Eat donuts. Good donuts. Choc-o-late, honey, straw-berry." He smiled broadly, nodding. "Good food. Good people. Good day."

"You're right, Dom," Veronica said, this time managing a cheerful voice. "Today's a very good day."

23

GROUSE MOUNTAIN

A long string of very good days followed Easter Sunday.

Veronica started working on her second scientific paper, one about the misadventure that had led to Dom being buried in a soon-to-be-frozen bog, dead yet, of course, not dead. After that she started writing up outlines for her books and dreaming of the day they would be published.

The first day of May turned out to be a big day. The NDA was lifted and Veronica sent her first paper out to *Canadian Anthropology,* although she expected the editor would contact her with a multitude of questions before daring to publish her mind-blowing article. She assumed Professor Sutherland would be in the same position once *Archaeology* received his paper on the artefacts found at Bennett Lake.

Dom continued working hard to improve his English. He would soon be legally literate, if not legal by any other definition. Veronica had him studying the geography of B.C. on Google Maps in hopes he might make a connection between his memories and the satellite images of the province.

Becky gave birth to a healthy baby girl she and Neil named Caroline. Veronica's parents and Kim came down from Kamloops to visit and meet their granddaughter-slash-niece. Once they exhausted their gushing over the baby and new mother, they inevitably began to press Veronica on the mysterious "project" that was taking up all her time and energy.

After making them promise not to mention it to anyone until

her first paper was published and Becky had the chance to start working on the documentary she was sure to want to do, Veronica sat Kim and her parents down in her living room—they'd come for supper—and told them who Dom was. She left out only the fact that the man had lived two prehistoric lifetimes, fearing this might prove just too, too much. As it was, they could hardly believe it.

"That's. Not. Possible," Kim said, each word a statement on its own.

"The fellow's obviously pulling your leg," her dad suggested. A retired science teacher, Bryan Booth needed empirical evidence if he were to believe anything. "He must be some Native American hunter or trapper who fell into the mud and—"

"No, Dad, he's not. We have enough proof even for you." She elaborated on all the scientific evidence and told them some of what Dom had told her. The mammoth was the game-changer.

Kim looked horrified, but Bryan sat up ramrod straight and said, "I want to meet him."

"You will," Veronica promised. "I'll bring him up to your place as soon as it's convenient." She found she was looking forward to it.

The best news of all, however, had nothing to do with Dom. Or maybe it did.

Gracie was making unprecedented progress. Her vision had returned. She was able to grasp objects in her hands and was beginning to speak. Her words, while mostly unintelligible as yet, were spoken with clear intent. She knew what she was saying even if no one else did. Her parents were going to bring her a laptop to help with communication.

Walter attributed the girl's stunning recovery to the fact that he was using the first batch of Dom's stem cells—the ones still containing a minute amount of the mutated *Bacillus F.*—in the secret solution he injected periodically into the girl's brain. Although he admitted he didn't know if the bacteria had anything to do with his success, he was determined to find the source of Dom's infection. If it proved not to assist in the healing of traumatic brain injuries, he would find a way to incorporate it into a product that would extend human lifespan and make him as rich and famous as Veronica's books were bound to make her. To this end, he began planning a trip to central and northern B.C. in August. He hoped that by then, they would be able to narrow down the search area to less than half the province.

"Wonderful," Veronica said after he let her in on his plans. "I think we should step up Dom's preparation for the trip. I want to take him on longer, tougher hikes than we've done before. You should come too." She let her gaze fall to his slight paunch. "You could use the exercise."

Walter barked a laugh. "I've been a bit too busy saving people's lives to go to the gym, Veronica. But you're right. I could. And I will—come with you, that is. It's a good idea."

They decided to organize hikes of increasing intensity beginning the coming Sunday at Stanley Park, and the following week on Vancouver's famous Grouse Mountain, weather permitting.

Veronica hurried to give Dom the good news. Not finding him in his room or the stationary bike in the therapy room, on which he'd been spending quite a bit of time lately, she had an idea where he might be this sunny afternoon.

She found him sitting on the grass near their usual picnic table, hands, palms up on his knees, seeming to meditate. But that wasn't what made her catch her breath and jog towards him.

"Dom! What've you done here?" she demanded when she was close enough not to have to shout.

"Dom make fire," he said, rousing himself. He gestured at the small pile of twigs and sprays of cedar burning in front of him, a grin spreading across his face.

"Why? How?" She didn't think he'd fabricated any kind of fire-starting tools.

He pulled a yellow plastic lighter from the front pocket of

his jeans. "Alex give Dom for make fire. Make easy fire."

"No kidding," she blurted. She snatched the lighter from him and shoved it into her pocket as she made a mental note to berate Alex the next time she saw him. "You can't have a fire here, Dom. We have to put it out."

Dom's face clouded and his voice was sharp with indignation. "No fire? Why? Law say no fire?"

"Yes, it's a law. You can't just make a fire wherever—"

Dom shot to his feet and started kicking the fire apart. "More laws," he snapped as bits of burning twigs fizzled out in the green grass. "Not go out night. Not touch store food. Not tell people Dom life. Not do. Not do. Not do!" His voice rose in volume with each word.

"Dom…" She reached for him, but he knocked her hand away.

"Leave Dom walk alone," he growled, turning away.

She made sure all trace of the flames was extinguished as she watched him march away. She was afraid he might go out into the street and was steeling herself to run after him, but he didn't. After stomping all the way around the yard, he let out a howl of frustration and plopped down on the ground below the dogwood tree near the patio.

Veronica scattered the remains of the fire until no evidence remained and perched on the picnic table, elbows on her knees, chin cupped in her hands, gaze fixed on Dom as she waited for him to calm down.

When she felt she'd waited long enough, she headed towards the hospital. She said a cheerful hello to Gracie and her mom, who'd come out to the patio to enjoy the sun, then went over to Dom.

"Dom sorry make fire," he said without looking at her. "Dom not know law say no fire."

"I know." She lowered herself to her knees. "It's okay. I'm not mad or anything." When he didn't respond, she went on, "I came out to give you some good news."

His shoulders rose and fell with his heavy sigh, and he

looked sideways at her. "What good news?"

"Well . . . I know you want to go to the mountains, so in two weeks we're going to start walking in the mountains close to here, to get ready for this summer." She pointed towards the peak north of the city, a white cap of snow lingering on the top. "Can you see that one? It's called Grouse Mountain."

Dom peered in the direction of the mountain, squinting and blinking and tilting his head left and right. "Yes, Dom see dark mountain, blue sky." He shook his head. "Not see good."

"Right. Well, come inside and I'll show you on my computer."

They returned to his room, where Veronica showed him photographs of the popular tourist site, explaining about the skyride, the trails, the bird sanctuary, and the grizzly bear habitat. Dom was, understandably, not keen on the bears, but he wasn't interested in anything else, either. All he wanted was to walk in the forest.

Two weeks later, after much planning and praying for good weather after some mid-week rain, Vee, Dom, Walter, and Ty rode in Ty's SUV to Grouse Mountain that Sunday morning. Chloe had bemoaned not coming, but she would've had the awkward task of explaining to her family why going out with friends was more important than attending her grandfather's eighty-ninth birthday brunch. Even though the NDA had been lifted, she'd agreed not to tell anyone about Dom until Veronica or Professor Sutherland's first paper was published.

As they emerged from the car at the base of the mountain, backpacks filled with water, juice, and granola bars, spare tee-shirt, raincoat, and other necessities, Veronica found herself growing excited. She and Walter had come here often as UBC students, but she hadn't been back for several years and only now realized how much she missed it.

Cautious as always, Ty insisted Dom carry his cane to help him with the anticipated rough terrain. Dom, seeing the sense of this, hadn't argued.

Veronica led them to the start of the BCMC trail which, while slightly longer, wasn't as steep and gruelling as the more celebrated Grouse Grind.

Despite his enthusiasm, the rocky, muddy path proved difficult for Dom. Focus as he might on where he put his feet, he stumbled repeatedly over rocks and roots, catching his breath in hisses of pain and falling once to his knees.

"Hey buddy, take it easy," Ty said, springing forwards and helping Dom to his feet. "You okay?"

"Yes, Dom okay," he said, disdain in his voice. He brushed mud from his jeans. "Not see good where walk."

"Maybe this wasn't such a good idea after all," said Walter, voicing Veronica's exact thoughts.

"What do you think, Dom?" she asked him. "Are you up to this, or do you want to turn back? Go back down?"

"No! Not go down," he replied immediately. "Go up. Yes, go up."

And go up they did. Stopping to rest and drink or eat a bit every twenty minutes or so, it took them five hours—roughly twice the normal time—to reach the developed area halfway up the mountain. By then they were all breathing heavily. Veronica's legs and feet screamed for rest. Walter was huffing and puffing and looked near to collapse. Dom's face was slick with sweat. He was limping noticeably on his left leg and leaning on his cane. When asked, he reluctantly admitted his feet and left leg hurt.

"No surprise there," Ty said. Going into nurse mode, he added, "Let me take a look at you." He sat Dom down on the ground, took off his shoes and socks, and examined his feet. "I was worried about your toes—well, where they were taken off, I mean—but they look fine. You've got a couple serious blisters coming up on your heels, though."

"Pretty sure I have some blisters too," Walter said as Dom

pulled his socks and shoes back on. "Dom? I can give you something for the pain, if you want."

Dom shook his head. "No. Dom not like pain pills. Make feel sick, head spin."

Veronica's stomach rumbled loudly enough for everyone to look at her. Dom smiled. Walter suggested a late lunch-slash-early supper at the Rusty Rail Outdoor BBQ and Beer Garden.

"Now there's an idea," Ty said with a weary grin. "Nothing like trekking up a mountain to work up an appetite."

They made a pitstop in the restrooms before heading to the rustic restaurant, where they took seats at a round table under a green parasol on the wide wooden deck. No sooner had they stretched their legs than a waitress brought them menus and asked if they wanted a drink.

"I could go for a nice, cold beer," Ty admitted.

"Oh, me too," Veronica agreed. "But Dom . . . Dom, do you want a smoothie?"

"Smoothie, yes," he replied.

Veronica ordered a strawberry smoothie for Dom while she, Ty, and Walter ordered beer and the waitress left them to ponder their menus.

Dom held his menu up close to his face for a moment, then tossed it down on the table. "Words too small," he said. "Dom no can read."

"I'll help you," Veronica offered. She hadn't thought to bring his glasses on this excursion. She pulled her chair closer to him and went through the entire menu with Dom who, not knowing what half of the items were, opted to eat whatever she suggested.

The waitress came back with their drinks and took their orders: BBQ pulled pork sandwiches with potato salad for the guys and a Caesar salad with chicken for Veronica.

They took their time over the meal, chatting between bites about their hike, the anticipated ride down on the gondola, and where they would go next week.

Walter generously paid everyone's bill and they were rising

to leave when a voice cried out,

"Professor Booth? Oh, I thought it was you!"

Veronica turned to see Anne Temple, the red-haired student from Professor Sutherland's Bennett Lake dig, with a tall African American guy in tow.

"Hi Anne," she said in a cheerful but careful tone. "What're you doing here?"

"We did the zip lines," she replied with a grin, but her face clouded as she looked from Ty to Dom. "Do I know you?" she asked, addressing Dom. "You look sort of familiar."

Dom gave her a long look before shaking his head. "No. Dom not know . . . uh—"

"That's funny, I could've sworn . . . Oh my God!" Her eyes opened so wide Veronica saw the white around the blue irises. "You're . . ." She turned to Veronica. "He is, isn't he? The guy from Bennett Lake?"

"The dude your crew dug out of the ground?" asked the guy, his brown eyes widening.

"You told him?" asked Veronica, incredulous.

"Well yeah, Franco's my boyfriend. I tell him everything. And it was before I signed that NDA." She looked across the table. "What's your name?" she asked. "Dom, you said?"

"Yes. Dom." He tapped his chest with his hand.

"Awesome. Professor Sutherland told me you'd recovered, but I didn't... You were so close to death, I couldn't believe anyone could've survived that."

"This is great," said Franco, grinning widely. "I'm a journalism major. I'd love, love, love to talk to you. Both of you." He looked from Veronica to Dom. "But especially to you, Dom. I'll bet you've got an amazing story to tell about how you ended up buried and how you survived."

"Not now," Veronica said before Dom could respond. They apparently didn't yet know where—or rather when—Dom had come from and she didn't want him to spill the beans. "Not here. Professor Sutherland and I both have papers pending. Once they're published, we'll be available for interviews."

"Sounds fair enough," Franco said agreeably, although he looked disappointed. "Can I give you my contact info?"

"Sure." Veronica keyed his name and number into her cell phone. Hoping to end this conversation before it got out of hand, she made to leave, wished Anne and Franco an enjoyable meal, and nudged Dom towards the stairs leading off the deck.

"What mean word 'int-er-view'?" Dom asked as they walked away from the restaurant.

"It means he wants to ask you a lot of questions," Veronica explained. "And you'll get a chance to answer them when it's the right time. Soon, okay? But not today. Do you understand?"

"Yes. Good. Dom too much tired for answer questions today," he said.

They continued in silence to the red skyride gondola that would take them down the mountain. Its capacity was one hundred, but there were only a handful of people on it when it started downwards.

"Dom know not fly," he said, his voice tense as he gazed out the plexiglass window at the trees below them. "Feel fly. Not feel good."

"We're hanging from a cable," Veronica reminded him. She placed her hand over his, which clutched the top of his cane, hoping her touch would instill some confidence in him. "Remember, I showed you pictures on my laptop?"

"Yes, Dom remember pictures. How much more long?" He cleared his throat, and suddenly Veronica feared he might upchuck his supper right there on the gondola floor.

She gave his hand a squeeze and glanced at her watch. "The ride lasts fifteen minutes, and it's been five, so—"

"Ten more minutes."

"Right."

Dom was shaky and chalk white by the time they disembarked, but he wasn't sick, and after a couple minutes standing on firm ground again, he'd recovered enough to say he was looking forward to their next outing.

24

FROM CAPILANO TO KAMLOOPS

He is tired and aching all over. This is a good feeling, one he knows well. It reminds him of who he is and things he has done. It reminds him also of things to come.

It took a few days, but by Friday Dom had completely recovered from his hike on Grouse Mountain and was eager for more. Veronica and Chloe picked him up that morning for a long walk at Cates Park, followed by lunch at a Subway restaurant and some grocery shopping at the supermarket on the way to her apartment.

Now that Dom understood he couldn't taste things before paying for them, Veronica told him he could pick up anything he wanted. Although he couldn't read the small print on boxes or cans, he was able to make out some of the contents from the images on them. His magnifying glasses weren't convenient in a setting like this as he couldn't see clearly to walk while wearing them. Having to whip them on and off was awkward at best, but she supposed he would have to do so if he were ever to go shopping alone.

Back at her place, she and Chloe put away the groceries while Dom unpacked his bag for his usual weekend stayover.

"We eat steak tonight?" asked Dom, joining the women in

the kitchen.

Veronica startled. As far as she could remember, it was the first time she'd heard him use a pronoun, which apparently didn't exist in his language.

"Dom choose good steak, veg-etables," he continued, looking at Veronica. "Help cut veg-etables?" He promptly produced one of his obsidian blades from the back pocket of his jeans.

Veronica realized with some concern that she had no idea how many of these he'd made. She considered confiscating them but then again, he wasn't going to attack her with one, was he?

"You can cut the vegetables," she said, "but wash that thing first, will you?"

"Yes," he said in a mock patronizing tone. "Dom wash *adi-choo* for Vee." He obediently washed it in the sink with soap and hot water, and then went about chopping vegetables for her stir fry.

After setting the table, he occupied himself by playing with the cats in the living room while Chloe and Veronica cooked. As they ate, they planned what they hoped would be a productive weekend.

Supper and the washing of dishes done, Veronica began coaching Dom on how to go about answering questions in an interview, something she was concerned would come sooner rather than later. Chloe played the role of skeptical interviewer to perfection.

"I have a question of my own, Dom," Veronica said eventually. "I've been wondering about something for a while. I know it's not an easy subject, but—"

"Yes, Vee," Dom said. "Dom answer all questions for you."

"Okay, well . . . What did your people believe about death? I mean, did they have any notion of what might happen after death?"

Dom's forehead creased as he thought this over. "*Taa*. One person dead. *Den-no-ny* cover body in ground. Many dead all one time, burn bodies for no more sick." He paused, certainly recalling the tragic time when Roo and their children had perished along with much of their tribe. "*Den-no-ny* say body dead." He said a few words in his language, shaking his head. He tapped his chest with one hand. "*Xat.* Person heart . . . no, not heart. Uh . . . Part no can see. *Xat.* Good person *xat* go . . ." He gestured upwards. "Go meet people dead long time before. Elders. Grandparents." He swallowed. "Mother, father, wife, husband, children. All together happy. Live in . . . sky? Stars? *Taa,* stars river."

He'd used the word "*xat*" before and she'd been confused as to whether it meant "me" or "you."

"You mean '*xat*' is like, your essence? Your soul?" she persisted. "Something inside you that—"

"Bad person *xat*," Dom went on, interrupting her. "Not go stars. Go animal. Bear. Wolf. Dog. Fish. Learn in nature how be more good. Come back person. Try again."

"We call that reincarnation," Chloe said, her voice hollow. "So your people believed that? You believe it?"

Dom nodded. "Yes. Dom good man, go see family dead long time before. Shay-shoo-wa, Me-shoo not go see family. Come back bad smell animal. Skunk? *Taa!*" He burst into a laugh. "Skunk, skunk. Many times skunk."

His laughter was contagious, but while they all giggled until they were breathless, Veronica thought she'd heard the slightest note of bitterness in Dom's voice.

Chloe was back at Veronica's place at 8:00 the next morning, breakfast and coffee from Tim Horton's in hand. After eating, they packed up their necessities and headed in Veronica's car to the lower end of the Capilano Pacific Trail at Ambleside Park in West Vancouver. On this walk, which was far less demanding than last week's trek, the women were going alone with Dom, although Walter had been informed and was on call should he be needed.

The path following the Capilano River took them along stretches of sandy beach and rocky shore, past canyon cliffs and through some West Coast rain forest, until they emerged three hours later at the Cleveland Dam more than two hundred metres above sea level. Just east of the dam was a park where they used the facilities and sat to eat their picnic lunch before heading back to the city.

Dom was already stronger than he'd been a week earlier, finishing the fifteen-kilometre round trip in good enough shape to return the next day to the Capilano River, this time at Suspension Bridge Park, which they'd glimpsed but had no access to the day before.

Vee, Dom, and Chloe met Ty and Walter at the entrance to the famous tourist attraction, where they strolled trails through the forest and visited Kia'palano Totem Pole Park. They filled up on waffles and coffee at the Sugar Shack Café before venturing out on the one hundred and forty-metre-long wooden suspension bridge that hung some seventy metres above the river.

Halfway across the bridge, Dom stopped so suddenly Chloe walked right into him with a muffled, "Ouf, sorry!"

"Dom? What's wrong?" asked Veronica, turning back when she realized he wasn't following her. "Are you feeling sick? Dizzy . . . um, head spin?"

He was peering over the waist-high Frost-type fence bordering the side of the bridge, left hand white-knuckled on the railing while his right hand clasped his cane. His face had taken on a faint, greyish hue.

"Head spin . . . *taa*," he murmured. He cleared his throat. "Bridge much high. Dom not like rocks far down." He blinked, gazing down at the river. "Like better ground under feet."

"We're halfway across," Chloe said, practically prying his hand from the railing and taking it between hers. "We're all here with you, Dom. You'll be fine. Just put one foot in front of the other and soon we'll be on the other side. Do you see the trees there?" She pointed ahead of them.

"Yes, Dom see," he said between shallow breaths. "Green trees."

A couple teenage boys pushed past them, giving them looks of disdain and muttering about how some people weren't meant to be out in nature, and if they were afraid of heights they shouldn't be on the bridge.

"I'll be in front of you," Veronica said, ignoring the boys, "and Walt and Ty are behind you."

"And I'm right beside you," Chloe added. "I won't let you go until we get off the bridge."

"Dom not afraid for today." He squeezed his eyes closed. "Remember long time before. Bad men hunt Dom. Dom fall far on rocks. Bad hurt."

"That's right, you told us about that," Ty said from behind him. "Try not to think about it, okay, buddy?"

Veronica recalled the rocky cliffs overlooking the place where Dom had been found at Bennett Lake. Things must have looked much like this in his day—a deep, narrow chasm between mountain peaks where any other man would have lost his life.

She reached out to lay a hand on Dom's shoulder. "It's not the same now, Dom. Nothing's going to happen to you here. You're with friends."

"Friends. *Taa.*" He nodded and opened his eyes. His breaths seemed to come more easily. He looked over his shoulder to Ty and Walter, to Chloe at his side, and finally straight ahead. "We walk across bridge. Friends together. Dom can do."

"Don't look down," Walter advised him. "Look straight ahead at Veronica's back and the trees beyond."

They walked slowly to the end of the bridge, Chloe holding Dom's hand all the way, and sat on the damp ground as soon as it was possible to do so.

"Dom sorry," he said once he pulled himself together. "Bad remember. Okay now."

"There's no reason to be sorry," Walter said. He hadn't been privy to Dom's recounting of his life, but Veronica and Ty had caught him up in the days following his revelations to them.

They wandered along some of the trails on that side of the bridge. Unfortunately, they had to cross again to get back to the parking lot and their cars. This time, however, the trip was uneventful, and if Dom felt anything more than vague apprehension, he managed to hide it from the others.

An hour later, before leaving Dom and his baggage at Cooper Medical, Veronica asked him if he would like to meet her parents and sister. She thought it would be good preparation for talking to strangers like media people.

"Dom meet Vee family? Yes," he said, his face lighting up. "Meet tomorrow?"

"No, not tomorrow. Next weekend. There's one problem, though; it's going to be a four-hour long trip."

He seemed to deflate as some of the enthusiasm left him. He frowned. "Four hours in car?"

"Yeah. Do you think you can handle it? If not, we can wait—"

"No. Uh, yes. Dom go four hours in car. Go meet Vee family in . . . Wait, Vee tell Dom before. Uh . . . Kam-lop?"

"Kamloops," she corrected, nodding. She was surprised he remembered, but maybe it was time she stopped being surprised by him. "That's right. We'll spend the weekend at my parents' house, if you feel ready for it."

"Yes, Dom ready." He yawned widely. "Need sleep now. Goodnight Vee. See you tomorrow."

"See you tomorrow, Dom."

By Thursday, Vee had the coming weekend organized. She hoped for an enjoyable time that wouldn't go down the drain when her understandably skeptical family realized Dom really was who she said he was.

Walter had offered to come but Veronica declined, thinking it might make things awkward, he being her ex-husband and his parents still good friends with hers, so she drove alone with Dom to her hometown Friday morning.

They stopped halfway to stretch their legs, use the restrooms, and eat lunch at a roadside McDonald's. Dom handled the trip better than Veronica had expected. In fact, by the time they arrived at her parents' house, he seemed quite relaxed, while she was growing increasingly stressed. If she couldn't get her nerves in order, she mused, she might have to take one of Dom's anti-anxiety pills.

"Veronica! It's so nice to see you again so soon!" her mother greeted them, opening the door before they'd even reached it. Her sharp blue eyes went straight past her daughter to Dom, just behind Veronica. "And Dom! My goodness, you look well."

Glancing back, Veronica had to agree. Bronzed from all his time outdoors, his cheeks filling out and a hint of muscle beneath his white tee-shirt, he looked nothing like the almost-dead man she'd met less than a year ago.

"Welcome," Mrs. Booth went on as they entered the house. "Veronica's told us something about you, Dom, but not nearly enough. I'm afraid we have quite a few questions for you."

Dom put his bag down at his feet. "Dom understand. Happy answer questions for Vee mother."

"Oh! Call me Andrea, please. That's my name. Andrea."

"Andrea." He nodded and tapped his chest. "*Xat* Dom."

"Where's Dad?" Veronica asked after she'd given her mom a hug. "His car isn't in the driveway."

"I sent him to the supermarket for provisions," Andrea said. "He should be back any minute."

"Oh, good! In the meantime, I'll show Dom around. His eyesight isn't great, and I want to make sure he knows where things are and how everything works."

"Of course. Have him put his things in Neil's bedroom. It's

all ready for him."

"Perfect, thanks." Veronica steered Dom upstairs to her brother's room. Once he'd put his clothes away in the chest of drawers, she took him around the house, explaining what each room was, where he could find the light switches, and how the sink and shower faucets worked in the bathroom.

By the time they finished the house tour, Bryan Booth was back with the groceries.

Veronica introduced him to Dom, who politely offered his right hand to shake.

Bryan's expression clearly said, *Well, at least he has some manners*, but Veronica suspected he still took Dom for a phony.

They spent the afternoon sitting on lawn chairs in the back yard, sipping ice-cold lemonade, enjoying the late spring sun, and chatting about safe subjects like the weather and baby Caroline. Questions would be left until Kim and her husband, Rick, were there so Veronica and Dom wouldn't have to answer them twice.

"Hey there, Dom, you want to help me with the barbecue?" Bryan asked after Kim and Rick had arrived and introductions had been made.

Dom's thick brows came together. "Barb-e-cue? What mean word, 'barb-e-cue'?"

"You don't know what . . . Oh, well, a barbecue is cooking on a grill over a fire. Surely you've cooked over a fire before?" His tone suggested this might be a trick question, but the nuance was lost on Dom.

"Uh, yes. Long time before, Dom cook over fire." He shot Veronica an accusing scowl. "Law say no more make fire."

"Hmm, right. Well, we can make a fire in the barbecue on the patio. Come on, I'll show you."

Bryan and Dom headed towards the house.

"That was nice of your dad," Andrea said to Veronica.

"Yeah, it was," she agreed, "although I'm pretty sure he has ulterior motives."

"Probably interrogating the poor guy as we speak," Rick

said. He looked sideways at Veronica. "Is Dom really who Kim tells me he is? I mean, come on."

"He really is," she replied. "You can ask him all the questions you like over and after supper."

"I will," he said, nodding.

And he did. They all did. Dom held up admirably well, answering all their questions about himself, his past, his people, and his struggles to learn English and adapt to modern life.

By the time dessert and coffee were over, Veronica could see that everyone had fallen under Dom's spell. Her family believed him and were clearly fascinated by him, and she felt Dom was ready to face the challenge of a debut interview with Becky, as soon as Becky was up for it. And then there was Franco, the journalism student, to deal with sometime in the near future.

After a leisurely home-cooked brunch the next morning, Veronica and Dom left for Kim and Rick's farm half an hour south of town.

With their two preschool-aged sons in tow, the couple showed Veronica and Dom all around their place. Veronica had been here before, of course, but Dom was intrigued by the small menagerie that included an Australian sheepdog named Jewel and her four two-month-old puppies, a pen full of rabbits, two goats, a cow, a couple barn cats, half a dozen chickens that roamed freely in the yard, and three Quarter Horses in a big, grassy pasture.

"Do you like horses, Dom?" Kim asked as he leaned over the post-and-rail fence to pat the friendly animals.

"Yes, beautiful. More big than horses Dom remember."

"You had horses back in your day?"

"Wild horses," Dom explained. "Good eat. Good skin. Hard hunt. Much run for hunt."

Kim's jaw dropped, but only for a second. "Right. Well, these horses are perfectly tame. Domesticated. We don't eat them, we ride them. Hey! Do you guys wanna go for a ride? We could go up into the hills, see the view."

"Sounds wonderful." Veronica turned to Dom. "Do you want to ride a horse? You've seen people ride on TV, haven't you?"

"Yes, Dom see." He thought for a moment. "Yes, go ride horse," he replied, although he sounded less than certain about the venture.

Half an hour later, Veronica, Kim, and Dom—with much help from Rick—had brushed and saddled their horses. Dom climbed with some difficulty onto Polly, the oldest and calmest of Kim's horses. Kim showed him how to hold the reins and how to make the mare walk, turn, and stop using his hands and legs.

Kim and Veronica mounted, and they set off at a sedate walk, Kim in front, followed by Dom and then Veronica on a gelding called Obelix. Veronica wasn't anywhere near the rider Kim was, but she'd been on a horse often enough to sit solidly in the saddle. Her heart stuck in her throat as she watched Dom sway from side to side for the first minutes, clutching the saddle horn with his left hand as best he could while holding the reins in his right fist, until he found his balance and steadied himself.

After forty minutes of trekking through alpine meadows and along a trail gradually leading uphill, they emerged from the trees to a magnificent view of the countryside. They stopped their horses and took time to appreciate the scenery.

"Ooh, beautiful place," Dom said after a moment of taking everything in. Looking up and then down at the valley below, he added, "Big sky. Big land. Good place. Make Dom remember *den-no-ny* homeland."

"It does?" Veronica said, thinking maybe Dom's childhood home hadn't been as far north as she'd presumed. "That's really nice."

And interesting. Very interesting.

They rode back to the farm, even daring a short, cautious lope across one of the meadows, and took care of the horses before turning them out again.

"Horse not horse," Dom commented as he led Polly back to

the pasture. He was limping slightly on his bad leg after the stretching it had on Polly, but he didn't complain. "Horse big dog. Good big dog." He chuckled, and Kim and Veronica laughed along with him. They pitched in with the kids to feed the animals before sitting down on the back veranda of the farmhouse to their own supper of pizza, salads, and French fries delivered from town.

The sun was setting by the time Veronica and Dom drove back to her parents' place.

"I have to say," Veronica began after a few minutes in the car. "I'm proud of the way you've handled things these past few weeks. The new people, the new experiences. You've done really well."

"Thank you, Vee," Dom said, no hint of teasing in his voice. "Dom proud too. Some days not easy."

"I know. You liked today though, didn't you?"

"*Taa*. Dom like ride horse." He paused. "Lil-lia here, Saawli here, Dom daughters here, all like ride horse on mountain."

This surprised her. Dom had barely mentioned his family in weeks and only talked about his people in general terms when replying to direct questions. She realized now that, while he didn't talk about them, the wife and children he'd left behind were probably never far from his mind.

Of course, they aren't. I don't know how I'd go on without Mom and Dad, Kim and Neil in my life. As much as I hate to admit it, I'd even miss Walter.

"What about your oldest son? Seen-ee? You don't think he'd like to ride?"

Dom shook his head. "Seen-ee not like ride horse. Seen-ee hunter. Like eat horse!"

"Seriously?" She shot a glance at him.

He shrugged, a wry smile on his face. A few minutes later he said, "Thank you, Vee, for make Dom good day."

"Oh! Well, thank you, Dom." She reached over and gave his arm a squeeze. "I'm hoping our best days are yet to come."

25

SO NEAR AND YET SO FAR

Wanting to enjoy a true vacation weekend, Veronica hadn't looked at her emails or any social media since Thursday night.

Only Sunday evening, upon arriving home after dropping Dom off at Cooper Medical, did she open her email inbox to find a message from Gerald Sutherland informing her that the Bennett Lake Neolithic artefacts article had been accepted and was awaiting publication in *Archaeology*. Another email from one Mary Roberts, the editor of *Canadian Anthropology*, requested she contact Ms. Roberts concerning her recent submission to the journal.

She whipped off a quick reply to Gerald, congratulating him, and one to Mary Roberts, saying she would call her in the morning. It turned out, however, she didn't have to.

Mary Roberts called her at 9:00 sharp Monday morning.

"I have your paper right here in front of me, Professor Booth," the editor said after they exchanged hellos, and something in the usually friendly woman's voice chilled Veronica's blood. "I admit I was quite taken aback when I read it."

"I know, it's amazing, isn't—"

"I can't publish it."

"Excuse me?"

"I'm sorry, but I just can't. As you are well aware, *Canadian Anthropology* is a highly respected, peer-reviewed journal. Many of our readers are experts in their field. Unlike previous papers you've submitted to us, this one reads more like science fiction than science fact—"

"Are you accusing me of making it up?" Veronica was incredulous. "I would never—"

"I'm not accusing you of anything, Professor Booth, but I am afraid you've become a pawn in an elaborate hoax."

"It's no hoax! I have DNA analysis, radiocarbon dating of his clothes and the artefacts found with him. Professor Gerald Sutherland is publishing a paper about the artefacts, and Dom—the subject—has told me incredible—"

"Yes, I read through the supporting evidence you sent. I can accept that a man from an unknown indigenous tribe was buried alive and found just in time to save his life. I can even accept that he had some Neolithic artefacts with him. I cannot . . . Professor Booth, I cannot accept that the man himself is 9,500 years old, regardless of what kind of prehistoric microbe might have been found in his body. Someone has made a terrible mistake or, as I said, is perpetuating one hell of a hoax."

"You're the one who's making a mistake," Veronica said. She was unable to keep the bitterness out of her voice, even as she felt the battle was lost. "Dom's the real deal. You're going to regret not being the first to publish about him."

"That's a risk I'll have to take," Mary Roberts said with a sigh of finality. "I hope you'll reconsider publishing your paper, Professor Booth. I'd hate to see you lose your good reputation and academic future over it."

"Don't you worry about me," Veronica said and ended the call.

She'd had papers rejected before, of course, early in her career, but this stung more than any other because she knew what she'd written was true. Knew it would blow up all previous assumptions about the longevity of human life, never mind the invaluable first-hand information about early indigenous people in North America.

"Damn consensus science!" she spluttered. She tossed her cell phone on the living room table, sending Rusty, who'd been lounging beneath it, scampering to peace and quiet in her bedroom. "She can't publish my paper because she doesn't believe it? How the hell is science supposed to progress if it rejects anything remotely outside the norm? Damn it!"

She was well aware that the scientific community had great difficulty—to say the least—when presented with evidence that defied current beliefs. She'd probably been foolish to think anything would change with the presentation of her paper.

On the rebound, she considered sending her article and collaborating evidence to the prestigious British journal, *Nature,* thinking perhaps she should have approached them first. Then she changed her mind.

No. No way. To hell with the scientific community. I'll write my book. I'll write it the way I want to for the world at large. Let the scientists make of it what they will.

Unwilling to subject Dom to her foul mood, she called Cooper Medical and asked he be informed she wouldn't be in today after all. Then she made a pot of coffee and sat down at her laptop to work on her book which would, she vowed, be accepted and published and become a world-wide best seller.

The unusually warm, clear weather ended overnight, and Veronica woke Tuesday morning to wind and a cold drizzle that perfectly suited her still grim mood. When she found Dom's room at the hospital unoccupied, she headed to the sunroom, where she found him, along with Gracie, watching television.

"Hey, Dom, I figured I'd find you here," she said. "Hi Gracie," she added, not expecting a response.

"Yes. Too much rain for go outside," Dom replied. "Where Vee yesterday?"

"At home. I'll tell you everything later."

"Hi. Are you Vee?" Gracie said, turning to look at her. Her words, while slurred, were perfectly intelligible. "Dom tells me about you."

"I am," Veronica said, her spirits raised slightly by the girl's words. "He does?"

The girl gave her a crooked smile. The right side of her face was still paralyzed, but she appeared far stronger than she had at Christmas time and was now sitting up in a regular wheelchair, no tubes or wires in sight. "He does." She giggled.

Veronica looked at Dom, who smiled and shrugged. She decided not to pursue the subject, at least for now. Gesturing towards the television, she asked, "What are you watching?"

"Animal doctor help dogs and cats," Dom said, rising from the sofa. "Vee come. Dom want show you new drawings. Bye, Gracie."

"Bye, Dom."

"I can't believe how much better Gracie's getting," Veronica said to Dom as they walked to his room. "Walter really is doing miracles here."

"Yes, Gracie good girl. Strong girl," Dom agreed. "Dr. Walter say she stand soon."

Back in his room, Dom pointed out a new drawing on one of the last virgin areas within reach on his walls. It was a reasonable representation of a man on a horse; the horse was dark brown with a white face and three white legs.

"That's you on Polly," Veronica observed. "It's very good."

"Yes," Dom said, looking pleased. "Dom draw more on paper." He showed her two landscapes. One was vaguely recognizable as the scene they'd viewed from horseback on Saturday.

The other was more detailed, showing a roughly diamond-shaped land mass bordered on the top and sides by a series of lakes or rivers. At the bottom of the page stood a number of steep green points topped in grey—Dom's depiction of a mountain range with snow-covered peaks. Near the centre of the diamond, three low mountains stood in an almost horizontal line. Below and to the right of these mountains were some trees and a long, narrow lake with several brown *isaah*—tipi tents—

standing nearby in a circle. Evidently, Dom could see more clearly in his mind's eye than he could with his present-day vision.

"*Den-no-ny* homeland," Dom said, tapping the drawing. "Dom boy here, grow man here."

"So, that's your first homeland? Why didn't you show me this before? You know we've been asking you for it, over and over again."

"Yes, sorry. Dom not remember. Remember when see . . . Kamloops place." He waved at the first drawing. "Make remember homeland."

"Right. Wait! How do you know what your homeland looked like? I mean, Google Maps gets its images from a satellite . . . um, a camera on a machine that flies so high in the sky we can't see it. How could you—"

"Dom not fly," he said matter-of-factly. "Not bird, not sat-light. Not fly, no." One corner of his mouth twitched with the hint of a smile. "Dom go high up mountain. Here." He pointed to the left-most of the three summits. "Here." He pointed to the middle peak. "Elders go up mountain high, close sky. Eat *roo-zaa ya-monni* . . . red dream plant . . . for dream awake. Talk to elders dead long time before."

"So... you became an elder and you ate some sort of hallucinogenic plant to convene with your dead ancestors?"

Dom frowned. "What mean word 'hallu-so'. . . uh?"

She waved it off. "Never mind. You went up that mountain and from there you could see your land?"

"Yes. See all *den-no-ny* land. Water. Mountains. Trees. Village."

"I guess that makes sense," she admitted, nodding. "Well, thank you, Dom. This is great. Oh! Do you remember from here . . . from your homeland, I mean, where the sky stone place is?"

He thought for a moment. "Yes. Dom remember." He picked up the drawing, studied it carefully, and pointed to the left-hand edge of the paper. "Sky stone place this way."

"Wonderful! This will help us a lot. Can I take this home?"

"Yes, Vee. Take." Before handing it to her, however, he asked, "Why Vee not come see Dom yesterday?"

"Oh! I was busy, writing my book about you. You remember, I told you about it?"

He nodded. "*Taa*. Dom can read book?"

"Well, it's not written yet. I've just started, but . . . yeah, I guess you can read some of the first part."

"Good," he said, nodding. "*De-ne-land*." Thank you.

Veronica had Chloe pick Dom up for his weekend at her place Friday afternoon. After a healthy supper of salmon steaks and tomato salad, the two of them spent the evening reading the introduction to her book.

It began with an overview of archaeological discoveries on Prince of Wales Island, B.C., and Old Crow Basin and Bluefish Caves in the Yukon that suggested a substantial human presence in northwestern North America after the end of the last ice age. It went on to explain how thawing of permafrost soil and glacial ice attributed to climate change had revealed incredibly well-preserved animal remains dated as old as 40,000 years. As opposed to the very dead animals, several strains of bacteria and viruses frozen for millennia had reportedly come back to life once thawed. If true, this was scientific proof that multi-celled lifeforms could survive being frozen for extended periods of time. Finally, Veronica had written, tempting the reader to turn the page, all of this paled to a discovery recently made at Bennett Lake, B.C.

The reading of the six pages took hours as it was filled with words far beyond Dom's vocabulary level, necessitating the use of the whiteboard on numerous occasions to get an idea across to him.

"That's an awesome introduction," Chloe exclaimed once they were done. "I already want to read more." Reaching for the mouse, she scrolled down to peek at the first page of chapter one.

"I'm so glad you think so," Veronica said, "but we'll save it for next time. It's almost midnight already." She glanced at Dom, who was wearing a decidedly unhappy frown. "Dom? What's wrong?"

"Dom not understand," he said, still frowning. "Vee say book tell Dom life. We read much . . . uh, many pages. Read animals dead long time before, germs alive long time before. Not read Dom name one time."

"Oh. I told you that's just the beginning," she explained. "It prepares people . . . um, gets them ready for the next part of the book. For your story. Do you understand?"

He nodded slowly. "*Taa*. Dom understand get ready. Read Dom story more pages?"

"That's right. We'll read the next part soon. Okay?"

"Soon, yes." He nodded again. "Dom want read more."

"Don't worry, you will."

Chloe went home after that, but she was back the next morning for a trip to the UBC Anthropology Museum. Veronica had hesitated in taking Dom there, but she felt now that he would understand enough to make visiting the exhibits worthwhile, and the cool, rainy day was the perfect occasion for the indoor activity.

While Veronica drove, Chloe explained to Dom what the museum was and what he should expect to see there.

They parked and entered through the entrance hall, heading for the Great Hall, famous for its collection of totem poles, Northwest Coast canoes, and other artefacts originating mostly from the nineteenth century. From there, they went inside. There was no way, however, that they would have time to see everything in one day, not the way Dom paused at every item, asking what it was and what it did, so Veronica guided them to the Multiversity Galleries, where thousands of Native American artefacts were displayed behind glass. Dom was fascinated by the textiles, masks, artwork, and other cultural items, and the women could barely drag him from one display case to the next.

Eventually, they came to a case featuring photographs of petroglyphs and pictograms from various locations in the province. Veronica's heart almost stopped at the sight of a black and white, eight by ten-inch photo labelled "Pre-Columbian petroglyph, North Central Interior, c. 1965."

"Dom?" She tried to call him, but her voice came out in a dry croak. She worked her tongue around in her mouth to produce some saliva and tried again. "Dom? Chloe! Come here, please!"

Dom joined her from the display case across the hall. Chloe had wandered further away down the hallway and apparently hadn't heard her. "Yes, Vee? *Oh-cho*?" What?

"Look. Can you see that?" She pointed to the photograph standing near the right-hand corner of the middle shelf. Her hand was shaking, although maybe not so much that Dom would notice.

He peered into the display case. "Dom see . . . pictures?"

"Yeah, pictures. But that one"—another stab with her index finger towards the image in question—"there in the corner. What do you see?"

Dom leaned in until his nose practically touched the glass. "Dom see grey picture. Uh, grey stone?"

"That's right. It's stone. Can you see what's engraved—scratched—on it?"

After a few more seconds of profound scrutiny, he straightened and shook his head. "Dom eyes not good. Not see good, sorry. What Vee see?"

"There's an engraving—we call it a petroglyph—on that stone. Dom, it's . . ." She stopped as Chloe joined them, a *What's going on here?* look on her face. "It's faint, but it looks like this." She raised her hands so that her thumbs and index fingers formed a diamond-shaped space, holding them out so Dom could see them clearly. Then she drew two concentric circles inside the space. "Exactly like you drew for us in your room at Cooper Medical. "Like your tattoos."

"*Taa.* Mark mean name 'Dom,' " he said as Chloe gaped at the photograph and a couple curious onlookers crept closer, attracted by the commotion. He tapped the tattoo on his right forearm with his left hand. "*Xat* Dom."

"And did you ever scratch your mark, your name, into a stone somewhere? Do you remember?"

He thought for a moment, his forehead creased as he searched his memory. "Yes, Dom make mark at sky stone place."

"You did?" Veronica wiped her palms, suddenly moist, on the hips of her jeans. "Is that the only place you left your mark? Or did you leave it everywhere you went?"

He looked hard at her. Blinked. "No. *Den-no-ny* boy make mark in place where become man. One place."

"Only one place! Do you know what this means?" She looked from Dom to Chloe, and back to Dom. "If we find the right area, the place we're looking for is actually marked." She grabbed his arms, barely refraining from jumping up and down. "Why didn't you tell us this before?"

"Dom not remember," he said simply.

"Seems like you forgot a lot."

"Veronica!" Chloe gasped, reproach in her voice. She shook her head.

"Yes," Dom agreed with a sigh. "Long time before, much time after. Dom forget many things."

"I know. I'm sorry." She took a deep, calming breath and let him go. "It's just that it's so important we find that place, and now we have two good clues. Your drawing . . . and this." She pulled her cell phone from her handbag and snapped a couple photos of the photograph. "I knew I'd seen that mark before. Obviously, I must've seen it here"—she waved towards it—"and just forgot about it."

"Vee forget things too," Dom observed.

"Of course, I do. I'm sorry I snapped at you. Come on." She took him by the elbow and steered him away from the display case. Half a dozen people were gathered nearby and she didn't want to draw more attention than they already had.

They worked their way around the gallery, not talking much, occupied by their own thoughts.

As they reached the end of the room, Dom said, "Dom hungry. We eat?"

"I'm hungry too," Chloe seconded. "There's the cafeteria here, but . . ." She wrinkled her nose. "It's kind of expensive for what it offers."

"How about the sushi place down the street?" Veronica suggested. "We can drive, or walk if the rain's stopped."

"Yes, sushi good," Dom said. "We walk. Dom not afraid rain."

As it turned out the rain had stopped, although the sky remained a solid grey, threatening more precipitation. They walked to the restaurant for lunch, but as they headed back to the museum the sky opened once again. They dashed through the rain as fast as Dom's toeless feet would allow, shrieking and laughing all the way, but they were soaked to the skin by the time they reached the car.

An hour later, dressed in dry clothes—Chloe always left a few things at the apartment—they sat down at the kitchen table with Dom's drawing laid out on the table in front of them and tried to figure out how far the meteorite site might be from his homeland.

Chloe was on her cell phone, looking up walking speeds. "So, let's say he walked for eight hours a day, at around three kilometres an hour, which this app says is an average hiking speed."

"Did you walk fast?" Veronica asked Dom. "Or was it hard going? Did you stop a lot?"

"Dom not walk fast. Much forest. Stop for hunt. Stop for sleep."

"All right. Let's say six hours a day then, giving him time to hunt and putter around. What?" she asked as Chloe pulled a face. "He was a fifteen-year-old boy. You don't think he got sidetracked once or twice?"

"Okay then. Six hours at three kilometres an hour," Chloe repeated. "That's eighteen kilometres a day. Six days would come to"—she keyed her calculator—"one hundred and eight. Let's say between a hundred and a hundred fifteen kilometres. That's like Vancouver to where?"

"Um, Chilliwack or thereabouts," Veronica said. "All we have to do is figure out where he started from."

"Awesome." Chloe sighed. "So near and yet so far."

"We'll find it. We have to. So much depends on it. Dom's people's homeland would provide virgin territory for archeological exploration. Can you imagine what we might discover? And then the sky stone—meteorite—site. If Walter could find some trace of that bacteria? It could originate a breakthrough in medicine like there hasn't been since . . . I don't know what. The discovery of vaccines? Antibiotics?"

Dom sat in silence while they talked past him, his face blank. Veronica suspected he understood much of what they were saying but for whatever reason, he chose not to participate in the conversation. She couldn't help feeling he was holding something back, although she couldn't for the life of her imagine what it might be.

He remembers more of his life in the long time before, remembers things long forgotten. The memories do not hurt as much as he thought they would. He does not know why, but he thinks this is because there are good people around him. Because soon, he hopes, they will find his homeland on that magical thing called google maps and they will take him home.

26

IN THE NEWS

"Have you seen the sun?" Walter asked without preamble Monday morning.

Cell phone pressed to her ear, Veronica peered out her kitchen window. "Um, no, the sky's completely covered—"

"The *Vancouver Sun*!" he barked. "Top of page three. Your mud man's in the news."

"Oh. God." She sank into the nearest chair. "What . . . who?"

"That character from Grouse Mountain—Franco Paulo— wrote a piece. Are you coming in today?"

"Yeah, I am. Give me an hour?"

"Grab a newspaper on the way."

"I will."

She did, sitting in her car in the convenience store parking lot to read it before continuing on to Cooper Medical.

Anne Temple's journalism major boyfriend had written what he could about Dom, which wasn't much. Professor Sutherland and the doctors at the Whitehorse and Vancouver hospitals had refused to comment, and Professor Booth, Franco Paulo said, had been unavailable, so the article consisted almost entirely of Anne's first-person account of the discovery of the man buried in the northern B.C. soil, up to the time he was taken—alive, against all expectations—by medevac to the nearest trauma center. A final paragraph stated that the writer had seen the man, who called himself Dom, with his own eyes only two weeks ago, completely recovered, walking and talking and having lunch on Grouse Mountain. There would be a follow-up, he promised, as soon as he could find Dom and sit him down for an interview.

The text was accompanied by a photograph no doubt taken by Anne of Dom lying inert and covered in mud in the boggy hollow near Bennett Lake. Another picture, taken from the side, showed him walking down the stairs of the Rusty Rail Beer Garden. In all truth, it was impossible to tell it was the same man.

"I didn't even see them take it," Veronica muttered, as angry with herself as she was with the students. She folded the newspaper and threw it down in disgust on the passenger seat.

By the time she reached Cooper Medical, she'd calmed down enough to realize Franco hadn't written anything revealing. A man resurrected from burial in the earth was an amazing story, to be sure, but he had no idea who Dom was, no concept of the miraculous set of circumstances that had combined to his surviving for thousands of years.

Still . . .

"It won't be long before that damn reporter digs around and finds more," Walter said when Veronica joined him in his office. "Dom will have to stay indoors, no more going out for hikes or walks on the beach, coffee at Tim Horton's, or whatever."

"What? We can't do—"

"I can't have a media circus showing up here, Veronica, reporters or photographers hoping for a glimpse of him. Do you understand?"

"Of course, I do."

He doesn't want anyone looking into what he's doing here, not until his experimental treatment of TBIs is approved.

"He'll go nuts if he can't go outside, you know he will. Maybe I could have him stay at my apartment. I'm not going to abscond with him, Walt," she said at the look of disagreement on the man's face, "but it would be the best solution."

"And when they find him at your place? What then?"

"Then we'll deal with it. I have something to tell you too."

She related her conversation with Mary Roberts, admitting her frustration at the unexpected obstacle to getting news about Dom out in a scientific platform.

Walter groaned. "This keeps getting better and better."

He sat at his desk, fingers tented in front of his face, for a long moment. "Okay," he said finally. "I'll do some tests on him tomorrow, make sure he's good to go health-wise, and take another round of samples. After that, you can have him." As if he were a puppy.

"Okay. I'll give him the news."

She found Dom in the physical therapy room, pedalling away on the stationary bike.

Everett was having a therapy session with Ty on the other side of the room.

"Hi, Everett!" Veronica said with deliberate cheer. "I haven't seen you in months. How're you doing?"

"Doing good,   Vee," said the young man, while Ty stopped his exercises to let him speak. "Thinking of going back to school in September. Social sciences." His speech was barely slurred at all.

"That's wonderful. Good luck!" she said, then turned to Dom and lowered her voice. "I have to talk to you."

"Good, Vee. Talk," he said, still cycling.

"Not here. In your room."

Dom sighed and stopped his cycling. "Come."

They went to his room, where Dom pulled off his sweaty tee-shirt with no regard for Veronica, and put on a fresh one. At least he kept his sweatpants on. Despite everything he'd learned these past months, personal etiquette seemed to be beyond him. He still refused to wear underwear, declaring it uncomfortable. Veronica pondered ruefully what he would do if she walked around topless in front of him.

Probably wouldn't bat an eye.

"Sit down, Dom, I have something important to tell you,"

she began. Once they were seated cross-legged on the bearskin rug, knees almost touching, she related the situation, leaving out only the reason why Walter didn't want the media sniffing around the facility.

"Dom stay Vee house?" he exclaimed. He jumped up, ready to leave on the spot.

"Yes, Dom, in two days. Okay? I have things to do to get ready."

"Two days. *Laa-tah*," he agreed happily. "Two days Dom go Vee house. Yes. Good."

"Hey, Veronica, did you see this morning's *Sun*?" Ty asked, coming into the room just then.

"Oh, yeah. We're making contingency plans now."

"Huh?"

"Dom's going to be staying at my place starting Wednesday, so Walter won't have any journalists snooping around here."

"Good idea," Ty agreed, nodding.

Veronica left shortly after that, to shop for provisions. Once the groceries were put away, she called Becky to get her immediately involved if she wanted exclusivity before things got out of hand.

"Neil told me about Dom as soon as the NDA was lifted," Becky said, "and though I have to admit I found him quite unusual at our Easter picnic, I can't believe he's what the two of you say he is. You'll have to convince me before I can commit to anything."

"Happy to," Veronica said. "Can I come by tomorrow?"

"Sure. Neil has to work, so I'll be home alone with the baby all day."

Veronica went for a jog the following morning, got the apartment ready for Dom's extended stay, then showered and dressed to spend the afternoon with Becky and Caroline. In between feeding and changing her little niece, cuddling her, and simply watching her sleep, she told her sister-in-law everything she could about Dom. She showed her the paper that *Canadian Anthropology* had rejected, as well as copies of the DNA and radiocarbon analyses, and had her listen to a few bits of the countless audio recordings she'd made of her conversations with the man in question.

"So . . . Do you believe me now?" Veronica asked after Becky had seen everything.

"I don't see any other choice, other than to think two of the people I care most about in the world are completely off their rockers."

Veronica chuckled. "And are you interested in making a film about—"

"Are you kidding?" she blurted, hazel eyes growing wide. "Good God! This is the opportunity of a lifetime! I'll start working on a proposal tomorrow to use in order to scratch up some funding. Don't worry, everything will be confidential. I'll prepare some questions and we can talk about them, you know, and make sure you and Dom are willing and able to answer them. And I'd like to get comments from the people who found him, and anyone else who—"

"Walter will probably want to stay out of it," Veronica cautioned her. "He's pretty private about what goes on at his facility."

"Fine. We'll say Dom recovered at an undisclosed location. Not a problem."

Neil came home shortly after that. Veronica helped Becky make supper and while they ate, she asked Neil how they could go about getting Dom some kind of legal status, a social insurance number and a B.C. Care card, which everyone needed to navigate the modern world. She'd been worrying about this for a while now.

"I'll look into it," Neil said, although he didn't appear hopeful. "I don't have to tell you his situation is unique. Maybe

Indian Affairs can do something, or . . . maybe Judge Chamberlain. Have you kept him up to date?"

"I haven't," Veronica admitted.

"I'll call him, see what he has to say."

"Thanks. Becky? I'll pick Dom up tomorrow to stay at my place for the foreseeable future. We could come by Thursday and chat, off the record, get a feel of what you want to do?"

"Sounds good," Becky said, as Caroline began to cry in her crib. "Oops, baby calls! How about you bring lunch on Thursday? Chinese? And we'll spend the afternoon together."

"Perfect," Veronica said, "and thanks. Both of you."

Dom was stiff and sore on Wednesday, having undergone a spinal tap and bone marrow aspiration the previous day, along with the drawing of blood, urine, and sperm, Walt's desperate effort to get as much out of him as possible before he lost daily access.

Veronica was angry but not surprised, and she didn't see the point of confronting Walter about it again. She helped Dom pack, realizing for the first time that, aside from clothes and the necessities of hygiene, he had no personal items to speak of. She gathered up the deer skins and bearskin rug as well as the whiteboard and markers, the drawing pad and box of crayons, the only things he could reasonably call his own. She would return tomorrow morning for his ferns and the little cedar trees.

She took multiple photographs of the walls, ensuring she had shots of all Dom's unique artwork, and hoped Walter would keep his promise not to destroy it.

"Dom go away, not see Everett again? Not see Gracie? Alex? Beatrice? Ty?" he asked as they prepared to leave. His voice rose a note with each name.

"Oh, of course you will," she assured him. "Ty's going to come give you your PT and take hikes with us, and we'll come back here and visit everyone. Okay?" It struck her that he might well refuse to leave. It wouldn't be any fun forcing him to go against his will.

"Yes, okay. Dom want say goodbye to Gracie before we go."

Veronica sighed, but this was a compromise she could make. "Okay. Come on." They found the girl with her dad in the sunroom. Dom said his goodbyes, they went back to his room to collect his things, and they headed for Veronica's apartment.

Once he was settled, Dom took a nap, foregoing lunch, but he rose for supper looking better than he had that morning.

They ate shrimp, Caesar salad, and multi-grain rolls, washed it all down with vegetable juice, and spent the evening watching television, a cat on each of their laps—Scout had taken quite a liking to Dom—exchanging only a few words.

Ty came over Thursday morning for Dom's therapy, continuing to build up strength and range of motion in his left leg and dexterity in his fingers. While he was there, Veronica made a quick trip to Cooper Medical for Dom's plants, which she placed in his bedroom. Afterward, she and Dom headed to Neil and Becky's house, picking up the promised Chinese take-out on the way.

Becky had just finished feeding Caroline when they arrived. Once she'd put the baby to bed, they sat at the dining room table to eat and discuss what direction Becky's documentary should take.

"I'd like for you to tell me what life was like for you and your people," Becky said to Dom. "How you spent your days. What you believed and what was important to your people. Maybe teach me a few words in your language. Can you do that?"

"Yes, Dom can do," he said readily enough, although Veronica suspected he didn't really understand what he was getting himself into. *How could he?*

"And show me, you know . . . Vee said you can make stone

tools and . . . Well, you made those lovely little crowns for us at the park and I still have mine, by the way. What else can you make?"

"Dom can make wood spear for hunt and fish, bone needle for sew clothes. Good drink from berries and honey. Medicine for make sick people better.

"That's right!" Veronica gave him a big smile. "I'd completely forgotten about that. Will you draw the medicinal plants for us?"

Over the past months, he'd drawn illustrations of things like strawberries, fiddleheads, lichen, and cat tails, which he said could be consumed like a vegetable or whose pollen could be used as flour for a sort of flatbread. He'd never mentioned medicinal plants.

He nodded. "*Taa*. Dom draw medicine plants tomorrow."

"Perfect." She and Becky wrote up a rough outline of what Becky wanted to do, and some of the questions she would ask Veronica and Dom. They were interrupted a couple times by Caroline, whose needs naturally came before anything else.

"Dom hold baby Caro-line?" he asked.

Becky had Caroline in her arms, wrapped in her pink blanket, but the infant was fussing and wouldn't stop crying. The new mother was clearly growing impatient.

"Oh, I don't think—"

"Yes! Give baby. Dom many times father. Hold baby good. Not fall."

"I think you can trust him," Veronica said.

"O—kay," Becky said slowly. She handed Caroline to Dom, making sure he supported the baby's head and had her firmly in his grasp before she let go.

Dom held the infant close to his chest and began to murmur a chant in his language in a low, sing-song voice. Within a minute, Caroline's wails faded to the soft cooing of a contented baby. A minute later, she was quiet.

"Oh my . . . I'm going to hire him as a babysitter when the need arises," Becky said, her voice filled with awe. "Thank you,

Dom." She gently retrieved Caroline and put her to bed. Then she insisted Dom teach her the little song, which amounted to the same dozen words repeated over and over.

"Words mean, 'sleep little baby, mother here, father here, sleep happy baby.' " Dom told them once they'd memorized his magical chant.

"It's beautiful," Becky said, tears shining in her eyes. "Your people obviously loved your children just as much as we do, and I'm sure you were a good father."

"Yes, Dom good father," he said proudly but perhaps, Veronica thought, a little wistfully too. She feared it would devastate him to know he would never be a father again. "Take good care children. Teach much."

Becky vowed to put Dom's lullaby in the documentary, and they talked for a while longer. Then Veronica and Dom left, promising to come back next week to continue planning what Veronica was already convinced would be a ground-breaking and award-winning film.

27

WHEN IN DOUBT GOOGLE IT

While Dom spent Friday morning drawing his medicinal plants on his drawing pad, Veronica sat opposite him with her laptop open to Google Maps, the illustration of his homeland laid out beside the computer. She'd already searched the regions of southern Alaska and the Yukon and northern B.C. Now, inspired by the caption on the photo in the museum, she headed south towards the centre of the province.

They stopped their respective work when Chloe arrived with submarine sandwiches and coleslaw from the bistro near her mom's apartment. Afterwards, not surprisingly, Dom wanted to go out.

"Blue sky," he said, peering out the kitchen window. "No rain. We go walk. Walk on mountain."

"We can go out," Veronica said, "but we can't go to the mountain. With all the rain we had this week, the trails will be muddy and—"

"Dom not afraid mud," he interrupted.

"Well, I am," she retorted. "If I break an ankle or God forbid, you do, we won't be able to go looking for your people's homeland or the sky stone place this summer. You still want to go there, don't you?"

"Yes, Dom want much," he said with a grumpy frown. "Go walk on beach? No mud."

Chloe giggled. "You're right, Dom, there's no mud on the beach. Veronica?" She raised her eyebrows at her mentor and friend.

"The beach is fine," Veronica agreed with a sigh of defeat.

They walked from her apartment to Kitsilano Beach, where they strolled along the sand, stopping occasionally to pick up an interesting bit of wood or throw a pebble into the water.

"Hey, what're you doing?" Veronica asked Dom.

He'd sat down on a log and was pulling off his running shoes. "Dom go walk in water. Good for... uh, make feel alive."

"You're right, it does," she said with a sigh. "Why did I even ask?"

"I'll go in with you," Chloe offered. She was wearing three-quarter length red leggings, which she hastily rolled up as far as they would go before shucking off her sandals. "Here, let me help you." She rolled Dom's jeans up past his knees.

"Have fun," Veronica said, laughing, as the two headed for the water's edge. "I'll be filming you."

She shot a video with her cell phone, thinking Becky might use it in her documentary to show Dom developing relationships and making a life for himself in the modern world.

An hour later, back in Veronica's apartment, Chloe and Dom sat in the living room with Chloe's laptop to practice his reading on an educational website. He was, Chloe announced with a grin, now reading at the third-grade level and doing simple mathematics.

"My thesis is almost finished," she added. "Well, the first draft, anyway. Veronica, will you read it when it's ready?"

"Of course. I'd be happy to."

While Dom was busy with Chloe, Veronica took the opportunity to look at his morning's work. There were five drawings, and above each image he'd written his best translation of their names, which also indicated their use. She compared them with images of medicinal plants on Google to identify them.

There was devil's claw, still used today to treat pain and inflammation, which Dom called, "no pain pink flower plant."

"Stomach good plant" was the stinging nettle. Intrigued, she read that some tribes of Native Americans used it in an infusion to treat stomach pain and dysentery.

"Breath good tree"—red cedar—could be boiled and the steam inhaled to help with respiratory problems. Now she understood why Dom had wanted to make tea from it when he was sick.

The fourth plant was the "sleep drink plant," Indian hellebore, used in ancient times to reduce blood pressure or— she read with a shudder—induce sleep, coma, or death.

It took her a while to identify the last one. It was a red-capped toadstool called fly amanita, which Dom called "red dream plant" and no wonder. Anyone ingesting it risked nausea, seizures, hallucinations, and—once again—death. This was likely the hallucinogenic plant Dom had ingested to "talk to elders dead long time before" and the one his son had used along with Indian hellebore in the concoction meant to give him a peaceful death.

She marvelled at the knowledge of plants indigenous people possessed so long ago, but she had to wonder how many had been sickened or died while trying to figure out which species had what properties, and which ones could safely be eaten or used in other ways—or not. She couldn't imagine living in such a precarious world and she hoped Dom would come to appreciate the safety in this one.

Saturday and Sunday dawned warm and sunny, and there was no chance of keeping Dom indoors for the weekend. With everyone else busy on Saturday, Veronica took him to Stanley Park, where they strolled the length of the sea wall before stopping for fish and chips at the park's Tea House. They spent the afternoon roaming some of the lesser-travelled trails and finished up in front of the totem poles, to which Dom was inevitably drawn every time they came to the park.

They spent the evening playing checkers—Dom beat Veronica three games to one—and retired early. Sunday morning, they packed up their back packs and met Chloe, Ty, and Walter at the base of Grouse Mountain for another trek up the BC trail. It was an easier trip this time, all of them in better shape than they'd been for their first climb, and Dom steadier on his feet. They reached the end of the trail without any mishaps and ate once again at the Rusty Rail Outdoor BBQ. This time, fortunately, they didn't run into anyone who recognized them.

After their meal, Chloe suggested riding the chairlift to the mountain summit. She explained the ride to Dom, promising him the freshest mountain air and a breathtaking view.

"Yes," he said eagerly, "Dom want go top of mountain. Go forest."

Ty shrugged. Walter groaned. Then they were off to the chair lift.

Despite his enthusiasm beforehand, Dom white-knuckled the fourteen-minute ride, sitting between Chloe and Veronica, clearly uneasy with having empty air beneath his feet. After a few minutes' recovery, however, he took in the crisp mountain air with a wide smile on his face.

"Beautiful place," he said, peering out at the view from the 1600-metre-high summit. Looking around closer to them, blinking to focus, he asked, "We go walk in forest?"

Another groan from Walter. "Half an hour out on a trail, then we turn back. I'm not getting lost out here on some unmarked path"—he looked up at the sky, which had slowly been growing overcast—"especially with those clouds moving in. Could be snow coming up here, for all we know."

"Sounds good," Veronica agreed.

They took their walk on a little-travelled trail without getting lost. Back near the top of the chair lift, Walter thought to ask Dom if the sky stone place was near the top of whatever mountain it was on, halfway up, or near the bottom.

"Sky stone place not far up side of mountain," he said to a

collective sigh of relief. His words came slowly as he thought about it. "One morning walk. *Taa*." He nodded, pleased with his assessment.

"Well, that's helpful," Ty said. "All we have to do now is find the right mountain."

"I'm working on it," Veronica replied. "Believe me."

"Make sure you are. Summer's coming fast," Walter said.

On Monday, Dom was weary enough from the previous day's hike to agree to a day indoors, especially as a light rain was falling from a dull grey sky.

Veronica got out her laptop and Dom's drawing of his homeland and sat with them in front of her on the kitchen table.

"Dom, will you look at this again?" she asked, pushing the drawing over to him as he pulled up a chair beside her. "Are there any details you could add to help us find it on the computer?"

He frowned. "What mean word 'details'?"

"Well, it means small things like . . . anything you maybe forgot? Like . . . Oh! If you're standing here"—she poked at the middle of the landform—"where is the sun?"

"Sun in sky," he replied logically.

She groaned. "Well, yeah. What I mean is, where does it come up? Here?" She pointed to her right, then to her left. "Or here? Do you understand?"

"Dom understand." He got up and went to his room, coming back a moment later with his box of crayons and his magnifying glasses. He took his time finding the yellow crayon, then he turned the drawing on its side and drew a sun with an arrow pointing upwards at the right-hand edge of the paper.

"Seriously?" Veronica exclaimed. "You mean I've been looking at this sideways all this time? Why didn't you tell me?"

Stupid, she chastised herself. *Why didn't you ask him which way it went? God damn!*

He gave her a blank look and shrugged. She suspected he still didn't grasp the concept of maps and directions, other than the sun and stars and landmarks he'd been familiar with.

"Okay, fine," she said with a sigh. "That'll help. Thank you." She moved the cursor further north and to the west and started her search again.

Dom stayed at her side for about an hour, peering hard at the screen as Veronica zoomed the image in and out, left and right. Then he pushed to his feet with a groan of frustration.

"Dom no good help," he grumbled, pulling off his glasses. "Look computer long time make eyes hurt. Make head hurt."

"I know. I'm sorry. You don't have to keep it up. Why don't you make us some sandwiches for lunch?"

He nodded. "Dom make lunch," he said, adding under his breath, "Woman work."

She wanted to say something to encourage him but couldn't think what, so she let it go.

After an uninspired lunch of toasted peanut butter and jam sandwiches, Dom sat in the living room on his bear rug, a deer skin over his lap, knocking flakes off a chunk of obsidian and chanting softly in his language.

Veronica put on a load of washing and went back to her laptop and Google Maps. Dom joined her for the afternoon, but after supper he bailed, choosing to play checkers with himself, Scout curled against his hip, until taking his shower and going to bed.

Dom's bedroom door was still closed when Veronica rose the next morning. This was unusual, but she figured she would let him sleep in. She made coffee and toasted a bagel, and sat down with both at the desk in her bedroom to have another go at Google Maps.

Less than an hour later, she spotted an area just east of the coastal mountains, roughly between Kitimat and Prince George, that looked almost identical to Dom's drawing, particularly the three low mountains standing in a vertical line near the middle of the almost-island.

"Oh! My. God!" She jumped up so abruptly she knocked over her coffee cup, which was by now, thankfully, empty. "Oh, Dom. Dom! I think I've found it! Your homeland! You have to come and see…" She was heading to his room as she called for him.

"Dom!" She knocked on the door but when she received no response, she pushed it open. "Dom, get up! You—" Her next words died on her tongue.

He wasn't there.

28

ZEROING IN

It took Veronica all of five seconds to confirm that Dom wasn't in her apartment. Not in the bathroom. Not on the balcony. Not anywhere. His clothes and bag were still in his room, which was a good sign, but his cane was gone, indicating he'd gone for a walk. That was more than worrisome—she couldn't envision him wandering the city streets alone.

Heart racing in her throat and temples, she shoved her feet into her flip flops and dashed outside in near panic, still wearing the white tank top and shorts she'd slept in. She only registered once the front door clicked shut behind her that she hadn't brought her wallet, cell phone, or keys. She would have to buzz a neighbour to let her in.

I'll find Dom and worry about everything else later. Now, where the hell could he have gone?

After jogging around the building to make sure he wasn't communing with the cherry trees out back, she headed for the nearest green space, a playground a couple blocks away. Not finding him there, fighting the panic of a mother searching for her lost child, she hurried to the next logical choice—Kitsilano Beach.

She found him sitting in the sand, back comfortably against a log, apparently meditating.

"Dom!"

He startled and looked up as she reached him. "Vee. Why you here?"

"Why . . . Are you friggin' kidding me?" she demanded, fear and relief making her words sound harsher than she meant them to be. "You nearly gave me a heart attack! What the hell are you doing here?"

"Vee asleep. Dom want go out. Buy good coffee"—he waved a hand to the empty Starbuck's cup in the sand near his knee—"walk on beach. Listen ocean."

"Jesus Christ!" Her legs gave out and she sank into the cool sand beside him, disconcerted to find herself holding back tears. "I thought you... well, I don't know what I thought. I didn't know where... Dom, you can't go out alone like that. Do you understand?"

He looked sideways at her. "Dom not go out alone. *Aatay*?"

"Why? Because you—"

"More laws?"

"No, not a law. Just . . . you're special. You know that, don't you?" She studied him for a moment. Dressed in a black tee-shirt, khaki cargo shorts, and running shoes, he looked like an ordinary Native American guy. Not special at all.

"Long time past, Dom go much alone. Hunt. Fish. Search medicine plants. Search good stones for make tools. Go many years alone."

"I know that, Dom, but things are different now. The world's different. You have to be careful. If anything bad were to happen to you—"

"No bad thing happen Dom!" He grabbed his cane, pushed to his feet, and slapped sand from his butt with his left hand. "Why Vee here?" he asked again. Before she could reply, he started walking away, forcing her to follow.

She snatched up his empty cup and ran after him. "I had something to tell you. I think I found your people's homeland on the map."

Dom stopped in his tracks and turned back towards her, cloudy brown eyes wide. "Vee find *den-no-ny* land?"

"I think so. I came to get you in your room, and that's when I realized you'd gone out. I was looking for you to tell you. I'll show you when we get back to my place."

But this was more easily said than done. After buzzing three neighbours to no avail—apparently everyone was out and about this sunny morning—the elderly woman who lived three doors down from Veronica finally let them in.

Celia Wolts was waiting expectantly for them in the hallway, still in her housecoat, her white shih tzu cradled in her arms. A retired civil servant, she was a devoted Baptist who frequently volunteered at a women's shelter. She was also the building's resident busybody.

"Is everything all right?" she asked, giving Veronica a long look up and down.

Suddenly embarrassed by her lack of proper attire, Veronica crossed her arms over her chest. "Oh . . . yeah. Like I said, I locked myself out. Silly me."

"Hmm. And this must be the fellow they're looking for." Celia continued speaking to Veronica while her gaze fixed on Dom, who for his part was squinting in disdain at the little dog.

"What? What do you mean?" Veronica asked. "Who's looking for him?"

"Oh, a young couple came by a week or so ago. Red-haired woman and a tall black man. Asked me if I'd seen your friend here, said they wanted to talk to him. Asked me not to tell you they'd been around, but now . . . Well, here we are and it doesn't seem right not to."

"What did you tell them?"

"What could I tell them?" Celia replied. "Said I'd seen the two of you come in and go out together enough times to suppose you're a couple, but I hadn't had the pleasure." She shifted the dog to her left arm and stuck her right hand out to Dom. "Celia Wolts. Nice to meet you."

"Name Dom," he said and shook her hand.

"Dom. Hmm . . . that's an unusual name. What band are you from, if I might ask?"

"One you've never heard of," Veronica replied hastily in his place. "Thanks for buzzing us in, Celia. You have a nice day, now." With a hand pressed to Dom's back, she got him moving down the hallway towards her door.

Fortunately, her apartment door opened as it could only be locked with her key.

"What old woman Celia say?" Dom asked once they were safely inside. "People search Dom?"

"Yeah, um . . . Anne and Franco. You met them at Grouse Mountain, remember?"

He nodded. "Dom remember. Anne and Franco want talk to Dom?"

"They do," she said as an idea came to her. "Forget about them for now. Dom, I'm sorry I yelled at you earlier. I was just... I was scared. I don't know what I'd do if something happened to you." She gave in to her impulse and embraced him in what she hoped came across as a motherly hug, Celia's remark about thinking them a couple ringing in her mind. "Please don't go out again without telling me," she said into his neck.

"Yes, Vee. Dom tell Vee when go out."

"Okay." She let him go and took a step back, realizing at the same time that he hadn't actually said he would ask for permission. "Now come on, let's take a look at Google Maps." She brought her laptop out to the kitchen and sat down beside him at the table to look at it.

She let him manipulate the map, let him study it for as long as he wanted.

After about ten minutes of zooming in and out on the image, he pointed to a wide area at the bottom of the screen, on the north shore of Tetachuk Lake and east of the southern base of the southernmost mountain, known as Wells Gray Peak. "*Den-no-ny* live here many years. Three mountains on *den-no-ny* land. Many lakes, many rivers around." He pointed to Wells Gray Peak. "Man Dom go up mountain here." He moved his finger northwards and slightly east. "People move here after red spot sickness." He pointed to the snow-capped peaks of the coast mountain range on the far left of the screen. "Much high mountains here." He looked sideways at Veronica and broke into a grin. "Vee find Dom homeland. Close Vancouver?"

"No, not close," she said, her voice shaking with excitement, "but definitely reachable. Hang on . . ." She reached for the mouse and explored the image for a minute. "It's a provincial park now, a protected area called Tweedsmuir North Park."

"Tweed-smeer North Park," he repeated carefully.

"Close enough. Dom . . . are you sure, absolutely positive this is the right place?"

For a moment he looked doubtful. Then his smile returned, even wider than before. "Yes, Dom sure. Dom know three mountains on homeland. Good place, Dom remember. We go?"

"Oh, yeah," she assured him, "but we can't just rush off willy-nilly. We have to plan our trip," she explained at the look of confusion on Dom's face. "First I need to tell Walter about this. Then . . . oh, God, there's so much to do. But don't worry, we'll go there this summer. You'll see your homeland again, Dom. I promise you."

By Friday evening, Veronica felt she was zeroing in on a number of targets.

To begin with—and most importantly, to be sure—Dom identified the site south and slightly east of his homeland where he said the meteorite had landed. If he wasn't mistaken, it was partway up the northwest face of a 2400-metre peak called Far Mountain, in what was now Itcha Ilgachuz Provincial Park.

She'd talked to Walter and Gerald Sutherland, both of whom had their own reasons for wanting to accompany Dom to his ancestral lands, and they'd agreed to meet at her place on Saturday to discuss how to proceed.

She and Dom had spent Thursday afternoon with Becky, slowly advancing her film project and getting Dom used to talking to a camera.

Finally, she'd contacted Franco Paulo and agreed to give him a debut interview in hopes of piquing interest in Dom's story before her book and Becky's film got any further along. If members of the scientific community weren't ready to believe in a living, breathing Neolithic man, she hoped the general public was. She and Dom would be meeting Franco at the sushi place near UBC on Monday.

On the bad news side of things, Neil was making no progress in acquiring legal status for Dom. While the man's facial structure and colouring made it obvious he was of Native American blood, without proof of birth it would be hard to acquire official recognition. Judge Chamberlain had suggested meeting with Veronica and Dom to discuss the matter, and Neil scheduled that for Friday of the following week. Veronica planned to tell him exactly who Dom was in hopes of cutting through some of the bureaucratic red tape.

Saturday afternoon found Veronica, Dom, Walter, Gerald, and Neil gathered in Veronica's living room to hash out a plan for visiting Tweedsmuir North and Itcha Ilgachuz Provincial Parks. Gerald, who appeared to those unacquainted with him to be a stuffy academic, had a touch of Indiana Jones inside him. He also had contacts all over B.C.; he would take care of finding a lodge or a campground and a guide to see them safely to where they wanted to go.

Veronica would make sure that she, Dom, Walter, and Chloe, whom she knew wanted to be part of the mission, had the clothes and equipment they needed. Neil didn't want to leave Becky and Caroline for any extended period of time, but a long call to Ty ended with him saying he wanted to join them if Amanda could get her sister to come and help her with the girls while he was gone. This meant they would be six, seven in all with the guide.

Walter, for his part, was willing to finance the entire venture in return, of course, for undisputed credit for the discovery of the life-altering mutated *Bacillus F*.

"What if we don't find it?" Veronica had to ask. "It's been 9,000, 10,000 years, Walt. It could be gone, dried up or dead or . . . I don't know. Just gone." She gave him a low look. "Are you going to send us all a bill for expenses?"

"I'm not," he assured her as the others looked on, "although I might ask you, Veronica, for a cut of the millions you're going to make with your book, in payment of Dom's medical care. We did talk about that, if you remember."

"I remember," she said dryly. "We'll talk about it again—with lawyers present—if the situation arises."

"Fair enough."

The meeting ended shortly after that with Gerald agreeing to join Veronica, Chloe, and Dom for a hike in the mountains the following morning.

29

QUESTIONS AND ANSWERS

Sunday's hike in Cypress Provincial Park had been enjoyably uneventful and, for Veronica, something of a blur as she was constantly preoccupied with thoughts of today's meeting with Franco Paulo. At first she'd considered bringing Dom along, then she decided against it in case Franco proved to be the sort of unscrupulous reporter she wanted to keep Dom away from. Not liking the idea of leaving him alone at her place any better, she'd asked Chloe to spend the afternoon with him.

Chloe had happily accepted, arriving at Veronica's apartment with the suggestion of taking Dom to see the outdoor exhibits at the Museum of Anthropology that they'd missed last time because of the rain. Veronica reluctantly succumbed to pressure from both Chloe and Dom, who promised to behave themselves—whatever that meant. She said she would join them at the museum as soon as she'd finished with Franco.

She parked across the street from the restaurant and met up with the journalism student already seated at a table on the outdoor terrace. She was pleasantly surprised to find him looking professional in dark jeans and a pressed red shirt, electronic tablet in hand.

They said their hellos and ordered lunch and Franco asked Veronica if he could record their conversation, promising her every word would remain confidential. He would send her the written piece to proof and approve.

She asked him to sign a document confirming this and then,

between sips of their wine coolers and bites of sushi, she began Dom's story with her being called to witness a discovery at Bennett Lake.

Franco knew what his girlfriend, Anne, knew, but little of what happened after the mysterious mud man was transported to the hospital in Whitehorse. Veronica gave him a brief rundown on the patient's condition and progress, admitting things had been touch and go at first, and that doctors considered it a miracle he'd survived at all.

"They had no idea at the time just what a huge miracle his being alive actually is." She went on to tell him that after the man had regained consciousness and the ability to breathe on his own, he was transferred to a private medical facility for his long-term care.

"To Cooper Medical, you mean," Franco said. "What?" he added as Veronica raised an eyebrow. "It wasn't hard to figure out, Professor Booth, given who your ex-husband is. I do my research, you know?"

"So, you do. You can't mention it, though," she warned, "or you'll have Walter's lawyer making sure you never write anything again."

He nodded and grinned, showing straight white teeth. "Fair enough. I won't. So the patient was transferred to an undisclosed private medical facility. And then what?"

"Then we discovered who he is.

"And that would be . . ." Franco's dark eyes narrowed, and he leaned slightly forwards across the table towards Veronica. "Anne says they dug him out of a sort of thawing bog determined to be thousands of years old. Professor Sutherland told her the artefacts found with him are thousands of years old."

"It was and they are." Veronica hesitated. She'd been worried that Franco wanted only to write a sensational article to grab himself some quick fame, but for the past hour and a half, he'd struck her as a serious and thoughtful investigative journalist. "There's a reason why the RCMP weren't able to identify him through any of the usual means, and why they thought the first DNA sample they'd taken from him was corrupted. Give or take a few hundred, Dom's the same age as the other stuff . . . 9,500 years old."

The young man's dark eyes grew wide and his jaw dropped. After a few seconds his mouth shut with a click of his teeth and he said, "He can't . . . that's . . . that's impossible. Professor Booth . . . do you realize what you're saying?"

"I do," she said, "and I have incontrovertible proof or I wouldn't have believed it myself." She went on to tell him about the radiocarbon dating and DNA tests done on Dom's shoe, clothing, and possessions. She assured him that she had all the results to back up her claim, not to mention Dom's second DNA analysis and his own incredible but undeniable testimony.

They concluded the interview with Veronica promising to give Franco more after he got this part of the story printed in the *Vancouver Sun* or another respectable newspaper. No tabloids, blogs, or social media, or the deal was off.

Franco turned off the recorder and picked up the tab, which Veronica thought was decent of him, and they each made their way to their cars.

Veronica texted Chloe, who said to join Dom and her out by the museum's famous reflecting pool. Twenty minutes later the three of them were together. They sat on the lawn near the Haida House to chat, Dom telling Veronica what he'd seen on his visit, and Veronica telling him and Chloe about the interview. Afterward, Chloe left in her car and Veronica drove Dom back to her place, stopping on the way to pick up groceries for the week.

True to his word, Franco Paulo sent Veronica his story by email Wednesday afternoon. After painstakingly reading it through with Dom, who insisted on it, and making only a few minor edits, she sent it back with her blessing.

Neil came over for lunch on Friday, and they prepared their meeting with Judge Chamberlain in his office at the courthouse. Too late, Veronica realized Dom didn't possess anything close to a suit. Any item of Neil's would be two sizes too big, so she had him wear his grey denims and a white tee-shirt, and she tied his hair tightly at the nape of his neck with a strip of leather he cut from one of his deerskins.

"It doesn't matter what he looks like," said Neil, who had on a dark business suit, while Veronica wore a colourful blouse and white slacks. "Once we tell Judge Chamberlain who Dom is, he's not going to notice anything else."

He was right.

After Veronica spoke for almost an hour, telling the judge everything she felt he needed to know, the older man sat back in his chair, hands clasped in his lap, bifocals practically hanging off the end of his nose.

"I've never heard such an incredible story in all my life," he said in a low voice. Somewhere amidst Veronica's tale, he'd lost all colour in his cheeks. Visibly shaken, he pushed his glasses up, rose from behind his desk, and availed himself of a shot of what looked like whiskey from a cut glass decanter standing on one of the bookshelves. This seemed to fortify him somewhat and he returned to his desk ready for more.

"So . . . you understand what the problem is?" Neil asked once the judge resumed his seat. "About getting a birth certificate, social insurance number, medical card, or anything?"

"I do indeed." Judge Chamberlain rested a long look at Dom, who'd sat in silence, fidgeting only occasionally during Veronica's oration. "Do you understand what's going on, son? Why you're here today?"

Veronica drew in a sharp breath. She'd coached Dom extensively for this meeting, but she wasn't sure how much he'd truly absorbed.

"Yes, Dom understand," he said carefully, as if thinking through every word. "Gerald find Dom dead not dead in ground.

Doctors make Dom alive again. Long time before, Dom father. Hunter. Healer. Elder. Good man. Now time, Dom . . ." He shrugged. "Law say not leg-al, no good. Dom want be good man. Be leg-al." He looked at Veronica and smiled broadly, clearly pleased with himself.

"Good." Judge Chamberlain nodded and leaned forwards slightly towards Dom. "That's good to hear." Looking from Dom, to Veronica, to Neil, he added, "This is far outside the realm of my usual responsibilities, but obviously, it's a unique case and . . . What is it they say? Extreme circumstances call for extreme measures? Let me make a few calls—discreetly, of course—and see what I can do." He looked back to Veronica. "You say the NDA has been lifted?"

"It has."

"What about the emergency guardianship of an incapacitated adult you filed last year?"

Veronica shot a sideways glance at Dom, who didn't know anything about that. "Um . . . It's still in place. Just in case . . ."

"Fair enough. Lastly, you say you're going public with Dom's identity?"

"I am. The news should break in the next few days."

"Well, I suppose that might help." The judge pushed to his feet, and the others followed suit. "I'll get back to you as soon as I can." He came around from behind his desk and stuck his right hand out. "It's a pleasure and an honour to meet you, Dom. I hope to see you again soon."

Dom shook hands with the judge, then Neil and Veronica did as well. They left the courthouse hopeful that they'd at least taken the first concrete steps towards making Dom a recognized and legal member of modern society.

Franco's story was published the next day in the *Vancouver Sun.*

On Monday, one week after her first conversation with the journalism student, Veronica sat down with him for a follow-up interview. This time, they were at the Starbucks café near her apartment and this time, Dom was with them.

After exchanging greetings, they ordered iced drinks and sat down at a table on the outdoor terrace, Dom to Veronica's left, with Franco across from them.

"I'm not sure how well you speak English, Dom," Franco began. "Professor Booth told me you do, but . . ."

"Yes, Dom speak English," he replied promptly. "Learn many words. Learn letters for write words."

"Oh, great then." Franco seemed flustered as he plunged ahead. "Well, it's great to meet you. That is, we met up on Grouse, didn't we, but we didn't get a chance to talk. You look good for . . . I mean . . . Shit, I'm sorry, I don't even know what the hell to say to you." He grabbed his mocha Frappuccino and took a long sip that made him gasp and cough when the iced drink hit his throat.

Dom looked sideways at Veronica, his forehead creased in confusion, and shook his head.

Veronica threw her hands up in an "I don't know" gesture and sipped her iced coffee.

Franco's right, though, she thought. In his grey denims and a taupe tee-shirt, his dark hair loose to his shoulders, Dom looked extraordinarily good for a man who'd been frozen solid for millennia.

Dom gazed across the table at Franco. "Franco want talk Dom? Ask questions? Dom answer."

"Oh. Right. Awesome." Franco pulled his tablet from his messenger bag and powered it up. "You, uh . . ." He looked at Veronica. "Do I have your permission to record our conversation?"

"You do. Same deal as last time," she replied.

"Great, thanks."

"Just take it easy. Use simple words and don't talk too fast, okay?"

"Right, got it."

They sipped their drinks, then Franco asked Dom what he remembered from when he woke up in the hospital.

"Dom remember wake up in hospital. Bad light, bad smell.

Dom not understand people words." He paused. "Dom much pain. Hands. Feet. Hip. Throat. Eyes. Much afraid."

"I can only imagine," Franco admitted, nodding sympathetically. "But in time, you started to get better?"

"Yes. Many days go, Dom better. Sit. Drink. Eat. Dom not see good. Not understand where place. . . First think Dom dead. After think Dom not dead. Think lost in faraway place."

"And you are, aren't you? Far away from your home physically, of course, and even further away in time. Now . . . um, now that you've adjusted somewhat, how do you like living in our time? In Vancouver?"

"*T-lay*. Dom not much like city Vancouver," he conceded with a shake of his head. "Much noise. Much bad smell. Many people. Many laws." He shot a sideways glance at Veronica, who'd been listening in silence, ready to intercede if necessary.

She felt herself swelling with pride and admiration for the man Dom was becoming. Or re-becoming, which was probably closer to the truth. She could only imagine what he would be in another year or two.

"There are some things you like, Dom," she encouraged him. She gestured towards his cup of iced coffee. "You like coffee, don't you? Sushi? Donuts? What else do you like?"

He thought for a moment. "Yes. Dom like coffee. Like elect-ricity make hot water for wash and light for see in dark. Like soft bed for sleep. Good doctor for make sick people better. Dom friends Vee, Chloe, Ty. Dom like much." He paused and turned towards Veronica. "Dom like car for easy go far away place. Soon go Dom people homeland."

"Really?" Franco asked, his voice rising in surprise. "You're going back to Bennett Lake?"

"Not Bennett Lake, exactly," Veronica put in before Dom could give away too much. "Another place further south where his people lived when he was a boy. I can't tell you the precise location, though. I'm saving that for my book."

"Dom show friends *den-no-ny* homeland," Dom went on, but his words slowed as he thought through what he was saying.

"Beautiful forest. Mountains. Good water. Good smell. Forest remain. Water remain. No *den-no-ny* remain. All dead long time before." He reached for his drink and took a deep swallow.

"Yeah, I know. I'm sorry about that, man." Franco was silent for a long moment.

"What's wrong, Franco?" Veronica asked as the silence grew uncomfortable.

The young man shrugged. "Just trying to imagine how I'd feel if I were in his position, waking up to find my whole world gone."

"And?"

"And . . . I'm not sure I'd want to go on"—he shook his head—"if I'd lost everyone and everything I cared about. I mean, he has, hasn't he?"

"He has," she admitted.

She waited until they finished their drinks before pulling out her cell phone and opening the file of photos she'd taken of the walls in Dom's room at Cooper Medical. "Dom drew all this," she said. "You can see his tipi tent, his family, his dog, scenes from his life."

Franco was scrolling slowly through the photos as she spoke. Suddenly he stopped and held the cell up so that Veronica and Dom could see it, although Dom certainly couldn't make anything of the tiny image from across the table. "That's a . . . what'd you call it? Woolly mammoth?"

"It is," Veronica said. "Dom, tell him about the mammoth."

"Uh, yes. Mam-moth." He nodded. "Dom go with hunters for kill mam-moth. Much meat, good skin, good iv-ory." He grinned. "Big day for Dom. Tell story to children and children of children."

"He has it all up here"—Veronica tapped her forehead while Franco gaped at Dom—"and he wants to share it with us. He wants to teach us all about it, about his time and his people. I'm compiling a dictionary of his language. He's shown me how to make stone tools and how to scrape skins. He's told me what plants his people ate and which ones they used for medicine, and . . . well, I'm sure it's just the beginning. As his English improves, he'll teach me—all of us—more than we could ever imagine.

"We want to tell everyone about his world. In addition to my book, we're shooting a documentary with Becky Booth—my brother's wife," she added at the puzzled look on Franco's face. "Before we get too far into those, however, I need to stir up some interest in Dom's story, and that's where you come in. As I told you before, it looks like the scientific community is holding onto the impossibility of Dom's existence, but as you can see and hear, he's exactly what I claim he is."

They ended the interview with Franco taking a couple photos of Dom and Veronica and promising once again to send his story to Veronica for her approval before submitting it to the newspaper.

"Dom talk good?" he asked Veronica as they walked back to her apartment. "Say good answers?"

"You did, yeah. I'm so proud of you for the way you handled yourself today." Having been careful until now to avoid making any gesture that might be misconstrued, she resisted the urge to slip her arm around his back and pull him in for a hug. Then she thought, *What the hell*, and did it anyway.

Dom slowed for a second, then he reciprocated, and they walked like that, in comfortable silence, the rest of the way home.

Saturday was July 1, Canada Day. Shops and businesses were closed for the national holiday, but touristic and historical sites were open. Gerald Sutherland had called Veronica the previous afternoon to invite her and Dom to visit the Fort Langley historical site with him, suggesting it would contribute to Dom's ongoing education.

Veronica agreed, so they met Gerald and his wife, Linda,

their eighteen-year-old son, Lucas, and his girlfriend, Maddy, at 8:00 Wednesday morning for the annual pancake breakfast held at the fort.

They spent the rest of the day touring the former Hudson's Bay trading post, taking in the stone bastion, the blacksmith's forge, the big house, and the servants' quarters. Veronica and Gerald explained everything to Dom while Linda and the teenagers mainly just gawked in awe at the revived Neolithic man. Gerald had got them up to speed about who Dom was, but while they clearly hadn't absorbed it yet, they'd neither ridiculed him for being a fraud nor run away screaming. Veronica could only hope the general public would be as charitable.

"White-skin England people and Europe people come in big boats? Come from far away land? Far side ocean?" Dom wanted to clarify after Gerald gave him a very brief history of Canada's early colonization by Europeans.

"That's right," Gerald said.

"Why they come?"

"Well, there's a good question. Some came to start new lives in a new place, some to be free of taxes and laws in their countries. Some were simply looking for adventure or a way to make money."

Dom thought about this for a moment. "England people meet Dom people?"

"No, Dom," Veronica replied this time. "Your people would have already been gone by the time Europeans got here."

He frowned. "Why gone? Where they go?"

"I don't know. Maybe there was another sickness, or some really bad winters where many died from cold and hunger. Maybe they left your homeland for whatever reason and mixed in with other peoples." She thought of the markers in his DNA that were also found in a number of Native American tribes, but she wasn't about to start explaining DNA to him here and now. "That's one of the questions we hope to find answers to when we go back there this summer with you."

Dom nodded, seeming to accept this, and they continued their walk around the fort without him asking any more difficult questions. He had no idea of the extent of devastation European explorers and colonists had wreaked on indigenous populations in both North and South America. No clue about the tragic "Trail of Tears" in the southeastern US in the nineteenth century. No notion of the thousands of unmarked graves of indigenous children discovered in recent years on the grounds of residential schools across Canada. Veronica hoped to protect him from this disgusting and heartbreaking knowledge, at least for a little while longer.

That evening, Veronica took Dom to Stanley Park, where they stood amongst a substantial crowd near the famous Nine O'clock Cannon to watch the fireworks emanating from the Vancouver Harbour, an enjoyable end to what she thought of as a good and productive day.

He is happy he talked to Franco the reporter and Gerald's family. Happy he talked about his people. He wants everyone in this now time to know about his people in the long time before. He is sad the white-skin people make museums and forts to remember time before, but no one, not even the brown-skin people like Chloe and Ty, remember his people.

30

FULL SPEED AHEAD

Veronica took Dom to Cooper Medical Thursday morning for a therapy session with Ty and a workout on the stationary bike.

While Dom was at it in the PT room, Vee met with Walter in his office, at his request.

"I've made appointments for Dom with Dr. Russell at her office, as she suggested when she was here," Walter began. "I also found a dentist who's willing to overlook the fact that Dom has no B.C. Care card—for the right amount of cash, which one of my investors has graciously offered to provide—and perform whatever repairs he needs done on his teeth." He handed her a paper with two dates written down on it.

She had two weeks to prepare Dom for these potentially stressful if not terrifying appointments.

"Thanks, Walt," she said, meaning it. "Between Christmas, Dom's illness, and the excitement of presenting him to the world, I completely forgot about this stuff."

What kind of guardian does that make me?

Walter joined Dom and her for lunch in the cafeteria. Then she and Dom visited with Gracie and her dad in the sunroom before heading back to her apartment. As it had begun to rain heavily around noon, they spent the rest of the day working on the dictionary that would be part of Veronica's book, Veronica forcing herself to speak a little bit of Dom's language as she wrote out his words phonetically.

Franco's interview with Dom came out in Friday morning's *Vancouver Sun* and that very afternoon, the media circus Walter had been worried about began.

Veronica and Dom had spent the damp but mostly sunny day with Becky and her three-person film crew, Chloe in tow, to talk about her experiences with Dom, on a quiet stretch of the beach near UBC. They'd all had supper together at the sushi restaurant near the university, and then Veronica and Dom had returned to her place.

"Professor Booth?" a woman's voice called out as they headed from Veronica's car to the back door of the building.

Turning, Veronica saw a petite Asian woman and a tall, bearded blond man with a video camera mounted on one shoulder striding towards them from the far corner of the parking lot. Both were neatly dressed in khakis and polo shirts, hers white and his navy blue. The red light on top of the camera indicated that it was rolling.

"My name is Lin Chen," the woman said, reaching them just as Veronica realized she recognized her, "and this is Rob, my cameraman."

Rob gave a thumbs-up in greeting but kept on filming.

"We're with Global's Vancouver affiliate, CHAN," Lin went on. "Do you have a few minutes to chat?"

Glancing sideways at Dom, who nodded, Veronica said, "Sure, we can do that." She looked up to see nosy Mrs. Wolts peering down at them from between the curtains on her window. "But not here. Let's go to the park down the street."

"Whatever you want," Lin said agreeably. She motioned for Rob to cut the camera.

Fifteen minutes later, they were sitting at a picnic table in the middle of the park. On the way, Veronica had warned Dom to let her do the talking, but she wasn't confident he would keep his mouth shut if asked a direct question.

"Well, I've been reading about Dom since the first piece came out," Lin began, as Rob started filming again, "and I believe his story deserves some news coverage. I think our viewers would be fascinated to see him and hear from him."

"I'm sure they would be," Veronica agreed. "I'm currently working on a comprehensive book as well as a documentary with an independent film maker, but I think a few minutes in the news would be a great way to stir up interest." Responding to Lin's questions, she explained how she'd come to oversee Dom's care and adaptation to the modern world.

"And what makes you—the both of you," she added, looking straight at Dom, "believe Dom actually spent . . . what was it? Over nine thousand years . . . in a frozen bog?"

Veronica rattled off the scientific findings she accepted as proof of Dom's origin without mentioning the mutated *Bacillus F.*, adding that as she grew to know the man, it became clear he was what he appeared to be.

"But he didn't come out of it unscathed," she finished. "He lost his toes, the tips of his fingers and most of one thumb, as you can see, and his hearing and vision are impaired. He also suffered seizures the first weeks, although he hasn't had one now in months."

Lin's eyes narrowed to brown slits. "Thousands of years," she murmured. Raising her voice in a tone suggesting disbelief, she asked, "And yet he speaks English?"

"Obviously, he didn't at first," Veronica replied. "But he's learning, far better than I'm learning his language, which he's trying to teach me."

"Fascinating," Lin said, nodding as her eyes went back to normal. "May I ask him a couple questions?"

"Depends what."

"Well, I guess I want to know . . . Dom? What has it been like for you since waking up and finding yourself in a whole new world?"

"New world," Dom said thoughtfully. "All things Dom world gone. Dom learn all things new world. Learn English words. Learn letters for write words. Learn food, clothes. Learn laws. Do, do, do. Not do, not do, not do."

Veronica groaned and shook her head, but Lin smiled.

"Do you have any idea why you survived being frozen for so long?" the reporter asked. "You do realize you're the only person in history who's had such an experience, don't you?"

Dom frowned the way he did when he didn't understand. "What mean word, 'survive'? Word, 'ex-pe-rens'? "

"Oh, um . . . Let me rephrase that. Do you know why you're alive today?"

Veronica tried to tell Dom not to answer with a discreet shake of her head, but he either didn't see or chose to ignore the gesture. "Vee say small germs inside Dom make Dom stay alive in ice ground much long time."

"Germs? Really?" Lin turned to Veronica. "Could you explain further, Professor Booth?"

Although she hadn't wanted to go into this, Veronica reluctantly told Lin how Dom's doctors suspected a bacteria found in his system may have played a role in his survival. She didn't mention the theory that it might have been mutated by a meteorite, nor that it had apparently extended his lifetime far past the usual years. She did say that a strong course of antibiotics had wiped them out and that Dom no longer harboured any trace of the bacteria in his body.

"Do you know where or how he became infected?" Rob enquired from behind his camera.

"We don't," Veronica replied before Dom could, "and for the moment we can't say anything more about it as its origin is still under investigation."

"I understand," Lin said, although she looked like she wanted more. "Well, Dom"—she turned to him, Rob and his camera following—"I'm glad to have met you. I wish you luck navigating modern day Canada and I hope to see you again soon."

"Thank you. Yes, Dom see Lin again. Talk more." He looked up at the clouds, blinking, and took a long, deep breath in through his nose. "Rain come soon."

Rob chuckled under his breath.

"Really? How do you know?" Lin asked.

Dom shrugged. "Dom know."

"Dom is far more in tune with nature than any of us are," Veronica told her. She pushed to her feet.

"Right. Okay then." Lin signaled for Rob to stop filming. "Thank you, Professor Booth. Thank you, Dom. I'll run this past my producer and see if we can get it on tomorrow's evening news."

They walked back to Veronica's apartment building, arriving just as the rain began.

"Dom, you're amazing!" Lin exclaimed, laughing, as she and Rob dashed for their car.

"You really like it, don't you?" Veronica asked Dom once they were inside. "Talking to people about your life?"

"*Taa*. Dom like talk to people. Tell people Dom life long time before." He grinned widely, his eyes shining between the nebulous spots.

They spent the evening sharing stories from Dom's youth and Veronica's childhood in Kamloops, the cats curled up in their laps, only going to bed when they became too sleepy to keep their eyes open or string more than two words together.

Walter called Veronica Saturday morning to let her know that with some help from Ty, whose cousin had a friend who was a wilderness guide based out of Williams Lake, plans for their trip were moving full speed ahead. He'd booked a vacation for himself from August 3 to August 16, hoping that two weeks would be long enough for them all to find what they were looking for. As much as he wanted to go, Ty had to decline as Amanda's sister wasn't able to come after all. However, his cousin's friend, Pat, was going to round up camping supplies and handle the logistics of the trip, including the charter of a helicopter or floatplane to get them from Williams Lake to as close to Far Mountain as possible. After spending a few days there and hopefully finding the site marked by Dom when he was fifteen, they would head north to Tetachuck Lake and Dom's homeland to scout out possible archeological sites for future exploration.

Veronica gave the news to Gerald, who admitted he'd been on the verge of informing her he'd had no luck finding a guide on such short notice. Ty had come through at just the right time.

She had a month to learn whatever other details she could glean from Dom and get him, Chloe, and herself ready for the wilderness excursion of a lifetime. Gerald, for his part, would take care of preparing Walter.

There had been too much rain the past few days to hike in the mountains, so Veronica and Dom took a brisk walk all the way around the Stanley Park sea wall. They got home just in time to turn on the 6:00 news. Only minutes later, Lin Chen's interview with Dom and her aired after a brief introduction by one of the news anchors.

Barely ten minutes after the newscast ended, there came a frantic rapping on Veronica's door. She had a good idea who was there before she squinted through the peep hole.

"I knew there was something peculiar about that man," Celia Wolts said as Veronica opened the door. She craned her neck to see past Veronica into the apartment. "Is he here now?"

"I assume you mean Dom?" Veronica asked, as if she could have meant anyone else. "He is. Do you want to see him?"

"I do not!" the woman exclaimed, grey eyes wide behind her glasses. "He's an abomination, Veronica! Our Heavenly Father never meant for anyone to—"

"Please, Celia," Veronica interrupted her. "You don't know anything about him."

"Well, I know you. And I know you're not a churchgoer, but I never would have imagined you'd be involved in anything as diabolic as raising the dead. Well, how could anyone . . . That man shouldn't be—"

"All good, Vee?" Dom asked, coming up behind her.

Celia gasped and took a step backwards into the hallway,

one hand over her mouth and the colour draining from her face, as if she faced a ghost or a demon.

"Everything's fine," Veronica said, her instinct to protect Dom kicking in. She slammed the door closed and locked it. "Celia Wolts just wanted to tell me she saw us on TV."

She called to order chicken for supper, then spent the time waiting for the delivery on the phone organizing tomorrow's hike to St. Mark's Summit in Cypress Provincial Park.

Chloe arrived at the apartment early Sunday morning, followed a few minutes later by Gerald Sutherland. They piled into Gerald's SUV with the day's necessities and drove to the parking lot near Horseshoe Bay, where they met up with Walter.

The trail was rugged and slick, the hike the roughest one yet, but if they wanted to be ready to trek through Itcha Ilgachuz Provincial Park in a month's time, they had to push themselves. They left the mountain exhausted and muddy, Dom limping slightly on his bad leg and Walter with a sore ankle and scraped hands from a spill late in the day, and parted for their respective homes.

"Oh, you've gotta be kidding," Chloe muttered as Gerald's car approached Veronica's apartment building.

Veronica peered from the middle seat where she sat with Dom to see eight or nine people gathered in front of her building.

"I wonder what that's all about," Gerald said.

"I'll give you one guess," Veronica replied. "Drive around back, will you?"

He did, but it didn't help. Before his three passengers could get out of the SUV, the group descended on them, cell phone cameras raised to capture the moment.

Several people called for Dom.

"Holy cow," said Gerald, something like awe in his voice.

"Why people call Dom?" Dom asked, turning in his seat to look out the side window.

"They probably saw you on TV, or read about you in the newspaper," Veronica said. "They want to meet you."

Like groupies hoping for a glimpse of a rock star.

"Ah." He grinned. "Dom talk people?"

"No. I don't think that's a good idea."

"Why not good idea?"

Why not, indeed? Veronica thought. *This is what I wanted, isn't it?* "Okay. Look, they'll probably want pictures more than conversation. Let me talk first, and whatever you do, don't say anything about the germs or the sky stone or how long you lived with your people. Do you understand?"

He nodded again. "Yes. Not talk bac-teria germ. Not talk sky stone. Dom understand."

"Okay then." She rested her hand on the door handle. "Here we go."

"Hang on," Gerald said suddenly. He drove slowly forwards to pull the SUV into the empty visitors' parking slot. "I'll come with you."

They disembarked and met with the group. What followed was half an hour of disorganized but not frantic exchanges. Veronica spoke first, controlling the narrative, and Gerald related how his students had found Dom in the thawing permafrost soil near Bennett Lake.

As Chloe chatted with the three younger women, Veronica heard snippets about what a kind and good man Dom was. About how smart he was, and how she was learning as much from him as he was from her.

Dom repeated what he'd said to Franco and Lin, that he was sad for the loss of his people and didn't particularly like life in the city. He showed them his hands and eyes and explained that, like his feet, they were hurt from being in the cold ground. He told them he didn't know why he was alive. As promised, he made no mention of things he shouldn't, despite one man's insistent, repeated questions. He posed for pictures—everyone wanted several, despite his muddy jeans and sweaty tee-shirt— and printed his name in large letters across the top of one young woman's newspaper.

Finally, the little crowd seemed satisfied and began to

disperse. Chloe, Veronica, and Dom collected their backpacks and Gerald left for home. Chloe accompanied Veronica and Dom upstairs, the three of them sharing their thoughts about the day's experience.

Too tired to cook, Veronica once again ordered supper, Thai this time. They showered and changed into clean clothes while they waited for the delivery. Dom donned only his black gym shorts, saying he was too hot for more clothes. Veronica immediately took his temperature but no, he wasn't sick, just looking for an excuse to flout the concept of etiquette in polite company.

"At least he put shorts on," Chloe said with a giggle. "I've seen the drawings of how his people dressed—or didn't dress—in summer."

As they ate, the women explained to Dom what a celebrity was.

He smiled and nodded, seeming to take it all in stride, but Veronica suspected he hadn't a clue what it all really meant. She wondered if any of them did.

After supper, while Chloe and Dom sampled her CDs, Veronica opened her email inbox to find a message from Mary Roberts, the editor of *Canadian Anthropology*. Given recent events, Ms. Roberts wrote, she'd changed her mind and would like to print Veronica's paper in the next issue.

Veronica wanted to tell Ms. Roberts just what she thought of that, but the truth was, she wanted to be published in a peer-reviewed journal just as much as she wanted to be rich and famous. After careful consideration, she replied with a politely worded message thanking the editor and saying she looked forward to seeing her paper in print.

Then she called Walter and told him what he'd missed.

31

ON THE WAY

The following three weeks flew by, the days filled with work on Veronica's book, Becky's film, and Chloe's thesis, which was now in the editing stage. Veronica, Dom, Walter, and Chloe took long hikes every weekend to get into the best shape possible, even tackling Grouse Mountain's famous Grouse Grind trail. Sandwiched between these activities were visits from independent journalists as well as news crews from CTV, CBC, and even CNN, all of them wanting an interview with Veronica but especially Dom, the man of the hour.

Chloe set up a Facebook page under the banner "DOM THE MUD MAN." She and Veronica wrote short entries, shared some photos, and responded to the growing number of readers posting questions or encouraging comments. They were careful to delete comments suggesting Dom should burn in hell or not exist at all, or accusing them of perpetrating an elaborate hoax before Dom could see them. Despite his difficulty negotiating the computer keyboard, he wrote a few words from time to time, mostly in answer to a question or sharing something innocuous about his day.

Veronica spent hours talking to Dom about his upcoming appointments, explaining the importance of them and telling him as exactly as she could what he should expect.

Everything went smoothly when she and Walter took Dom to Dr. Russell's clinic. The specialist and her assistants gave his eyes a thorough examination using all the high-tech instruments at the ultra-modern facility. Unfortunately, after reviewing the results, Dr. Russell retracted her earlier suggestion that surgery might be a possibility to improve Dom's vision.

"Do you understand?" Veronica asked when Dr. Russell finished her explanations. Remembering how he'd reacted last time, she was concerned about his receiving more bad news.

"Yes, Dom understand," he said, surprising her with is casual tone. "Dom eyes no good. Stay no good. No more talk heal Dom eyes."

And that was that.

Three days later, the visit to Dr. Chase, a middle-aged dentist with Native American traits, ended on a happier note.

Dom declined the offered IV sedation and white-knuckled it through x-rays, examination, freezing, and the filling of three teeth fully conscious, although with his eyes tightly closed much of the time. Walter insisted everything be done in one sitting as he was afraid Dom wouldn't return for a second visit. By the end of the afternoon, Dr. Chase was pleased with his work and Veronica couldn't have been prouder of the way Dom handled it all.

The fourth week of July, Neil got back to Veronica with mixed news concerning the procedure to get Dom legal status. There appeared to be a path for him, but it began with acquiring something called a Secure Certificate of Indian Status. Since he didn't have a birth certificate, however, Dom needed a guarantor. Veronica, Neil, Walter, and Judge Chamberlain all qualified, but said guarantor must have known the person concerned for at least two years. Therefore, paperwork would be on hold until next summer.

Veronica almost laughed aloud at this. *If things go as planned, the entire world will know Dom's identity by next summer, legal status or not.*

When she gave Dom this news, he asked if he had to be legal to go to his homeland.

"No," she told him. "We should be okay without that, as long as nothing unexpected happens. Just don't get sick or hurt yourself."

He gave her a thin smile. "Dom not get sick. Not hurt. No worry, Vee."

As time went by, it wasn't unusual to run into three or four of Dom's increasingly dedicated followers hanging out near Veronica's apartment building. Apparently, it wasn't difficult to find a UBC associate professor's address. She and Dom always took time to speak to them for a few minutes, pose for photos and, in some cases, sign a photo or a newspaper article.

Veronica took Dom to Cooper Medical that Thursday for a final medical exam before the trip. They stopped to visit with Gracie, who proudly showed them how she could now walk down the hallway using a walker, and Beatrice, who had been put in charge of a new patient in the ICU.

As they left the medical facility, they were met by a rowdy crowd of over a dozen people in the same mind as Celia Wolts, causing such a disturbance outside the lobby that Walter would subsequently forbid any of them coming back—Dom and Veronica included.

"Why people shout at Dom?" he asked as they drove away after pushing through the mob of protesters with some help from Ty and Bill, the security guard. "People not like Dom?"

"Everyone likes you once they get to know you," she said, while keeping her eyes on the road. "But some people don't understand you. They don't understand how you can be alive and that scares them. People are scared of things they don't know. Scared of people who are different from them. But you know that already, don't you?"

"Yes, Dom know," he said, sounding so miserable Veronica guessed he was thinking of how he'd been expelled from his second tribe and the family he'd made there. "Dom different from all people."

She glanced sideways at him. "You're different in a good way, Dom. Don't ever forget that."

"Different in good way," he repeated, not sounding any less miserable. "*Taa.*"

After Dom's less than pleasant although necessary visits to the ophthalmologist and dentist, Veronica had a much more enjoyable outing planned. The last Friday in July, Chloe came over and the three of them drove to Vancouver's Alpine Start Outfitters store. Pat Browne, the wilderness guide, had sent Veronica an email with a list of gear they needed. He would supply cooking equipment, water purification tablets, emergency rations, first aid supplies, and one three-person tent. They would stock up on food in Williams Lake when they met there. Everything else was each individual's responsibility. Gerald Sutherland, who'd camped out numerous times over the years, offered to lend whatever necessities he needed to Walter. Chloe and Veronica had some things but needed more and, of course, Dom had nothing to prepare him for two weeks of modern camping.

Their appearances in the newspaper and on television led to Veronica and Dom frequently being recognized in public. Today was no different and they'd barely set foot inside the store when a salesgirl with a bobbing pink ponytail gravitated towards them.

"Hey there, can I help you?" she asked, the smile on her freckled face growing as she got a good look at Dom.

"You absolutely can," Veronica replied. Pulling her shopping list from the pocket of her cargo shorts, she added, "We'll start with this and go from there."

The girl's eyes popped wide as she read the list. "Right-o," she said after a moment. "We can get you all fixed up, no problem. My name's Lexie, by the way." She looked each of them over, but her eyes lingered on Dom.

"I'm Veronica. This is Chloe and Dom."

Lexie nodded at each name. "Dom," she said. "I've seen you on TV. It's so cool to meet you in person."

"Thank you," Dom replied. "Nice meet . . . uh . . . ."

"Lexie," she repeated.

"Lexie. Beautiful name." He smiled. "Beautiful pink hair."

Veronica noticed the colour rising in Chloe's cheeks as her lips pressed into a thin line.

Is that what I think it is? she wondered, then forgot about it as they got busy shopping.

They spent three hours in the store, loading the counter with deluxe backpacks, hiking boots, rain gear, dishes and utensils, a sleeping bag, pad, and pillow for Dom, a lightweight, three-person tent, and various other items, including the indispensable mosquito repellant.

Lexie was clearly smitten by Dom. She gave them all a twenty percent discount on their purchases and asked if she could have her picture taken with him. Veronica took it on Lexie's cell phone after paying for their purchases with a Visa card Walter had given her. She hadn't asked him whose account it went on, assuming it belonged to one of his nameless investors, perhaps the same one who had paid Dr. Chase's bill.

"You're a celebrity already, Dom," Chloe said as they lugged their gear out to the car. "I can't imagine when the book and movie come out. It's going to be epic!"

"Epic good?" Dom asked when they reached the car.

"Oh, yeah," she said, giving him a firm hug around the waist. "Epic is definitely good."

With an eye to teaching Dom how to set up the tent, Veronica arranged for the two of them to camp at Gerald Sutherland's place the following Monday.

Veronica's sister, Kim, came to visit that weekend, spending Saturday with Dom and her at Stanley Park, and Sunday with Neil and Becky and little Caroline at their house. Veronica and Dom joined them all for brunch before driving to UBC, where they met with Chloe in Veronica's increasingly cluttered and neglected office.

She promised herself she would come in more often once she got back from the Cariboo, but today they were here for a reason.

"We'll probably get in trouble for this," Chloe began, "but Professor Sutherland helped Veronica get hold of these, so we're all in it together . . . Hold out your hands, Dom."

Looking confused, he held out both hands, palms up.

Chloe took something from the front pocket of her denim shorts, placed it in his hands, and closed his fingers around it. "Professor Sutherland's students found these in the ground where they found you. They're yours and you should have them back," she said.

"Iv-ory beads," Dom said, opening his hands and holding them up to look closely at the six two-centimetre wide, yellowish balls.

"I put them on a cord so you can wear them around your neck the way you used to. If you want to, I mean," she added hastily.

"Yes, Dom want. Five beads for five children. Two beads for Lil-lia and Dom. Count seven beads. Why six beads?"

"Oh, I'm so sorry! One of them was destroyed—um, broken. We could only get six."

Dom lifted the cord over his head and dropped it around his neck. "Dom wear beads all days. Thank you, Chloe."

"It was Veronica's idea. She had one of the beads and Professor Sutherland snuck the others out of storage. I only put them on the cord."

Dom looked at Veronica, his eyes wet with tears he managed to blink away. "*De-ne-land.* Much big thank you, Vee. Dom happy today. Much good day."

Gerald's wife, Linda, invited Veronica and Dom for supper, so on Monday the four of them cooked burgers and potatoes outside on the Sutherlands' fire pit, and set up their tent in the middle of the back yard.

They actually put the tent up and took it down twice, giving Dom the chance to become competent at the task, before setting it up for the night.

As the sun dropped towards the horizon, they roasted the requisite marshmallows on long, metal forks over the dying flames. Gerald told stories of his adventures as a young man backpacking down the west coast as far as San Diego in search of Native American artefacts and experts in the field with whom to discuss them.

Dom seemed content to munch s'mores and listen quietly rather than share any stories of his own. Veronica didn't push him to talk, but she found herself hoping that once in the Cariboo wilderness, he would be inspired to open up and tell them things he'd never told them before.

Wednesday morning, Veronica took Rusty and Scout in their carriers, along with their food, bowls, litter box, and favourite toys, to Chloe's mom's apartment. Mrs. McLean, a veterinary assistant, had kindly offered to foster them while Veronica was away. She'd also mentioned wanting to meet Dom, so he accompanied her to the apartment in the Vancouver suburb of Burnaby. After a short visit over coffee and cookies, they kissed her kitties goodbye and headed to Ty's house, as Dom insisted on seeing him before leaving on their trip.

They ended up eating lunch with Ty and his family, before saying their goodbyes and hurrying home to finish packing and preparing for an early departure Thursday morning.

Walter arrived as previously arranged, toting his baggage in a backpack borrowed from Gerald, to spend the night.

Veronica ordered their go-to Chinese food and they opened a bottle of red wine, reminding each other that this was probably the last civilized meal they would have for two weeks. Dom drank half a glass, grimacing at every swallow, before giving it up for a tall glass of cold water.

They did the dishes and tidied up, took their showers, and went to bed early. Walter and Veronica shared a brief but intimate liaison, falling asleep in each other's arms shortly afterwards.

At least Walter slept, as evidenced by the regular rise and fall of his chest and occasional grunt of a snore. Veronica, too anxious about tomorrow's trip, lay staring at the ceiling for hours, thoughts racing through her mind, until exhaustion overtook her and she shut down.

Gerald arrived at 6:00 on the dot the next morning. They loaded everything in the back of his SUV and got away before any of Dom's fans or haters showed up. They picked Chloe up, then hit the Trans-Canada highway for the seven-plus-hour drive to Williams Lake.

They stopped twice on the way, the first time in the town of Hope, on the shore of the Fraser River, for a bathroom break and late breakfast at Tim Horton's, and coffee to go. Their second stop was in Clinton, just south of the Cariboo Plateau, where they took a fifteen-minute stroll to work the cramps out of their legs, snacked at the Junction Coffee House, and filled the gas tank in the SUV.

Veronica had worried about how Dom would handle the long car ride, but he seemed all right, spending most of the time gazing out the window at whatever he could see of the countryside. He even dozed off briefly a few times, his head falling forwards so that his chin rested on his chest.

The rest of them took turns driving, about ninety minutes each, while the others chatted, listened to music, and texted friends and family.

They pulled into the town of Williams Lake just after 4:00 and easily found the Best Western Hotel where Walter had rented two rooms—one for the girls and one for the boys, he said with a chuckle, as if they were all twelve years old.

Fifteen minutes later, they were checked in and relaxing in their rooms on the second floor. Veronica called Neil to let him know they'd arrived safely. She called Pat as agreed and arranged for them all to meet in an hour at the Laughing Loon Pub located a short walk from the hotel. Then, because she'd been thinking about it for weeks now and couldn't find the right way to say it, she blurted,

"Chloe? Do you like Dom?"

"Do I like him?" Chloe had stretched out on her back on her bed, but she sat up and swung her legs over the side before replying, "Of course I do. Don't you?"

"Oh, yeah. Far more than I should like anyone I'm involved with professionally. I'd say my feelings are maternal, though, as if he were my son or kid brother. I want to protect him, help him have a good life. Ridiculous, I know, given his age." She laughed softly. "I see the way you look at him though, Chloe. Hear the way you talk to him and he talks to you. I saw your face when he said Lexie had a beautiful name and hair. If that wasn't jealousy, please tell me what it was."

Chloe took in a deep breath and let it out in a long sigh. "I can't help it. I haven't had a boyfriend since I dumped Andrew, that two-timing loser, last summer. I've been trying not to . . . not to think of Dom that way. I know he's, like, fifteen years older than me if we count the normal way, never mind the rest, but my grandfather's twenty-one years older than my grandmother, and they've been happy together for nearly fifty years. And Dom . . . He's—"

"He's special."

"He is. He's smart and kind and honorable. But to him, he just lost his wife and family not even a year ago. There's no way he's over it yet, and I don't have a clue how to let him know I feel . . . the way I feel about him."

Veronica sat down on the edge of the bed beside Chloe, who looked at her with tears in her eyes. "Maybe when we get home after this trip—"

She nodded. "Yeah. I'll find a way. If he's not ready, I'll wait. And if he's not interested, then I'll settle for being the best friend he's ever had." The young woman sighed again, the sound cutting off abruptly when she startled at a knock on their door.

"Vee? Chloe? All good?" It was Dom.

"Oh, God, don't let him see me like this!" Chloe fled to the bathroom.

Veronica opened the door. "I called Pat," she told Dom. "We're going to meet him in the restaurant just down the street in"—she glanced at her watch—"forty-five minutes. Chloe and I are just getting washed up. We'll come to your room when we're ready."

Dom nodded and stepped back, and she closed the door.

She washed up when Chloe came out of the bathroom. Before they left to meet the guys, Chloe made her promise not to say anything about their conversation. Then they joined the others and the five of them walked to the pub, where they found Pat Browne waiting for them at a table for six.

The wilderness guide was a tall, wiry Native American of around forty, with cropped black hair and an easy smile.

Introductions were made, hands were shaken, and they all sat down.

While they waited for a server to bring them menus, Pat asked the usual questions: How was the drive up? Did they like the hotel? Were they hungry? He didn't ask anything in particular of Dom, even though Veronica knew Walter had told him who Dom was and why they were coming up north. He had, of course, been asked to sign an NDA concerning everything to do with their mission.

Dom wasn't able to read the tiny print on the menu. Thinking he wouldn't need them in the wilderness, he hadn't brought his magnifying glasses, but Chloe, sitting to his right, read the entire thing to him and explained when necessary what an item was. Once everyone ordered—sirloin steaks for Dom, Pat, and Walter, pork chops for Veronica and Gerald, and salmon for Chloe, various craft beers for all except Dom, who opted for iced tea—they got down to the business of planning the next stage of their trip.

By the time they finished their meal, everything was settled. They would take their complimentary continental breakfast at the hotel tomorrow morning. Then they would meet Pat at the Safeway supermarket to pick up provisions for a week and drive to a dock on the lake to rendezvous with the chartered float plane at noon. The plane would take them to Eliguk Lake, the closest body of water to Far Mountain that was long enough for it to safely land and take off. After that, they would be on their own until the plane returned in one week's time to take them to Tetachuck Lake and the second part of their journey. Their only connection with the outside world would be Pat's satellite phone.

Veronica fervently hoped he wouldn't need it.

32

INTO THE WILDERNESS

Veronica was already wide awake when the first pink light of dawn peeked in around the edges of the thick hotel room curtains, but she forced herself to remain quiet until she noticed Chloe stirring in the other bed. Then she rose to take her last hot shower for a week, dried her hair with the hotel blow dryer, and dressed in a tee-shirt and khaki cargo pants while Chloe took her turn in the bathroom. Once Chloe was washed and dressed in a tee-shirt and jeans, her wet hair twisted into a long braid down her back, they took the stairs down to the hotel restaurant and sipped coffee, casually chatting about anything but Dom, until the men showed up.

They ate their complimentary breakfast of toast, eggs, and sausages, draining glasses of orange juice and refills of coffee before returning to their rooms for their bags and checking out.

By the time they reached the supermarket, Veronica's stomach was jittery, and she wished she hadn't consumed such a hearty breakfast.

Pat arrived with a list of essentials—flour, sugar, salt, powdered eggs, powdered milk, powdered orange juice, peanut butter, coffee, canola oil, granola bars, packets of dried soup, rice, a few cans of the inevitable baked beans, and so on—which, once purchased, had to be evenly distributed amongst their six backpacks. He hoped to catch some fish and find berries, mushrooms, and other edibles in the forest, and Dom volunteered that he knew how to find food.

"Of course, you do," Pat said, nodding. "We'll make a great team then. You might even teach me a thing or two if you . . . um . . ."

If you really are who they say you are, Veronica read on his face.

"If you find anything good," he finished, colour rising in his bronze cheeks. "So . . . let's go, eh?"

They got everything packed away and followed Pat's battered 4 x 4 around the lake that gave the town its name until they reached the dock where the float plane would pick them up.

Veronica and Chloe had spent hours showing Dom photos and videos of airplanes, in particular float planes, but that didn't stop him looking like he might have a heart attack when the plane landed on the lake and coasted to a stop beside the dock.

"It's okay, Dom. It's the plane we told you about." Veronica gave his arm a squeeze. Walter had upped Dom's daily dose of anti-anxiety meds a week ago in anticipation of this trip, but she wondered suddenly if it would be enough to keep him calm in the air.

"Y'all my fare to Eliguk Lake?" asked the pilot, a robust man in jeans and a red lumberjack shirt. He spoke with a distinct American drawl. He strode towards the group on the dock. "Hey, Pat." He stuck out his hand and the two men shook.

"Everyone, meet Casey, bush pilot extraordinaire," said Pat. He made introductions all around.

Casey's gaze barely lingered on Dom, making Veronica wonder whether he didn't know who Dom was, didn't believe it, or didn't care.

"Let's get loaded up," the pilot said. "It's gonna be a tight fit with y'all and all your gear." Once everything was packed in the cargo hold, he asked, "You sure you don't wanna go to the lodge on the north shore of the lake?"

"Nope," said Pat. "We want the south shore. You said there's a dock?"

"There is," Casey assured him. "So, let's get y'all in. Pat, you wanna ride up front with me?"

He did, but as Walter and Gerald embarked, Dom stepped backwards away from the plane. "No," he said, shaking his head. "Dom not want go in big bird airplane."

"We came all the way here for you, Dom," said Chloe, turning around to face him.

That wasn't strictly true—they each had their own reasons for coming—but Veronica didn't want to interrupt the young woman's attempt to encourage him.

"It's perfectly safe. We've all been on airplanes before. So have you. You just don't remember because you were asleep the first time, when you were brought to Vancouver. We'll be fine, I promise."

"Tick tock, people," Casey said briskly, hopping down from the plane and giving them a stern look. "We gotta go. I wanna get home before dark." His gaze returned to Dom. "There's a couple barf buckets under the seats if you need them."

They got into the plane, Veronica propelling Dom forwards with a hand pressed to his back. Pat sat in the cockpit beside Casey while the others squeezed into seats in the passenger section of the plane.

"Fasten your seatbelts, everyone!" Casey called out. "And I suggest keeping them on. You never know out here."

Veronica glanced at Dom to see if he'd caught this, but fortunately it didn't seem he had.

Casey put on a headset and mic and handed one to Pat so they could converse without shouting, and started flipping switches on the console.

Dom was fumbling with his seatbelt. Veronica leaned over to help him fasten it as the plane's engines hummed into action. From the corner of her eye, she noticed Chloe extracting an empty ice cream bucket from beneath her seat.

The plane moved slowly away from the dock, then picked up speed until it was moving fast enough to rise from the lake.

"Ooh, Dom not feel good," said Dom, his face taking on a greenish hue that almost matched his tee-shirt. Beads of perspiration stood out on his wide forehead, and he slapped one hand to his mouth. "Feel sick."

"It's okay, it's just the feeling of the plane rising," Veronica leaned close to make sure he heard her over the rumble of the vehicle engine and gave his arm an encouraging squeeze.

"It'll level out in a few minutes."

Should've given him some Dramamine or something, she thought. *Damn! Too late now.*

"Much sick," Dom gasped, as Chloe plopped the bucket in his lap. Not two minutes later, he emptied the contents of his stomach into it.

The acrid smell of vomit mixed with the odours of fuel and the pine-scented air freshener hanging in the cockpit, making Veronica feel slightly nauseous herself. Holding her breath and making a concerted effort not to look at it, she removed the bucket from between Dom's thighs and placed it beneath his seat.

Casey and Pat were chatting through their headsets and didn't seem to have noticed Dom's distress.

Hands on his knees, Dom began chanting in a low monotone, but whether he was praying for a safe flight or attempting to occupy his mind, Veronica had no idea.

It doesn't really matter, does it? Poor guy, this is just about too much for him.

Casey called back to them a few times, pointing out what he felt were interesting landmarks, until three hours later, the plane began dropping in altitude and the pristine blue surface of Eliguk Lake rose to meet them.

They disembarked at a dilapidated wooden dock on the edge of the lake. Dom dropped to his knees to throw up again as soon as his feet hit the rocky shore.

"Sorry," he said after rising and taking a long breath of crisp, fresh air. "Dom stomach not like fly in plane."

"You don't have to apologize," Veronica said gently. "I was feeling pretty sick myself."

"Okay, guys, we're on our own," said Pat, raising his voice

over the rev of the engine as the plane pulled away from the dock. He'd spent a few minutes conversing with the pilot as the others unloaded the gear. "Casey will be back for us right here next Friday afternoon. We have exactly seven days to hike to Far Mountain, find the spot you're looking for, and come back. I suggest we get a couple hours in today, then set up camp. First night's always the hardest, till you get the hang of it. We'll head out in earnest early tomorrow morning."

"Sounds good," said Gerald, as everyone nodded in agreement.

They pulled on their backpacks. Gerald and Pat verified the direction with Pat's compass, and they set off towards the forest on a fairly discernable path presumably made by animals coming to drink or hunt at the water's edge.

Pat was right. Once they picked a camping spot beside a shallow but briskly flowing creek, it took them a ridiculous amount of time to set up their tents and bed rolls, hang their food safely in the trees a short distance from the tents, and get themselves organized enough to prepare a meal. Additionally, Pat insisted on designating a toilet area a good fifty metres into the forest from the campsite, marked by a short trench he dug with his trowel and a roll of toilet paper hung on a broken tree branch. On their way back, they collected wood for a fire that Pat started with a lighter, then Dom took over as without doubt he'd had more experience maintaining campfires than all the rest of them together. Pat poured a pouch of beef and barley soup into boiling water, and Gerald whipped up biscuits, which he fried in a bit of oil.

They didn't talk much, everyone seeming as preoccupied by the day's events and tomorrow's prospects as Veronica was. She'd only begun to realize how different this trip was going to be from the university-sponsored archaeological digs she'd been on in the past. By 8:30, the sun was setting, and they were all ready to hit the sack. They took turns going two by two to the toilet area. Chloe and Veronica changed from their day clothes into tank tops and leggings that would pass for pajamas, while the men put on tee-shirts and sweats—except Dom, who opted for sweats only. Each of them would take turns sitting up to watch the fire. Pat would be first tonight, followed by Walter, Veronica, Chloe, Gerald, and Dom. Then Dom would sit up first the next night, and so on.

Squeezed in between Chloe and Dom, Veronica was lulled to sleep by a chorus of cicadas and frogs. She woke up with a start when Walter came to fetch her at midnight. She grabbed her flashlight, pulled on her hoodie against the cool night air, shoved her bare feet into her sneakers, and crept out of the tent.

The fire was low but warm. She added a few twigs and then a larger chunk of dry spruce. She sat close to it, Dom and Pat having insisted it was better to sit close to a small fire than far away from a large one. She soon found herself listening to the gentle crackling of the flames and gazing at the multitude of stars in the black sky, happily imagining triumphant scenarios of finding Dom's sky stone place, chasing any thought of failure from her mind.

Breakfast consisted of porridge, orange juice, and coffee, all of it tasting slightly of the purification tablets Pat had put in the bucket of water he'd collected. Although the creek looked perfectly clear and clean, they would take no chances, to Dom's great disenchantment.

"Creek water good," he objected. "Smell good. Pure pill water taste bad. Make food taste bad."

"It doesn't matter," Walter told him in his voice of authority. "We can't risk anyone getting sick out here. You will drink water from the bucket. You will not drink directly from any creek, river, or lake we come across. Do you understand?"

Dom pouted. "Yes, Dom understand," he grumbled, but Veronica didn't see how they could prevent him doing anything he wanted to do. Not really—they were in his world now.

They made good progress that day, despite Dom's difficulty on some of the rougher terrain. Although he'd stopped using his cane months ago when walking in the city, he took it on hikes as it was easier for him to grasp than a trekking pole. Despite the cane, and focus as he might on where he put his feet, he stumbled repeatedly over rocks and dips in the ground, catching his breath in hisses of pain, occasionally muttering, "Eyes no good," or, "Feet no good," but never asking for help or even a pause.

When they stopped for breaks approximately every two hours, Dom spent much of the time on his hands and knees, searching for edible plants. He and Pat collected white mushrooms they swore were safe to eat for their evening meal, while the others picked wild blackberries for dessert.

They stopped on the pebbly shore of a small lake at 5:00, three or four hours by Pat's calculation from the base of Far Mountain, which loomed to their south. While everyone else set up camp, Pat pulled out a collapsible fishing pole and endeavoured to catch their supper.

Gerald made some more of his biscuits.

When Veronica admitted concern about the mushrooms, Dom promptly popped two of them into his mouth, his face practically glowing with delight as he munched and swallowed.

"Fine, you've convinced me," she said with a laugh. She and Chloe got to work washing the mushrooms and berries, while Dom had Walter help him pull up several cattails, the stalks of which he said could be sliced up and cooked up with the mushrooms while the heads could be roasted directly over the fire.

Pat caught two small rainbow trout that at once cleaned weren't much in themselves, but added to the rest made a more than adequate meal for everyone. The cattail stalks, deftly peeled by Dom using an obsidian blade he'd extracted from his backpack, as well as the roasted brown heads, turned out to be quite tasty, although Walter passed after taking one bite of the latter.

"Walter not know good food," Dom said with a *tsk-tsk* and a shake of his head, and everyone laughed.

"I feel like I'm on vacation," Chloe observed after supper. They'd washed their dishes in Pat's collapsible bucket and were relaxing around the fire with cups of coffee in hand and the bag of blackberries, which Dom called *maa-shaw*, making the rounds.

Pat spent half an hour admiring the three obsidian blades Dom brought, while Gerald recounted how Dom had shown Veronica and him how to make them.

"I feel like I'm back in my Boy Scout days," Gerald added with an easy chuckle. "We'd drink hot cocoa, roast marshmallows, and tell stories—mostly ghost stories, you know, to see who could scare the rest of us." He sighed happily at the memory. "Anyone have a good story to tell?"

"There's a story I'd like to hear," Pat suggested. He fixed Dom across the fire from him with a stare. "Dom? How about telling us—well, me, at least, if everyone else knows—why we're going to Far Mountain? All I know is it has something to do with you."

"Uh, yes. Dom tell Pat. Tell everyone."

Veronica expected the same story he'd told her and Ty, but she hurried to fetch her cell phone from her backpack in order to record him, just in case it turned out to be something else.

It did.

"Elders say much long time before Dom time, long tail star fly in sky," Dom began. "People see star break in many pieces. Many fires in sky. Sky stones fall, make fire many places. Much forest burn. People go mountains for be safe. After fire, much water come. Animals die. People not go mountains die. After water much cold come. Bad time for hunt. People on mountains die. Few people not die, go . . . go beach. Go more warm place.

"People make children. Children make children." He made a rolling movement with his hand to indicate that this continued for a while. "People make *den-no-ny* homeland long time before Dom time."

"My people have a story something like that too," Chloe said when Dom paused. "I remember my granddad telling me when I was a little girl. It's one of the reasons I got interested in anthropology."

"It sounds like collective memory handed down by his ancestors of a time called the Younger Dryas," Veronica offered. "A growing number of scientists believe pieces of a comet impacted the northern ice cap twelve or thirteen thousand years ago, initially causing fires, then floods from a rise in sea level, followed by a drastic drop in global temperatures. It took a good thousand years for conditions to improve."

"I admit that's real interesting," Pat remarked, "but what does it have to do with us being here now?"

"Ah." Dom grinned, apparently relishing Pat's interest. "Dom people see fire in sky. *Grr-pffft!*" He made an exploding sound. "Stone fall from sky. Make fire. Elders say bad. Say big water come. Big cold come. Dom people wait. No big water come. No big cold. One year more . . . uh . . . after. Dom fifteen years." He paused as an owl hooted nearby. "Dom want go sky stone place. Elders say no, not go. Bad place. Father say no, not go. Dom not afraid. Not listen. Not tell mother, not tell father. Bad Dom!"

Walter chuckled. No one else made a sound, rapt as they were by Dom's tale. Chloe sat beside him, her gaze fixed on his face, clearly hanging on every word.

"Dom go. Walk six days. Find sky stone circle place. Trees burned. Find cave for be safe. Dom stay one month. Find good stone for make tools and points. Hunt, eat berries, mushrooms, cat-tails." He glanced at Walter. "Drink good water. Feel good. Feel strong. Before go home, Dom make mark say Dom here. Go sky stone place boy. Go home man.

"Dom bring home good stone. Women happy. Hunters happy. Mother happy, father happy. After happy, angry. Mother cry. Dom sorry make mother cry." He gave a wry smile and shrugged.

"She was afraid for you, Dom," Chloe said.

He nodded. "*Taa. Dom say-a.*" Dom knows.

"All righty. And this place where you went," said Pat, getting back to his initial line of thinking. "We're trying to find it . . . why, exactly?"

At this point, Walter spoke up. "Let me explain. No offense, Dom, but I want to make sure he understands."

Dom nodded. "Walter understand germs for teach Pat. Walter tell Pat why we go mountain."

Pat's thick eyebrows shot up. "Germs? What's he talking about?"

Having pretty much been cornered, Walter told Pat what he suspected Dom had inadvertently found at the site of the meteorite impact. He explained the effect the mutated bacteria had on the teenager and the reason why it was so important to find the exact location again. He reminded Pat that he'd signed an NDA and couldn't reveal anything he learned during the trip until he was given leave to do so.

"So, you think that's how he survived," Pat murmured after Walter was done. "Jesus . . . That's freakin' amazing." He stared at Dom for a moment, then pulled himself together and asked, "If we come in contact with that bacteria, do you think it could . . . I don't know . . . make us live longer or something?"

"I have no idea," Walter admitted, "although I doubt Dom was infected through casual contact. More likely prolonged ingestion of contaminated water or food sources, maybe even through his blood as he sustained some minor injuries while he was there. What I'm hoping to do is dig up a sample of the bacteria and take it back to the laboratory for study—if it's even there after all this time. If it is"—he shrugged—"who knows what its medical applications might be."

Who knows? Veronica thought as she turned off the recording. *Who knows what any of us will get out of this quest?*

33

FAR MOUNTAIN

Sunday dawned sunny and warmer than the previous morning. It began with porridge topped with the last of the blackberries, juice, and coffee, followed by the dismantling of their campsite. After hiking for a couple hours, the group emerged from a mossy forest path inhabited by roaming clouds of minute, black flies, into rolling green and golden grasslands that spread out below the smooth northern flank of Far Mountain.

The view was spectacular—and cause for concern.

Dom's memories of this place might be clear, Veronica thought as she took in the expansive landscape, *but his eyesight certainly isn't. What if he can't lead us to the right place in the limited time we have here?*

"Oh, look!" exclaimed Chloe, pointing ahead and to their left. "Are those . . . mountain goats?"

The animals were mere whitish specks in the distance, barely distinguishable from the rocks dotting the ground, but Pat confirmed,

"They are. We might see caribou too, though the population has really fallen over the last few years."

Squinting in the direction Chloe was pointing, Dom shook his head. "Dom not see goats. Too much small far away."

And there we are, thought Veronica, but she kept her worries to herself.

They took a break before heading towards the mountain,

reaching the edge of the grasslands and the beginning of the volcanic basalt slope at noon.

"Do you recognize this place, Dom?" Walter asked as they snacked on apples and granola bars and drank purified water from their bottles.

"What mean word, 'reco-nize'?" Dom asked back.

He groaned. "It means, do you know this place? Do you remember it?"

"Ah. *Taa*. Dom remember walk mountain sun go down side. Find . . . uh . . . long, deep place where trees and water. Dom go up, see trees burned dead. Find sky stone place."

"He must mean a sort of gouge in the side of the mountain," Pat suggested. "We have to skirt it to the west."

"Now there's a plan," Gerald said. "Better than climbing up the barren north face for no reason."

"Sounds good to me," Walter agreed. "Dom, can you take us to the place?"

Veronica found herself holding her breath while Dom thought for a moment. "Yes. Walk half day, find long deep place."

"Wonderful!" Walter exclaimed. "Are we all done eating?" he asked, looking around at them. "Let's go."

Poor eyesight notwithstanding, Dom's memory proved to be accurate. Four hours later, they came upon a sort of chasm leading gently up the mountain. Mixed trees, ferns, and other foliage lined both sides of the slope. A dry creek bed ran down the centre of it.

"Place where go up," Dom said, pointing with his chin.

"You're sure?" Pat asked. "You said there was water."

"Yes. Dom sure. No water now. Water in Dom time."

"Okay, guys," the guide said to everyone. "It's getting late. I suggest we camp near that creek we saw half an hour back. Get a good night's sleep and tackle the mountain tomorrow."

"That sounds good," Veronica said. "I don't know about the rest of you, but my legs are killing me."

They all agreed, Walter moaning that his legs had had

enough for the day too, and even Dom admitting his feet hurt. They backtracked to the creek in question, where they set up their tents and other necessities. Dom got the campfire going while Pat set up the bathroom area. Veronica and Gerald cooked up baked beans, scrambled eggs, and some more roasted cattails for supper. They took turns discreetly washing with water warmed up in a saucepan while they still had the light of day. Then they sat around the fire with their coffees, the women sharing anecdotes from various archaeological digs or school field trips.

"What was that?" Walter asked suddenly, interrupting Chloe's story telling.

"What was . . . oh!" Veronica said as she heard a faint howl in the distance.

"It's a wolf," Pat said calmly. "Don't worry, guys, they won't come near the fire."

A second howl, answered by a third, this one closer and echoing slightly off the mountain, coming, it seemed, from somewhere south.

Dom sat up straighter, his eyes widening.

"Dom? You heard that one?" Chloe asked.

"Yes, Dom hear. Wolf." He nodded, smiling. "Wolf good."

"Good?" Walter repeated doubtfully. "I don't think—"

"*Taa*. Dom people say, '*Ooh-shay lah-taa ke-we.*' Wolf good sign. Mean good hunt."

"That's right," Veronica said. "In many Native American traditions wolves symbolize courage, strength, and success in hunting."

"Loyalty and strong family in Haida culture," Chloe added.

"Lovely," Walter said. He peered worriedly out into the dark.

"I'm telling you, they're more afraid of us than you are of them," Pat assured them, his voice so steady and confident that Veronica suddenly wondered if he had a weapon in his backpack. He told Gerald, who had first watch that night, to come get him if he heard or saw anything unusual.

"Don't worry, I will," he said, and the others went to bed.

Walter roused Veronica at 3:00 for her turn. She pulled on her hoodie and grabbed her notepad and pen, and between the light of the low flames and her flashlight, she wrote up notes on the trip so far. Ninety minutes later, she woke Chloe for her turn and went back to sleep in the tent.

It is good to be here, in his world. He had been afraid it was gone, but the forest, grasses, mountains, running water, big open sky are the way he remembers them. The smells and the sounds are the same, even if he doesn't hear as much as before.

He told the others he can find the sky stone place but he is not so sure he can find the place to turn towards the cave where he left his mark. But the wolves are a sign. A sign of a good hunt, and this is what he is on, is it not? A hunt for the place where he became a man. The place where Vee, Walter, Gerald, Chloe want to go.

He falls asleep and in his dreams he follows the wolves.

"Where's Dom?" Veronica asked, looking around after she emerged from her tent, blinking in the early morning sunlight. "Chloe said he came out before dawn and swapped places with her."

"Haven't seen him," Pat said. "He wasn't here when I came out."

"What?" Her heart skipped a beat and proceeded to race in her ears.

"What's going on?" asked Gerald. He covered a yawn with one hand as he emerged from the guys' tent, Walter just behind him. They both still wore their pajamas.

"Where's Dom?" Veronica repeated.

"Maybe he's gone to the bathroom?" Walter suggested. "That's where I'm headed."

The bathroom. Of course. He'll be back in a few minutes.

But Dom wasn't back in a few minutes. He wasn't at the toilet area, nor down by the creek, nor anywhere nearby, and a quick search of their tent revealed that while his bed things and backpack were still there, his cane was gone.

"He's gone off ahead of us." Veronica tried but failed miserably to keep the panic out of her voice.

"I'm so sorry!" Chloe wailed. "It's my fault. He offered to swap places with me. I'd heard the wolves and I was scared so I said yes, thank you. I never thought—"

"It's not your fault," Veronica said. "He has that devious streak ingrained in him, you know?"

"We'll catch him up," Pat said. "He can't move all that fast."

Walter and Gerald got dressed. They all gobbled a hasty breakfast of granola bars and the last apples. They filled their water bottles, packed a few necessities, kicked the fire out, and hurried away in the direction of the route up Far Mountain that they'd found the previous afternoon.

They pressed ahead as quickly as they could and caught up with Dom about half an hour after turning to head up the side of the mountain.

"Dom! Hey! Wait for us!" Veronica called out as soon as she caught sight of him.

He was struggling on a section of loose rocks, practically on his hands and knees, his cane clutched awkwardly at his side. He didn't stop or look back until he was on solid ground about thirty metres above them.

"Vee!" He turned around to peer down at them. "You follow Dom?"

"Of course, we followed you!" Walter yelled back. "What the hell did you think we were going to do?"

Dom didn't answer, but he sat down, legs stretched out

between the ferns, to wait as they scrambled across the rock scree to join him.

"What were you thinking, Dom?" Pat asked. "You, of all people, should know it's not a good idea to go off alone in the wilderness."

Getting to his feet, he replied, "Dom live many years alone in wild-erness."

"And you ended up getting mauled by a bear, didn't you?" Walter reminded him. "Almost killed?"

Dom turned on him. "Bear come for Dom join new people. For Dom take wife Lil-lia. Wolf come night before for tell Dom come. Search. Find good place. Walter white-skin. Not understand." His voice rose in frustration, then fell again, so low they could barely make out the words. "Dom people listen animals, listen forest, listen mountain. White-skin people not listen. Kill animals. Kill brown-skin people. Make bad concrete city where good forest long time before."

"You're right," Veronica said, stepping closer to him. "We don't understand your people. That's why we're here with you, so we can maybe discover something to help us know them better." She half-expected him to point out that Walter wanted something else entirely, but he only huffed and turned to continue on his way.

They trailed after him, breaths coming in painful gasps, legs burning from the climb, until Dom stopped so suddenly that Chloe, following close behind him, bumped into him.

"Sorry!" she said with a giggle. "Let me know next time you're stopping, eh?"

"Uh, yes. Stop here," he said, slapping a massive boulder on the left side of the fissure in the mountain that passed for a trail. "Dom remember big stone. Turn here."

"Really? You're sure?"

"Yes. Come." He led them off through a stand of scraggly pines that had somehow found purchase in the rocky ground.

They continued for an hour, pushing through mixed forest and crawling over lichen-covered rocks, until they came upon a mild slope with a sort of overhang in the mountain to their right.

Dom put down his cane and began inspecting the rock face, parting ferns and shrubs in search of something. "Come help Dom search cave."

They shed their backpacks and began to search, spreading out to inspect the wall of rock.

"Here!" Pat shouted ten minutes later. He stood, pointing at the rock wall. "I think I found it!"

They all hurried to join him.

"*Taa*!" Dom exclaimed. He pushed aside the ferns and bracken, revealing a shoulder-high hollow about two metres wide and going back some three metres.

He crouched and stepped inside. Dropping to his knees, he began feeling around the sides of the space with both hands, tactile memory perhaps serving him best in the dim light inside.

"This is it? Are you sure?" Veronica asked. She walked in bent over, hands on her thighs, but this position proved too uncomfortable to maintain so she knelt down in the coarse sand and dry pine needles on the floor of the cave. "Do you remember where you left your mark?"

"Dom make mark . . . uh . . . close here." He patted the right-hand side wall of the cave. Peering owlishly at the stone, he shook his head. "Not see."

"Hang on," she said, and called for a flashlight.

Gerald shimmied in on his knees and handed her one. He was, of course, acutely interested by the archeological promise of this place.

Even in the dimness, Veronica could see the excitement in his eyes. She supposed he could see the same in hers.

She shone the light at the flat part of the wall. At first she didn't see anything, then a thin line harbouring a few tiny specks of black caught her eye. "Found it!" she squealed. "It's faint, but . . . oh God, it's beautiful. I've never seen anything like it." Turning to Dom she added, "You scratched it into the rock— your mark, I mean—and then you . . . what? Painted it? There's a bit of black in it that doesn't come from the rock, I don't think."

He nodded slowly, remembering. "Yes. Dom paint mark black for see long time."

Veronica sat there with Dom, enjoying the moment, and somewhere along the way realized she was clasping his arm. Gerald went out and came back with his camera, Chloe on his heels. She let go of Dom's arm and pointed the flashlight on the petroglyph.

The professor took half a dozen photos of the cave walls, in particular the handprints made by Dom over 9,000 years ago.

"So, now you've found your cave," Walter said when the four of them finally emerged, "how about showing us where the sky stone landed?"

"Yes, Walter," Dom replied, his tone just the slightest bit condescending. "Come." He took them down the slope from the cave about fifty metres and stopped. "Sky stone place here."

Veronica looked around. The flattish area was thinly forested with a mix of spruce and aspen trees, the ground covered with mulch, moss, and ferns.

Gerald marched decisively between the trees, around and around in an increasingly large circle, until coming back to the others. "I'd need to see satellite images and maybe talk with someone in UBC's geology department, but I'm fairly certain we're standing in an impact crater."

Looking around them, Veronica realized they were in a shallow hollow about thirty metres in diameter. "I think you're right, Gerald."

"Are you sure?" asked Walter, his voice rising with excitement. "So this is really it? We've found it?"

"Looks like," said Pat. He grinned. "I've gotta tell you, I didn't believe we would." He clapped Dom on the back. "You did good, man. Really good."

They spent the rest of the day at the site, exploring and taking photographs. Humming happily under his breath, Walter extracted numerous samples from different depths of soil. He took scrapings from moss and trees and even collected a couple live beetles and some ants, which he put into vials he'd brought for just this purpose.

"I don't see any water around here," Pat remarked at length. "Dom? Where did you drink when you were here?"

"Time Dom here, water run close." He walked away through the trees, followed by the others, and stopped after about five minutes. "Water here."

Veronica couldn't tell if there was a dry creek bed beneath the foliage, but she trusted that he remembered correctly.

Walter dug up additional samples of earth from where Dom indicated the water had been. Veronica, Chloe, and Gerald returned to the cave to search for any artefacts Dom or other inhabitants might have left behind. They worked carefully, as if it were an authorized archaeological dig, and came up with several stone flakes that looked to have been made by human hands, along with a good number of small animal bones, some petrified scat, and two teeth that looked canine. This indicated that Dom hadn't been alone in using the cave as shelter over the years. Dom confirmed that the teeth were, in fact, the teeth of a wolf. They put everything away in labelled zipper bags for study and cataloguing back at UBC.

"This is amazing," Veronica said through a smile. "I feel like a little girl at Christmas!"

"And hopefully it's only the beginning," Gerald said, grinning just as widely. "Next week we'll be going to Dom's people's homeland. Imagine what we might find there."

Reminding them that there was no water nearby, Pat suggested they return to their campsite before they got caught out in the dark.

They reached their tents well before dusk and made a hearty meal of chicken soup, biscuits, and mushrooms once again collected by Dom, with some help from Chloe. Their mood was celebratory; if they'd had a bottle of champagne, they would have opened it.

As they finished their coffee, Dom said suddenly that he wanted to make paint.

"You what?" asked Walter with a chuckle.

"Dom want make black colour paint," he repeated. "Make new mark. We make mark say we come here."

"That might sound like a good idea to you," Gerald said, "but it amounts to desecrating an archaeological site. We can't do—"

"*Taa*! Yes, Dom can do!" he insisted. "Dom find cave long time before. Make mark. Find cave today, make mark. Why no can make mark?"

Walter gave a discouraged sigh and shook his head, but Chloe spoke up.

"Dom's right. Why not? It's not an identified archaeological site—not yet, at least—and if anyone has a right to mark it, Dom does. We all came here for a reason, didn't we? Maybe this is his reason, or one of them."

"All right, then," Gerald said after a moment. "Go ahead and leave your mark, Dom, if you feel you must. But only you. The rest of us will abstain."

Dom frowned. "What mean word 'abs-tain'?"

"It means we won't leave our mark," Veronica said. "But we'd love for you to show us how you make your paint." She would regret that request soon enough.

Dom retrieved the smallest of their saucepans and put in some charcoal from their fire, which he crushed to powder with a rock. He didn't have the animal fat he said he'd used in the past, so he used some of their canola oil.

"Need one more thing," he said once he was satisfied with the lumpy paste he'd made from the oil and charcoal. Before anyone realized what he was doing, he unzipped his jeans and added a few drops of hot urine to the mix.

An acrid odour rose around him as he stirred the mixture with a stick.

"Well, I guess that proves that theory," Veronica said with a chuckle.

Walter wrinkled his nose and huffed. "We're not cooking in that pot again, are we?"

"Pee make good paint," Dom said matter-of-factly as he zipped up. "Tomorrow Dom make new mark in cave."

"I feel like we're in living history," Chloe said through a wide grin. "No offense, Professors, but it's way better than any class I've ever taken."

"No offense taken," Veronica said. "In fact, I agree with you one thousand percent."

34

ULTIMATE GOAL

The group expected rain to fall at some point during their trip and fall it did, beginning around midnight and continuing into the morning. By the time they arrived at the cave once again carrying essential items only, they were muddy, miserable, and shivering beneath their rain gear.

"You go do your painting, Dom," Walter said. "I want to go down to the impact site and collect some water samples. There must be a couple puddles there by now."

Pat accompanied Walter while Chloe, Veronica, and Gerald crowded into the cave with Dom, who ceremoniously extracted his zipper bag of viscous, black paint from his backpack. After chanting under his breath for a few minutes in prayer or benediction, he used his right index finger to trace around his left hand, which he'd placed on the rock wall opposite his original mark. Then he changed hands and traced his right hand. Finally, he drew his signature double concentric circles in the space between the two and sat back on his haunches, admiring his work. A minute later, he stuck his finger into the bag again and put a dot below his handprints.

"Vee," he said, his tone so solemn it gave Veronica the chills. Another dot, close beside the first one. "Chloe." Another. "Gerald." And another. "Ty." He paused, thinking about it, then made his decision and plopped a fifth dot on the wall. "Walter."

"Oh," said Chloe, although it was more a breath than a word.

"Dom friends for all time," he said, nodding his satisfaction at this job. He tapped the blanket of dirt and pine needles beside him. "Ty not here." He touched his forehead. "Ty here." Touched his chest over his heart. "Here."

"That's so sweet, Dom, so thoughtful," Veronica said over the lump in her throat. Although she'd known it for a long time, this was further proof that Neolithic man was as caring and sentimental as anyone living today. Probably more than many.

Gerald took photos of the image on his camera and Chloe took some on her cell but Veronica, wanting to save her battery for recording, refrained from taking any. The others would share theirs with her anyway.

Walter came back from his trip to the impact crater, half a dozen little vials of water in hand.

"Pat's waiting for us up ahead," he said. "He wants to get off the mountain before this rain makes the going treacherous."

Unfortunately, it was already too late for that. The way down the chasm was slick with mud and swiftly flowing water. Chloe and Walter slid a good way on their butts. Dom fell twice to his knees and, judging by his torn jeans, would need some first aid when they got back to their campsite.

They eventually reached the camp and gratefully changed into dry clothes. Walter had Dom go into his tent to get his scraped knees cleaned up with material from Pat's basic first aid kit.

Dom returned to the tent he shared with the women and they hunkered down, munching on a lunch of trail mix. Despite the rain and his injuries, he was in a boisterous mood, recounting numerous exciting and even humorous stories of hunting and vision quest-type trips he'd been part of, and sharing traditions of what animals such as caribou, moose, and eagles meant to his people.

Veronica recorded his tales until her cell phone died, in need of recharging when they got to the lodge on Friday.

The rain stopped late that afternoon, and the sun quickly burned through the remaining clouds. They ventured out into their misty, sodden campsite to hang their soaked clothes and socks on a cord Pat strung up between two nearby trees. Fortunately—or more precisely, with brilliant foresight—he and Dom had stored a pile of twigs and firewood in the tents, so they were able to get a campfire going. While Pat started supper, Dom and Chloe prowled amongst the trees, coming back with more wood that Dom stacked around the fire to dry and be burned later. They ate their fill of scrambled eggs and baked beans, followed by first and second cups of coffee.

Walter boiled water in the saucepan Dom had used for his paint until he was confident it was sterilized and once again fit for its intended use.

Veronica pulled out the bag of marshmallows she'd bought for an evening like this. They were mostly squished flat but perfectly edible. Pat cut thin, green branches from nearby trees with his hunting knife to be used as skewers, and they devoured roasted marshmallows for dessert. It was their most relaxed evening yet, the urgency to find the ancient impact site and Dom's cave removed from their shoulders.

"Ooh, much good supper," Dom said, munching on his fifth marshmallow and nodding his approval. "Good day today. Good see sky stone place. Good food. Dom much happy."

Watching the sun go down in a beautiful red and purple sky, Veronica thought that about summed it up for everyone.

They broke camp early Wednesday morning and began their journey back to Eliguk Lake. This time they took it easy, partly for the sake of Dom's sore knees and feet, and partly so they could enjoy the landscape and take some photos with Chloe's cell phone and Gerald's camera, both of which still had some battery life left in them.

The trip was pleasant and uneventful, and they arrived late Thursday afternoon at the lake, not far from where they'd begun their quest a week ago.

"How's the water?" Chloe asked, gazing out over the lake. "I mean, it's not polluted, is it?"

"I wouldn't think so," Gerald replied, "but I wouldn't go drinking it without Pat's little pills in it."

"Oh, I don't want to drink it. I want to go swimming. I told Dom I'd teach him back in Vancouver, but we haven't got around to it yet. It's warm enough this afternoon. Pat?" She turned to their guide. "What do you think?"

He shrugged and smiled. "Sure. Sounds like a good idea. Just don't swallow any water, don't pee, and if you're thinking of washing, don't use soap."

Gerald took a pass and offered to start setting up camp. The rest of them shed their vanity along with their clothes, stripping to their underwear—except for Dom, who had neither vanity nor underwear and readily hopped into the water in his birthday suit.

The water was cold, but not numbingly so. Veronica and Walter swam out towards the middle of the lake, turning around after five minutes or so and heading back to the shore.

Chloe and Pat had Dom doing a rudimentary crawl stroke in waist-deep water, the three of them laughing and splashing and having what looked like the time of their lives.

Veronica was glad to see Chloe enjoying a nice, normal activity with Dom and hoped there would be more to come for them in the future.

As Gerald started collecting wood for the fire, they got out of the water and dressed, refreshed and clean despite the no soap rule.

Once again, Dom found a fair quantity of mushrooms—the rain brought them up, he said—as well as some fiddleheads to add to the packaged vegetable soup Pat got going.

"This has been an amazing experience," Walter said as they ate, "but I have to admit I'm looking forward to the luxury of the lodge. Hot showers, soft beds . . ." He sighed happily in anticipation.

"A day and a half at the lodge," Veronica reminded him,

"and three days out wherever Dom wants to take us. You promised, Walt"—she gave him the stink eye—"and don't you forget it."

"Don't you worry," he said. "I know how much you all want to find Dom's homeland and search for archeological sites that'll keep you busy for years to come. I wouldn't think of depriving you of that." He glanced at Dom. "Any of you."

They hiked to the old dock the next morning and Casey flew in just past noon, as scheduled. He took them to the Tetachuck Lake Wilderness Lodge, where Walter had rented a cabin for the week. Dom handled this shorter flight better than the last one, managing to keep down his lunch of fried rainbow trout caught earlier that morning, although, clearly, his constitution was not made to handle air travel.

Walter, it turned out, was right about one thing—the lodge was indeed luxurious after a week in the wilderness.

Their cozy log cabin had a sitting room with a wood-burning stove, a bathroom, and two bedrooms. Chloe and Veronica claimed the smaller room with two twin beds, while the guys took the larger room with a double and twin bed. That still left someone sleeping on the sofa; Pat and Dom generously proposed to take it one night each, solving the problem.

They took their dirty laundry to the lodge owner, who kindly offered to wash them and hang them out to dry. They showered and washed their hair—Veronica had never appreciated hot water and shampoo so much—and strolled to the rustic dining room of the main house for a delicious, home-cooked supper. About a dozen other people were there, including a middle-aged couple with two teenagers, and a group of seven guys and girls in their twenties. The atmosphere was amiable and after their meal they lingered to drink coffee or hot cocoa and chat. The older man admitted he recognized Veronica and Dom but, like the lodge owners, he kindly didn't make a big deal of it.

Saturday was devoted to the three Rs—relaxation, recovery, and writing. While her cell phone recharged, Veronica sat on the cabin porch and filled most of her notebook with details of their trip back from Far Mountain and some of Dom's stories that she hadn't been able to record. After lunch, she hit the outdoor hot tub along with Walter and Gerald, followed by Chloe and Dom. Walter and Gerald then spent some time in the small library in the main house while Chloe and Dom sat together on the quiet beach, sipping iced tea from the kitchen. Veronica wondered what they talked about, but when they came in she didn't ask. Pat slept most of the day, recharging his batteries, Veronica supposed, for the next trip into the woods.

Walter arranged for them to rent two canoes, so Sunday morning they set out eastward on the water, Gerald, Veronica, and Walter in one canoe, the others together in the second boat. Taking turns at the oars, they made far better time than they would have on foot. They pulled in at noon for a cold lunch of sandwiches and potato salad graciously provided by the lodge, then paddled on for another four hours before Pat called out that they should stop and make camp for the night.

They found an inviting spot, beached the canoes, and set up their tents. Dom was in a foul mood. He'd tried to take his turn paddling the canoe but couldn't manage the oar with his damaged hands. He insisted on making the fire and maintaining it all evening to make up for his frustrating inability to help out on the water, and this eventually cheered him up.

Pat and Gerald went fishing and came back in no time with a huge trout caught by Gerald, which they ate for supper along with the rest of the potato salad and whole grain rolls from the lodge.

True to his word, Dom stayed up until midnight minding the fire, after which time Pat, then Walter, Vee, and finally Gerald took over, seeing them through until morning.

Dom had been shown the location of the lodge on Google Maps back in Vancouver, and he'd confirmed that it was indeed on *den-no-ny* land, although the shoreline of Tetachuck Lake had certainly changed over the millennia. More precisely, the lake and even the flow of the water had been altered with the building of the Nechako hydroelectric reservoir in 1952.

Still, having calculated the distance with Pat Saturday evening, they stopped at noon and beached the canoes when Dom thought they were close to where his people's main village had been when he was a boy.

They spent the afternoon searching the area for indications of human habitation. Since they had no permit or permission to undertake an actual archeological dig, this was limited to a superficial inspection of the ground, looking for flakes of stone or bits of cut bone amongst the pebbles or surface soil. Veronica used her dinner knife to scrape moss and lichen from boulders she assumed had stood where they were for thousands of years in search of petroglyphs, to no avail.

They moved from one area to the next, heading slowly westward as Dom admitted they'd perhaps gone too far, until Pat suggested they stop and make camp for the night.

After their supper of scrambled eggs—the powdered ones supplemented by half a dozen small, speckled eggs Dom had collected during their explorations—and the last of the rolls, Gerald took up on Veronica's effort and began scraping off a thick layer of moss from a large chunk of granite halfway between their tents and the toilet area Pat had set up.

"Well, will you look at this!" he exclaimed suddenly. Straightening from his work, he called, "I think I've found something!"

They all gathered around to peer at the spot where Gerald pointed. Looking closely, Veronica was able to make out three straight lines, close together, about fifteen centimetres long, etched into the stone.

"Dom? What do you think? Do you recognize this?" she asked him.

Squinting to focus and leaning in until his nose was almost touching the stone, he studied the area in question. Then he straightened and shook his head. "Dom eyes no good. Not see."

"Here, let me show you." She took his right hand and slowly drew his good thumb along the three lines. "They're faint but . . . can you feel them?"

"Ah, *taa*," he said, his eyes widening. "Three lines mark." He nodded. "Yes. Three lines for elder Mo-shooma. Mo-shooma small boy, bad hurt finger. Three fingers, three lines."

"So, you're saying the elder, Mo-shooma, made this mark?"

"No. Mo-shooma dead. People put in ground. People work for put stone over Mo-shooma."

"You mean he's buried here?" Chloe asked, her eyes wide.

Dom nodded. "Yes. Buried here."

"How do you know?"

"Dom know. Mo-shooma son Dom father."

"He was your grandfather?" Veronica asked.

"Yes. Dom small boy, remember grandfather Mo-shooma. Remember people bury. Put stone over."

"We're close to where your village was, then?" Gerald asked.

"*Taa*." Dom nodded again. "Village here. Many *issah* here." He gestured around them with both arms. "Dom boy home here." He grinned widely.

"I can't believe no one ever found this place," Chloe said.

"No one was looking," Gerald replied. "We'll get a permit and set up a proper dig next summer. With Dom to guide us, who knows what we'll find?"

They stayed up late that night, only going to bed when they were yawning and couldn't keep their eyes open any longer. Pat offered to sit up first.

Walter woke Veronica up at 3:00 to take her turn watching the fire.

"So, how did it feel to sleep in your people's homeland?" she asked Dom when he crept out to join her ninety minutes later.

He'd only slept a few hours, but he looked and sounded invigorated and ready to start the day.

"Feel good. Dom happy come home." He put a couple branches on the fire, a wide smile on his face. "Much happy."

An hour after dawn, everyone was up and dressed. They ate porridge and drank orange juice and the requisite coffee, and continued their search for artefacts. Dom showed them places where he thought people had sat to work stones or bones into tools. They stopped for lunch, then, as previously agreed, they began breaking camp in order to head back to the canoes.

Leaving the others to work, Dom walked away into the woods. Veronica figured he was going to the toilet area, but when he wasn't back in thirty minutes, she went in search of him.

She found him sitting cross-legged on the ground with his back against Mo-shooma's tombstone. He'd undressed and hung his jeans and green tee-shirt over a nearby tree branch, his socks and boots placed neatly below them. His cane leaned against the tree trunk.

Oh, dear God, this can't be good.

"Hey, Dom, what're you doing there like that?" she asked as she approached him. "You need to get dressed. We're . . . um . . . we're ready to leave." She dragged her eyes from the four white scars on his chest, up to his face.

His eyes were closed as if he'd been meditating. He didn't open them. "No, Vee. Dom not go."

"What do you mean, you're not coming? I know you missed this place, but we'll come back next year and we'll stay longer. I promise."

"No," he said again. "Dom not go." He pushed to his feet with a low groan and when he opened his eyes, Veronica was shocked to see tears brimming in them. "Grandfather here. Mother, father here. Children here. Roo here. Only Dom not here. Dom alone in faraway place."

He held something in his right hand and now, with a skip of her heart, Veronica recognized it as one of his obsidian blades.

"Hey, guys? We have a situation here," she called over her shoulder, as loudly as she dared without upsetting Dom more than he clearly already was. Reaching out with one hand, she said, "Dom? How about you give that to me? Put your clothes back on, and we'll talk about . . . Oh! Don't!"

In the two seconds it took her to reach him, he'd drawn the razor-sharp blade across the side of his neck almost to his Adam's apple.

"No!" she screamed as bright blood spurted. "Walt! Help!"

Dom stood there in silence while blood ran down his shoulder and arm.

Veronica grabbed his hand as he dropped the blade. She clapped the palm of her other hand against his neck in a desperate effort to stop the flow of warm blood.

"What have you done?" someone yelled as everyone seemed to arrive at once. She realized dimly that it was her.

"What the hell?" Walter's voice rang out behind her.

"Walt! He—"

"I see!" He yelled, "Pat, bring your first aid kit. Quickly!" In the meantime, he pulled off his tee-shirt and tossed it to Veronica, who pressed it against Dom's wound.

Dom was trembling now in an effort to remain on his feet. Veronica followed him down as he sank to his knees. His chest and her tee-shirt were already stained with dark red blood, as were his six ivory beads, the only thing he'd kept on his body.

"Oh, God, Dom, no," Chloe cried. She knelt on his other side and took his hand between hers. "Why? Why would you . . ." Words failed as she choked on sobs.

"Dom stay here. Stay with *den-no-ny*," he said casually, as if he were offering to make coffee or a sandwich.

Pat arrived with the first aid kit and Walter elbowed Veronica aside to press a wad of gauze to Dom's neck.

Dom tried to pull away. "No, Doctor Walter. Please not help Dom."

"You can't do this, Dom!" Chloe wailed. "You can't leave us! We . . . I . . ."

"No cry, Chloe," Dom said. He pulled his hand away from hers and reached out to stroke her tear-streaked cheek. His voice was a whisper now and he was starting to sway. "Chloe good woman. Dom much like. Sorry for leave you." He left three short, red lines of blood like war paint on her face when his hand dropped, trembling, to his side.

"Keep him still, damnit!" Walter hissed.

Chloe grabbed his shoulders, but he managed to turn towards Veronica. He looked at her, blinking to focus.

"Thank you, Veron-ica, for bring Dom home." His eyelids fluttered and closed. Seconds later, his body buckled, and he collapsed onto his side.

"No!" Chloe screamed as Walter struggled to keep the pressure bandage on Dom's neck.

"I'll get on the sat phone, call for a medevac," Pat said. "If you could stitch him up or something, Walter. Buy him some time until he gets to the hospi—"

"No." Gerald spoke up at last. "Let him go. Don't you realize this is why he brought us here?"

"It was his goal all along," Veronica agreed, forcing the painful words out through tears and trembling lips. The coppery scent of blood was so thick in the air, she could taste it. She looked down to see she was holding Dom's hand. She didn't realize she hadn't let go. "Walt... you can't save him. He wouldn't want you to."

"I can't just let him die," Walter argued. "I'm a doctor, for God's sake. I took an oath to save lives."

"You took an oath to do no harm," Gerald reminded him.

"All good, Walter," Dom rasped. He opened his eyes, but he seemed to stare past them at something only he could see. "Dom eyes good now. See Roo. See Lil-lia. See... children... Po... Beauti-ful... stars. Dom... go..." He took a long, hitching breath, and let it out in a weak cough. Despite Walter's efforts, blood pooled on the moss and leaves beneath him. "*Dom... esk... so-ko.*"

"Dom go   happy," Veronica translated, the words half-smothered by the lump in her throat.

The faintest smile curled the dying man's pale lips, his cloudy eyes fixed on the stars only he could see, and then he was still.

He has come at last to the end of his too long life.

For a moment, he hears nothing. Sees nothing. Then he sees the stars and all the people he loved who went before him. They have waited for him all this time.

Now, his spirit will join them.

That is good.

He is happy.

35

AFTERMATH

They sat or stood there for a long time, silent except for the occasional sniffle or sob or clearing of a throat, motionless except to wipe away tears, everyone looking as horrified, stunned, and sad as Veronica felt.

Finally, Pat coughed softly and ventured, "You say this was Dom's goal all along? To come here and die where his people lived?"

"I'm sure of it," Veronica said miserably when she realized the questions were directed at her. "He told everyone he didn't like the modern world... the city, the noise, the laws... I should've told him there are places where people live simple lives close to nature. Maybe if I had... Why didn't I realize he'd do something like this?"

"Because like you said," Gerald reminded her, "he's... he was... devious."

"He asked me what it meant to be a celebrity," Chloe said, her voice cracking, "and after I explained it, he said he didn't want to be one. When we talked on Saturday, he kept saying how happy he was to be home, to see the forest and lakes and smell the good air. He said he wanted us to tell everyone about his people and his time. I never thought he meant he wouldn't be around to tell them himself. That he wanted..." Choking over her words, she shook her head and fell silent.

"No one did, Chloe," Gerald said. He reached an arm around the young woman's shoulders in a comforting, fatherly embrace. "He fooled us all."

"Now what do we do?" Walter asked. He'd closed Dom's eyes and left the bandages covering the gaping laceration on his neck. He rose from his knees and wiped his blood-covered hands on his equally bloody trousers. "We can't exactly bury him, we don't even have a damn shovel."

"Seriously?" Veronica lashed out, her pain and sorrow dripping from her words. "All you ever cared about was having him as your goddamn guinea pig!"

"That's not true!" Walter declared, then lowered his voice. "At first yes, all right, I admit it. But I grew to respect and care deeply for him. I didn't want this, Veronica, not in a million years."

"Of course, you didn't," Gerald said. He looked from Walter to the others, his eyes red and brimming behind his glasses. "Pat has his trowel. The earth should be soft enough after the recent rain. We could dig a shallow grave and cover it with—"

"Rocks," Pat said, "the way Dom's people would've done."

"Right," said Veronica, nodding. "He'd like that."

"First, though," Gerald went on, "we need to document everything. We came out here with Dom and we're going home without him. There will be questions. The authorities—"

"Don't tell me they'll think we murdered him!" Chloe found her voice. She glared at Gerald. "How could anyone possibly think—"

"Gerald's right," Walter said. "Dom had no official identity, at least not yet, but he was pretty visible. People saw him on TV and read about him in the newspaper. There are bound to be questions."

"Oh, God," Veronica moaned, her face in her hands. "You're right, of course."

Gerald went to his tent, followed by Walter. The professor came back minutes later with his camera and took a number of photos of Dom where he lay, the blood-soaked bandages still stuck to his throat and the obsidian blade on the ground beside him. A couple shots of Dom's clothes, still where he'd placed them, except for his tee-shirt, which Veronica had draped over his genitals to give him at least that much dignity. Then Walter returned wearing latex gloves, a zipper bag in hand. He picked up the blade while mumbling something about fingerprints, slipped it into the bag, and took it back to his tent to be safely put away, presumably in the protective box with his other precious samples.

Pat fetched his trowel and went to work digging behind Moshooma's tombstone. Gerald found a flat stone he could use as a spade, and he knelt down to help. In the end, they all took turns digging with branches or stones or even their bare hands. They collected stones to pile on top of the grave. From time to time one of them took a few photos or filmed for a minute or two, recording the tragic event for posterity and if necessary, the authorities.

They placed Dom in the grave, arms crossed over his chest the way they'd found him a year ago, and covered him with earth and stones.

Chloe stumbled away in the direction of the tents and came back with Dom's little bag of black paint.

"There's not much left," she said, fighting to hold back fresh tears, "but I think there's enough." She knelt down and proceeded to recreate Dom's mark on the largest of the stones, a weather-worn chunk of granite, using her own handprints and drawing his concentric circles between them. "There... I don't know how long it'll last, but at least for now it's not an... unmarked... grave." She lost her battle, burst into heartbreaking sobs, and hurried away to solitude in her tent.

Although they'd planned to leave and everything but the tents was packed up, Pat said it was too late in the day to start out into the forest. They wouldn't make it to the canoes before nightfall, he explained, and the others reluctantly agreed.

Soiled by blood or earth or both, faces streaked with drying tears, they trudged to the pond they'd passed about half a kilometre back to wash it all off as best they could, their need to cleanse themselves physically and emotionally overriding any of the usual concerns about polluting the pristine water hole.

Feeling as if her arms and legs weighed ten times what they should, Veronica struggled to wash and dress and later eat a few bites of the chicken soup Pat cooked up. Then she excused herself, put on her pajamas, and went to bed.

Chloe joined her in their tent about twenty minutes later. She'd collected Dom's jeans, socks, boots, and cane from where he'd left them. Without a word, she put them down on his bed roll, changed into her pajamas, and crawled into her sleeping bag. Veronica wanted to say something to comfort her student and friend, but she could find no words even to comfort herself.

They spent the next day on Tetachuck Lake, Veronica with Chloe and Gerald in one canoe, Pat and Walter in the other with Dom's backpack, bed roll, and cane stored along with their own things. They paddled all day under a darkly overcast sky that matched their mood, subsisting on granola bars and water, too shocked and heartbroken for conversation or the eating of proper meals. They didn't stop until they arrived at the lodge just as the sun set in a blaze of orange and red between the clouds.

Walter, bless his lukewarm heart, explained to the lodge owners why Dom hadn't returned.

They were understandably horrified and saddened, but admitted that given the circumstances, Dom's choice wasn't a complete surprise.

It was a surprise to us, Veronica thought bitterly as she went to bed. She didn't sleep, though, instead spending her hours in the dark tossing and turning, reliving the special moments Dom had given her over the past year, and regretting not having realized how much pain he'd been in.

Casey picked them up at ten the next morning as scheduled.

This time, it was Pat who explained Dom's absence.

"Jeez Louise, you gotta be kidding," the pilot said under his breath. He shook his head in commiseration. "That's awful. Don't know what else to say."

No one else knew what to say either, and the flight back to Williams Lake was marked by a heavy silence although Pat, sitting up front with Casey, appeared to be filling the pilot in on the details.

Once settled in the hotel they'd stayed in ten days and a lifetime ago, Veronica called Neil. Doing her best not to break down in tears but not quite succeeding, she told him what had happened and, at Walter's insistence, asked for legal advice.

"Don't say anything more than you have to to anyone until you get home," Neil advised. "Then we'll prepare a cohesive statement. Since Dom has no one to report him missing or accuse you of any wrongdoing or crime and since, in fact, he wasn't even officially… well, anyone, I guess… there shouldn't be a problem."

Once home in her apartment, too miserable and drained to do more than let her kitties out of their carriers and dump some dry food into their bowl, Veronica sat on the edge of Dom's bed and leafed slowly through the drawing pad he'd left on his pillow. There she found his final drawing, apparently made the evening before they left Vancouver.

On a background of dark blue, he'd drawn a winding river of silver stars. Across them, he'd written in large, white letters, "DOM."

He really was planning to kill himself all along. She clutched the drawing to her chest, the realization that her suspicions had proven true sitting like a rock in her stomach. *That's why he wanted so badly to find his homeland. Why he was so happy when we did. He had no intention of coming back with us.*

Fortunately, as sad as it was, Neil's assessment also proved correct. When the police came to investigate Dom's disappearance as signaled by Celia Wolts and others who were paying attention, Veronica and the others' version of events stood, backed up by the photographic evidence, the obsidian blade that had only Dom's thumbprint on it, and Dom's final, telling drawing.

After multiple interviews with everyone involved and some fancy legalese by both Neil and Walter's lawyer, Fiona Harrison, the authorities were satisfied there had been no foul play. Questions from reporters like Franco Paulo and Lin Chen became fewer and far between. Franco, for his part, wrote a lovely tribute to Dom that was printed in the *Vancouver Sun* and picked up a few days later by Reuters to be published worldwide.

Veronica donated Dom's clothes to a local men's homeless shelter, but she kept all his drawings and the stone tools he'd made. She also kept his cane, which she gave back to Ty so he would have something to remember Dom by. She told him about the mark Dom had made in his cave, how he'd painted a dot for each of his friends, and how he'd included Ty even though he wasn't physically there with them.

"Thanks for telling me," the big man said, his voice husky. Tears stood in his eyes. "And thanks for the cane. Not that I need it. I'll never forget him."

"I know. I'm sure none of us will."

Days and weeks passed and weeks turned to months, and although they certainly didn't forget, the aching holes in their hearts created by Dom's death slowly grew smaller and less painful.

Chloe earned her bachelor's degree in anthropology, thanks to the thesis based on her comprehensive work with Dom and her earnest conclusion, painfully arrived at after his death, that teaching someone to speak, read, and write a new language didn't necessarily mean they would assimilate that culture unless they truly desired and made a conscious effort to do so.

Becky edited her documentary to Veronica's satisfaction, adding a bit at the end about Dom's demise, and found herself not looking for a distributor, as she'd initially feared, but having the luxury of choosing who would best do her film justice. It would later go on to win most of the awards a documentary could win.

Walter had succeeded in finding a minute quantity of mutated, living *Bacillus F.* in one of the samples he'd collected at Dom's sky stone place. He was able to cultivate it in the laboratory, negating the need to return to Far Mountain. He had high hopes of receiving approval for clinical trials of his revolutionary treatment for traumatic brain injuries, as well as opening a whole new branch of study into the possibility of extending human life. Although he, along with everyone else concerned, had signed an NDA stating they wouldn't divulge the whereabouts of Dom's cave nor his grave, he suspected that eventually he would be required by health or other authorities to disclose the location where he'd found the miraculous bacteria. Until that happened, the secret was safe with him.

Gerald decided not to pursue any archeological exploration in the vicinity of Dom's original tribe's homeland. Instead, he headed an expedition the following summer into the region southwest of Bennett Lake, where he calculated Dom's second tribe had had its summer village. He would eventually discover conclusive evidence of habitation that would fuel exploration for years to come.

Veronica found herself being drawn to a kinder, more compassionate Walter. They'd both come to the realization that as important as their careers were to them, human connections were even more essential. They decided to give their relationship a second chance, starting slowly and figuring out together where to draw the line between their professional and personal lives.

Dom was posthumously recognized and given full status as a Native American by the British Columbian and Canadian governments. UBC's Museum of Anthropology set up a small space commemorating Dom, his people, and his time, displaying his drawings and stone tools, along with the pieces of his spear and other artefacts unearthed at Bennett Lake—all except his beloved ivory beads, which had been buried with him. Veronica had the wall panels from his room at Cooper Medical removed and erected at the museum. Photos she'd taken of Dom were printed and displayed, audio recordings were made available, and a few short texts written by Chloe, Gerald, and Dom, himself—taken from his Facebook page— were laminated and presented as well. They even put in his ferns and dwarf cedars and took care of them so they flourished.

Veronica thought Dom would be happy to see it all, pleased to know that he and his people would be recognized and remembered.

She finished and published her book, titled *Dom, the Mud Man*. It would eventually become a critically acclaimed best seller, making her rich and famous enough to satisfy her appetite in that regard. But there were no triumphant book tours, talk shows, or sold-out conferences. Rather, she returned to teaching at UBC after being offered tenure in the anthropology department. She often spoke fondly and with great reverence about Dom in her classes and she answered all the questions her students asked, but for the most part, she was content to let him rest in peace the way he'd intended so very long ago.

About the Author

Donna Marie West is an educator, translator, author, and freelance editor. She has published close to 500 drabbles, short stories, and non-fiction articles in a variety of Canadian and American magazines, web sites, and anthologies. She loves the unusual and unexplained, often finding ways to weave those themes into her stories.

In 2019, she co-authored a collection of horror-themed short stories and poems entitled *HAUNTED HORROR*, which is currently out of print as the publisher closed its doors. Her first novel, *NEXT IN LINE*, was published in September 2020 by an independent American publisher. The sequel is scheduled for release later in 2022. *THE MUD MAN* is her third book.

Donna spends her free time reading, writing, and researching for projects. She lives in Québec, Canada, with her long-time partner and two beloved kitties.

You can follow her on her Amazon author page and her public Facebook page, both under her name.

CPSIA information can be obtained
at www.ICGtesting.com
Printed in the USA
LVHW020257110422
715852LV00008B/344